CALLED
to JUSTICE

CALLED *to* JUSTICE

A
QUAKER MIDWIFE
MYSTERY

EDITH MAXWELL

MIDNIGHT INK
WOODBURY, MINNESOTA

FIRST EDITION
First Printing, 2017

Book format by Cassie Kanzenbach
Cover design by Ellen Lawson
Cover illustration by Greg Newbold/Bold Strokes Illustration
Editing by Nicole Nugent

Midnight Ink, an imprint of Llewellyn Worldwide Ltd.

Library of Congress Cataloging-in-Publication Data
Names: Maxwell, Edith, author.
Title: Called to justice / Edith Maxwell.
Description: First edition. | Woodbury, Minnesota : Midnight Ink, [2017] |
    Series: A Quaker midwife mystery ; #2
Identifiers: LCCN 2016033194 (print) | LCCN 2016054081 (ebook) | ISBN
    9780738750323 (softcover) | ISBN 9780738750811
Subjects: LCSH: Midwives—Fiction. | Quakers—Fiction. |
    Murder—Investigation—Fiction. | GSAFD: Mystery fiction.
Classification: LCC PS3613.A8985 C35 2017 (print) | LCC PS3613.A8985 (ebook)
    | DDC 813/.6—dc23
LC record available at https://lccn.loc.gov/2016033194

Midnight Ink
Llewellyn Worldwide Ltd.
2143 Wooddale Drive
Woodbury, MN 55125-2989
www.midnightinkbooks.com

Printed in the United States of America

For midwives everywhere, who gently and professionally help women birth their babies in the safest, most effective environment possible, whether in a West African hut, a contemporary European home, or a birthing center in a modern American hospital. Mothers thank you, this one included.

AUTHOR'S NOTE

While I was writing this book, I trained as a docent at the John Greenleaf Whittier Home and Museum, which is only a few blocks from my home. The Whittier Home Association has been generous and helpful in providing information about Whittier and his life, particularly Susan Herman with her extensive grasp on the facts of Whittier's life. I used Edward Gerrish Mair's notes on the life of Lucy Larcom, a distant relative of his. A visit to the historic Strawberry Banke Museum in Portsmouth, New Hampshire, gave me several new ideas about life and homes in the late nineteenth century.

The Amesbury Carriage Museum is an invaluable resource with their collection of carriages from the period in which I set this series. I've been lucky enough to help move them around town on several occasions and to pick the brains of some of the active members, particularly Susan Koso. I also was delighted to be able to ride in a carriage at the Carriage Barn in South Hampton, New Hampshire, tour their collection of antique conveyances, and listen to owner Ann Miles share some of her extensive knowledge. Susan Koso also took me riding in her antique runabout in Ipswich and taught me quite a bit more about carriages, horses, and roads of the day. She read a draft of this book and set me straight on several matters of terminology and practice.

I consulted a number of historic references for this book, including Ruth Goodman's *How to Live Like a Victorian* (2013), Marc McCutheon's *Everyday Life in the 1800s* (1993), *The Letters of John Greenleaf Whittier, Volume III 1861–1892* edited by John B. Pickard (1975), and *John Greenleaf Whittier: a Biography* by Roland H. Woodwell (1985). I was also excited to obtain replicas of several historic texts, including the *Montgomery Ward & Co. Catalogue and Buyers' Guide* from 1895, the *Sears, Roebuck & Co. Consumers' Guide* for 1894, *The Massachusetts Peace Officer: a Manual for Sheriffs, Constables, Police, and Other Civil Officers* by Gorham D. Williams (1891), and *A System of Midwifery* by William Leishman, MD (1879). I check the Online Etymology Dictionary frequently to see if I can use a particular word or phrase, or if its first attested occurrence was after 1888. I also poke around all over the Internet on Pinterest and other sites too numerous to mention looking for pictures and names of hats, what kitchens looked like, information on illnesses, current events in the rest of the world in 1888, and much more.

Quaker writer and historian Chuck Fager once again helped with Friend practices from the late nineteenth century. Alison Russell shared some of her extensive knowledge about the Civil War, which helped me understand Akwasi's past and how he got to Amesbury. KB Inglee again read for historical details and corrected several of my errors; Sam Sherman also contributed her historical knowledge. And Allan Hutchison-Maxwell again caught several anachronisms. Obviously, any remaining errors are of my own doing.

This book cites portions of Friend and abolitionist John Greenleaf Whittier's poems "One of the Signers" and "The Meeting." Whittier was on the building committee for the Friends Meetinghouse where my protagonist, Rose Carroll, and Whittier himself worshiped. Details about the 1888 Independence Day parade and dedication of the Bartlett statue (which still stands downtown) are taken directly from a written account of that day in the *Daily News*

(1888, Newburyport), which I am able to peruse on microfiche at the Newburyport Public Library.

It's always a delight to walk through the streets of my town and imagine life almost a hundred and fifty years ago. The Bailey family lives in my house, built in 1880, and I walk to worship, as Friends have over the centuries, to the Meetinghouse portrayed in this novel. Many of the original nineteenth-century buildings in town remain standing and in use, and the same noon whistle blows as did in 1888. I hope, as you read, that you feel that same sense of walking through history.

ONE

The day had seemed an unlikely one to include death.

On a sunny, hot Independence Day, citizens from miles around had flocked in carriages, by trolley, even on bicycle to the streets of Amesbury, Massachusetts, to celebrate our country's one hundred and twelfth birthday. Colorful buntings hung from buildings, including John W. Higgins, Boots and Shoes, across from where I stood. I strained to keep my place at the edge of Main Street that morning while others jostled for an advantageous spot from which to watch the parade.

I'd walked down from the modest home where I lodged with my late sister's husband and his five children. My beau, David Dodge, was taking me to watch the fireworks tonight, but he needed to make rounds at the hospital today so I was on my own for the morning.

I was laughing along with the crowd at one of the horribles, a policeman dressed as a British bobby pulling an outhouse on a cart labeled Amesbury Lockup, when someone tugged at my sleeve.

"Rose," she whispered.

"Hannah," I said to the young woman at my side. Hannah Breed was a Quaker like me and one of my niece Faith's fellow employees at the Hamilton Mill. The smile slid off my face when I focused on her pale visage and drawn, frightened eyes. "What's wrong?"

"Faith has said thee is a midwife."

"I am." I touched her shoulder. "Thee is troubled."

"I need to talk with thee."

I barely heard her, because the drums and brass of the Newburyport Cadet Band struck up a tune. The band was followed by the marchers of the Eighth Regiment. The soldiers, walking purposefully in step, wore purple hats and carried rifles with bayonets. I had no desire to watch such a display of militarism, so I took Hannah's hand and pushed through the crowd behind us until we gained the relative quiet of Currier Street.

We moved down the hill until Currier joined Mill Street and opened up to the rushing lower falls of the Powow River. I stood facing Hannah in the welcome shade of one of the Salisbury Manufacturing Company's buildings.

"Please tell me what ails thee," I said, although I suspected the cause. She attended Amesbury Friends Meeting, as did I, and I'd detected a change in her the last couple of months.

Hannah gazed at the embroidered handkerchief she twisted in her hands. As she glanced up at me, a roar erupted from the crowd we'd left behind.

"I'm in trouble, Rose. I don't know where to turn, what to do."

I clasped my hands and waited without speaking. As a member of the Religious Society of Friends, I was accustomed to silence. When we gathered in worship, we sat silently, waiting on the Light.

"I have not been well. I'm sick often throughout the day. I thought it was a touch of illness." She paused, lifting her chin. "But then I missed my monthly."

As I thought. "How many times?"

"Three." She laid a hand on her belly. "I have felt it move." Indeed her simple forest-green dress strained around her chest and waist. So far her figure only appeared thickened, but it wouldn't be long before the bulge of a growing child in the womb would be unmistakable.

"Is the father of thy baby a boy thee knows? A beau?" I asked, speaking as kindly as I could. I wasn't an elder of Amesbury Friends Meeting, but rather a midwife only nine years older than Hannah's seventeen. I wasn't in the business of judging a woman with child no matter how she came to be in that condition.

"No." She shook her head slowly and stared at the ground. "And I can't tell thee the identity of the father."

"But thee knows." I reached out to lift her chin with my finger. "And the father knows of thy state."

"Yes." She cried out and turned her back, bending over to retch into the weeds, her slight body heaving with the effort. She straightened and dabbed her mouth with her kerchief before facing me again. "I'm sorry."

"No need to apologize, my dear." I drew out my own handkerchief to wipe perspiration from my brow. "Does thy mother know of thy condition?"

"No. Both my parents would be so very disappointed in me."

Hannah's family was a large one, residing in Nantucket, and a less-than-prosperous family, at that. Faith had told me Hannah's father had obliged her to travel to Amesbury for work in the mill.

She lived in Virginia Perkell's boardinghouse, sharing a room with other mill girls.

Hannah tucked a limp curl of hair the color of straw back under her bonnet. "Whatever am I going to do?"

"I'll think upon it, dear Hannah. The best option would be for the father to stand up and marry thee."

"But he won't. He's ..." She stared at the tumultuous river foaming furiously over the rocks. "We can't marry." A sob escaped her as she met my gaze. Fear and anguish mixed on her face.

I prayed this pregnancy wasn't as a result of someone taking advantage of Hannah, or worse, violating her. I knew the terrible effects of that experience from my own past, when I was about her age. The degradation had been wrenching, and the shame I felt about it, even worse.

"It would be best if I simply died." She took a step toward the steep river bank.

I laid my arm across her shoulders and turned her back toward the street. "Now, now. No talk of that. Together we'll figure a solution. Come back to the festivities. We'll find Faith and Annie, and the three of you will enjoy this day of respite."

We trudged back up toward the parade. Though I knew my heart couldn't be as heavy as hers, the thought of finding a way for her to bear her child in dignity was ponderous enough to cloud this glorious day. At times like this my twenty-six years felt like forty or more. My calling as midwife included acting the role of counselor almost as often as being the protector of a mother's health and that of her baby.

TWO

THE PARADE WAS OVER and orations in honor of the newly erected statue had begun by the time Hannah and I rejoined the fray on Main Street. We strolled behind the crowds until I spied Faith, her friend Annie Beaumont, and another girl laughing with tall Zebulon Weed, Faith's beau. I dispatched Hannah into their care.

"Thee'll be fine. Do forget thy troubles for today," I murmured in her ear, praying she would be fine, in fact.

Hannah smiled wanly, then squared her shoulders and turned to the girls, who were acting as happy and carefree as young women should be—at least until work started up at the mill again tomorrow. I headed to the area around the statue, grabbing a small corner of shade in which to stand. Josiah Bartlett had been a native of Amesbury, a delegate to the Continental Congress, governor of New Hampshire, and the second to sign the Declaration of Independence. Amesbury luminary Jacob Huntington, who some say was the father of our world-renowned carriage industry, had donated land near his home and funded the creation of the statue, which was being dedicated today.

After an hour, my feet duly ached from standing for the speeches and honoring of the assembled Bartlett descendants. As the speakers droned on, I thought about Hannah. The best thing for her would likely be to return home to her parents, despite the prospect of their disappointment. In the spring I'd attended the birth of another unwed mother, but she'd had the full support of the baby's father even though he was married to another. The new mother had tragically been murdered only a week after giving birth, and the well-off father had taken over the care of the newborn. I wondered how little Billy was faring. I'd try to stop by for a visit one day soon.

I waved my small Oriental fan in front of my face, but it barely cooled me. Finally the moment I'd waited for was at hand. Fellow Friend John Greenleaf Whittier was summering at his cousin's in Danvers at present, but the elderly poet and abolitionist had penned a poem for this occasion. A professor from Andover, the assigned reader, rose and cleared his throat. "'One of the Signers,' by John Greenleaf Whittier," he said. I listened as he read the familiar cadences, which ended thusly:

> *O hills that watched his boyhood's home,*
> *O earth and air that nursed him, give,*
> *In this memorial semblance, room*
> *To him who shall its bronze outlive!*
> *And thou, O Land he loved, rejoice*
> *That in the countless years to come,*
> *Whenever Freedom needs a voice,*
> *These sculptured lips shall not be dumb!*

That was just like John, my friend and mentor, to make sure freedom was mentioned. After the applause died down, the assembled dignitaries rose and streamed toward the opera house, where they'd be served a gala dinner. Myself, I was due on the banks of Lake Gardner for a picnic with my friend Bertie Winslow, so I made my way against the throngs toward High Street. I found myself following some paces behind a tall colored man whose jaunty gait looked familiar.

"Akwasi," I called. "Is that thee?"

He halted and craned his head to glance behind him. "That it surely is, Rose. What a delight to see thee." He pivoted and held out both hands to greet me, squeezing my pale hands in his when I arrived. His smile was broad and white in his dark face, and smiling made his ears stick out farther than they usually did. He was a warm and generous member of the Society of Friends, but he hadn't always been. John Whittier had sheltered a teenaged Akwasi in the hidden quarters in the cellar of the Meetinghouse as part of the Underground Railroad during the last year of the War for the Union. Akwasi had chosen to stay on in Amesbury even though not all local residents had welcomed him. He'd been diligent about his studies, mentored by John, and had become a member of the Meeting.

"Did thee hear the poem of Friend John?" I asked.

He released my hands and laid his right hand on his heart. "'Whenever Freedom needs a voice, These sculptured lips shall not be dumb!' Let us hope that comes to pass, Rose. Let us pray it does."

"How is thy business?"

"I'm kept quite busy creating fine furniture for our more prosperous citizens. It goes well, and I have been able to employ several lads to assist me. Keeping the books for the business is almost an additional job." He shook his head. "I'm thankful every day for John's help teaching me to read and cipher all those years ago."

"He helps so many. Well, I'm off to a picnic. I shall see thee on First Day, no doubt."

"Or at mid-week worship tonight, perhaps."

I laughed. "With all the commotion of the fireworks, it won't be a silent worship. I dare say I'll not attend."

"Thee has a point. Perhaps I shall attend the fireworks display, myself." He tipped his hat. "Good day, Rose."

I raised a hand in a wave as he turned up Friend Street. Despite it being decades past the war between the North and the South, and despite our location firmly in one of the most anti-slavery Northern states, I knew some in town did not favor the success of Akwasi's business. Few other colored people lived in town, and most held more menial positions like that of servants or railway workers. Akwasi had started his own woodworking business precisely to avoid being in that situation, and his hard work and head for numbers had stood him well. I hoped they always would.

———

I waited under a maple tree by the banks of Lake Gardner, the tree's wide leaf-lined branches providing welcome respite from the midday heat. Unbuttoning the collar of my dress, I tried to cool myself with my fan. I soon heard a clop-clop-clop on the paving stones behind me and turned to see Bertie ride up on her horse. She was postmistress of our town of Amesbury, and a true unconventional spirit I was glad to call friend.

"Whoa up, Grover," she called, pulling on the reins of the horse she rode astride. She carried a basket balanced on the pommel of the saddle.

I always smiled to hear her refer to a large animal by the name of our country's president. And Bertie was one of the few women I knew who rode astride instead of sidesaddle, although she did wear long bloomers under her dress for a modicum of modesty.

"I bring sustenance," she announced and handed down the basket before sliding off the horse. "How is my favorite Quaker midwife?"

"I'm well," I said. "And famished."

Bertie threw me a cloth to spread on the ground and set to drawing paper-wrapped packets and two bottles out of the basket. "See here? Cold meat pies, dilly beans, berry tarts, even a bottle of ale." She glanced at me. "Not to worry, I brought lemonade for teetotaler Rose." Bertie poured a metal cup of ale for herself and handed me a portion of tangy lemonade. "How were the speeches?" she asked, raising her perfectly arched eyebrows as she unpinned her beribboned boater and threw it on the cloth.

I bit into a meat pie. "Mmm, perfect crust, delicious filling," I said once I swallowed. "Thank thee, Bertie. The speeches were, well, speeches."

"You won't catch me listening to a lot of blowhards on a fine day."

I laughed. "I'll admit, several of the orators struck me as exactly that." I took a sip of lemonade. "Where's Sophie today?" Bertie lived with Sophie, a hard-working lawyer, in what most called a Boston Marriage. I knew it was more like a real marriage than simply two spinster ladies sharing a household, but I kept that fact under my bonnet. "It's a federal holiday. She can't be off working as usual."

"Sophie's mother is ailing. She went down to Cambridge to sit with her." She sipped her ale and let out a satisfied breath. "Did you get to listen to Mr. Whittier's poem?"

"I did. It was very fine, as usual. Afterward I spoke with Akwasi. The last line of the poem, where John mentions freedom, meant a great deal to him."

"A former slave? I should think it might. And where is the Bailey family today?"

"Their father took the younger three children to watch the parade, but they might have gone home by now. Frederick is taking them all traveling tomorrow, so perhaps he is busy preparing their bags. I know Faith is off somewhere with her friend Annie."

"And the beanpole Luke?" Bertie asked.

"He must have absconded with his pack of thirteen-year-old friends."

We ate and chatted for most of an hour. A family also picnicked a little ways down and we watched as the children splashed in the water. A song sparrow entertained us from a nearby bush while a breeze brought a semblance of water-scented coolness off the lake, which was really just the Powow River backed up behind the Salisbury Mills dam.

I laid back on the cloth for a rest while Bertie read one of A.M. Barnard's scandalous tales. I'd only recently learned they were actually penned by Louisa May Alcott herself. Giggles awoke me from my nap and two hands covered my spectacles when I opened my eyes.

"Guess who?" a voice asked.

"Thee will have to do better than that, Faith Bailey." After the hand slid away, I sat up to see my niece as well as Annie, Hannah, and the other girl from earlier all plopped down on the edges of our cloth. They threw off hats and bonnets and used them to fan themselves. I was pleased to see Hannah with color in her cheeks again and a shy smile on her face. Annie, as was her habit, wore several brightly colored ribbons tying back her red hair.

"We came to go wading," Faith said. "It's much too hot in town." A slender young woman, she smoothed tendrils of brown hair up off her neck with one hand.

"Rose, Bertie, this is Nora Walsh," Annie said. "She's only been here a couple of months. She works with us and rooms at Mrs. Perkell's with Hannah."

Nora flashed a quick look at Hannah. "Not my choice, that. But we live with what we have to," Nora said in a brogue. "Pleased to meet yeh, ladies," she added, looking at Bertie and me with the kind of light eyes set off by milky skin and dark hair I associated with the Irish.

Perhaps Nora and Hannah did not get on well. "Likewise, Nora," I said. "Bertie, does thee know Annie Beaumont and Hannah Breed?" I removed my glasses and polished off Faith's fingerprints with my handkerchief.

"I've met Annie." Bertie smiled. "You're of the Nantucket Breeds?" Bertie cocked her head at Hannah.

Hannah wrinkled her nose. "How does thee know that?"

"My uncle lives on the island. Obediah Winslow," Bertie said. "He knows everybody. He's an ornery old coot, but I adore him."

"I know of him," Hannah said. "My younger brother Asa wants to apprentice to him to learn blacksmithing."

"Uncle is tough but fair," Bertie said. "I'll wager you girls are happy to have the day off from mill work."

"Indeed," Annie said. "It's becoming quite tense at the Hamilton Mill. One of the supervisors, Mr. Colby, has been harsh with us girls of late."

"He's terrible, Rose," Faith added, as she unlaced her shoes. "Mean for no reason."

"I wonder if his own supervisor is exerting pressure on him about his work." I peeked at Hannah, who hadn't said a word. She'd paled again and sat staring out at the lake.

"Well, I'm on holiday today and I'm not going to think about him. We're going to cool off now and watch the fireworks show tonight." Annie pulled off her stockings and jumped up. She set her fists on her hips. "Come on, girls. Last one in is a cow's tail."

Faith tugged off her stockings, then elbowed Hannah until her feet were also bare.

"Aren't you coming, Nora?" Faith asked as she stood.

"I don't know how to swim," Nora said. She crossed her arms. "It's dangerous, yeh know. And I'm not after all the gents fancyin' me legs."

"We're not swimming, silly," Faith said. "Only putting our feet in. Isn't thee hot?"

Nora's expression changed to one of relief. "Well, I suppose it can't hurt." She removed her shoes and stockings.

I watched as the four ran down to the water. Annie and Faith lifted their skirts and plunged in up to their knees, with Nora tip-toeing in after them. Hannah peered back at where we sat. She was too far away for me to see the expression on her face, but her stance wasn't a happy one.

"I know Lester Colby from several dealings at the post office," Bertie murmured, staring at the girls as they frolicked. "He's no good."

"Oh? Then how'd he get to be a manager at the mill?" I listened to a grinding, crackling sound as the picnicking family cranked an ice cream freezer.

"Men." She snorted. "They take care of each other. I believe he's distant cousin to the mill's owner."

"Cyrus Hamilton? He has always been decent to our family."

"Sure, but I'll wager he doesn't keep track of the details on the floor. He's a businessman, Rose. He cares about making money."

THREE

An hour after sunset, David steered us through the crowd of carriages, buggies, and wagons full of citizens eager to watch rockets and stars explode against the night sky. I'd never seen so many conveyances on Lions Mouth Road west of town. The Little Farm was a perfect place to celebrate the end of Independence Day. The extensive dairy farm featured acres of open fields, as well as a hill sloping gently up toward the south. The organizers of the extravaganza staged their lighting station in another field across the road so all could "ooh" and "aah" in safety as the fireworks went off.

We'd chosen to walk, as David's mare Daisy did not take well to explosions. He'd left her and his buggy at my house, but he carried a thick blanket for us to sit on.

"You're sure you'll be comfortable?" he asked as we walked up the hill. "Whoa, there, lads," David said as three boys chased by without caring if they bumped into adults as they passed.

"Of course I will. And it's a warm night." We'd been courting, this gentle doctor and I, for some months. His kind manner and lively intelligence appealed to me, despite the differences in our social class and religion. He was on staff at the recently built Anna Jaques Hospital across the Merrimack River in Newburyport, and I sometimes consulted with him on difficult births. But I much preferred spending enjoyable hours like these in his company. "We'll be fine. We have each other, after all." I squeezed his arm while we picked our way through hundreds of town residents already sprawling on blankets.

"For which I'm ever thankful." He covered my hand with his, dropping the blanket in the process.

"It appears this is our spot." I laughed, glancing around. In fact, it was an open area on the freshly mown pasture.

He spread the blanket and in a moment I sat leaning against his knees. I stayed carefully on the cover in case farmer Jonathan Little's cows might have been grazing and doing other business here recently. The air was filled with the sounds of laughing and talking, accompanied by the clink of glass here and there, no doubt from liquor being hoisted. I heard the pops of firecrackers from one quarter and young people shrieking with delight. I hoped no one would be injured. Every year more than one reckless soul was hurt or even killed by a prematurely exploding rocket or the careless celebratory firing of a gun.

"The children didn't want to come along with us?" David asked.

"Of course they did. But the younger ones are too young, and Frederick forbade even Luke. They're all going off early to Mother and Father's tomorrow—all except Faith, that is."

"You and Faith will rattle around in the house by yourselves."

"I shall delight in some peace and quiet. Don't get me wrong. I'm grateful to have lodging with my brother-in-law." Frederick, a teacher, had offered me the use of the parlor for my office and as lodging after my older sister passed away last year. "But the household is always full of the noise of growing children, not to mention Frederick's moods." After Harriet had died, her husband's moods had become increasingly erratic. I wasn't sure if it was simply the result of grief and the responsibility of being the sole parent to five growing children, or if it was some kind of mental ailment. Regardless, I was glad Frederick was off to a pedagogical training for the rest of the summer while the children spent a healthy month at my parents' farm some twenty miles southwest in Lawrence. A break from his moods would be most welcome.

"Why isn't Faith going?" David asked.

"She has her job. And she's excited to meet the author Lucy Larcom on First Day. John Whittier is returning from his sojourn in Danvers to meet with Lucy and then travel to New Hampshire with her for the rest of the summer. John agreed to introduce Faith to his author friend." I patted my forehead with my handkerchief. Even though it was evening, the temperature had hardly moderated, and being in close proximity to so many other people kept the air from cooling.

"First Day being Sunday, correct? Tell me again why you Quakers don't use the same names for the days and months as the rest of us?"

"It's because many days and months are named after gods. Norse gods, Roman gods. We choose to be simple, as in other areas of life, and say Fourth Day instead of Thursday, after Thor. First Month instead of January, which honors Janus. And so on." I caught sight of an Amesbury police officer picking his way through the seated townspeople, hands behind his back. In any outdoor evening event like this one, it was best to have law enforcement about in case anyone decided to take the festivities a little too far.

"Now I remember. So Faith wants to be a writer, I think you said." His deep voice was alluring, as always.

"Yes, very much so." When I spied a girl in the distance who reminded me of Hannah, I pulled away and twisted to face David. "David, a young woman—a girl, really—in my care is in a desperate situation." I spoke softly so only he could hear. "She is with child, several months gone, and unmarried. She says she can't name the father, or will not, more likely. She's about Faith's age. I'm not sure how to help her resolve what to do."

"What about her family? Surely they'll support her." His dark blue eyes gazed at me with concern.

"No. The girl lives in a boardinghouse and works at the Hamilton Mill. Her family lives on distant Nantucket, and Han … the girl told me her mother would be deeply disappointed if she knew." I smoothed out a wrinkle in the cloth as I lowered my voice. "She could be pregnant because she was violated."

"Raped?" he asked in a whisper.

"Maybe she is afraid of the man and that's why she won't identify him." Although she'd seemed more upset than fearful when she'd asked me for help. I let out a breath. I glanced up to see Akwasi stroll by with a lovely colored woman on his arm, her back straight, her hat tastefully decorated. "Good evening, Friend," I called.

Akwasi stopped and peered down at us before a smile lit up his face. "Rose, thee joins me in mid-week worship, I see. May I present my friend Esther MacDonald? Esther, this is Friend Rose Carroll."

David scrambled to his feet and gave me his hand to stand, too. "So pleased to meet thee, Esther," I said. I was about to introduce

David to both of them when I paused. "Akwasi, I don't believe I know thy surname."

"Ayensu." He lifted his chin. "My previous, shall we say, employer, had called me by his family's name. White, if thee can imagine, and dubbed me Kenneth, as well. But I always had a family name, and unlike many freed slaves, I did not choose to take the surname of an American founding father. I also have always known my own given name in the Akan language, the name my mother gave me. Once safe here in the North, I let it be known I am Akwasi Ayensu." He extended his hand to David.

David shook it, introducing himself, and tipped his hat to Esther.

"Does *Akwasi* have a particular meaning in your language?" I asked.

"It means I was born on a Sunday, on First Day. In our lore men named Akwasi are leaders, and also keepers of secrets."

Esther gave Akwasi a shy smile. "We are to be married," she said, glancing at me. "So I'll be Ayensu, as well." Her pink cheeks shone through her skin, which was colored like melted chocolate with plenty of cream mixed in, and her lashes were dark, full, and curly.

"Let us both congratulate you," David said.

"Yes, that is splendid news," I added. What good fortune for Akwasi to find such a beautiful and gracious woman to make his wife.

"Rose is a midwife, Esther. And she serves all in the community." Akwasi extended an arm around Esther's waist.

"Indeed I do." I expected we'd see some little Ayensus in the next few years. I smiled at Esther. "Please come to Friends worship with Akwasi. We would welcome thee."

We all said good-bye before they moved on. David sat again, and I once more leaned back against his knees. A woman sitting nearby glared at me before looking away. She probably thought I was either being too familiar with David or overly friendly with the coloreds. Either way, it didn't concern me.

A crack split the air and red streaked upward, ending in a golden flower suspended for a moment against the starry night. "Oh, look, David!"

He pulled me close with both arms, murmuring in my ear. "It's beautiful, but not as lovely as you, Rose."

After several more rounds of rockets, I noticed a gray-haired man pacing nearby, his arms wrapped around his chest. Every time a new firework exploded he stopped and looked around fast, almost in a panic. At a particularly loud explosion, he dove for the ground, nearly knocking over two boys running past. David jumped up and went to him. He helped him stand and I watched as they conversed softly. At last David seemed to convince the man to leave, and he shuffled off down the hill. David sat on our cloth again.

"What was that?" I asked.

"I believe he has neurasthenia. Sometimes we call it soldier's brain. He's a veteran of the War for the Union, and loud noises like these can shock some former soldiers so they think they are back on the battlefield."

I watched another display go up. "I suppose these fireworks do mimic the sounds and sights of war. I never thought of it that way."

"How fortunate we are that this is a pleasant summer diversion, and not a battleground," David said softly.

We watched for at least twenty minutes more, with each display growing more fantastical, although my enjoyment was somewhat tempered by my new awareness of the show's similarity to violent conflict. The show of lights paused for a moment, during which the murmur of conversation rose. A raucous party of dandies on a nearby cloth grew louder as they passed a flask and shot a gun into the air until they ran out of ammunition.

I narrowed my eyes at these foolish young men. "Don't they know how dangerous that is?"

"Do you want to move, my dear?" David asked.

"There really isn't a spare piece of ground. We'll keep a watch out for them."

Another series of cracks went off at once. Accompanied by the smell of sulfur, we watched three tremendous bursts of color fill the sky. A chorus of admiration rose around us.

"Does thee think those are the last ones?" I asked.

"I'd say so."

The lights piercing the night were crumbling into darkness when a shout went up.

"Help! Someone's been shot," a man cried out. "Is there a doctor?"

David and I stared at each other. He sprang up.

"Wait. I'll come with thee." I extended my hand for him to pull me to standing. I lifted my skirts several inches as we hurried toward a growing crowd a few yards distant. Some incautious celebrant must have let loose a stray bullet or gotten careless with a firecracker or a rocket.

David pushed his way through the cluster of folks all peering toward the center. "Let me by," he urged. "I'm a doctor."

I followed in his wake as he knelt over a woman crumpled on the ground. Horrified townspeople leaned in to see from all sides. David's hands were stacked, pressing on the slight woman's chest. The light from the waxing moon showed a growing stain on her gown. The moonlight revealed that the dress was plain of adornment and dark green. *No. It couldn't be.* I clapped a hand to my mouth, hurrying to kneel at David's side. But it was. Hannah Breed lay on the ground with blood pouring out from between David's fingers.

FOUR

THE POOR THING. How had this happened? Where were Faith and Annie? My heart thudding, I glanced around but saw no sight of the other girls.

David gave me a quick look. "Check the pulse in her neck."

Hannah gasped in shallow gulps as if she couldn't get enough breath. I extended two fingers to the vital spot below her jawbone. Her pale skin, as soft as a child's, yielded only the faintest of beats. As I felt, even those ceased, and the terrified look in her eyes froze to an unseeing one. The gasping stopped. I shook my head slowly and sat back on my heels. This wasn't the first time I'd seen a person's life force ebb away. I'd lost newborn babies as well as recently delivered mothers, and I'd been at my sister's side when she died. But I'd never witnessed a death from violent means.

"David, this is the girl. The one carrying a child," I whispered.

He cast me a look. "How far along was she?"

His use of the past tense hit me like a wave. "Three or four months. Much too early to try to save the infant with a Cesarean section, I fear."

David nodded, sorrow filling his eyes, then he sat back, too. He rubbed the blood off his hands on the mown grasses, then pulled out his pocket watch.

"Time of death, nine thirty-six." He reached over, gently smoothing down Hannah's eyelids. His finger smeared a line of blood on her cheek.

The onlookers drew back, some gasping, some muttering. I saw Akwasi's head above the rest, his eyes wide.

"Will someone please go for the police?" I called out.

David surveyed the crowd. "Who among you reported the shot?"

A few men exchanged nervous glances. One nudged another, who said, "What's that?" as he rubbed his ears.

"He wants to know who reported the shooting," the first one shouted.

The other man stepped forward. "'Twas me, sir. Sorry, my ears are ringing something fierce because of the noise. We was all just a crowd, though. I didn't see who done it. I only heard it. Came at the same time as them rockets went off." The man, wearing a sack suit that had seen better days, rubbed his forehead with a grimy hand. "You know, all our eyes was on the sky up there. Didn't want to miss the pretty lights. But then I looked down and there she was, just lying on the ground."

"Surely this young woman wasn't here alone," I said. I surveyed the group, their faces a little too much like eager vultures for my taste. "Wasn't she with several others her age? Did any of you see who shot her?" Had Faith and Annie been shot, too? My worry mixed with fury at all the stupid men clowning about with drink and weapons.

The sack suit cupped his hand to his ear to listen, frowning, then shook his head fast. Others on the perimeter murmured, "No," and another chimed in with, "We didn't see nobody with no gun."

A robust older woman with a reddened face pressed her lips together. "I wouldn't put it past those mill girls to be up to all kinds of mischief. Out here at night alone? Why, their boardinghouse matron ought to either be chaperoning them or locking them up after dark."

"Now, you wait a minute." Another woman pushed through from the back of the crowd and stepped forward, her sensible black ladies' trilby firmly pinned to slate-gray hair. Not a tendril escaped a tightly wound bun. "I am Mrs. Perkell and I manage the girls in my house quite well, thank you very much." Virginia gazed down at Hannah's body. She brought her hand to her mouth and her expression softened. "The poor dear thing. Miss Breed was in the company of three other girls and a respectable young man when she left tonight. They'd all promised to stay together." She seemed to shake off her sorrow as she folded her arms across a broad chest and stared at the first woman, who narrowed her eyes but turned away.

"Virginia, greetings," I said. I myself had lived in Virginia Perkell's residence prior to my sister's death, and I knew she ran a tight ship, but a fair and caring one. "Was Hannah with Faith and Annie when she left?"

"That she was. And Miss Walsh, as well, along with that nice boy, Zebulon Weed." She knelt and drew off her shawl, covering Hannah's face and torso. She straightened the shawl with care, even as the blood on Hannah's chest soaked through the blue cloth in a dreadful bloom illuminated by the moonlight.

"Did you see her shot?" David asked.

Virginia stood again. "No. I heard in the crowd it was a girl and thought I'd better see for myself. What happened? It must have been some kind of accident."

I tried to look for the weapon on the ground, but with the shadows cast by the crowd, I could see nothing. "How did she end up here alone?" I said, more to myself than to anyone else. Hannah had been so despondent about her circumstances. Could she have obtained a gun and ended her own life? But why do it here in the midst of hundreds? Another crack split the air and I startled, crying out. Was the shooter responsible for her death still about? I turned my head quickly in one direction and another, but saw no threat, only everyone's heads tilted upward.

"Only another rocket, Rosie, dear." David reached out and patted my hand.

His hand was damp where it touched mine. I shuddered. It must have been Hannah's blood still on his skin. The sky was, in fact, again infused with sparks of colored light. I couldn't admire them, though, and fervently hoped that was the last display of the night.

"Move aside, move aside," a man's voice shouted. The crowd parted for a uniformed police officer rushing toward us. "What's the problem here..." Guy Gilbert, a young officer I knew, halted as he caught sight of Hannah's body, and his voice trailed off.

"There was a report of a person shot," David said, standing. He reached a hand to me. "We tried to save the life of this poor young woman, but we were not able to."

"Miss Carroll, Doctor Dodge. Looks like a gunshot wound. Anybody find the weapon?" He narrowed his eyes and gazed from face to face in the crowd. Sack Suit threw his hands open and shook his head, while others murmured they hadn't seen the gun.

"Do you know the girl's name?" Guy asked.

"Hannah Breed, Guy." I'd helped his wife and him through a difficult period in the spring. A couple of years younger than I, he was a competent officer. "She's a mill girl."

"She's a respectable girl who rooms with me," Virginia added. She lowered her voice, addressing Guy. "If this wasn't an accident, her murderer is still about. We could all be in danger."

I stared at her. Not an accident? Murder? But who would murder an innocent mill girl? And why would that even occur to Virginia?

Guy, a tall, thin man, rubbed at his chin. "Back up, everyone. Give us some room." He gestured with a pushing movement to the bystanders as a cloud pushed away the moonlight. The people edged back, but their collective murmur grew louder, with "murderer" and "weapon" arising here and there.

Since Guy was occupied with asking questions and controlling the crowd, I again examined the ground around Hannah for the gun, but it was difficult to see in the darkness. I realized she couldn't have killed herself. The weapon would have still been in her hand, unless someone seized the opportunity to obtain a free weapon and had stolen it. But that was unlikely. So whoever shot her, whether accidentally or with malice aforethought, would have absconded with the weapon.

"Now, see here," a burly fellow said as he pushed into the clearing. When the moon reappeared, it illuminated a face glistening with sweat, at least the part not covered by an impressive set of side whiskers. "What's this about a girl being killed?"

"And who might you be?" Guy stepped between the man and Hannah's body, holding his arms out to the sides. "Step back, please, step back."

"Name's Lester Colby, officer. I'm a manager at Hamilton Mills. I supervise a great number of girls. Wondered if the unfortunate victim was one of them." He pushed his lips into a knot and blinked at Guy.

So this was the supervisor. "Yes, she is," I said. "I mean, was. Hannah Breed is her name." I watched him.

He removed his bowler. Holding it over his heart, he peered around Guy, who'd dropped his arms. "God rest her soul," Lester said in an officious tone.

Guy cleared his throat. "All right now. I'll need the names and addresses of all you who were near the victim when she was shot." He pulled a pencil and a small notebook out of his pocket. He licked the pencil lead and looked up expectantly.

Half the crowd had already melted into the darkness, but Guy focused on the man in the sack suit. "Name, sir?"

The man frowned but provided Guy with the information. "But I didn't see nothing. And that's the truth."

Several others echoed what the man said.

Where was Faith? I prayed she was still with Zeb and Annie. Perhaps they were safe at home already. Tomorrow was a work day, after all. The wind blowing the clouds around had picked up and the moonlight came and went capriciously. "There was a woman here," I said, thinking of the one casting aspersions on all mill girls. "Where has she gone?"

Nobody seemed to know, although one fellow offered up the woman's name and address.

"Thank you, sir," Guy said. "I'll need to be providing all the information I can to our detective." He squinted at the notebook and muttered, "Can't see a thing in this darkness."

"Kevin will be taking on the case, then?" I asked. I'd worked with Kevin Donovan after the murders in the spring, and we'd come to a tenuous friendship.

"Yes, of course. Glad it won't be me leading the investigation." He wiped his forehead with the back of his hand. "All the details of tracking down a shooter, whether a careless one or one with purpose, make my mind spin."

Lester leaned toward Guy and spoke in a low voice. "There's a Negro in the back there." He pointed at Akwasi. "He could have killed Miss Breed. You ought to get his information. Or better, throw him in jail tonight."

Guy frowned, but he beckoned to Akwasi, who stepped forward, Esther still on his arm. Two men in the crowd murmured to each other as they watched.

"I can vouch for him," I told Guy. "Akwasi doesn't even swat mosquitoes. He's a Friend."

"The police don't care who your friends are, miss." Lester glared at me.

David stepped closer and took my elbow in a protective move.

"He is a friend, a good friend," I said. "But he's also a respected member of the Religious Society of Friends, and I'll not have thee maligning him." I stood tall and met his glare straight on with my own, as his height was no greater than my own five feet eight inches.

Lester rolled his eyes, then turned toward where Guy stood speaking with Akwasi and Esther.

"No, sir, I saw nothing," Akwasi said calmly. "We only heard a commotion. We stood well outside this inner circle." He gave over his address, and slowly spelled both his first and last name for Guy.

"All right, you can go," Guy said.

Akwasi tipped his hat at me, then shepherded Esther away toward the road.

"Best not go far, you hear me, boy?" Lester called after him.

Akwasi and Esther kept walking, Akwasi swinging a clenched fist.

FIVE

I STOOD ON THE steps to the side door the next morning. I waved to Frederick and the children as they headed down the path for the early train to Lawrence and my parents' farm. It was good the little ones would have a month of fresh country air in which to play under care of their loving grandparents. I was also glad the children would get a respite from their moody father, as he would be attending a course for teachers in Lowell during the vacation.

Each child carried a satchel or a haversack with their belongings for the month, even eight-year-old Betsy. If I knew my mother, the children would come home with several fresh pieces of clothing she'd make for each of them. And a good thing, too, at the rate they were all growing. Their father toted his valise for his studies as well as the sack of savory pies and fruit I'd packed for the family to eat as they traveled.

The day promised to be warm again, and the air already pressed in, full of moisture, even though it wasn't yet six o'clock. I yawned. The tragedy of last night had kept my brain too busy to fall asleep for some time after David had returned me home. I hadn't spoken of Hannah's death this morning, so as not to upset the children or Frederick prior to their journey.

I turned back into the kitchen to find Faith doing the washing up from the family's breakfast. "Let me finish that, Faith. Doesn't thee need to prepare for thy work?"

"I can do it. I have time. Will thee stir the porridge? I made a second pot."

"Surely."

A few minutes later we both sat at the table, bowing our heads for a moment of silent grace before dipping into our bowls of oat porridge, onto which I'd sprinkled raspberries and poured fresh milk.

"I'm very excited about meeting Lucy Larcom." Faith's face shone. "I told thee she is coming to visit with John Whittier, and he said he'd introduce us, didn't I?"

"Thee did. That is wonderful, Faith. Thee will talk with her about her writing, I dare say."

She bobbed with excitement. "I want to be a writer like her. And like Louisa May Alcott, and Margaret Fuller."

"And like Harriet Beecher Stowe. Thy mother was named after her."

Faith fell silent, her spoon motionless. "I miss Mother so much, Rose. It's been over a year, but the pain is still so sharp at times."

"I know. I miss my sister, too. I wish she were here to guide all of us. Thee knows how proud she would have been of thee, leaving school, taking on the burden of her mill job to help the family." Harriet had been eleven years older than I, but we'd always been close. And it was when I helped at Betsy's birth eight years ago that I'd met midwife Orpha Perkins and had asked her to take me on as apprentice. "And most of all she'd be proud of thee for resolving to leave mill work, as way opens, and instead do what thee loves."

"I hope I will know when way opens, when the time is right." Faith's smile was wan, but it was a smile. A pity I needed to tell her about the current death.

"Thee watched the fireworks display, didn't thee?" I asked. Faith had been fast asleep by the time I'd come in. I needed to ask her about Hannah, but I hated to upset her. Still, she would certainly hear the news once she arrived at the mill.

"For a little while. But we all needed to rise early today and so we made our way home. Zeb saw me safely to my door." She blushed a little.

Hannah, the same age as Faith, had been assaulted. I wondered if Faith and Zeb, both healthy young people, were exploring their own physical urges. Maybe I could gently inquire of her during this month when we would have plenty of time to speak in confidence of matters close to our hearts. "Was Hannah with thee at the Little Farm?"

Faith frowned. "She was at the beginning. We all went up there together. Hannah spoke to the fellow who's been courting her, and then we lost them in the crowd."

The fellow? "Who is the young man?" This could be the father of Hannah's baby, but I wasn't going to tell Faith that. Surely she would have let me know if Hannah had confided to her the fact of her pregnancy.

"Tobias Cartland. He is a Friend from New Hampshire. He moved here last year to work at Clarke's Carriage Manufacturer. Tobias attends Meeting for Worship, and is a kind soul who adores Hannah."

"I'm not sure if I can place him." Surely a young Quaker man would not resort to violence. I prayed not. I swallowed. I had to tell her. "Faith, something terrible happened last night up at the Little Farm."

She lifted her head and waited.

"Hannah was shot." I reached for her hand.

She gasped. "No! Hannah?" Her face went pale. "Is she all right?"

"I'm afraid she isn't. Faith, her spirit was released to God last night."

"But how? Who shot her? Who would?" Her brown eyes filled, eyes like her mother's. And like my own. "It must have been an accident. Poor sweet Hannah. No older than I."

"We don't know who shot her. It was likely an accidental shooting."

"Thee and David saw her?"

"Yes. It happened nearby to where we sat. A man called out for a doctor, so David and I rushed to see if we could help, but she died almost immediately. She seemed to be alone in the crowd." I shook my head and pushed a raspberry around with my spoon. Through the open windows I heard a mockingbird warble through its repertoire of four other birds' songs without heed to a girl's death, and horse hooves clopped along the beaten dirt way that served as our street.

"This is the very worst news," Faith said. She sniffed and wiped her cheeks.

"I know. I hated to have to inform thee."

"I'll have to tell the other girls."

"I'm sorry thee has to carry such sad tidings." I took a bite of porridge and swallowed before continuing. "The manager thee dislikes appeared afterwards. He is an unpleasant sort, I have to agree."

"Lester Colby." Faith's lip curled. "So he already knows."

"Yes. He apparently was at the farm watching the fireworks like everyone else. When word spread through the crowd, he pushed forward wondering if the victim was one of 'his girls,' as he put it."

"I know it isn't Christian of me, but I do not like him. Not a whit." Faith gazed at the table. "Is it possible Hannah shot herself?" She sat up straight and swiped at the tears on her cheeks.

"I doubt it," I said. "The gun would have been in her hand, and it wasn't. Surely someone wouldn't steal a weapon that a poor girl had just used to kill herself."

"Yes, and Hannah wouldn't take her own life."

"I spoke with her yesterday morning. She seemed quite despondent."

Faith narrowed her eyes. "She has been acting a little odd lately. Moody. But not so much as to end her life among us. I'm sure of it."

————

After Faith walked down the hill to the Hamilton Mill for her seven o'clock shift, I cleaned up the kitchen and took stock of our food stores. What a relief to have the always hungry family away for a time. The work of cooking, cleaning, and laundering fell on Faith's and my shoulders, and it became onerous, especially when my birthing schedule grew full, as it was now. The two of us could make do for a month, but I was determined to talk Frederick into hiring a kitchen girl upon his return. He'd resisted doing so since my sister died, but it wasn't fair to Faith or to me to lay it on our shoulders. I knew of a few men, mostly Quakers, who helped in the business of running a household, but my brother-in-law wasn't one of them. Faith was too young to be saddled with such a burden, and I was called away to births too frequently. Harriet had been in charge of the household before her death, of course. I remembered one maid she'd hired who quit after Frederick had exercised one of his moods on her. Maybe Frederick knew he didn't have it in him to be civil to a hired girl. Or perhaps taking over the role of household manager would be one more painful reminder that his wife was dead.

When I was done, I set to work reviewing client files in my room. I had three ladies coming this morning for their antenatal visits. In the afternoon I was due to go to the home of a new client, to assess the residence's readiness for a birth. I attended women from all walks of life, from the very richest to the most abject poor. I helped them labor in finely appointed bedchambers with servants hovering as well as in the crowded tenement buildings where immigrant workers often lived. As long as the room and the linens were clean, and there was boiling water to be had, infants could be birthed safely almost anywhere.

I perused my records, noting that one of my women, due to deliver in two months, had gained what seemed like excessive poundage. Some of it was water, as indicated by her swollen ankles. But it could also mean she was carrying twins, although I'd never heard more than one heartbeat. Or she might have a diabetic condition, which could lead to an overly large baby and a difficult birth. I'd have to monitor her closely, and perhaps recommend she give birth at Anna Jaques Hospital instead of at home.

I gazed out the windows at a factory worker trudging by, his metal lunch bucket swinging as he walked. The sight of him brought to mind the boy Faith had mentioned, Tobias Cartland.

Also a factory worker. Had he learned of Hannah's death? And would Kevin Donovan have been informed about Hannah's pregnancy? No. I imagined no one knew about that but me. I glimpsed the clock on the mantel. With a shooting to investigate, I was sure Kevin would already be at work at the police station, and my first client wasn't coming until nine o'clock. I could also tell him about Tobias's connection to Hannah. I ran a hairbrush through my thick dark hair and pinned it up. I pulled on my cycling bloomers under my gray work dress, tied on my bonnet, and headed down the road on my trusty steel steed. Buying a safety bicycle in April had been one of the smartest purchases I'd ever made.

Five minutes later I leaned the bike against a lamppost and ran up the steps to the police station. I was halfway up when the outer door pushed open. Kevin himself stepped out, looking rather worse for the wear. He saw me and groaned.

"Miss Carroll. I am not surprised to see you so bright and early this morn. I would have sent for you in any case. I've just been reading Gilbert's report." Moisture beaded on his ruddy face, and the buttons on his high-collared uniform shirt strained over an ample belly.

"Kevin, thee knows I prefer to be called Rose." Quakers did not hold truck with titles, but it was often hard to convince non-Friends to adopt the same practice of equality. I sometimes thought I should wear a small badge with *Please call me Rose* lettered on it, for all the times I've uttered those words. "I have several pieces of information—"

"About Hannah Breed's death." He made a tsking sound. "You were there."

"Yes."

He surveyed up and down the busy street. The horse-drawn trolley clattered by, filled with people on their way to the day's work. A matched pair of chestnut mares pulled a graceful Bailey carriage, and a jay squawked from the tall swamp oak on the corner. He gestured to a bench on the bricked walkway.

"Have a seat. I need to interview you, since you are a witness to the facts of last evening. You ended up quite helpful to me in the murders of last April. You know I can't involve citizens in my investigation, but if you have information to share, I'll gladly hear it."

After we both sat, I turned to him on the bench. "Is thee thinking this is also a case of murder?"

"That hasn't yet been determined."

I gazed at him. Murder, not an accident. That he was even entertaining the thought meant he had reason to believe Hannah's death might be homicide. But why?

"I know Officer Gilbert asked you last night, but let me ask again," he said. "You didn't see anyone in the vicinity of the body who was acting suspicious? Didn't see a weapon about?"

"No to both questions."

"Your niece is a mill girl, too. I expect she knew this Miss Breed. Do you know if the girl had been in trouble, had jealous suitors, that kind of thing?"

"Not that Faith has mentioned. She worked with Hannah, and was friendly with her outside of the mill, as well. Thee knows Hannah was also a Quaker, I assume."

He nodded. "You know, I need to question Dr. Dodge, as well. Gilbert said the two of you were together at the fireworks. Dodge wouldn't happen to be a beau of some kind, would he?"

I felt my cheeks warm. "In fact, yes."

Kevin frowned. "Is he a good man? Kind to you, respectful?"

I laughed. "Thee sounds quite protective. Yes, he is very good, very kind, very respectful. And he comes from a good family over in Newburyport. Thee doesn't need to worry."

He cleared his throat. "That's all very well, then. I suppose he's one of your Quakers, too, then."

"No, he's not."

"Is that so?" His eyebrows ascended nearly to his hat. "You can't go marrying someone outside your church, now, can you? My mother would have throttled me if I'd ever even thought of doing such a thing."

I gazed at Kevin. He was older than I, a devout Roman Catholic, and a man who, while intelligent, didn't often look beyond the boundaries of what he thought was conventional and usual.

"Did I say anything about marriage?" I kept my tone light. This was not the time to begin a discussion of the changing times and the gradual opening of the Society of Friends to new ways, nor of David's mother's unfavorable view of me.

It was his turn to laugh. "No, you didn't. And I will retreat from trying to act the detective about your private life. Now, what brought you down here this morning?"

"I came because I wanted to tell thee that I spoke with Hannah yesterday morning. She was in a bit of trouble. She told me she was in the family way."

Kevin's eyes flew wide. "The girl couldn't have been more than eighteen. Not married, either, I'll wager, not if she worked in the mills."

"She wasn't married, and she was seventeen."

His jaw clenched as he shook his head.

"She wouldn't tell me who the father was," I said. "She said she couldn't."

"Couldn't or wouldn't?"

"She said she couldn't," I repeated.

"Huh. I'm surprised she didn't want to hold him accountable. Unless he was a married man." He narrowed his eyes.

That would explain why Hannah had said they weren't able to marry. "Does thee know her family lives on distant Nantucket Island?"

He pursed his lips. "Yes, I was informed of that fact by her landlady. More's the pity."

"My niece Faith told me this morning a young man by the name of Tobias Cartland was courting poor Hannah. A Quaker from New Hampshire, she said. He works in Clarke's carriage factory."

"Aha. The suitor. That's good to know. Thank you, Miss Ca... Miss Rose." He grinned at me. "I've told you my sainted mother rolls in her Irish grave every time I address you by your Christian name, now, haven't I?"

I was glad for a moment of levity. "Thee has."

Two ladies dressed in fine summer gowns bustled by on the walkway. The older of the pair cast me a disapproving look, as well she might. A young woman sitting on a public bench laughing with a police detective before eight o'clock in the morning wasn't a generally approved social activity. Good thing for me I didn't care.

SIX

I'D POPPED THE LAST bite of cold chicken pie into my mouth when the noon whistle sounded. My morning appointments had gone well and I'd be heading out shortly for the home visit.

Someone pounded on the front door with great urgency. "Midwife!" a male voice called.

I rushed to open the door. I faced a thin man of about my own age turning his cap in his hands. An open gig and horse sat in the roadway.

"Miss Carroll? We need a midwife. My wife's time has come. You must help us. You've got to help Pearl." His curly black hair was damp, and red spots flared in his acne-scarred cheeks.

I searched my memory for a client named Pearl. "What's the last name?"

"Hoyle, miss." Sweat dripped off his chin. "I'm Patrick Hoyle."

"Is she a client of mine? Have I seen her before?" I was sure I hadn't.

"No, miss. She didn't get care ahead of time. But she's screaming something horrid. Will you come? We're just up the hill on Lake Street." He gestured. "The big brown house."

"I know that house. Yes, I'll be along shortly. Why doesn't thee head back and let her know I'm coming. I need to prepare my birthing bag."

"I can stay and drive you. It'll be faster that way."

"All right, then. I won't be long."

I hurried back in and made sure my satchel was ready. I splashed cold water on my face and neck, washed my hands, tidied my hair, and secured my bonnet. I could have walked the few blocks to the house, but it was straight up Powow Hill and I'd arrive a lot fresher if I accepted the ride. I wrote a quick note to Faith that I was at a birth and left it on the kitchen table for her. The family was used to me disappearing at all times of the day and night, and not returning home for a full day's cycle at times. But since Faith would be alone, I wanted to reassure her. I was about to close the door behind me when I remembered my afternoon client. I blew out a frustrated breath, and then realized I could send this fellow along with a message for my client after he'd delivered me to the home. I ran back inside and quickly penned a note at my desk about postponing the visit, waving it in the air to dry as I made my way to the gig.

Five minutes later, after he dropped me off and drove away to deliver my message, I climbed the steep front stairs of the Lake Street home and rapped on the front door. The house was wide and substantial perching on the side of the hill, with rounded bow windows upstairs and down in the middle of the building. When I turned to look behind me I could see all the way down to Market Square, with the steeple of the Baptist Church, the smokestack at Walsh Manufacturing, the tower at the Hamilton Mill, and the brick edifice of Saint Joseph's dominating the horizon.

A woman opened the door. "Oh, thank the Virgin Mary you've arrived, Rose. The poor girl is in agony."

"Catherine Toomey, what is thee doing here?" I asked. I usually saw her behind the counter at Sawyer's Mercantile, where we were congenial acquaintances but not what one would call personal friends.

"I'm Pearl's mother-in-law." Her rosy cheeks and silver-streaked black hair covered with a kerchief gave her a homey, welcoming appearance as she extended her hand. "She's been laboring since dawn. I'll be the one who was after sending for yeh." Her Irish way of speaking was more pronounced than usual.

"Thy son. It was he who fetched me?"

She smiled. "That's me Patrick."

"But he is so much older than thy twins, and he has a different name." I'd delivered her twin girls four years prior. She was an older mother but hadn't experienced any problems with the girls' births.

"Twenty-three years older." Catherine laughed. "Patrick was from Mr. Hoyle, me first husband, who crossed the dark river these many years past." She crossed herself.

"Well, I'm happy to help." I shook her strong, broad hand. "Thy home is lovely. And with a splendid view."

She laughed. "Oh, it's not me own home. It belongs to the Colby family. Now come along upstairs, Rose." She led the way into the vestibule and up a gracefully curving staircase.

"May I ask, is this the household of Lester Colby? A manager at the Hamilton Mill?"

Catherine paused on the landing. She frowned and peered at me as if trying to judge my intent. "Yes, that it is. It's his daughter Pearl who's now laboring to birth her baby, hers and me son's." She closed her mouth, opened it to say more, then sealed it shut again.

"I see. Where is Pearl's mother?" I thought it passing odd the mother-in-law should be attending to this birth in the home of the girl's own mother.

"Marie is here. But she's not so well, yeh know. We get along fine, and I'd agreed to come and help out when Pearl's time came."

A shriek sounded from the second floor.

"And it's most definitely her time." Catherine turned and hurried up the rest of the stairs, surprisingly light of foot for one with a filled-out figure such as hers.

I followed, appreciating the finely turned banister, its rich dark wood glowing in the sunlight, and the delicate yellow-sprigged wallpaper. I made my way to the open door of the room at the front of the house, but no sunlight or fresh air streamed in through the bow window. Heavy drapes were drawn and the air was stifling from the heat and from the lit gas lights. A pretty woman about my age lay in a bed big enough to sleep a family. Her white lawn nightgown was dark with the damp of perspiration and her sandy-colored hair lay in a long limp braid. She gazed at me, panting. Catherine wiped Pearl's face with a cloth, then rinsed the cloth in a basin of water and laid it on her brow.

I moved to Pearl's side. "I'm Rose Carroll, the midwife. Is this thy first baby, Pearl?"

"Yes," she whimpered.

"I'm going to take care of thee, but I'll need light and air. Catherine, will thee please open the draperies and the windows, and turn off the lamps?" A fear of fresh air was a thing of the past, wasn't it? Surely everyone now knew that a closed environment was not healthy. Or maybe not.

Catherine raised her eyebrows but did as I asked.

"And I'll need a stack of clean linens and a fresh basin of water. I understand thee received no antenatal care, is that correct?" I asked Pearl.

Pearl wrinkled her nose. "What about my auntie?"

"She means did you see a midwife in the months leading up to now," Catherine said with a kind smile, but she shot me a sideways glance.

Pearl shook her head quickly. "My mama said I didn't need one." She lowered her eyes to her huge belly.

"When did thee miss thy first monthly?" I drew out my Pinard tube to listen to the baby's heartbeat, but another pain hit Pearl before I could. "Breathe, Pearl, and blow air out through thy lips." I rolled up my sleeves.

She grasped the iron bedstead behind her head and hung on, her arms straining with the effort of the pain. "It hurts," she wailed between gritted teeth.

When the pain subsided, I checked the watch I'd pinned to my bosom and noted the time. Catherine came back in the room with her arms full of neatly folded cloths.

"Good. Catherine, please help her sit up more, with plentiful pillows behind her back. Pearl, I need to examine thee. And tell me when it was thee missed thy first monthly." The pains were coming close enough together that I decided not to waste time listening to the baby's heart. I drew back the coverlet and lifted her gown onto her swollen belly, the skin stretched tight. The size looked to be at full term, or close enough to be safe for the baby, of which I was glad. I'd lost a newborn to prematurity not long ago, and it was a sad, difficult thing for a new mother to accept.

"It was in October. Or November? I can't quite recall."

Close enough. I knelt on the bed. "I'll be putting my hand up thy passageway to assess the opening. Thee might feel discomfort. Try to breathe down to my hand. It can help." My nostrils flared as I removed her drawers and parted her legs farther. There was a putrid stench about her. But I'd smelled worse. I slid in my hand, being as gentle as I could. The opening to the womb was nearly ready, at four fingers' width.

"Good. Thee will meet thy baby soon. Thee isn't quite ready, but it won't be long."

When I drew my hand back out, I had to fight not to grimace. My fingers were covered with a thick yellowish discharge. I rose and turned away, searching out the basin Catherine had used when I first entered the room.

Catherine watched me wash my hands. She narrowed her eyes and moved to my side. "What is it?"

"I fear she has a gonorrheal infection. The clap. No wonder she's in so much pain." The birth passage would be terribly painful with the constant irritation of the infection. Patrick must have either given the disease to her or gotten it from her.

Catherine gasped and brought her hand to her turned-down mouth. "The poor thing."

Perhaps she didn't know of the transmittable nature of the infection, and that her son was surely also infected. But this wasn't the time to talk about that. "Indeed. But there's something worse. The disease can affect the baby's eyes. There's nothing to be done about it now." I'd seen babies end up blind from passing through a birth canal infected with the clap. I prayed this one wouldn't suffer thusly.

"That's an awful thing." Her nostrils flared. "The wee baby's eyes? May our sainted Mary watch over them." She crossed herself.

"I'll need soap and several basins of clean water, if thee will," I said to the accompaniment of a long guttural groan from Pearl. Catherine rushed out of the room as I took up a cloth, dried my hands, and spread the cloth in front of Pearl's buttocks. I wet another one and cleaned her as best I could. I didn't know if such a measure would help, but it couldn't hurt.

Catherine hurried back in again with two stacked basins holding a bar of soap, as well as a large teakettle. "This just boiled." She set the kettle on a chest at the end of the bed and brought a pitcher of cold water over to it.

I stood and assembled warm water in one basin, and washed Pearl again, this time with soap, after the pain subsided.

"What are you doing with all this washing?" she complained. "That ain't necessary, is it?"

"We want to give your baby its best chance at good health and a long life." Even if it did end up with damaged eyes.

————

Traces of light-colored hair were visible inside the opening to Pearl's birth passage twenty minutes later. "I can see the baby's head." I said. I used a knuckle to push my spectacles back up the bridge of my perspiring nose. It was only marginally cooler in here with the windows open, but at least there was some movement of air, and it was no longer stale and oppressive. "With the next pain, go easily. Pant for me instead of bearing down. Little breaths are best."

Catherine pulled out a string of rosary beads and stood fingering them as she silently mouthed what I expected was a prayer.

Pearl complied, as if she were blowing out a candle, over and over. As the contraction seized her body, the top of the baby's head slowly emerged, and then it was out.

"Good, Pearl. Very good," I said, as I wiped the baby's face clean and swept my finger through the mouth to clear it of mucous. "I hold thy baby's head in my hands. Now, the next time thee feels the contraction, bear down with all thy might," I said, keeping my tone encouraging. When I heard murmuring near the door, I peered in that direction.

In the doorway next to Catherine stood a woman with beautiful features but a near-skeletal figure. Pale blond hair showed under a lacy house cap and dark shadows lined her eyes, which carried a yellowish tinge I could see even from here. This must be Pearl's ill mother, Marie, experiencing some kind of wasting disease.

"Thank you, Miss Carroll, for helping my girl," Marie said. "I'm her mother, Marie Colby."

This was no time for the niceties of introductions, or even to ask her to call me Rose.

"Mama," Pearl wailed. Her nostrils flared as the next pain began. She squeezed her eyes shut.

Marie moved slowly to Pearl's side, as if walking hurt her, and stroked her daughter's forehead. "You'll be fine, my sweet. Do as Miss Carroll tells you."

"Push, now, Pearl." I kept one hand under the baby's head and the other ready for the torso that would soon appear. "Push with as much effort as thee can muster."

"I can't! It hurts."

"You have to, Pearl," Catherine urged. "Your travails are almost through and you've done very well."

Pearl grunted, her face reddening with her effort. It was an effort with a grand reward, as the baby's shoulders cleared one after another, and a little boy slid into my hands. Grateful he was of a healthy size, I held his new soul in the Light of God as I took a clean wet cloth to his eyes and dabbed them as free of the discharge as I was able. I then tied off the umbilical cord and used the clean blade from my kit to cut free the tough silvery cable, a lifeline no longer necessary.

I held him up. "Thee has a son, Pearl Hoyle."

The infant, whose skin was pinking up nicely, filled his lungs for the first time and let out a suitably loud cry.

Pearl laughed. "My son is alive!"

"A boy, my sweet," Marie said, leaning down to kiss Pearl's forehead. "A blessed son."

Before I laid the baby down on the linen Catherine had set out, I saw tears of joy seep down Pearl's cheeks, tears matched by her mother's.

Catherine wrapped the tiny boy, beaming down at his face. "Hello, my wee grandson."

His dark eyes gazed up at her with that look of calm wisdom all newborns seem to possess. I only hoped he'd be able to actually see his grandmother's face in the future, as well as the rest of his world. I thought of Hannah's baby, who could not live. A generation stopped in its tracks, neither mother nor baby surviving the terrible attack. I shook off the thought—my work here was not yet done.

"Pearl, the afterbirth will come out with the next pain. Don't fear, but do give a push when thee feels another contraction." There was still the risk of bleeding and infection, particularly with Pearl's gonorrheal case.

Catherine brought the baby over to Marie, who stroked his cheek but did not reach out for him. Marie's face suddenly paled even more than before and she sank into the chair beside the bed. When Pearl reached up her arms to Catherine for her son, I shook my head.

"Wait until the placenta is born, please," I cautioned.

With a high-pitched cry, Pearl expelled the mass of the afterbirth, and then exhaled a noisy breath of relief. I was similarly relieved to find the placenta intact, without tears or pieces missing, and I was easily able to stanch the small amount of blood that followed after it. With several of the most important hurdles of childbirth cleared—an unobstructed birth, an apparently healthy baby, no postpartum hemorrhaging—I began to clean up.

In the best way of it, women at the end of their pregnancies go down into death and bring forth life, but the birth process did not always end up as happily as it had today. I held the baby and his new family in the Light that each of their lives would be healthy and long.

SEVEN

"THEE CAN COME UP now," I called downstairs to Patrick some minutes later. He sat slumped in a chair in the front hall.

He lifted his head and stood. "Is my Pearl all right?" he asked. "She was screaming something awful."

I smiled at him. "She's fine, and so is thy son." I would speak to him of the infection later.

"A son!" He slid back onto the seat with a look of wonderment. "A son?"

"Most assuredly. Does thee want to meet him?"

Patrick tore out of the chair and ran up the stairs, taking them two at a time. I have seen many first-time fathers become overwhelmed with joy when they meet their baby, although not all are happy about starting a family. Patrick won the prize for delight and adoration, though. He knelt at the bedside and stroked the newborn's cheek with one finger, then made the same motion on Pearl's face.

"Look at him, husband," she said, her gaze on the child. "Ain't he just perfect, then?"

"He's perfectly perfect." He glanced up at his mother. "Isn't he, Ma?" He laughed. "We'll have to call you Granny now."

The baby had two grandmothers, but Marie had returned to her room. I thought I might inquire about her health before I left. I could at least discern if she was receiving adequate medical attention.

"You can hold him, Paddy," Catherine said.

"Oh, no." He shook his head, frowning. "I wouldn't want to hurt him."

"Thee won't hurt him. Make sure to support his head." I liked it when a father felt a bond with his infant, and I had a suspicion holding the baby when it was new could help that bond become stronger.

"You'll have a lifetime of holding him, my boy, God willing." Catherine beamed at the threesome.

"Then I'll wait. You're not injured, Pearl?" Patrick asked her.

"I'm a bit sore, you know, down there. But Rose and your mother helped me through."

"She's going to be fine," I said. Except for the infection. "She's going to suckle the infant now, Patrick. Thee should leave us. I'll call thee when she's finished."

He turned in the doorway with a longing look.

"Off with you now, son." Catherine shooed him out and shut the door, then busied herself tidying up the room.

I was helping the baby latch on to Pearl's breast for the first time when the door burst open. Lester Colby stood there, a wide smile on his ruddy face, but the smile slid off and his eyes widened as he focused on Pearl. She grabbed for her shawl and covered her breast as well as the newborn.

Catherine hurried over to him. "Mr. Colby, your girl's feeding the wee babe," She said, taking Lester's elbow. "You'll have to go on out, now."

"But Patrick said I have a grandson, Mrs. Toomey!" He blinked. "My first grandchild."

"Thee does," I said, smiling. Although perhaps I shouldn't be smiling, based on how he'd glared at me last night when I defended Akwasi's character. I decided Lester hadn't quite registered who I was, and I might as well leave it that way for now. This family had more important priorities.

"Oh, Papa. Come and meet him." Pearl lifted the baby out from under the shawl.

I didn't stop her, since the tiny fellow hadn't begun to suckle yet. In four swift strides Lester was at the bedside. He reached for the baby and cradled him in his arms, and he clearly knew to support the head.

"Does he have a name?" Lester asked, gazing into the baby's eyes.

"Not yet. Patrick and me, we couldn't decide."

"Lester, do you know the midwife, Rose Carroll?" Catherine asked.

He focused on me as if for the first time and narrowed his eyes. "I've seen you before today."

"My niece, Faith Bailey, works for thee. And I attended the fireworks last night." I watched him to see if he'd remember.

He blinked a few times and nodded his head once in acknowledgment. "You came to the defense of that African. You can't trust them, you know."

"I believe attributing negative traits to an entire people is false and wrong." I stood tall. "Akwasi, and many others who have descended from African blood, are entirely honest and trustworthy. And I might mention I have encountered many with skin as pale as thine who are deceptive and act in hurtful ways. We are all children of God."

"Hmph. Well." He cleared his throat. "That's neither here nor there." He didn't meet my gaze. When his grandson let out a cry, Lester rocked him and cooed to him until the little fellow quieted. Lester Colby certainly was possessed of a kind and gentle side, despite what the girls and Bertie had said about him. Like other Friends, I believe there is that of God in each person, although some seem to hide it more deeply than others. In my experience, everyone has at least a kernel of good in them, if we are patient enough to wait for it.

————

After Lester went back downstairs and Pearl had successfully nursed her child for the first time, she and the baby nestled in to sleep. I packed my satchel, and Catherine and I went into the hall, leaving the door ajar in case Pearl called for help.

"I can't thank you enough, Rose, for coming to our rescue. I don't know why that foolish girl and her mother didn't want to have the care of a midwife before her labor began. Pearl had a notion I could help her birth the baby." She pressed her lips together. "When the screams set up, I told Patrick in no uncertain terms he needed to go fetch you. We'll find Mr. Colby now and get your payment."

"I'd appreciate that. You'll need to watch the baby's eyes for infection."

"Mother of God." Catherine crossed herself.

"I hope his eyes will not be affected, but keep watch for extra discharge and call for me immediately should you see it."

"I shall."

"I'd like to say good-bye to Marie before I leave. Which is her room?"

Catherine led the way down the hall to a room at the back of the house. She knocked lightly, and when we heard a faint bidding, she pushed the door open.

"Mrs. Colby, Rose here is going now."

Marie sat on the other side of the gracefully proportioned room in a plush armchair, her feet up on a hassock. A rich maroon blanket covered her lap and legs despite the heat. The leaves of a tall elm outside the window barely stirred. I caught sight of the brilliant red of a cardinal in the tree.

"How is the baby?" she asked in a soft voice.

"He is well." I approached her chair. I could wait to discuss his eyes if and only if a problem arose. "He and thy daughter are resting at present. Is there anything I can do to make thee comfortable before I leave?"

"I don't think I'll ever be comfortable again, Miss Carroll. But I appreciate your asking. I now thank God for every additional day He lets me stay among the living, and am grateful I was able to meet that grandson of mine."

Catherine bustled over and helped Marie sit up a little straighter, plumping the pillows behind her. The contrast between the well-fed, rosy-cheeked Catherine and the gaunt, pale Marie was even more shocking seeing them side by side.

"We're an odd couple, aren't we?" Marie laughed, but without any energy behind it. "I never expected my daughter's mother-in-law would become one of my best friends."

"And I expect we're going to stay best friends for a long, long time," Catherine said. "I don't want to be hearing any more of your talk about additional days, now, Mrs. Colby."

"Miss Carroll—" Marie began.

"Please call me Rose."

"Very well. Rose, did you hear of the terrible murder in town last night?"

"Murder?" I said. "I don't think the police have determined that yet. But yes, I did." Did I want to talk with this very sick woman about witnessing Hannah's death? No, I certainly didn't.

"I'm not able to get out, but the maid told me this morning…" Her voice trailed off when the door opened and Lester strolled in carrying a pipe.

"What did the maid tell you, missus?" He smiled at her and walked over to plant a kiss on her forehead. He tapped the pipe and drew out a safety match.

"Lester, please don't smoke that horrid thing in here," Marie said. "I've asked you so many times not to."

He sighed and laid the pipe and match on a low table. "How has your day been, my sweet? And did you meet our little fellow?"

"Yes, I've met our grandson," Marie went on. "And my day has been no worse than any other, for which I'm blessed. Indeed, it's a large measure lighter because of Pearl and the baby both surviving with their lives and their health."

"I'm going to get you down to that cancer hospital, Marie, I swear it." Lester's voice had taken on a hard edge.

So it was cancer she had—one of the worst and least curable diseases, one afflicting people from all walks of life. "The New York Cancer Hospital?" I asked. "I have heard of it, with its curved walls and healthy air. Will thee be seeking a cure there, Marie?" David

55

and I had discussed the hospital, built only four years ago after former President Grant died of the disease. The hospital featured innovative architecture designed to eliminate the sharp corners where dirt and disease could lurk. Patients' heads could be farther apart in the round wards, and special ventilation systems kept the air fresher.

"It's terribly expensive. And I may be too ill to travel." Marie waved a hand weakly.

"Nonsense." Lester folded his arms. "I'm determined to find a way."

I wondered, if he was so determined to get Marie there, why he didn't insist on open windows and fresh air here at home.

Catherine looked at him. "Mr. Colby, Rose here needs payment for attending the birth. She's a professional midwife, and even when she's called into service at the last minute, she should be paid."

"Of course, of course. What's the charge?"

"Two dollars, please," I said.

He pulled a roll of bills out of his pocket and peeled off two one-dollar greenbacks. "We thank you, of course, for taking good care of our Pearl."

"I'll be back tomorrow to check on her." I turned to Catherine. "Make sure Pearl drinks plenty of fresh milk and boiled water. Even ale is fine, and it's good for her milk production. And send for me before then in case of fever or excessive bleeding."

"We will. And thank you so much for taking care of her."

"But wait, Rose," Marie said. "I was asking what you knew of the killing."

"Now, dear, you don't want to be talking about unpleasantness." Lester frowned at his wife. "It'll only make you sicker."

"Yes, I do want to." Marie lifted her chin. "And no, it won't make me more ill. You don't know what it's like to be confined to a house, to a room. I need to know what's happening out in the world."

I caught a flicker of what must have been a lively and vital personality before the illness drained it of energy. Lester obviously hadn't told his wife about seeing Hannah's body last night, and just as obviously, she wanted to know. But why hadn't he told her?

"A teenaged acquaintance of my niece was shot and killed in the crowd at the Independence Day celebration last night at the Little Farm," I said. "A physician and I were nearby but were unable to save her life."

Catherine gasped and crossed herself.

"What a horrific thing to witness," Marie said, her mouth pulling down.

"Indeed. The girl was only seventeen," I said. "She worked in the mill for thy husband, as a matter of fact. But the police have not determined if it was murder or an accident. I don't know why someone would kill Hannah, and in such a public place. There were plenty of guns going off in foolish celebration, so perhaps her death was accidental. Either way, it's a great waste of a young vibrant life."

Lester gazed out the window for a moment, then turned back to us. "That young miss shouldn't have been out in public alone. God only knows what kind of riffraff she was consorting with."

I frowned at him essentially blaming Hannah for her own death, but I wasn't going to argue about it in front of Marie. She had enough troubles.

———

In the street in front of the Colby home, I met Patrick pulling a shiny red child's wagon full of packages. In his other hand he grasped a huge bouquet of summer flowers: daisies, zinnias, and dahlias.

"Look, Miss Carroll, I got gifts for my boy." He was breathless with both the heat and his excitement. "A wagon for only a dollar, and cast your eyes on this." He laid the flowers on the wagon, grabbed a small flat paper-wrapped package, and ripped the string off it. A moment later, beaming, he held out a little sailor suit in navy blue with short pants and white piping.

I laughed. "Splendid, Patrick. That'll fit him in about a year's time. Maybe he can wear it on his first birthday." Or second, more likely.

Patrick picked up the flowers again. "These are for my girl. She worked so hard." His smile transformed into a worried look. "She's all right, isn't she? I know you said she was, but is she truly?"

"I'll check on her tomorrow, Patrick. If she stays quiet and drinks plenty of liquids to make milk for the child"—and if nothing unexpected happened, I didn't add—"she'll recover from the birth. But I must speak with thee. Thee wants Pearl to be a healthy mother to thy son and wife to thee, I assume?"

"Of course." All the cheer slid off his face as he gazed at the ground for a moment. He looked up with a determined set to his mouth. "Are you talking about the infection?"

"Yes. Thee must have it, too. Has thee had treatment?"

"No. My case seems to be in abeyance. But poor Pearl's symptoms have not gone away. I must have gotten the clap from the one wretched time I visited one of those houses down by the train station. Before I was married, I assure you." He twisted his hands together over and over as if scraping off the shame.

"I know of an antiphlogistic treatment I can administer to both of you. It isn't always effective, but it sometimes helps to reduce the inflammation of the disease."

"Oh, please do. I will make sure Pearl takes it. I have felt guilty ever since I learned I'd passed the clap to my dear wife."

"I'll bring the medicine next time I come, then. It's an extract from a tropical tree, the copaiba. I have some at home."

"We'd be grateful." His face lightened again. "I'd better get me upstairs again, then." He reached for my hand and clasped it in both of his. "I can't thank you enough."

I extricated my hand while it still retained feeling. "Go then, and be a proud father." I shooed him away with both hands and watched as he lifted the loaded wagon and ran up the stairs to the house. I probably should have told him about the baby's eyes, but at least Catherine would be watching for infection. And maybe they wouldn't be harmed. I wouldn't cross that bridge until I came to it, as the poet Longfellow had said. Unfortunately, I was sure balsam of copaiba shouldn't be given to babies. Adults had a hard enough time digesting the extract from the South American tree. And as I'd told Patrick, it had only irregular success. Although some success was surely better than none at all.

I wondered at Patrick's occupation. He'd been present or nearby all afternoon. Was he not gainfully employed? If not, how could he afford to venture out and bring home a toy wagon full of gifts?

He halted and looked back. "Miss, I must pay you!" He looked at the load in his hands, at the door, and back at me. He set his things on the stoop and clattered back down the steps, hand in his pocket.

"No." I shook my head. "Pearl's father paid my fee. The business is settled."

He frowned. "Are you sure? But why would he pay for my wife's delivery? He's always saying he doesn't . . ."

"Doesn't what?"

Patrick blew out a breath. "It's this way, see. Me, I've got a good head for numbers. Got it from my da, who died these ten years ago. He left me some funds, a portion of which I've invested in the new stock exchange, and I make a good wage at the Counting House and from my other accounting jobs, too. But Mr. Colby—well, he's not so well set."

I couldn't help my eyes from straying to the large house.

"I think he went into some considerable debt moving into this residence, I'll tell you, Miss Carroll." He cleared his throat. "You're sure he paid you in full?"

"He did."

"I'll make it good with him, then. He'll appreciate that. Good day, Miss Carroll." He tipped his hat and made his way into the house.

Perhaps the job of a mill manager didn't pay as good a salary as one might imagine. Nice that Patrick seemed well set in life, though. I still found it odd Pearl hadn't sought prenatal care. Perhaps it was a lack of funds, if what Patrick said was true, although he didn't seem short on money. It was also curious that Pearl seemed uneducated compared to her husband or even her own parents. Maybe she was simply a little deficient in the intellect. But then why had a congenial, competent man like Patrick made her his bride? I shook my head. Orpha had often said we could never know what went on in other people's marriages, that it wasn't our place to analyze or criticize. I did my best to follow her advice.

I made my way down Lake Street, thinking once again of Hannah Breed's unborn child, which brought to mind the question of the baby's paternity. If I happened to appear at the Clarke Factory at shift's end, I might be able to find Tobias Cartland and query him about Hannah.

My watch read three thirty. Possibly enough time to make that home visit I'd canceled. Given the heat, on top of the intense nature of attending any birth, particularly a first, I decided instead to give myself the rest of the afternoon off. We had lemons at the house. A nice tart, sweet lemonade would slake my thirst, and Faith's, too, later. And maybe I would have received a note from David in the afternoon mail, which always brought a smile to my face.

EIGHT

WHEN THE CLARKE'S CARRIAGE Factory's shrill whistle blew at five o'clock, Faith and I were in position outside the gates on Chestnut Street. I'd picked up Faith at the end of her mill shift at four. She'd come along to identify young Tobias, since I couldn't match a face to that name, even though I'd searched my memory of last First Day. We talked as we watched the flood of men as well as a goodly portion of women pour through the gates. Faces bore fatigue and sweat, but a cluster of men joked and laughed, and a couple of young ladies linked arms as they walked. Overall the workers looked healthy and with energy. I knew Robert Clarke treated his employees with respect and dignity, from their working conditions to their pay. There would be no strikes at this factory, unlike those currently taking place in New York City.

"How did the other girls take the news of Hannah's death?" I asked my niece.

"We all worked with sadness today, Rose, and with some fear, too. Does thee think the detective will soon find the person who killed Hannah? What if he has a penchant for shooting mill girls?"

"I pray that is not the case, dear Faith." That thought had not occurred to me. Perhaps it had to Kevin. "And while we don't yet know if someone killed her purposely or by accident, it might be prudent not to travel about alone. Make sure thee has a friend with thee until the police put this death to rest. I can accompany thee to work in the mornings."

"I guess that'd be wise."

"Does thee know of other suitors Hannah had, besides Tobias? Maybe someone more difficult?"

She shook her head. "But Nora mentioned something dreadful today." Faith's brows knit together. "I thought one isn't supposed to speak ill of the dead, but she didn't seem to care about that."

"Oh?"

"She said Hannah was stealing from her and from others in the boardinghouse."

"What an accusation. Does thee imagine it was true?" I twisted out of the way of a man in such a hurry to get home he wasn't watching his step.

"I don't know." She pointed. "There he is. There's Tobias." She stepped forward and waved. "Tobias! Tobias Cartland."

A young man swung his head in our direction, then hurried toward us, carrying his jacket over one shoulder, swinging his lunch pail with the other hand. He stood only an inch or two taller than I. His unlined face sported what looked like his first try at a mustache and nut-brown hair poked out from under his tweed cap.

"Faith," he said. "Does thee have any news?" His hazel eyes widened and blinked in a gesture that would have looked hopeful if it wasn't overlaid with sadness.

"News?" Faith looked puzzled.

"About Hannah's killer. Thee mentioned last month thy aunt is a kind of investigator." He blinked at me and tipped his hat. "Tobias Cartland, miss."

Faith laughed. "Tobias, this is Rose Carroll. My aunt."

"I have seen thee at Meeting for Worship, Tobias, but I don't believe we have spoken before now. Thee should know I'm a midwife, however, not an investigator."

"I have seen thee at Meeting, too. But thee is too young to be Faith's aunt. I'd pictured an older lady, perhaps a spinster, who would go along with a magnifying lens and such and deduce things from clues. Like in that new story I read by Mr. Doyle, *A Study in Scarlet*. My uncle sent it over from England for me."

A spinster I was, at least so far, but I was young enough to be Tobias's big sister.

"Rose, I told Tobias about thy role in solving the murders in April." Faith hunched her shoulders a bit. "I hope thee doesn't mind."

"Of course not. But I didn't do much, in truth. I simply kept my eyes and ears out for the actual detective, Kevin Donovan." I looked at Tobias. "I'm so sorry for the loss of Hannah, Tobias. I understand you two were courting?"

His mouth turned down. "With emphasis on the *were*. We'd been sweet on each other. But then she started acting strangely. She pushed me away, said she couldn't see me anymore. I didn't understand why."

"Did you ask her?" Faith asked.

"Of course. She wouldn't tell me. Only said it wasn't meant to be. We're both Friends, so it couldn't have been a matter of religion."

"How long ago was this?" I asked

"About a month ago. It broke my heart." He stared down at his battered tin lunch pail, its lid askew.

About when Hannah would have known she was pregnant. But she clearly didn't tell him of her condition. And she'd said the father knew, so I was sure it wasn't Tobias. Poor boy.

"So thee has no new information about who shot my Hannah?" Tobias's eyes sagged at their outer edges.

"I'm afraid not. Thee would have to ask the police for that." A flash of blue caught my attention. "And speaking of Amesbury's finest, here is the detective himself."

Kevin strode up in the Amesbury Police uniform of blue serge, silver buttons, and a bowler-shaped helmet. Except on him the buttons strained across his middle, and the helmet perched almost comically atop his large round head.

"Did I overhear my title mentioned, Miss Rose?" He touched his hat, then clasped his hands behind his back and rocked on his heels.

"Thee did," I said. "I was telling Tobias here if he wants information about Hannah's death, he needs to talk with thee."

"Might you be Tobias Cartland, young man?" Kevin pursed his lips.

"Yes, I am. What can thee tell me about the man who shot Hannah?"

Faith raised her eyebrows and looked both expectant and worried. "I'm also interested. We mill girls are concerned it might be a deranged person who is after us, one by one."

"Is that so?" Kevin asked. "Mr. Cartland here is one of the very persons I myself am interested in. I'll need you to come with me down to the station and answer some questions, young man."

Tobias looked at Faith and at me. "But why? I don't know who killed my girl. And I wouldn't own a gun. I'm a Quaker." His mouth turned down as if in horror at the thought.

"You were walking out with Hannah Breed, were you not?"

"I was. But she had cut it off with me."

"Precisely the reason we'd like to have a word. Now, if you'd be so kind." Kevin took Tobias's elbow and gestured with his other hand at a police wagon waiting a few yards away.

The last workmen exiting the gates stopped and watched.

"But..." Tobias twisted to look at me. "Rose, can't thee tell him I didn't hurt Hannah?"

"I'm sorry. I'm certain of thy innocence, Tobias. But thee must go with Kevin at this time. I'm sure thee will be out and home within the hour. Isn't that right, Kevin?"

"Ladies." Kevin walked Tobias to the wagon.

I watched as he made Tobias get in the back, like a common criminal. What an awful thing to do to a young man, haul him off in front of his place of work.

"That don't look good for the lad," one of the workmen muttered. His friends shook their heads and they all walked on.

Faith took my arm. "Isn't there anything you can do?"

I tamped down my annoyance with Kevin and patted her hand. "Wait for justice to be served." And maybe do some asking around of my own. It was looking more and more as if Kevin was searching for a murderer, not a person with a gun who happened to miss the sky during the fireworks and instead fired a celebratory shot into Hannah.

———

I rang the bell of the wide white three-story building that was Virginia Perkell's, situated near the Powow upriver from the bustling mill area closer to the center of town. Faith had come with me. Over our supper I'd suggested we go ask Virginia about Nora's allegation of Hannah stealing. Faith had readily agreed.

Virginia pulled open the door and smiled. "Well, if it isn't the Quakers coming to call. Come on in with you, then." She stepped back, wiping her hands on a flowered apron and ushered us into the parlor at the front of the house. The clatter of forks on china, along with murmured female conversation, drifted forth from the rear of the house, and the air was fragrant with the smell of savory meat. "The girls are just finishing up their supper. What can I do for you? Will you sit down?"

I glanced at Faith. "We won't take much of thy time, Virginia. Faith, tell her what Nora said." I remained standing, as did Faith.

"Nora Walsh?" Virginia asked, narrowing her eyes.

"Yes," Faith said. "She told me Hannah Breed, God rest her soul, had been robbing her."

"I have heard Nora say that, too. I told her she might consider holding her tongue if she didn't have proof of this crime. I'll not have my girls slandering each other." Virginia folded her hands at her waist and tapped a finger. "However, I myself have noticed a few small items around the house go missing of late. A spoon here, a small snuff box there. Nothing of great value, mind you, but gone, nonetheless."

"I would guess thee has asked thy lodgers about these wayward possessions," I said.

"Nobody claims to know where they went. Including Hannah as recently as Monday."

"Does thee clean the rooms?"

"The girls are responsible for that. But I'm just about ready to go exploring up there. I can't have it spread about town that my boarders are petty thieves, not even one."

"Has Hannah's family been notified of her death?" I asked. Someone at Meeting might have done so, I realized.

"That Detective Donovan said he notified them. Sent a telegram. I suppose they'll be up to fetch the girl's body."

"And for the memorial Meeting for Worship, too?" Faith asked.

"I'm not sure about that. It'll be up to the family to decide if they want to hold such a meeting here in Amesbury," I said. "I'd say it'd be more likely they would conduct the service back at home."

"Nantucket's pretty much awash with Quakers, I have heard." Virginia cocked her head. "Involved in the sailing industry, aren't they?" She pointed to a splendid painting of a clipper ship above the mantel, its sails full with wind. "My uncle painted it during a stay on Nantucket some years back. He was quite the artist, and thought the light was different, special, on the islands."

A voice called out, "Mrs. Perkell," from the back.

"One moment," she called. "Is there anything else I can help you with?" she asked. "I've my own family to feed yet."

"Thee has been very kind. I think that's all," I said.

A girl bustled down the hallway toward us. "Mrs. Perkell, we're after needin' more ..." Nora Walsh trailed off and came to a halt when she saw us. "Hallo, Faith, Rose. What brings yeh here?" Her striped shirtwaist was rumpled, and her hair was done up in a messy knot on her head.

"We're asking a few questions relating to Hannah's death," I said. "I understand thee thought she was stealing from thee."

Nora set her fists on her hips. "And that she was. She took the coins I was savin', and me Gran's silver ring. Gone like a leprechaun spirited them away." Her eyes flashed.

"Miss Walsh, I have already instructed you not to speak further of this matter." Virginia's nostrils flared. "I'm responsible for you girls while you're away from home. Unless you saw her take those things, or have found them among her possessions, you're to stop accusing the poor dead girl. Do you understand me?"

"I think we should have gone to the police about it," Nora said. "Now Hannah's dead, I'll never get my things back."

"Miss Walsh." Virginia's tone was stern.

Nora rolled her eyes. "Yes, ma'am." She dragged the two words out. "I'll see yeh tomorrow, then, Faith," she said and headed back down the hall.

Virginia shook her head. "She never did like Miss Breed and I'm not sure why. I wouldn't be surprised if Miss Walsh hid her own things just so she could cast blame on Hannah."

Gazing down the hall after Nora, Faith opened her mouth to speak and then shut it again. It wasn't until we'd said good-bye and were walking down the sidewalk that she spoke.

"I think Nora is sweet on Tobias. Maybe she was trying to get Hannah in trouble so she could have Tobias to herself."

"Does he return her feelings?" I asked.

"No, not at all," Faith scoffed. "He had eyes only for Hannah, and truly pined when she shunned him. He used to stand at the entrance to the mill on Seventh Day when we were dismissed at the noon whistle, because he works only five days a week. He'd come around and wait for Hannah. Even after she'd rejected him, he still came, always hoping she'd change her mind, I guess. But she never did, and the hurt look on his face was painful to see."

NINE

I sat at my desk at eight the next morning penning a return letter to David, who had, in fact, sent a note to me yesterday. I told him about Pearl's birth as well as the few facts I'd learned about Hannah's death.

A quick thunderstorm had blown through during the night and the temperature was blessedly cooler today. I glanced up when I heard a furious rapping at the front door. I rose, opening it to find a distraught Esther MacDonald in front of me.

"Oh, Rose, you have to help us." She stood as straight as when I'd met her during the Independence evening festivities, but her hat sat at an odd angle and an escaped strand of hair frizzed in front of her ear. Tears filled her eyes.

"What's wrong, Esther? Do come in."

She looked at the street and then at me. "All right. But we need to go soon."

After she stepped inside, I closed the door and led her to my office. "Go where?"

"They've taken my Akwasi. The police, they've taken him to the station. I think they're arresting him."

"This is dreadful news. How did thee learn of it?"

"I was there, at his office in the shop. I'd stopped in on my way to my job to bid him a good morning and bring him some berries I picked. A detective arrived with two other officers. The detective laid his hand on Akwasi's shoulder and said he needed to go with them. Rose, they handled him rough. Akwasi! He's the gentlest man on this good earth."

"Oh, dear. Did he try to resist them?"

"Well, in a way. He stood tall and asked them their reasons. He said he possessed rights under the law."

"And that he does." I signed the letter, set down my pen, and grabbed my bonnet. "I agree, we should get ourselves to the station and make sure they are not further mistreating him. I'm glad thee came for me." I had no morning clients today, and only needed to check on Pearl later and then be at my rescheduled home visit at one o'clock. Luckily the police station was only a few blocks distant. I quickly addressed the letter to David and left it out for the postman.

We hurried down the path to High Street, where phaetons and farm wagons clattered past, and the thrum of mill wheels turning in the rapid waters of the narrow Powow River filled the air.

"After we assess the situation, we can decide if he needs legal counsel," I told her as we walked.

Esther simply nodded. She seemed focused only on the street and the task ahead.

Before long we stood facing Guy Gilbert at the front desk of the station. The tall windows lining the office behind him let in plentiful light, and two of the battered wooden desks were occupied by officers bending over report forms. On the wall hung one of the new telephones.

Guy stood when he saw me. "Miss Rose." His gaze traveled over to Esther. Guy was a hardworking, well-meaning young man, but I didn't know if his good nature was free of prejudicial feelings toward those with darker skin.

"Guy, this is Akwasi Ayensu's fiancée, Esther MacDonald. Esther, Guy Gilbert."

"Officer." Esther's hands kneaded a handkerchief.

"Miss MacDonald, I'm sure you're here about your man." His tone conveyed sympathy. "And you too, Miss Rose."

"We are." I'd relinquished hope of ever getting Guy and Kevin to discard uttering a title in front of my name. At least he wasn't calling me Miss Carroll today.

"Detective Donovan has him in an interview room, Miss MacDonald. It's a matter of gathering information." He leaned both hands on the desk in front of him and lowered his voice. "But between us? I think you might want to retain a lawyer."

"It was Lester Colby who accused Akwasi, isn't that right? Was Lester down here this morning demanding an arrest?" I pressed my lips together.

"I can't tell you that, Miss Rose."

"Is Kevin going along with this negative opinion of colored folks?" I asked. I slid a glance at Esther, whose eyes were filling again.

Guy sighed. "Detective Donovan has to question anyone who might have seen or known something of the crime."

"He took young Tobias Cartland at the end of his shift yesterday. I assume Kevin let him go home."

"That he did. Mr. Cartland was most cooperative. It's a shame Mr. Ai … ai … What in blazes is his name again?"

Esther swiped at her eyes and took a deep breath. "Ayensu." She spelled it in a clear voice. "Ayensu," she repeated.

"Yes, that. It's a shame he resisted our officers."

"But he didn't!" Esther protested. "He merely asked for information on why he was wanted for questioning. I was there."

Guy lifted a shoulder. "If the man did no wrong, he'll be free soon enough."

Esther turned her back. I saw her struggle to contain her upset emotions, which looked to be warring with a good dose of anger. Guy's statement struck me as naive. Colored people were often treated unfairly, even when completely innocent of wrongdoing.

"Of course he did no wrong," I said in as firm a tone as I could muster. "He couldn't have killed Hannah. He was with Esther every minute of the evening. We'd like to see him now, please."

"I'll go back and see if the detective is done with him. If he is, Mr. Alwenzu will either be out here in a minute or in a jail cell."

Esther whirled. "It's Ayensu."

"Yes, ma'am. You'll be able to talk with him soon, whichever it is." Guy hurried out of the room.

I took Esther's hand, marveling at her smooth, cool skin. "We'll get him out. Please don't worry."

She lifted her chin, her deep brown eyes holding decades of stories. "Rose, I know you mean well. I know your church has helped Akwasi in so many ways. But you don't know about worry."

———

When Kevin emerged alone from the back, I knew the news would be bad.

"Kevin, we must see Akwasi Ayensu," I said. "Thee is holding him under false pretenses."

He ignored me. "Esther MacDonald?"

73

"Yes." She looked distraught, but she stood as straight and proud as ever.

"Your, uh, betrothed—is that correct?"

"Yes, we are pledged to marry."

"Well, he is accused of murdering young Hannah Breed. An eyewitness saw him fire the shot."

Esther gasped and brought her hand to her mouth, shaking her head.

"Kevin, this is preposterous and impossible." I folded my arms. "For one thing, he was with Esther during the entire evening of fireworks. Second, he had no reason in the world to shoot a mill girl. Finally, he is a fine, honest, person, better than most in this town. I demand thee release him at once."

Kevin cast me a look but once again addressed Esther. "Miss MacDonald, is it true you never left Mr. Ayensu's side during the evening?" He tapped a pencil on a pad of paper on the desk.

Esther looked at the floor. She looked at me, as if she were asking a question with her eyes, but I couldn't decipher it. She looked at Kevin and swallowed before speaking.

"Not the entire evening. I'd seen someone I work with and had strolled over to greet her. Akwasi stayed observing the show."

My heart grew cold. "When was this?" I asked.

Kevin groaned. "Miss Rose, I'll ask the questions, if you don't mind." He focused on Esther. "Miss MacDonald?"

"It was right before the commotion. When I saw the crowd gather, I rushed back to Akwasi's side."

"Exactly as he said." He slapped the pencil down on the desk with a crack.

It spoke to both Akwasi's and Esther's integrity they didn't lie for each other. And even if they had, even if they'd agreed on a

74

common story, surely honest eyewitnesses on the scene could testify the couple had been apart for a few moments.

She lifted her chin. "He would never, ever hurt another human being. He has the kindest soul I have ever met, despite the cruelest past you can imagine."

I knew Akwasi had been whipped and beaten as a child before he managed to escape to the north at age fifteen.

Kevin raised his eyebrows. "Maybe the lessons learned in his past aren't buried so deep."

"Tell us who made this slanderous accusation," I demanded, my second such an aggressive statement in as many minutes. "Was it Lester Colby?"

"Now how in tarnation did you know ..." Kevin shut his mouth and shook his head. "I mean, I'm not at liberty to say at this time."

"So thee has arrested Akwasi," I said. I felt a decidedly un-Quakerly anger rise up in me. "And what does thee posit as his motivation to kill? Doesn't thee have to take him before a magistrate today?"

"Miss Rose, I'm not answering any more of your questions. You said you and Miss MacDonald wished to see the prisoner. Follow me."

I took Esther's hand, now not cool but frigid, and followed Kevin through the heavy door. We passed several empty cells and one with a man snoring on the rough cot with the smell of alcohol in the air. A moment later we stood in front of the bars that separated us from Akwasi. When we arrived, he was pacing back and forth within the short confines of the space. After he saw Esther, he paused and took one long step to the barrier. His cheek bore a bruise and his shirt was torn at the shoulder. It looked like the officers had been rough indeed.

Kevin turned to us. "Now, I'm going to leave you ladies alone here, but it's only because I trust Miss Rose, you hear? You'll not be trying to set him free or some other kind of tomfoolery. I'll be right down the hall."

I turned toward Kevin to give the other two a moment of privacy. "I appreciate that, Kevin. But if thee thinks Hannah's death was a murder, thee should be devoting thy energy to finding the real killer. This man didn't murder that girl, and he will not hang for it." I emphasized *will not hang.*

"Justice will be served." Kevin spun on his heel toward the door.

"Yes." Akwasi's deep resonant voice sounded loud and clear behind us. "Let justice be served."

TEN

After ten minutes, Guy came in to the cell area and made us leave. Esther and Akwasi held hands through the bars in silence for a moment, their gazes locked, before Guy escorted us to the lobby. He wouldn't say another word about the arrest, despite my prodding.

"I'll go directly and seek the advice of John Whittier," I told Esther once we'd gained the sidewalk. "He'll find legal assistance for Akwasi. I know it."

"How can I thank you, Rose?" Her expression was somber and she kneaded one hand with the other. "You and the other Friends are the kindest souls I have ever met."

"Stay strong and hopeful. That'll be thanks enough."

"I'd already planned to convert to your religion. Now I shall, as soon as I'm allowed. Or should I say, *thy* religion?" She smiled for the first time this morning, but it was a pale relative of the beam she'd displayed the first time we'd met.

"I'm pleased to hear that."

Esther took my hand and squeezed it. "I must be off to my job."

"Where is thee employed?"

"I stitch upholstery for the company that supplies Bailey Carriages with their seats, and I'm already almost two hours late." She tucked a stray hair behind her ear and repositioned her hat, a summer boater wrapped with a brilliant green ribbon, before hailing the passing trolley.

I fervently hoped her employer wouldn't penalize her for her tardiness. She and Akwasi seemed made for each other. When I saw them interact back in the jail, they appeared to understand each other's thoughts and concerns without speaking. David and I enjoyed each other's company, but ours was a more verbal closeness. We talked about everything and anything, and I was glad of it. I hoped I could find a time soon to discuss all this recent business with him.

Glad I'd scheduled no appointments this morning, I made my way up a busy sidewalk on Friend Street to John Whittier's home only two blocks distant. He'd stayed away at his cousin's in Danvers during the July Fourth observances, likely because of the attention that would be foisted on him. He was a widely known poet in great demand, and had had an important and fiery career as an abolitionist in earlier days, as well. And I knew he didn't enjoy public speaking. But I thought he'd be back in Amesbury by now, it being already Sixth Day. Perhaps Lucy Larcom would arrive a day or two early. I wouldn't mind meeting the famous author and journalist, myself, despite having no aspirations whatsoever to become a writer.

As I walked, I thought again about Hannah's pregnancy. Who could be the father? That was what Kevin should be focusing on. I

stopped so suddenly someone behind bumped into me. A woman with a small child holding each hand excused herself and made her way around me, casting a glance back as she shook her head. What had made me stop was the idea that maybe Akwasi, counter to every notion I had of him, had impregnated Hannah. Akwasi wasn't yet married, but maybe Hannah had felt she couldn't marry a colored man. And perhaps Esther, out of jealousy, had shot Hannah when she'd parted from Akwasi at the fireworks. It was a horrible thought, though, and I couldn't see how it had any credence. I had to believe neither Akwasi nor Esther would act in such ways.

I knocked the clapper on the front door of John's plain white two-story home, and smiled when John himself appeared in the doorway.

"Friend Rose, do come in. I always welcome the sight of thy lively, intelligent visage." His tall figure bent over somewhat with age, John made his way through the open former kitchen and back to his study. I took a moment to examine the portrait of Lincoln hanging above the mantel and then followed him.

John sank into his rocking chair and gestured for me to take a seat, as well. His small desk bore evidence of recent scribblings, and his shiny black hat sat at the ready, as always. During the building of the latest addition to the house, he'd specified a window be installed in the door to the street. If he spied unwelcome admirers coming to call, he'd grab his hat and say he was just going out, a practice I found delightful in such an aged and esteemed man.

"Now, what ails thee?" he asked. "I discern thee has come to me with a problem."

"I have, indeed." I perched on the edge of the chaise.

"Then let us take a moment to hold this matter in silent prayer before we commence our discussion." He folded his hands and closed his eyes.

I did the same, but found great difficulty in stilling my worried thoughts. When I heard him rustle a couple of minutes later, I opened my eyes.

"Please, lay out thy issue so we may view it in the Light of God." He looked at me expectantly.

"John, a girl named Hannah Breed was killed on the evening of the fourth during the fireworks. She was a Friend from Nantucket, and worked at the Hamilton Mill with Faith."

He frowned. "I have heard of this crime, and I hold in my heart the sadness of the release of the girl's spirit."

"It is most definitely sad. But almost worse is that Akwasi Ayensu has been arrested for the murder this morning, not more than an hour ago."

John sat up straight. "What's that thee says? Akwasi? *Our* Akwasi?"

"I'm afraid so. It's possible the killing was accidental, because there were so many reckless men firing guns into the air that night. And I believe this accusation is a false one made by a man who harbors great resentment against coloreds. Still, Akwasi is in jail at present. I just came from there and he needs help. Can thee—"

"I shall summon my good friend Benjamin Lehigh of Newburyport. He's a skilled criminal lawyer, and a Friend. He'll see to it that Akwasi is first freed and then absolved." He leaned over to his desk, selected a sheet of paper and a pen, and began scratching out a message.

"I hoped thee could help in this way." I watched as he wrote, and wondered how dashing off a quick letter differed from the process of composing a brilliant poem like "Snowbound."

"But of course I'll help. I regard Akwasi almost as a son. He has survived great travails in his life, and he does not deserve even a minute more in a state of misery because of deceptive allegations."

"Does thee know his beloved Esther?"

John smiled, his dark eyes twinkling. "Now there's a match made in heaven, wouldn't thee say?" He finished his note and waved it in the air for the ink to dry.

"They appear well suited. And are possessed by a similar sense of honesty." I explained about their being apart for the critical few moments during the time of the killing, and how they'd both told Kevin the truth.

"I'd expect no less of Akwasi, nor of his beloved."

"Esther says she'd like to join the Religious Society of Friends." I didn't know of anyone converting to our faith in the current time. Clearly many had converted back when George Fox had started his protests against the hierarchies of established Christian faiths, saying we all have that of God within us and do not need an intermediary of any kind. "I hope that will be possible."

"Of course it is possible, with sufficient study and after being judged ready for membership by a clearness committee."

"Good. Did thee know she and Akwasi plan to marry?"

"I did. I'll give them my blessing and will attend their Meeting for Worship for Marriage, no matter what time of year." He handed me the note. "Will thee give this to Mrs. Cate on thy way out, please, and ask her to post it forthwith?"

"Of course." For a Friend who advocated equality at every turn, I thought it passing strange he used a title for his housekeeper. Perhaps she would have it no other way.

"I have pressing work to do before Lucy arrives, but I have no doubt Benjamin will arrive at the police station well before the end of day today. Do not fear, dear Rose. Justice shall prevail."

ELEVEN

I SPENT AN HOUR or more at home doing paperwork, but always in the back of my mind were thoughts of Akwasi in the jail cell. Nora with her accusations about Hannah. Lester's bigotry with regard to Akwasi. Patrick's hint about Lester's finances. Tobias's confusion at being abandoned. The question of who was responsible for Hannah's pregnancy. I had no answers, and that made for an unsettled feeling.

The morning mail brought a note from David—our messages must have passed each other going over the Chain Bridge—asking if I'd like to step out for some supper at the restaurant in the new Grand Hotel tonight. The invitation made me smile, as I very much wanted to have a chance to talk through the current situation with him and I always loved being in his company. He said to ask Faith if she'd like to come along, too. I wrote a reply and left it out for the afternoon mail.

I stoked the stove, extracted some leftover soup from the icebox for my midday meal, and warmed it. After I ate and packed the medicine in my satchel, I mounted my bicycle to ride up the hill to Pearl's. My home visit after that was across town on the Merrimack River, and the cycle would make the trip much easier.

Once at the Colby house, I looked at it more closely in light of Patrick's comments. It was definitely in need of paint here, repairs there. The railing on the front porch would leave splinters in a hand trailing along it, and a front window displayed a crack in the glass. After I knocked, Catherine again opened the door.

"Does the new mother fare well?" I asked. "It's a good sign thee didn't need to call me for anything urgent."

"She seems well. The little fellow is suckling nicely, too."

"Excellent. I'd like to mention a couple of things to thee, Catherine."

"Surely."

I beckoned her outside to the landing and lowered my voice. "Your daughter-in-law seems a bit, well, simple. And Patrick is quite acute and articulate. It seems an odd match."

She nodded slowly. "He's been sweet on her since they both were young. He's always felt protective of the girl, too. But you're right. She's not his intellectual equal by any means."

"If they have love and are happy, that's all that counts. But there is the matter of the infection I mentioned. The clap. Thee didn't know Patrick is also infected?"

She bit her lip and looked away. "I thought he might be ailing in that way a year ago, but he's seemed fine since. I wasn't going to ask a grown man about, you know, things like that."

"I spoke with him yesterday about it. I've brought a kind of medicine that might help the both of them."

"Bless your heart, then, Rose." She gazed back at me with hope-filled eyes.

"We'll see if it's effective. Unfortunately it's the only remedy available." I took a breath. I didn't like prescribing a cure that wasn't a cure, but it was all I could offer.

"And will it help the wee one's eyes, then too?"

"I'm afraid not, unless some of the effects are passed through Pearl's milk."

"More's the pity." Catherine made a tsking sound.

"Let me go up and check Pearl now and then I'll be off."

Catherine led the way upstairs. In the bedroom, Patrick's flowers were arranged in a vase barely containing them, and today the draperies were open and the windows, as well. Marie sat holding the baby in a chair next to the bed, where Pearl sat up with pillows behind her. Marie's color looked better today, and Pearl appeared in good health, too.

"Good morning, ladies," I said. I first moved to the infant. "How is our lad today?"

Pearl greeted me as Marie gazed down at the sleeping baby.

"He is quite sweet," Marie said. "But do you think he looks a bit yellow?" She held him up to me.

I took him to an upholstered chair near the window and sat. I unwrapped his blankets. His cord stump was healing well, but his face and torso did have a very slight jaundiced appearance. At least his eyes were clear. I glanced up at the women.

"Perhaps a little. Many newborns experience infantile jaundice. Two things can be done for that. Make sure thee is nursing him often, Pearl. And leave him unwrapped here in the rays of the sun. It'll help his body rid itself of the toxins."

"Toxins?" Pearl's voice rose in alarm. "Ain't that like poison?"

"It's perfectly normal, Pearl. It's his blood system finding its own equilibrium after having been attached to yours all these months.

Thee shouldn't worry unless his color becomes worse, not better. It can take a few days, though. Make sure thee gives him a sunbath several times each day."

"I'll see to it that happens, Rose," Catherine chimed in. "My Patrick had the same condition when he was born. She's right, Pearl. Don't be worrying or you could make yourself ill, and that wouldn't serve little Charlie, here."

"Thee has named him?" I asked. The baby awoke and let out a lusty cry. I rocked him in my arms and he quieted.

Pearl laughed. "Charles Lester Hoyle," she said with pride. "Patrick was set on naming him for his daddy who died."

Catherine crossed herself. "May my late Charlie rest in sight of the Holy Virgin."

Marie rolled her eyes. "You can imagine Lester isn't too pleased with being relegated to the second name. I told him to be quiet and take it like a man." She shook her head but smiled, looking happy to be here in the company of women.

I imagined she might not have many more such days in her life. I briefly held her in the Light for as many of them being happy ones as possible.

"Let's let Charlie have his first sunbath now, shall we?" I stood, laying him on the chair, and motioned for Catherine to come over.

She took him onto her lap in the sunlight. She cooed to him and stroked the bridge of his nose until his eyes drifted shut again.

I sat on the bed next to Pearl. "I'll quickly examine thee now. Is thee still bleeding some?"

"A little. Less than during a monthly, though."

"Good. That'll subside sometime in the next few days, but could linger on lightly for a few weeks. Nothing to worry about unless it increases or gives thee pain. I'm going to palpate thy belly now."

After Pearl nodded her agreement, I pulled down the coverlet and pressed in firmly but gently with both hands, exploring the womb within. "Good. Thy uterus is already firm and beginning to return to its normal size. Now tell me about giving Charlie the breast."

We discussed the details of nursing for a few minutes, with Catherine adding her advice, and Marie looking on, a satisfied look on her thin face.

"Pearl, I noticed during the birth that thee has a severe discharge. I believe thee has gonorrhea." I glanced at Marie

"Gone oh what?" Pearl asked, wrinkling her nose.

"It's the clap." Catherine looked up from the baby as she spoke.

Pearl's eyes became saucers. "The clap?" she asked, her voice rising into a squeak. She shook her head, hard. "I don't got no clap. Where'd I get something like that? Only whores get the clap."

"I spoke to Patrick and he acknowledged that he has the disease, as well, acquired before thy marriage to him," I said. "He passed it on to thee, and feels terrible about doing so."

"Why didn't he tell me? I just thought I had an itchy twat. Ain't there no medicine for it?"

I also wondered why Patrick hadn't spoken of the infection to Pearl. What was past was past, though. "I have brought a kind of medicine. It is not always effective, though, and I should warn thee it might cause some stomach distress." I extracted the box of gelatine capsules from my satchel. "You should each take one capsule three times a day. The medicine is embedded in liquorice to make it more palatable."

"I'll take one right this minute," Pearl said, and she did, washing it down with a swig from a tankard of ale that sat on the bedside table.

Charlie voiced his unhappiness by and by, so Catherine handed him to Pearl. I watched as she gave him the breast.

"Ow." She looked up at me. "Should it hurt when he first begins to suck?"

"That's normal. Thy nipples will grow accustomed to him. It'll hurt less and less in the coming days, until thee feels like thee has been feeding a baby forever."

"But so little milk comes out."

"That too will change. What thee feeds him now is perfect for his age and size. In a day or two the true milk will come in, and thee will have much more volume. God has created a clever system for women's bodies. The more the baby suckles, the more milk thee produces. When he grows and becomes hungrier, the milk increases, too." I never ceased to marvel at the natural balance of the quantity of breast milk and the infant's needs. I hoped her gonorrhea wouldn't hinder the milk flow, but I didn't believe it had that effect.

Catherine held up the little sailor suit and laughed. "That son of mine is delirious at being a father. Charlie will be walking before he can fit into this."

"Mr. Colby was just the same when Pearl was born, too." Marie chuckled softly. "Some men adore being fathers."

"Patrick was quite generous, bringing all those gifts yesterday," I said. "I met him outside when he'd just arrived home."

Pearl looked up from her nursing. "He's like that. And he earns a good steady income, doing the books for several businesses here in town. We're right blessed for a young family."

"Indeed you are," Marie said to her daughter, but the light went out of her expression, as if she was struggling with a wave of pain, and she turned her face toward the outside.

"All is in order here," I said, standing. "I'll be back for my next visit in two weeks time." I walked over to Marie and lowered my voice. "If I can help thee in any way with thy condition, please send for me."

She met my gaze. "I'm grateful for your assistance, Miss Carroll."

"Please call me Rose."

"Rose, then. I wondered if my girl had an infection. Do you think if she'd seen a midwife earlier she could have been cured before the birth?"

"There is no real cure, I'm afraid, just the copaiba balsam I gave her, which could lessen her symptoms. But why didn't Pearl seek out antenatal care?"

Marie let out a ragged breath. "I have been so ill that my strength to manage anything almost doesn't exist. And my husband is so difficult. I was partly afraid of his wrath if he found out Pearl had the clap. I didn't want him taking it out on her or on Patrick, who is so good to my girl. In addition, I would have had to arrange all Pearl's midwife visits and such. She's just not capable of doing things like that on her own. Patrick is busy with his work, and besides, pregnancy is the women's realm. I now see how wrong I was."

"We'll hope for the best."

"That we will. Rose, I hope Mr. Colby did not short you in your payment. I wish I had some extra token I could offer you ..." She studied her hands.

"He paid me in full. And I need no token other than seeing thy daughter and her baby well taken care of, of which we have direct evidence in front of us. Be well, Marie." I extended my hand. When she matched the gesture, I felt I was gently shaking the hand of a skeleton.

———

After I left the Colby household, I made an antenatal visit to a home in the Salisbury Point neighborhood and then cycled back along Main Street. The road bordered the wide Merrimack about five miles from where it merged with the Atlantic Ocean. The river's level and current came and went with the tides even this far inland.

All had been well at the visit. It was the third pregnancy for the mother, who'd experienced no problems in her earlier deliveries. The house, one dating from the Colonial days, was clean and airy, and the husband held a position in the shipping business that paid a more-than-decent income, judging from the tasteful decor of the home as well as the several servants in the family's employ. My client even said they would send a carriage for me when the labor began, a service for which I was grateful. Being summoned to a birth in the wee hours of the morning and then having to ride my bicycle several miles wasn't one of my favorite experiences—especially considering this baby would likely be born in November, when pleasant cycling weather had given way to sharp winds and short, dark days.

I neared Lowell's Boat Shop, a robust industry that built dories and skiffs. Slowing, I gazed at the boats anchored in the river near the shop. They were sturdy, well-crafted wooden boats, the same sort Lowell's had been manufacturing here for almost a hundred years. Two men stood in front of the shop, conversing and gesturing, one in workman's canvas overalls and the other in a neat suit. I looked more closely at the one in the suit, then braked to a stop near them.

"Why, Rose Carroll, what are you doing down here?" Patrick asked, tipping his hat.

"I made a home visit down the road there. And thee, Patrick?"

"I do the accounting for the shop." Patrick held the handle of a leather business valise in one hand.

The other man touched his hat and bade Patrick farewell, disappearing into the building, from which emanated sounds of sawing and hammering.

"It looks like business is thriving," I said.

"Indeed it is."

"I was with thy wife and Baby Charlie an hour earlier. They are both thriving, too." I told him about the slight jaundice and what I'd prescribed as treatment.

"You're sure it isn't serious?" His eyebrows joined in concern. "I can take him across the river to the hospital. I can afford the cost." He set his valise down and folded and refolded his hands.

I laughed. "No, it isn't a serious issue. It's perfectly normal. The women will watch and make sure the condition clears and does not worsen. In fact, thy mother informed me that thee experienced the same condition and remained a perfectly healthy baby."

"Good. I'll watch, too, of course. I don't know what I'd do if something happened to my son."

"We'll all do our best to ensure Charlie's good health. And speaking of health, I left the medicine for thee and Pearl. The dosage is one capsule three times per day. She already took one. I was surprised thee hadn't spoken with her about the disease."

"I tried to when her symptoms first appeared, but she didn't seem to hear me. I'll make sure she takes the capsules every day, and I'll take them myself."

"Good." I gazed at the river flowing by, and then back at him. "Thy mother-in-law seems very ill, and after the birth there was some discussion of the New York Cancer Hospital. Will she be going there?"

"Cancer is exactly what she has. Nobody has a real cure—I've investigated—and while Mr. Colby seems determined to take her to New York City, I know he can't pay the cost. I have offered to help, but he pushes me away each time."

"Then I'm afraid she may not have too many more days to enjoy being a grandmother."

He nodded gravely. "Pearl will be devastated, but at least she has her child."

"And thee." I patted his arm. "Are there other siblings in the family?"

"No, none."

"Mr. Colby has a good job at the mill, though, doesn't he? Why does thee suppose he is so lacking in funds?" I knew this was not the kind of question one asked in polite company, but these circumstances were all out of the ordinary. And I wanted to know.

"Are you sure he paid you in full?"

"Yes, he did."

Patrick cleared his throat. "Let us simply say he made some mistakes in his past which he has been forced to reckon with."

As I cycled homeward, I wondered what Lester, an apparently devoted family man, had done that ended up impoverishing him.

TWELVE

On my way home, I made my second visit that day to the police station. I felt obliged to tell Kevin about Nora's suspicions of Hannah stealing from her. I also wanted to share Faith's idea that Nora wanted in return to steal Tobias's affections away from Hannah. I doubted Nora would kill her roommate over such a trifling, but the Irish girl seemed to have a temper, and it was Kevin's job to investigate the shooting. Perhaps he also should be made aware of Lester Colby's reduced circumstances. Maybe by accusing Akwasi, Lester hoped to gain financially from ... from whom? John Whittier? Stranger things had happened. Bertie had mentioned knowing something about Lester's character. I reminded myself to ask her more about him. I also wanted to inquire about bringing Akwasi meals of a better quality than the usual tasteless overboiled jail fare from a local boardinghouse, as Bertie and I had done for her cousin in the spring.

When I walked into the station, I saw a thin, fair-haired man of about fifty in the waiting area. He wore a well-cut three-piece linen suit and a bright blue cravat and sat with one leg crossed over the other on the bench. He looked thin from good health, though, not illness, as he had color in his face and projected an energetic attitude. An attitude of a person who clearly didn't like to be kept waiting.

No one sat at the reception desk, and several other officers in the large room behind the desk appeared engrossed in whatever they were working on. The thin man slid over to make room on the bench, so I took a seat, smiling my thanks. I removed my bonnet, then pulled out a handkerchief from my pocket and patted my perspiring neck and forehead. Despite the morning's coolness, the sheer strength of the early afternoon sun blasted the air. Combined with the effort of cycling uphill from river's edge for two miles, my heated condition was enough to make me wish I'd not made this stop. I hoped to have a respite at home to refresh myself before my supper date.

"A busy department, this one, isn't it, miss?" the man asked with a surprisingly deep voice. He smiled at me.

"Indeed it is. A terrible crime happened on Independence Day, which added to their burden."

He stopped smiling. "The shooting of the young Friend. Did thee know her?"

I looked at him more closely. "Yes, I knew Hannah Breed. My niece worked with her. Thee is also a Friend, I gather." I didn't recognize him from Amesbury Meeting. His clothing was certainly richer and more colorful that I was accustomed to seeing on Friends, too.

"I attend Newburyport Meeting." He tilted his head, regarding me. "Thee is the midwife who asked John Whittier to help our colored Friend."

"Yes, but how—"

"I am Benjamin Lehigh, attorney-at-law. Rose Carroll, isn't it?" His smile returned and he extended his hand.

I shook it. "The same. I'm pleased to make thy acquaintance, Benjamin." Maybe attorneys needed to wear more conventional dress to make a visual impact in court.

Kevin pushed open the door from the back of the station and Benjamin stood.

"Mr. Lehigh? I was told you wanted to see me. I'm Detective Kevin Donovan." He caught sight of me and groaned. "And Miss Rose. What conjectures have you for me this afternoon?"

"I had a couple of small things to inform thee about," I said as Benjamin approached Kevin to exchange a hearty handshake.

"Benjamin Lehigh, attorney. I was just getting to know my fellow Quaker, Rose," Benjamin said to Kevin. "I represent Akwasi Ayensu. I request an interview with thee about the exact charges and the evidence they are based on, and then I'll need time with my client. Since Rose was instrumental in engaging my services, I formally request she be allowed to sit in on the interview."

This friendly Friend was all business when it came to defending his client's rights, and I was glad of it. I also guessed I wasn't getting home anytime soon, but plenty of time still remained in the afternoon for rest. This was far more important.

"Whatever you say, Counselor. Please come with me. Yes, Miss Rose, you may come, too." Kevin beckoned to us to follow him back through the door. A minute later we three took seats at a wide table, Benjamin and I on one side, Kevin on the other. I'd sat here last April when a possession of mine had been stolen and used as a murder weapon. Being in this room again brought back unpleasant memories, but I took a calming breath and kept my attention on the present.

"A respected member of the community came forth and said he witnessed Mr. Ayensu shoot Miss Breed to death during the display of fireworks on Wednesday evening the fourth of July." Kevin drummed the fingers of one hand on the table. "There are no other eyewitnesses, and Mr. Ayensu was separated from his companion at that moment."

"What says my client in his defense?" Benjamin asked.

"He denies it, of course."

"Was this witness alone? Has he anyone to back up his claim?"

"Yes, and no, I don't believe so," Kevin said.

"Has thee found the weapon with proof showing my client had obtained it for this purpose? Has thee connected the killing shot to this same gun?" Benjamin folded his hands on the table and fixed his stare on Kevin.

"We have not yet located the weapon, but we are still searching."

"What would be my client's motive to kill this young girl? She was a member of his own religion, I might add."

"That is yet to be determined." Kevin was starting to sound defensive.

"So thee has come up with no reason for the killing and has discovered no evidence whatsoever of my client's guilt other than the accusation by this . . ." Benjamin consulted a paper he pulled from a leather portfolio. "This Lester Colby. Whose charge has no independent confirmation. It's his word against my client's."

I felt I was watching a game of lawn tennis, with the remarks bouncing back and forth before my eyes.

"Mr. Colby is a well-respected member of the community," Kevin said. "He is a family man and a manager in one of our local mills."

"And a new grandfather, as well." When the men looked surprised, I added, "I assisted in the delivery of his first grandchild only yesterday."

"Lester Colby's standing in the community is irrelevant, Detective. Thee has not brought him before a magistrate as required by law, and thee has not a shred of physical evidence against my client, not even enough to bind him over for trial. I request thee release Ayensu into my care immediately. It's a disgrace to have locked up a man who is also well-respected in the community, who owns his own business, and who harbors no ill will against the race which enslaved him for the first fifteen years of his life."

Kevin slapped his hands on the table with a scowl and pushed up to standing. "Very well. If my superior approves."

"I imagine he will," Benjamin said smoothly. "My good friend, the judge Ezra Putnam, would be happy to agree with me."

"But if sentiment in the community is running high against the colored man, he might be safer right here in a cell," Kevin said.

"Shall we seek out thy chief?" Benjamin raised his eyebrows, his lips pressed into a flat line. "A jail cell is no place for an innocent man."

———

I waited alone on the bench for some minutes. Would Kevin's superior agree? Benjamin seemed to be a persuasive lawyer, but his comment about his friend, the judge, struck me as somewhat un-Quakerly. Perhaps he felt he had to deliver that kind of threat in the name of freedom for Akwasi. But what if Kevin was right, and Akwasi would be in danger by going free? I hated to think of Amesbury's residents turning hatred on my friend solely because he was colored. And why was Lester making untrue statements? What did he have to gain by doing so?

Finally Kevin escorted Akwasi out from the cell area with Benjamin following close behind. I stood and extended my hand to Akwasi.

"Rose, I know thee played a part in this miracle and I thank thee." Akwasi pumped my hand, but his expression was serious rather than joyful. The abrasion on his cheek still flared red and swollen.

"Be well, Akwasi," I said. "Esther will be well pleased to see thee."

"Friend Rose, we shall meet again." Benjamin also shook my hand.

"I'm sure we will." I said good-bye to both of them and watched them leave the station.

"Satisfied, Miss Rose?" Kevin asked.

"Of course. Benjamin made several valid points, didn't he?"

He cleared his throat.

I turned back to face him. "Akwasi had no reason to wish Hannah dead. And thee wouldn't have been able to convict Akwasi without evidence. So why hold him in a cell?"

"Pressure from my superiors. I know Colby's going to speak to the chief and he'll have my hide. I did try to find a magistrate but one was unavailable today."

I wasn't sure I believed that, but Kevin had always followed the law. Perhaps he was telling the truth.

"And then there's the matter of Mr. Ayensu's safety out in the community," he went on.

"Thee thinks that is a real problem, I gather."

"It could be. I hope not, but there is plenty of anti-colored sentiment that remains among us despite the emancipation of the slaves more than twenty years ago. We wouldn't want any mob violence in Amesbury." He frowned at me. "Did you come here with the lawyer?"

"No, I simply happened to meet him here. I brought two other matters I wanted to discuss with thee. May we do that now?"

Kevin gazed at the big clock on the wall. "Yes, but I need to be getting down to Market Square. It's my wife's birthday, of all days, and I ordered up a special bracelet for her."

I looked closely at him. "Is thee blushing?"

"Be that as it may." He laughed. "Men aren't supposed to be talking baubles, are we now? I do cherish the lady, though, and always strive to keep her happy."

"Thee sounds like a loving and attentive husband, and that sounds like the recipe for a successful marriage. I approve."

"Will you walk with me toward the jeweler? We can talk as we go." He called out to an officer at one of the desks that he was going out on an errand before holding the door open for me.

"Surely." We headed down the steps and I grabbed my cycle, walking it along next to me. "Now thee has lost thy prime suspect, thee must be looking into other friends of Hannah's, or others with a cause to end her life."

"We interviewed young Tobias. He could have killed her. You know, because he was heartbroken she'd rejected him, perhaps he was even the father of her baby and didn't want to be, that kind of thing. He claims he was out with a few other fellows, and we need to track them down before ruling him out."

"Did thee tell him Hannah was carrying a child?"

"No, I didn't go that far. Perhaps I should have. I can always summon him back in." Kevin rubbed his broad forehead.

"Here's another idea. Hannah roomed with an Irish girl named Nora Walsh at Virginia Perkell's Boardinghouse for Ladies." I told Kevin about Nora's accusations. "Faith also said Nora was sweet on Tobias. I suppose she could have killed Hannah out of anger at the theft, which would also remove Hannah from Tobias's affections."

"Seems a long shot. Where would a mill girl get a gun, and would she know how to fire it? But I'll look into her. I appreciate the tip."

I steered around a pile of manure as we walked down Friend Street toward the square, passing the stately Merrimack Opera House and the public library.

"What else have you got for me?" Kevin asked.

"It seems Lester Colby, despite having good employment, is hard up for money. His wife has an advanced cancer and he can't afford the hospital." I glanced in the window of Gladden Books and News, reminding myself to come back and select a work of Lucy Larcom's as a gift for Faith. Perhaps the author would autograph it for her when they met. "His house is becoming rather run-down, as well."

"So why would he kill Hannah? He wouldn't gain any funds from that."

"True." I wrinkled my nose. "But his impoverished state could be connected with his accusing Akwasi. Maybe he'd planned to extort money from John Whittier in exchange for dropping the charges." I laughed. "I happen to know he wouldn't have a lick of luck with that idea. John maintains high standards of integrity."

"I'll wager he does. He's a fine example of a man who stands by his principles." Kevin lifted his hat to a couple of gentlemen strolling by, then lowered his voice. "Of course, one of the most important things is to locate the cursed weapon, even though it could be deep in Merrimack River by now. We might never find it. And another is to determine the paternity of Miss Breed's baby."

We neared the post office, newly rebuilt after April's massive conflagration. The terrible fire had been set by an arsonist whose identity I'd been able to uncover. Bertie stepped out, her hand shading her eyes against the three o'clock sun.

"Well, look who's here. The Quaker and the detective." She laughed with a delighted look in her eyes. "Sounds like the title of a Pinkerton detective novel, now, doesn't it?"

———

Faith arrived home half an hour after I did, shortly after her four o'clock shift's end. I'd forgotten I'd said I would meet her there and walk her home. I wasn't being a very responsible auntie. My mind must be too full of crime-solving ideas these days.

"I'm going to do nothing until tomorrow." She plopped into a kitchen chair and stretched her legs out.

"Good. I made some refreshing lemonade." I'd never gotten around to it the day before. "Can I pour thee some?"

"Please."

I handed her a tin cup full of the cold drink. The current block of ice in the ice box was half gone already, but I'd chipped off what I needed to cool our refreshment. I poured my own cup and sat across the table from her. Luckily a breeze wafted over us from the northern window to the one on the south. This room became uncomfortable when the wind blew in the opposite direction, because, in this season, the sun shone full on the southern side of the house.

"Faith, David has invited me out to supper at the new hotel tonight. He wondered if thee would like to accompany us."

She gazed at me for a moment, and then shook her head. "No, you go on and have your romantic evening." A smile played around her lips. "The animals went onto the Ark two by two, Rose. Anyway, I only want to sit and be at ease. It has been a difficult week."

"If thee is certain. We have foodstuffs aplenty thee can consume without lighting the stove for thy supper, and I won't be late." I sipped my lemonade, savoring the tart, sweet drink. "It has most surely been a difficult week. Much happened even today." I told her about Esther coming by, and about Akwasi being in jail and then out. I said I'd told Kevin about Nora's suspecting her roommate of theft.

"Thee should have seen the attorney-at-law John Whittier arranged for Akwasi," I went on. "He was very impressive, and he's a Friend, too."

"I'm not surprised." Faith raised one eyebrow and sat up straight. "Did the detective say what transpired after he took Tobias away last evening?"

"Not definitively. He needs to check whether Tobias was in fact with the fellows he said he'd gone out with that night. But he did let Tobias go home."

Faith stared at her folded hands on the table. "I can't believe Tobias would kill Hannah. He adored her. But then, it's hard for me to believe anyone would take the life of their fellow man." She gazed up and grinned at me. "Or fellow woman, as Granny would insist on saying. I wish I'd gone to the farm with the younger ones. I so wanted to hear Granny's stories of attending the International Women's Congress last March. It's not the same in letters." Faith set her elbow on the table and rested her chin onto her hand with a dreamy look in her eyes. "She says she'll take me with her next time. Imagine mixing with members of the National Women's Suffrage Association, Rose, and meeting Susan Anthony and Elizabeth Stanton!"

"That would be an unforgettable moment, I do agree."

A small gray blur darted out from under the stove toward the far corner of the kitchen.

"A mouse!" Faith let out a little shriek and pulled her knees up, wrapping her arms around them.

I laughed. "And more afraid of thee than thee is of him, I dare say."

Faith frowned at me, and then shook her head with a smile. "Of course. It's a tiny creature, after all. But we don't want mice in the house, do we?"

"Most surely not."

"Zeb said their kitchen cat gave birth to kittens. Maybe I can get one for us." She wrinkled her nose. "But Father won't like it, I suppose."

"Better to keep vermin out of the home than to worry about pleasing thy father." I waited a moment. "Thee is going to meet a famous person on First Day. I bought thee a gift to prepare for the meeting." I drew the wrapped book out of my bag and handed it to her.

She tilted her head. "It isn't my birthday or anything. What has thee gone and done, Rose?"

"Open it. I can give thee a present in celebration of thy life and dreams, can't I?"

Faith ripped off the string and tore open the paper. She gazed at the cover of *An Idyl at Work*, turned it over, looked at the inside, and clapped it shut.

"Thee can ask Lucy Larcom to inscribe it for thee, if she's willing," I said.

"I love it. Thee is the best aunt in the world." Faith jumped up from her chair and ran around the table to give me a tight embrace. When she straightened, I was surprised to see tears on her cheeks.

I pulled her, nearly as tall as I, onto my lap and smoothed the hair on her brow. She laid her head on my shoulder. I was nine years older and had watched her grow from a newborn, while I was still a child myself, into this strong, caring, spirited young woman. I felt more like a big sister to her, but someone needed to take the place of her mother, and her father wasn't capable. "Now, then, what's wrong, dear Faith?"

"Giving me that book is exactly the kind of thing Mother would have done. I thank thee, Rose, with all my heart. It just makes me miss my mama."

We sat there, the two of us, missing Harriet Carroll Bailey, until the five o'clock whistle blew.

THIRTEEN

Faith had tucked her feet up in a comfortable upholstered chair to rest and read the Larcom book, while I'd closed my eyes on my bed for twenty minutes or so. I was rested, washed, and had my hair neatly done up when David pulled his buggy in front of the house at precisely six o'clock. He jumped out to help me up.

"Have fun," Faith called, waving at us as we drove off down the hill toward the town proper.

I waved back, then turned to David. He wore a pale blue coat with white trousers and suede shoes. It looked quite striking on him with his dark hair and brows and his deep blue eyes. But once again I was stabbed with doubt about the wisdom of our feeling so strongly about each other. A Quaker man wouldn't have worn such eye-catching, fashionable attire—well except for Benjamin, perhaps, although the suit I'd seen him in had been of a simple cut, just an elegant one in expensive cloth. I myself was clad in my nicest summer dress, but it was a pearly gray poplin with a matching bonnet, both garments as plain of adornment as all my other clothes. David had insisted over and over he didn't care. He always said he admired my faith and my strength of commitment to Friends' values, among which was plainness.

"Thee looks fresh and summery," I said.

"These are the coolest clothes I own, short of a bathing costume, which doesn't seem quite appropriate for dinner out with the smartest and prettiest girl in Essex County." After he transferred the reins of Daisy, his sleek mare, to his right hand, he reached over and covered my hand with his while I colored at the compliment.

"Our messages crossed in the mails this morning," I said. "After I received thine in the same post in which I sent mine to thee, I imagined the letters waving and calling to each other as they passed on the Chain Bridge."

He threw back his head to laugh, as was his wont. "You have a delightful imagination, Rosie dear."

"But wouldn't it be so much easier if we could answer invitations instantaneously rather than send pieces of paper back and forth across the river? Oh, I suppose we already have the telegraph, but even that takes some time and effort to convey information."

"It's called a telephone, my dear. It's quite the invention." He headed up Friend Street past John's home, then past the Friends Meetinghouse with its graceful, simple lines and tall, wide windows.

"I know about that, naturally. But who can afford one? And the wires are not in place everywhere, are they?"

"They're putting up new poles and wires every day, at least in Newburyport. My father installed a telephone in our house, you know."

"Did he really?"

"Indeed. He's quite taken with the contraption." He clucked to the horse. "More seriously, imagine how useful it'll be for notifying hospitals of emergencies, accidents, patients who need urgent care."

"Of course."

"If you had an expectant mother needing your assistance, you could go directly to her instead of waiting for a messenger to find you. Or if a lady in labor entered a state of distress, you could call for emergency transport."

We'd almost reached the Little Farm when David took a right turn and drove the buggy up a steep hill.

"I know," I said. "Except we don't have one in our modest home and most homes of the women I attend don't, either. Until the system becomes widespread, I can't see it supplanting the written word."

David directed to the horse to slow up as we approached a tall, stately four-story building perched on the top of Whittier Hill. *Le Grand Hotel* was inscribed in carved lettering on the lintel. I'd read about the building of the hotel in the newspaper. Rather than being one of the establishments catering to travelers, as were springing up near the railway station, this was more of a resort for vacationers. The breeze high on the hill stayed fresh and free from pestilence, and additions such as tennis courts, elaborate gardens, and bathing pools were designed to attract the well off.

David pulled up to a line of fine carriages and buggies from all the major Amesbury carriage manufacturers: Bailey, Clarke, Parry, Ellis, and more. He slid out of the driver's seat and handed the reins to a waiting footman, then came around and helped me down.

"I think you'll like this eating establishment," he said, offering me his arm, which I was happy to take. "It's new, but the chef is up from Boston, and it's said he was trained in France. *Nous allons manger comme des rois.*"

"*Mais bien sûr,* we will eat like kings," I answered.

David looked both surprised and pleased.

"*Oui*, I studied French," I said. "For several years. It comes in handy when I have a newly arrived French-Canadian mother who as yet speaks no English but needs help birthing her baby. Although that's an experience which transcends language, as thee well knows." I picked up my skirts with my free hand before we ascended the front steps.

David pulled open the heavy ornate door.

"Oh, my." I halted just inside. The interior of the hotel was stunning. A shiny mahogany reception desk faced us, with a wide staircase curving gracefully upward next to it. To the right was a sitting room resembling a library, and to our left I spied an elegant dining room. White tablecloths were topped with fine china, lit pink tapers, and sparkling silver flatware. Rich maroon swags swooped over the tops of tall windows, and the heavy furniture was embellished with carved flourishes.

I almost turned around and walked out. David must have sensed my reaction to such opulence, because he took my hand and tucked his elbow close to his side, thus trapping my arm through it.

"It'll be fine, Rose," he murmured. "Stay with me. Please?"

I wasn't afraid of the finery, or of the rich folks certain to be the customers eating here. Rather, I didn't believe in it. Friends' strong views about plainness made much more sense to me. The fancy dinner dance I'd attended as David's guest last April had been an ordeal which I'd survived, but barely. His mother had insisted he attend, and wanted him to escort his silly society cousin. He'd invited me, instead. I'd had to get special dispensation from Friends in the person of John Whittier to wear a fancy pink dress, albeit a simple one. And the issue of the differences in our class and religion kept arising, time after time. Like tonight.

David approached an obsequious man in a formal black suit, and said, "A table for two."

The man raised his eyebrows.

"On the Newburyport Dodge account," David added.

"Ah." The man's eyebrows elevated almost into his greased hair and he blinked as if that would convey his favor. "Please come right this way." The man selected a piece of paper from a stack and led the way. We passed couples, tables of four, and a large group of pipe-smoking men before we arrived at a small table near the convergence of two wide windows. Our guide pulled out the chair for me and helped me sit.

I thanked him, then gazed outside and smiled, despite my discomfort. We overlooked the countryside for miles around. On our right, the Powow River snaked away from the upper reaches of Lake Gardner, disappeared out of sight, and then reappeared in a much more narrow profile down in the fields on our left.

"Look, David." I pointed. "Did thee know the Powow traveled such a circuitous route?"

"I can't say I did. We were right across the road from there for the fireworks, though."

I rubbed a finger down the handle of the silver knife as David perused the paper. My dissatisfaction with this fancy place was melting away amid the tantalizing smells wafting about and in the face of one of my favorite people across the table. A small portion of guilt stabbed at me for enjoying such a non-simple pursuit, knowing it was not available to all, by any means.

"What are you hungry for?" David asked, glancing up with a wicked smile. He turned a simple question of supper into an inquiry of much more than that, and my cheeks reddened.

I gazed at him with a tiny smile. I felt his shoe gently rub my calf under the tablecloth, a delicious caress that sent my heart aflutter and my skin atingle. "What have they to offer?"

He handed me the piece of paper. On the top was lettered MENU, and it listed two soups, delicious-sounding dishes from beef to lamb chops to duck, and all manner of mouth-watering desserts.

"How can I possibly decide?" I asked, regaining my composure. "Every dish looks like it would be the best thing I've ever eaten."

"Might I suggest the striped bass *à la Bordelaise*?" said a deep voice at my side.

I looked up with a start to see Benjamin Lehigh standing there with bright eyes.

David stood and pumped Benjamin's hand. "Mr. Lehigh, how are you?"

"Now, David, thee knows better than to address me as Mister."

"Old habits die hard," David said.

"You two know each other?" I asked, slightly bewildered at this connection.

"Indeed," David said. "Despite my youth, I barely beat him at tennis."

"In fact, thee often doesn't." Benjamin smiled.

"As you can hear, he is a fellow Quaker, Rose." David beamed. "Rose Carroll, may I present Benjamin Lehigh of Newburyport?"

"I know, we met this afternoon. Hello, Benjamin." I went on. "I was going to tell thee, David. John Whittier engaged Benjamin's services to act as counsel for the falsely accused Akwasi Ayensu—"

"Whom we met at the fireworks?"

"Yes. Kevin arrested him for Hannah's murder, but Benjamin here was able to get him released after only a few hours in the jail cell."

"That detective should not have detained Akwasi on such a flimsy charge," Benjamin said, looking disgusted.

"My, my, you had a busy day, Rose." David then addressed Benjamin. "Mr. Lehigh, will you join us for supper?"

"I thank thee, but I'm dining with my elderly parents." He gestured across the room. "We three should gather socially at another time, though." He smiled at me.

"I'd like that," I said. "Enjoy thy repast."

Benjamin thanked me, nodded his head at David, and headed back to his own table.

"What a surprise to find thee is acquainted with him." I tilted my head. "Tennis, is it? Does Benjamin travel in thy social circles, then?" This surprised me, but I wasn't quite sure why. Plenty of Friends lived in far more comfortable circumstances than my family, and most who did used their wealth to benefit charitable causes in line with Quaker values.

"Yes, as a matter of fact. Benjamin is friendly with my parents. It's quite sad that Benjamin's wife passed away a few years ago, but he seems to have recovered his natural good humor."

"That is very sad, indeed. Does he have children?"

"Two girls, now in their teen years. To Benjamin's credit he has kept them home with him rather than sending them off to live with an aunt or a sister, or to boarding school. He has household help, of course."

Of course. That was a given for people of a certain level of means. I might have known any Friend wearing an expensive suit like Benjamin's would be a wealthy one. I didn't care, as long as he was a good lawyer. Akwasi was going to need that.

FOURTEEN

I'D SPENT SOME TIME telling Faith all about the evening after David brought me home. We'd chatted like pals about David and Zeb, about the menu at the restaurant and her cozy evening reading at home.

"You love him, don't you, Rose?" she'd asked, her eyes bright.

I'd nodded. "Yes. And I do believe he loves me back."

I'd hoped to sleep into the morning, but my eyes flew open before first light. What was that racket? I peered out the window to see a carriage in front of the house and a man rapping on the door. I surely was being summoned to a birth again, so I threw on a wrapper and answered the door. The uniformed driver on the front step asked politely but firmly for me to accompany him to the stately Clarke home only a block away on Powow Street for his mistress's birth.

"Give me five minutes and I'll join thee." I wasn't about to ask him into the house with only Faith and me in residence. I hurried

113

to wash, dress, tear off a hunk of bread, and eat it as I scribbled a note to Faith. Coffee would have been nice, but I didn't like to keep laboring women waiting. Such is the life of a midwife.

A sweet-faced maid let me into Georgia Clarke's house. "Please follow me, miss." She led the way up one of the grandest staircases I'd ever traversed. Robert Clarke was a good man who'd led the other factory owners in resolving to rebuild immediately after the disastrous fire on Carriage Hill last April.

I stepped into the bedchamber. Georgia, not a young woman, stood leaning on the back of a sturdy upholstered chair, her forearms flat on its top, her feet spread wide. She peered at me.

"I'm so glad you're here, Rose. I can't lie down, it's much too painful." White streaked through her brown hair, which lay in a long braid down her back, and the lines around her mouth were deepened by her travails.

"She's having a tough time of it. Not like with her earlier births."

I turned my head toward the familiar voice coming from a chair near the window where Virginia Perkell sat rocking and knitting. "Virginia, hello."

"She's my sister," Georgia said with a weak smile. "You didn't know that?"

I laughed. "I did, as a matter of fact, and I'm glad to see a familiar face here helping out." I had attended Georgia's most recent labor two years ago but not the prior ones, and Virginia had not been present at the youngest child's birth. I set my satchel near Georgia's chair. "How far apart are the pains?" I rubbed her shoulders and upper back.

"She has only a minute or two respite between them." Virginia stood and laid down her knitting.

"I'll check thy progress and the baby's well-being after the next pain, then. And it's no matter thee can't recline. Standing actually helps the baby to come down. It's a good position as long as thy legs feel strong enough."

"Here's one now." Georgia hung her head over her arms and groaned softly.

This was her fifth baby, so I didn't have to worry giving birth would frighten her. I'd kept careful watch on her health because of her age, and all had seemed well throughout the pregnancy. Georgia moaned with the contraction but did not cry out.

I removed my bonnet and pushed up the sleeves of my dress, then drew out a cloth and the Pinard horn so I'd be ready to listen to the baby's heart as soon as this pain had ebbed.

Georgia blew out a noisy breath and opened her eyes. "I think it's getting close."

I knelt to press the listening tube against the thin, fine cloth of the nightgown covering her belly, now large and taut. I listened carefully for a moment. "The heart sounds healthy." I laid the horn on the floor. "I'll check the opening now."

"Do I have to lie down?"

"No. I can do it here, and catch the baby here, too. Spread thy feet a little wider, please, and bend thy knees a bit." After she complied, I inserted my hand and found the womb wide open and the head already in place to come down. I slid my hand out and wiped it on the cloth. "Good. As I remember, thy last child came with great dispatch, didn't he?"

"Yes. As did his three older brothers."

"Then let's ready ourselves for this baby. Virginia, please bring me the linens for the birth." I'd noticed a stack of folded cloth next to two basins full of water as well as an empty one. I stood and brought back one full basin, then prepared the area beneath Georgia. "Now, Virginia, come and act as ballast on the chair, and help Georgia stay on her feet. After the baby emerges, thee can assist me."

Virginia handed me the cloth, then knelt on the chair's seat facing the back. She hooked her hands under her sister's armpits. Georgia clenched her hands on the upholstery. Bending her knees, she half squatted. Three mighty grunting pushes later, out slid the infant into my waiting hands. I held it up off the floor so it wouldn't tug on the cord.

Virginia peered down. "It's a girl, Georgie," she said, beaming up at her sister. A tear trickled down her cheek.

I'd never seen Virginia be anything but businesslike and brisk. A daughter must mean a lot to Georgia. I'd been at my niece Betsy's birth, and remembered how delighted Harriet had been to produce a second daughter after three boys. How I wished my sister hadn't died when she did. How I missed her. However, I had a job to do.

"Virginia, please come around here and hold the baby up like this," I instructed.

The newborn took her first breath, opened her mouth, and wailed. Georgia remained leaning on the back of the chair. A flash of Hannah's pregnancy once again passed through my mind, a reminder of one newborn who would never have a first cry.

"What a lovely sound," Virginia said, hurrying to kneel and take the infant. After I tied and cut the cord, Virginia grabbed a piece of linen and sat back, cradling the baby in the cloth and wiping her clean. The newborn quieted and stared at her aunt.

"I think the afterbirth is coming," Georgia said. She grunted again, pushing out the placenta, along with a gush of blood. The slippery mass slid out of my hands onto the floor. Georgia straightened and stared down, the hem of her gown now stained with crimson. Blood streamed out of her onto the white cloth beneath.

FIFTEEN

"WHAT IS HAPPENING?" GEORGIA asked in a panicked tone as the pool widened.

Virginia scooted backward with the precious bundle, eyes wide. I pushed up to my feet.

"Lie down, quickly." I helped Georgia to the floor. "Lie down with thy head flat. Bend thy knees and raise thy hips."

I grabbed all the pillows at the head of the bed even as I held her in the Light. Let her not bleed out. Please, dear God, let her not bleed out. We had not been able to save Hannah's life. I must save Georgia's.

I stuffed three fat pillows under her hips so her pelvic area was elevated. I rushed over to grab the softest cloth in the stack, then hurried back to kneel and press the cloth against her opening. If she'd retained a piece of the placenta in her womb, her body would keep pumping blood into it, but this time the blood wouldn't circulate through the infant. Georgia could die. The blood could also be coming from a tear in the birth canal or at the opening, although that usually didn't happen with a fifth-time mother. The baby girl, while a healthy weight, wasn't so overly large as to cause lacerations.

I needed to keep calm. How I wished my teacher, Orpha Perkins, was still able to be at my side. What would she do? What had I seen her do?

I kept one hand in place trying to stanch the blood, and palpated Georgia's stomach with my other hand. Her uterus was still spongy, so I massaged it deeply. I didn't want to increase the flow, but hoped for another contraction to expel the piece, if that's what the problem was. I also needed to check the placenta itself for missing chunks. Georgia's face was nearly devoid of color.

"Virginia, is there a nursemaid in the house?" I asked. My spectacles had slid down the bridge of my nose but I didn't have a spare hand to push them up with.

"Yes, the younger children's. I'll call for her." Virginia stood, shifting the baby into her left arm, and pulled a knob set into the wall.

A moment later the same maid who had taken me upstairs peeked in. Her eyes became saucers. "Oh, my." She stood with mouth agape, as well she might with blood all over the floor and her mistress lying in a strange position.

"Girl, run and fetch Nursey," Virginia said in a stern voice. "We're in need of her help right away. Tell her not to bring the little ones with her under any condition. And then wait in the hall. We might need you for something else."

"Yes, ma'am." Quick footsteps tapped away from us down the hallway. A very long two minutes later, a stout woman in a white-bibbed apron pushed into the room.

"I had to leave the boys in the kitchen with Cook," she began, and then stopped, staring. "Gracious, Mrs. Clarke."

119

"Please take the baby away for the time being," I instructed her. "Thy mistress isn't at all well, and I need Virginia's help."

The nursemaid stretched out her arms for the infant Virginia handed her, then headed for the door. Before she left, she turned back. "Perhaps we need to call a proper physician." She pressed her lips together.

We might still need to do exactly that, I thought, but didn't voice it. If she weakened further, or lost consciousness, we'd have to summon an ambulance carriage with great dispatch and transfer Georgia to the hospital for care and even a blood transfusion.

"That will be quite enough." Virginia glared at her and waited until the door clicked shut. "What should I do?" Now she sounded more scared than firm.

"Come here. Wait, grab a clean cloth first." I showed her how to apply pressure to the opening. The flow did seem to be diminishing a bit.

I heard her murmuring to Georgia as I slid the placenta into the empty basin. I picked it up with both hands, turned it, and examined it for integrity. I exhaled in relief when I could find nothing wrong with it. That had been one of the worst threats to Georgia's life, and I was grateful I could eliminate it as a cause for her hemorrhage. I rinsed and wiped my hands before I returned to Georgia's side, where she lay with eyes closed. *No.*

I bent over her face. Good, she was breathing regularly. "Georgia, I need thee to keep thy eyes open." I patted her cheek several times, almost slapping it.

"I'm so tired," she whispered, but at least she forced open her eyelids.

"Is thee feeling pain?" I asked.

"A dull ache in my womb, but nothing sharp. And it stings near the opening. Why am I bleeding so much? Am I dying?" Her eyes filled. "I haven't even met my daughter yet."

Virginia stared up at me, her face communicating how worried she was about the bleeding.

"No, thee is very much alive. I had a particular concern about the cause, but I was able to rule it out. I want thee to breathe deeply and rest, but do not let thyself fall asleep quite yet."

"All right. I trust you, Rose." She swiped at her eyes. A trace of pink was returning to her cheeks.

I smiled at her. My mothers did trust me. I took over for Virginia. "Let's see what's going on here." I patted away the blood. The cloth wasn't soaked through, which was a good sign. I turned it and held it to Georgia's opening for another moment, then pulled it away. I gently felt the tissue inside and out and found only small rips in the passageway and in the opening. These were common and would heal on their own. I didn't encounter anything torn enough to warrant stitching it up. The hemorrhage must have come from the placenta tearing away, but the womb contracting back to its pre-pregnant size would heal that. "Good. Thee is going to be fine, Georgia. The danger is past."

"Thanks be to God," Virginia said.

Amen to that.

————

After all was cleaned up and put to rights again, with Georgia resting comfortably in bed, we summoned the nursemaid to return the baby. I watched a weakened but alive Georgia give her little girl the breast with an experienced hand.

"I'll be going, then," I said. "Thee knows to take plenty to drink, and this time please partake of rich meats like beef liver to replenish thy blood." I stood by Georgia's side.

"I will, Rose."

"Keep thy pelvis elevated on one pillow as it is now for the rest of the day and night, and do send for me in case the bleeding starts up again."

"I can't thank you enough. You saved my life." Georgia stroked her baby's head as she regarded me.

"It's my job and I'm happy to do it." I ran a finger along the baby's soft cheek.

"I'm going to name her Rosie." Georgia watched me. "It's the least I can do."

"Thee doesn't need to go that far." I laughed. "I'm sure thee had a name already selected in case the baby turned out to be a girl."

"I didn't like Edna, anyway." Georgia rolled her eyes. "It's Mr. Clarke's mother's name. Rosie here will have to have it as her middle name, instead."

Virginia walked me out and down the stairs as a tall clock in the hall struck ten. We stood on the wide covered front veranda.

"You did save her life, you know," she said.

"I suppose. It's all in a day's work." The sun was well up by now, and a breeze rattled the leaves on a nearby aspen. My knees felt a bit rattly, too, after all that tension and the need to act quickly. I had saved Georgia's life. One bad birth, or one dead mother—particularly a rich one—and I could have the community turn against me. It was a fact of life that not all births ended up with a happily alive mother and a thriving living baby. But it could be hard to convince the public of that fact. In addition, some physicians were beginning to maintain they should manage the work of birthing babies instead of midwives.

Virginia patted her chest. "I was afraid there for a while. She never had that kind of bleeding with her boys."

"She's getting older. The body isn't as strong as we age, and damage can be done more easily. It isn't exactly my business to advise Georgia not to become pregnant again, but that would likely be the safest path for her."

"She'll be protected by feeding her baby for the next year or two, I dare say."

"It's not a sure protection, I'm sure thee is aware," I said.

"Of course not. But she might go through the change soon, anyway. Our older sister Carolina stopped having her monthlies when she was forty-three." Virginia leaned against one of the porch pillars.

"Carolina? Are you all named for states in the Union?"

She laughed. "That we are. Our other sister is Indiana, and our only brother is called Rhode. Don't ask me why."

"No Vermont in the bunch? Or a Jersey?" I smiled, glad for the chance to be lighthearted.

"Thank goodness, no." Virginia snorted. "Say, I heard from Hannah's father yesterday. He's coming today to carry her body home. I thought you'd want to speak with him, being as how he's a Quaker and all. And he might want to talk with you about Hannah's manner of death, since you and your doctor friend were the last ones to see her alive. God rest her soul."

I nodded slowly. "We were. I'd like to speak with her father, although I'd hate to have to describe her last moments. I wonder if he plans to hold a memorial Meeting for Worship here. We would welcome him."

"Couldn't tell you. He sent a telegram saying he'll be arriving this afternoon around two."

"I'll come by at that time, then. Thee will stay on to help Georgia here?" I stifled a yawn. My body was feeling the aftereffects of the rush of spirit and feelings that always accompanied a worrisome situation.

"Yes. I asked a friend to put on the boarders' dinner when they get home at half past twelve today. But I'll have to go back to the house by two to receive Mr. Breed, and I'll stay to make supper before I return."

"Make sure someone sits with Georgia when thee leaves, please. We don't want the bleeding to resume unnoticed. I'll stop back tomorrow to see how she and the babe are doing. Do send for me if she takes a turn for the worse. But if she should happen to lose consciousness or the bleeding starts up again, don't bother with me. Just summon an ambulance carriage and get her to the hospital at once." At the look of alarm on her face, I added, "But I don't think that will happen. I believe she will remain well."

"I pray so. Thank you again." Virginia extended her hand. "Oh! Your fee. We need to pay you, of course. I think Mr. Clarke is at the factory, though."

"I'm happy to be remunerated tomorrow when I return. I know where they live, after all."

She laughed. "That you do, Midwife Carroll, that you do." A fine sidebar buggy drawn by two black steeds clattered into the drive, its high narrow wheels graceful, its brass fittings sparkling. "Oh, there he is now," she added. "He never uses a driver. Can you believe it, a man of his stature? Says he makes the carriages, he wants to drive them, too."

Robert Clarke secured the horses and hurried toward us. "Mrs. Perkell, I was sent word of my Georgie failing. I came along as soon as I could." His high brow accentuated worried eyes behind owlish glasses, and his clean-shaven face was damp with sweat.

"Don't you be worrying, now, Mr. Clarke. Georgia is stable, and delivered of a lovely daughter, as well. This is Rose Carroll, the midwife who made it all go right. Rose, my brother-in-law, Robert Clarke."

He extended his hand to me. "Was she in danger? I told her I would have paid for her to go to the hospital or to be seen by a physician, but she wasn't having it." His voice was thick.

I'd seen him in town but we'd never been introduced, and I hadn't met him at his youngest son's birth. I shook his hand, which was damp with both the summer temperatures and his concern, I could tell. "She experienced a bit of difficulty, Robert, but she and thy daughter are both quite well now, and I believe they will stay that way."

He startled a little at my use of his Christian name, but I was used to that.

"How can I ever thank you, Miss Carroll? My wife is very dear to me, and ..." He clasped his hands.

"You can pay her fee, for one." Virginia winked at me.

"Of course, of course. How much do I owe you for your services?"

"It's two dollars, please." I clasped my hands on my birthing satchel.

He pulled out a silver money clip and extracted a twenty-dollar greenback. "I thank you very much. I must go up and see my girls. It's my first daughter." His eyes filled and he cleared his throat then pulled open the front door.

"Robert," I said as I stared at the bill in my hand. "This is too much by far."

He waved it off and clattered up the stairs.

"I can't take so much in excess of my fee," I said to Virginia. "I shall bring him the change tomorrow."

"Oh, leave it, Rose," she scoffed. "You earned it. And he has plenty more where that came from."

SIXTEEN

I TOOK THE REST of the morning to tidy up around my house. Robert tossing off so much money had struck me as a bit demeaning and left me with a sour taste. Because he had so much more than that, it wasn't really a sign of generosity. So the straightforward physical work of putting my house in order helped to restore my heart and head to order, too.

I stripped all the beds except mine and Faith's and left them to air unmade. At least Frederick had consented to hire out the laundry so I didn't have to spend my Second Days scrubbing linens, shirts, and undergarments. After I dusted and swept, I filled the tub with tepid water and gave myself a long cool bath. I didn't enjoy the feeling of my skin being clogged with the perspiration that warm temperatures brought. This morning's work had added the sour scent of nerves, which didn't go away even when Georgia's crisis of bleeding had passed.

Wearing a fresh lightweight dress, I sat on a stool under the shade of the big sugar maple behind the house, brushing out my wet hair. Frederick's gelding, Star, munched on his hay from within the open door to the shed that doubled as his stable. Faith trudged up the walk, her shoulders slumped, her brow creased, her bonnet hanging down her back by its strings. She sank onto the stump next to me.

"Shall we have a moment of blessed silence, my dear?" I asked, touching her knee.

She nodded even as she closed her eyes. The world continued around us, but the noises of machines and horses and children playing became more distant as we sat. I held this niece of mine in the Light, along with Georgia, her new baby, and Hannah Breed's family. And Kevin, too, praying that his search for the shooter might result in a resolution sooner rather than later.

Finally Faith let out a breath, and I opened my eyes. "Is it the long week and hard work on top of thy friend's death which troubles thee, or something in addition?" I asked.

"Something new."

"Let me bring cold drinks and some dinner for us first."

A minute later I carried out a tray of lemonade and small meat pies and set it on a second stool. Faith had removed her bonnet and her shoes and lay stretched out on the clover that grew under the tree. She sat up and drank deeply of the lemonade, then stood and washed her face and hands at the pump next to the shed. When she returned, she downed half a pie before speaking.

"I saw something odd at the mill today." She gazed in the distance before looking at me again.

"Go on."

"It was near the end of my shift. Well, right after the noon whistle blew. I happened to glance to the corner where the manager's office is. A man was slipping a stack of greenbacks to Lester Colby."

"Is thee sure it was money?"

"It couldn't have been anything else." Faith frowned.

"Why did thee find that odd? Couldn't it have been someone paying off a personal debt? Or perhaps making a purchase?"

"I doubt Lester would be settling personal business on the job, and we don't sell cloth out of the weaving room. We make the cloth but it is sold elsewhere. I couldn't even say where."

"Did thee recognize the man?" I asked.

"No. Also, Lester looked around quickly as if checking to be sure no one saw the transaction, which made it doubly odd. I tried to get my eyes off him but I wasn't successful. He saw me watching. The man left, and Lester stormed over to me and began yelling."

"What did he say?" I divided my hair into three strands and began plaiting it.

"That I was lazy, that I was his worst employee, and that if I wasn't careful, I wouldn't have a job anymore."

"All untrue, I assume."

"Except I might soon be without employment. And thee knows Father relies on my income to supplement his own." Faith downed the rest of her lemonade. "Rose, Lester was livid. I'd have been even more scared if fifty other girls weren't working nearby."

"I might advise thee never to be alone with him if he displays that kind of temper." Lester Colby, the adoring grandfather, clearly had a dark side to his personality.

"Don't worry, I won't. But I want to find out why money was changing hands." She narrowed her eyes. "How can I do that?"

"Thee could ask thy friends there if they have ever caught sight of a similar transaction, or if they know who the man was."

"Yes," Faith said. "I could. Like a Pinkerton detective." Her eyes gleamed and her fatigue seemed to melt away.

———

I bicycled over to Virginia's boardinghouse at a few minutes past two o'clock. A wagon and driver were parked in the shade of a wide elm, the driver apparently asleep with his hat tilted over his eyes. Before Virginia showed me into the parlor on the north side of the house, she whispered, "The poor man's beside himself."

A man holding a bowler in his hands whirled when we entered the room. He hurried toward me.

"Rose Carroll, is it?" The same luminous green eyes as his daughter's carried a deep sadness.

"I am Rose. Is thee Hannah's father?"

"Yes. Edward Breed of Nantucket."

"May I convey my sympathies at the passing of thy daughter? It's a great loss."

"I thank thee." He swallowed hard. "I want my girl. I thought she'd be laid out here where she lived, but—"

"I told you she's with the police, Mr. Breed." Virginia folded her arms but her expression was soft. "Rose can take you down there and introduce you."

"I can, of course," I said. "Will thee be staying long in Amesbury? We can hold a memorial Meeting for Worship for Hannah in our Meetinghouse, if thee likes."

"But why would I stay?" He gazed from Virginia to me and back. "I simply want to take Hannah home. Our family is there. We'll have the memorial Meeting on Nantucket in our own Meetinghouse. It is kind of thee to offer, though."

A bell pealed. Virginia excused herself, and I heard the front door open and voices murmuring. A moment later, she returned with John Whittier in tow.

"I heard thee was coming to town, Friend Edward," John said. "I wanted to pay my respects."

Virginia looked a bit flustered, perhaps at the thought of entertaining the famous poet, but she gestured to the settee and several chairs. "Please sit down, all of you. I'll bring some iced tea and some sweets."

"Thee doesn't need to bother," Edward said.

"I insist. You've had a long trip, and it's hot out." She bustled out of the room.

Edward waited until I sat before sinking down onto the settee. The shades were drawn, keeping the quiet room at a comfortable temperature.

John took another chair. "Let us hold Hannah's released spirit in the Light of God together," he said, closing his eyes.

I listened to the men breathing, to muted female voices coming through the ceiling above, to horses clopping by outdoors. A choked sob sounded from Edward's direction. I wasn't surprised. In my practice I'd seen the cruel effect the loss of a child had on a parent. We prayed in silence until the clink of china indicated Virginia's return. I opened my eyes to find her poised in the doorway.

"Come in. We only were sharing a moment of grace." I gestured for her to enter.

She set the tray on a low table in front of the settee. Moisture dripped down the sides of the glasses and a plate held crispy molasses and sugar cookies. She invited us to partake.

"I thank thee for this refreshment," Edward said. "Indeed, I traveled since yesterday morning by ferry, then by coach to Boston. I stayed with Friends near the Meetinghouse on State Street last night and made my way on the Boston and Maine up to Amesbury today."

"You are welcome to it." Virginia turned for the door.

"Please stay, Virginia," I said. "I'm sure Edward wants to hear about his daughter's life here." I expected he also wanted to know about her death, painful as it might be.

"Yes, if thee pleases." Edward drank long from his glass. "Tell me everything about her."

"Your girl was a sweet, hardworking boarder," she said, perching on the edge of a chair. "She helped out around the house when she could. She kept her room clean and her belongings tidy. I didn't have any complaints about her, if that sets your mind at ease."

"And my niece, Faith Bailey, enjoyed her friendship with Hannah," I added. "They worked in the Hamilton Mill together."

"What's this about the Hamilton Mill?" Nora appeared in the doorway. Despite Virginia's look of disapproval, Nora stepped into the room.

"Nora, this is Edward Breed, Hannah's father," I said. "Edward, Nora Walsh also worked side by side with thy daughter." I hoped she wouldn't speak about her suspicions of Hannah's thieving.

"Hannah had stopped writing letters to us in recent months," Edward said after greeting Nora. "It worried my wife and me no end. Was she ill with something?" he asked, searching first Virginia's face, then Nora's, then mine.

Nora blinked. "I couldn't say."

"Hannah seemed a little moody of late," Virginia said. "But if I'd known she'd stopped writing to the family, I would have insisted she pen a letter to you."

And what was I to say to his query? I felt a moment of panic. Did Edward need to know of Hannah's pregnancy? I didn't want to distress him by revealing the truth. Maybe there was no need to do so. Quakers had a long tradition of speaking truth to power.

But what about speaking truth to a grieving parent? Kevin might inform Edward of Hannah's state, however, and tell him I was the source of the knowledge, and then what could I say? My concern must have evidenced itself on my face, because John fixed his intense dark-eyed gaze on me. He raised one eyebrow almost imperceptibly. I finally discerned that it was kindness which needed to preside here, not cruel honesty.

"I believe she'd recently ceased stepping out with a suitor," I said softly. "Perhaps that had upset her."

"I'd like to speak with this young man," Edward said. "What would his name be?"

"Tobias Cartland." I explained his origin. "Faith might know where he resides. Or does thee, Nora?"

A smile flirted on her lips. "Of course I do. He's sweet on me now Hannah's gone. Has been since she began puttin' him off."

I examined her. This did not comport with Faith's description of Tobias's behavior toward Hannah.

"Miss Walsh," Virginia said sharply. "You'll take care to mind your manners now."

"I was simply after answerin' the man's questions, Mrs. Perkell. Tobias boards in Mill Village, the gentlemen's house there on Summer Street."

"I can take thee to see Tobias, Edward," I offered.

"Now that yer here, will yeh be payin' me back the value of my things what Hannah stole?" Nora set her fists on her hips.

"What? My girl wasn't a thief." Edward looked both horrified and bewildered.

"That'll be quite enough, now, Miss Walsh." Virginia jumped to her feet. "You already told me you don't have a shred of proof about those items. I'll thank you to leave this room immediately and cease spreading rumors about our deceased friend." She took a step toward Nora.

John didn't speak, but I noticed him watching this breech of manners and goodwill carefully.

"I'll go." Nora sauntered toward the door. Before leaving she added, "Ask her daddy if she was sending home extra money now, will yeh?"

After Nora was gone, Virginia sat again, shaking her head. "I'm terribly sorry, Mr. Breed. I don't know what's gotten into the girl. She mentioned this crazy idea recently, that Hannah had taken her coins, but she never saw her do it and she hasn't discovered them in the room they shared."

"I shall hold the soul of this unhappy girl in the Light of God," John said.

John could be right. Maybe Nora was unhappy being so far from home. As Hannah surely had been, too.

"I will, as well." Edward's expression was pained, though.

"Edward, how can we help thee?" I asked. "How will thee transport Hannah's body back to Nantucket?"

"I have made arrangements with the Lake Gardner Ice Company to pack her coffin with ice immediately before we depart," he said. "Which I hope will be on this evening's train."

"A wise move, in keeping with Friends' values, as we do not hold with embalming," John said. "But this transport must be costing thee more than a few pennies."

"Indeed. I needed to borrow the funds from my brother, who has a successful sailmaking business." Edward was silent for a moment, then said, "Can any of you tell me the exact circumstances of my girl's death? Where she was, if she experienced pain? The telegraph from the police only said she was shot to death. Could it have been an accident?" His tone rose as if grasping for a wisp of hope.

I closed my eyes for a moment, seeking for the right words. I opened them again and outlined in the gentlest possible way the evening of the fireworks and the extent of her injury. "No one has come forward claiming to have caused an accident, and as far as I know the police have also not located the gun which fired the shot." I was not about to tell him of Lester's false accusation against Akwasi. John peered at me and gave the slightest of nods, as if he approved of my decision.

Edward sank his face into his hands.

"Edward," John said, "thee knows Hannah is now in a place of peace. She is filled with Light and surrounded by it. Let that be thy solace as way opens, without regard to the means by which she passed into the hands of God."

SEVENTEEN

EDWARD HELPED ME DOWN from his hired wagon in front of the police station and then extracted my bicycle from the back.

"Please wait again," he addressed the driver. "I hope I'll not be long in fetching my precious cargo, then we can return to the train station."

"Before we go in, I'd like to tell thee something in private, because thee has been very kind to me," Edward murmured. He touched my arm and beckoned to me to stand with him under the same swamp oak where I'd sat with Kevin only two days earlier. "I said that Hannah had ceased writing to us of late. But that girl's accusations are worrisome to me."

I waited for him to go on.

"Hannah is a good girl. Was a good girl. Her elder brother Jacob is ill in the head and he needs special care."

"I'm sorry to hear this."

"Yes, he became seized with the illness when he was about twenty. Jacob hears voices and feels he is being persecuted. We needed to put him into an institution on the mainland. It broke his mother's heart, I'll tell thee."

"How difficult it must be for thy family."

"That it is, Rose. My Hannah—she's my eldest daughter—saw the need to come here and work to help support her big brother. She always did so without complaining. But last winter she began sending us funds a bit in excess of the usual portion of her pay. I don't know where she obtained them."

"Does thee think perhaps she was stealing from Nora, after all?" How confusing. At first it'd seemed Nora had fabricated the story of the thefts. But where would Hannah have gotten extra money? Maybe Faith knew if she'd worked extra hours at the mill. The girls worked so much as it was, though. I didn't know where Hannah would have found the time or energy to do more. Maybe Virginia knew.

"I don't know what to think, Rose. I truly don't."

"For now, let us ascertain where Hannah's body is being kept, shall we? Kevin Donovan is the police detective, and he is a friend of sorts to me. He might have certain questions for thee, too." I motioned toward the steps leading up to the station.

"All right." Edward seemed to be treading in thick mud, it looked that difficult for him to lift and lower each foot again and again.

Not three minutes later we followed Kevin down the hall to the interview room. He directed Edward and me to sit at the wide wooden table, and he took a seat across from us, laying a notebook and pencil on the table in front of him.

"Mr. Breed, please let me convey my sympathies on your daughter's untimely death."

Edward seemed to steel himself as he lifted his chin. "Please call me Edward. I thank thee, Kevin."

Kevin shot me a look. I could almost hear him muttering to himself, "Another Quaker."

Edward continued. "I'd like to know where her body is being kept. I plan to take her back to Nantucket on tonight's train."

"I'm afraid that won't be possible. She's in the morgue, see, and the coroner was sent to Lowell on a special case. He won't be back until tonight."

"Why does she need the presence of a coroner?" Edward asked. "Thee knows she's no longer among the living."

"He needs to perform an autopsy on her."

"What is that?" Edward asked.

I knew well what it was, but I supposed if one hadn't been around suspicious death much, it might not be a term bandied about in Nantucket Quaker circles.

Kevin looked at the door for a moment, as if figuring out how to explain this indelicate topic. "It's a kind of surgery where they explore her body for the cause of death." He held up a hand. "Yes, I know she was shot and killed. But the coroner might be able to find the bullet within her, and then we could match it with the weapon, when that turns up."

"You mean they cut her open?" Horror and disbelief colored his voice.

"Yes, Edward." I kept my voice soft. "But they are decent and respectful about it, and they repair the incision as neatly as they can. When she's dressed properly again, thee won't detect it." I'd never witnessed the procedure, but Kevin had explained it to me.

"I don't want my girl cut open like that."

"I'm sorry, sir." Kevin drummed his fingers on the table. "It has to be done."

Edward studied his hands. "Very well." He glanced up. "This coroner will be able to do the job tomorrow, despite it being First Day?"

"He said he would," Kevin said. "Will you be wanting her embalmed afterwards, it being summer and all?"

"Oh, no. Friends don't hold with that." Edward explained about the ice for the transport.

"Good," Kevin said. "Now, I need to ask you a few questions about your daughter. I'm hoping you might be able to provide some information on who could have had motivation to want her dead."

Edward nodded. "If it'll assist thee to find Hannah's killer, I'm willing to help."

Kevin turned his gaze on me. "And I suppose you can stay, Miss Rose."

"I appreciate that, Kevin."

"Now, did Hannah have any enemies, anyone she didn't get along with?" Kevin asked.

"Enemies? Good man, she was a seventeen-year-old girl, and the sweetest one who ever walked this earth." Edward's eyes filled. "No, she didn't have any enemies. If she had quarrels with the other girls, she never told us about them." He sniffed and blinked away his emotion.

"If I might speak, one of the other mill girls has expressed some conflict with Hannah," I said. "I'm sorry to have to mention it, Edward."

"Who is that?" Kevin asked, pencil ready at the paper where he'd been taking notes.

"Nora Walsh," I said. "She has claimed on several occasions that Hannah was stealing from her."

Edward just looked at the ground and shook his head. "Never. My girl never would have done that."

"Nora lives at Virginia Perkell's," I went on. "But Virginia has no proof of this theft, and Nora couldn't offer any, either."

"All right. Mr. Breed, was Hannah sending funds home beyond what you would have expected?"

"A bit," Edward admitted. "But I know she came by it honestly."

Kevin watched him for a moment, then took in a breath like he'd resolved something in his head. "And Hannah didn't have enemies back home?" he asked. "That you know of?"

"No."

"Had she told you about this boy she was apparently sweet on, a Tobias Cartland?" Kevin asked.

"Not a word." Edward shook his head. "The first I heard of him was an hour ago at her boardinghouse."

"Did she harbor ill will against coloreds?" Kevin asked in a casual tone.

"Of course not." Edward frowned. "But what has that to do with her death?"

"One of our suspects is an African named Akwasi."

Edward faced me. "Tell the man we are Quakers. We believe in equality. We do not attend to the color of a man's skin, only to the Light within him." His voice rose in exasperation. "We have Africans in our Nantucket Meeting congregation. They are our equals, our friends."

"Akwasi is a member of our own Amesbury Meeting. And Kevin knows very well he isn't a plausible suspect," I said to Edward. I looked Kevin in the eye. "I demand thee stop treating him as one."

Kevin kept his voice even. "Demands will get you nowhere, Rose Carroll. You have been helpful in my investigations in the past. But I'm still the officer in charge of finding this girl's killer, and I'll go where the trail leads me."

EIGHTEEN

"EDWARD, I'LL TRY TO arrange lodging for thee with a Friend for the night, since thee is not able to return home until after the autopsy." I held out my hand.

"I'm grateful for that, Rose." He clasped my hand in both of his.

I left him in care of Kevin. He had consented, after Edward insisted on viewing Hannah's body, to take him to the morgue. I cycled to Althea's home, a Friend who was the Clerk of our Women's Business Meeting. She agreed both to find lodging for Hannah's father and to let him know he had a place to sleep. If Frederick had been at home, we could have offered him a bedroll on the floor. With only Faith and me in the house, such an offer would be unseemly.

Outside Althea's house I remounted my bicycle but kept one foot on the ground, unsure of my destination. I closed my eyes and held the entire complicated situation in the Light, hoping to discern how way would open.

"Yer blockin' the whole walkway, lass," a rough voice exclaimed.

I opened my eyes to see a red-faced man pushing a cart holding bushels of oranges and bananas. The man's odor was a mix of alcohol and unwashed sweat, and the fruit also smelled overripe. "Pardon me. I'll get out of thy way."

I began to cycle aimlessly. My thoughts muffled the clop-clop of a horse pulling a wagon piled high with hay, the clatter of the trolley, the cries and splashing of children in a quiet eddy of the Powow as I rode over the Pond Street bridge.

Kevin still considered Akwasi a suspect. I needed to find Akwasi and ask him why. The new information about Hannah sending additional money back to the family also troubled me. I hoped she hadn't been robbing her housemates, as Nora had suggested, or hadn't also been taking valuable items from Virginia. I wanted to speak more with Tobias Cartland, too, to see if he had any idea that the reason Hannah rejected him was because she'd been with child from another man. Those additional investigations would have to wait, though. I set off for Akwasi's home, also the site of his furniture making business.

Coasting down the hill on Main Street, I passed Patten's Pond. A welcome breeze came off the water and cooled me. I turned right on Carpenter Street, where I faced the same kind of slope going up as I'd just ridden down. I dismounted and pushed the bike up the hill, smiling at the name of the road despite the effort I was exerting to ascend it. I'd have to ask Akwasi if he'd chosen this street on which to build his modest cottage because of its name matching his occupation, or whether that was simply a coincidence.

After I arrived at his house, no amount of knocking produced him. "Akwasi?" I called. "It's Rose, and I'd like to speak with thee." I rapped on the front door again and then went around the back to the small building housing his business. I thought I caught a glimpse of a man disappearing around the side of the shop.

"Akwasi?" I followed around the side but saw no one, so I went back to the shop door. It was locked, though, and the shutters on the windows were closed up tight. I detected no sounds of sawing or hammering. Where could he be? With Esther, I supposed, possibly out enjoying themselves at Lake Gardner or on the river.

Now what to do? My mind roiled liked the lower falls of the Powow, where the water crashed and boiled over the rocks. I'd like to go home and rest, and I'd love to talk through all my ideas with David. But he'd told me he needed to pay a call with his father this afternoon—something to do with the shoe company his father owned—so he wasn't available. David was going to pick me up for a drive tonight, but not until seven o'clock. I resolved to go and speak with one of the wisest people I knew.

Orpha Perkins raised her eyebrows when she opened the front door of the house she shared with her granddaughter and her family. "*Bonjour, ma chère.*"

"*Bonjour, ma tutrice.*" We'd studied French together.

She smiled broadly. "Come in, my dear. I guess it's my day for callers." My former midwifery tutor and now elder adviser turned and made her slow way down the dark hallway to her sitting room.

I followed her in to see Akwasi and Esther seated in two chairs near Orpha's rocker. "Exactly the people I wanted to see. Besides thee, Orpha, of course," I added.

Orpha lowered herself into her chair. "I had a sense you'd be showing up about now."

"These senses of thine are always correct," I said. "In fact, I was looking for thee, Akwasi, and I'm glad to see thee here. But I didn't know thee was acquainted with Orpha. Greetings, Esther."

Esther smiled her acknowledgment.

"Orpha's a wise woman, and she and I have a connection of which few are aware," Akwasi said.

Orpha had told me in confidence some years ago she'd had an African ancestor. Even though her skin was quite fair and her features more European than Negro, it was in her wiry hair and deep brown eyes one might detect the relationship with her parentage. Was that the connection to which Akwasi referred?

"Sit down, Rose." Orpha pointed to a chair. "And tell me why you seek out our friend Akwasi."

"I can answer that," Akwasi said, the smile sliding off his face. "It's because the detective still thinks I killed that girl, is it not?"

"I believe he does." I studied him as I sat. "Akwasi, had thee had any direct dealings with Lester Colby prior to Independence Day?"

Leaning his elbows on his knees, he clasped his hands and studied the floor. "Yes." He raised his head. "He cheated me out of a good deal of money several years ago. He'd ordered an armoire built, and I crafted it to his specifications using only the finest cherry wood with delicate mahogany inlays and quite difficult joins. It was one of the most beautiful pieces I'd created up until then. After I delivered it, he claimed I'd cheated him and built it in a shoddy fashion. None of it was true. Not a word."

"What happened?" I gazed at the anger in his eyes.

"He told me to take it away. I tried to sell it, even taking out an advertisement in the newspaper. But he'd ordered it specially constructed to fit in an oddly shaped corner, so no one else wanted it. I finally sold it at a great loss. The price didn't even cover the cost of the wood, not to mention my time and the damage to my reputation when he went and told his cronies." His jaw worked despite his closed mouth.

Given what I'd learned about Lester's finances, it was possible he rejected the armoire because he couldn't afford to pay for it. In that case he never should have ordered it, although maybe he did so before he learned of his wife's cancer.

Esther reached out and stroked Akwasi's shoulder. "And you didn't go to the law about it, either?"

He shook his head, sitting erect again with flared nostrils. "A former slave takes on a factory manager? I didn't believe I would succeed."

"I advised you at the time, if you recall, to enlist the help of long-time residents like Mr. Whittier and myself, did I not?" Orpha asked in a gentle tone.

"Thee did," Akwasi agreed. "To be frank, I didn't want to think about Colby for a moment longer than necessary. I turned the other cheek as Jesus taught us to do and let the money go."

"But Kevin now thinks thee holds a grudge against Lester," I said.

"If I did, then I would have shot *him*! Why would I kill a poor mill girl I didn't even know?" Akwasi stood and paced across the room to the door and back. He usually moved his tall, powerful body with grace, but today he was more like a tightly coiled spring. "None of it makes sense because it's all fabrication." He clenched his fists until his knuckles paled.

"Kevin didn't give thee any idea as to the evidence he thinks he has?" I asked.

"No. But I believe he'd like to get me back in jail. Thanks to Benjamin Lehigh, he can't."

———

When I arrived home at around five, Faith and Zeb were sitting outside on the landing at the side of the house. A small cloth was spread between them holding a dish of boiled eggs and pickled cucumbers, slices of ham and bread on a plate, and a dish of raspberries. Zeb held a metal cup and another rested on the first step. It had taken some persuading for Frederick to let Faith spend time with Zeb unchaperoned. I'd convince him that they were both trustworthy young people and that he should allow it. They might raise a few staid eyebrows in public, but Quakers were used to that.

"Is this supper I see?" I asked before stowing my bicycle in the shed. I took a moment to stroke Star's nose and left the door ajar.

"It's much too hot to cook." Faith laughed. "But we have plenty. Come and join us." Her feet were bare and she'd unpinned her hair, leaving it to hang loose down her back. Her hair was much like her mother's and my own—thick, brown, and wavy.

"I will after I wash up." I gazed back at Star. "Someone should take him out for a ride. He must be getting restless with three days of not moving about."

"We shall a little later on," Zeb said. "Thee can ride in front of me." He gazed at Faith with tender eyes.

I slipped past them not even trying to hide my yawn and went indoors. All I wanted to do was to lie down and calm my thoughts, but my stomach had developed other plans once it spied the food. I also wanted to talk with Faith and make sure she was feeling better after her encounter of the morning. With clean hands and face and a loosened collar, I filled my own cup with cold water and headed back outdoors. I sank onto a step and accepted a slice of bread topped with ham from Faith, listening to the two banter with each other while I ate.

About to ask Faith how her afternoon had been, I stopped when I saw Nora Walsh turn up the path at the side of the house. She carried a flat packet and moved with a tentative gait.

"Nora, what brings thee here?" Faith called.

"I brought yeh a gift, Faith," Nora said.

"Me?" Faith stood, brushed the crumbs from her lap, and ran down the steps. "Why did thee bring me a gift?"

Nora extended the packet to Faith. "Yer always sayin' how much yeh like to write. So I got this for yeh."

Faith smiled ear to ear and bounced on her heels. "I thank thee kindly, Nora." She reached out and hugged Nora for a moment, then stepped back. "Can I open it now?"

"Of course." Nora's own smile wavered as if nervous Faith wouldn't like her offering.

I watched as Faith tore off the string and then the paper to reveal a slim leather-bound book. She flipped through the pages, then looked up at Nora with her brown eyes asparkle.

"It's a blank book. A diary! What a perfect, thoughtful gift. I can't wait to start writing in it." She turned back to the stairs. "Look Rose, Zeb." She handed me the book, then grabbed Nora's hand. "Come and sit with us, Nora. Has thee eaten supper?"

The leather on the book's cover was smooth and soft. It was indeed a perfect gift for Faith, even better than the Lucy Larcom book I'd given her yesterday. Nora had seemed prickly and almost mean earlier. I was happy to see she was also capable of being generous and considerate. But the book must have cost a pretty penny. Where had Nora found the money?

Nora sat next to me and accepted an egg and a slice of bread.

"How does this heat compare to that in thy home country?" Zeb asked.

"Oh, by the blessed Virgin, it's never this hot in County Cork." Nora gave a small smile as she gazed into the distance. "In the warmest part of summer I'd go huntin' in the woods with my da. The trees kept us cool, and we brought home meat for the family." She leaned toward us and whispered, "He's part of the rebellion, you know, the Land League. That's why he has a gun."

I stared at her for a moment, then looked away before she noticed. So her father was a rebel. She knew how to shoot. And she'd had arguments with Hannah.

"Is thee the eldest?" Faith asked.

"That I am." Her voice grew wistful. "With nine wee ones below me. They're Seamus, Mary, Katie, John, Culkin, Bridget, Keira." She ticked them off on her fingers. "Rowan, and baby Fiona."

"Many mouths to feed," Zeb said.

"I miss the littlest ones the most. It was almost like they were my own babes."

Many mouths, indeed. Nora's mother had been busy. Not quite one baby every year, but giving birth ten times in a row took its toll on a woman's body. And that good Catholic woman might not be done yet.

"Which is the reason I'm here workin' and after sendin' as much money home as I can." Nora nibbled on her bread.

"As was Hannah Breed, poor soul," I said. "Her elder brother suffers from a malady for which he is institutionalized."

Nora stared at me. "Oh?"

"Yes." I nodded. "The cost is high, her father told me, and Hannah helped as much as she was able."

"She never once told me that," Nora said with a frown. "The poor lass."

The poor dead lass with her poor dead unborn child. Too bad Kevin wasn't making much headway in figuring out who'd killed her. Nora seemed more concerned about Hannah today than she had on earlier occasions. Because Hannah also had a need in her family?

NINETEEN

THE AIR HAD BLESSEDLY cooled by the time David clucked to Daisy after picking me up.

"Where are we off to tonight?" I asked.

"Let's traverse the length of the Merrimack River. We'll find a nice breeze by its banks, I dare say."

"The Merrimack it is. Although I doubt you mean the full length. I believe it originates halfway up the length of New Hampshire to the north."

He laughed in that infectious way that made me laugh, too. "No, I certainly don't. How about its length only to the western boundary of Amesbury?"

"Much more manageable."

We set off down the same Main Street hill I'd descended on my bicycle earlier in the day. The image of visiting Akwasi's shop and my conversation with him at Orpha's popped into my brain, but I banished it. Despite my earlier yearning to talk through my ideas about the shooting with David, I now wanted to have a light-hearted, enjoyable evening, instead.

"A penny for your thoughts?" He glanced at me.

I swallowed. Because I didn't want to lie to him, I switched my thoughts as fast as I could. "How went the call with thy father this afternoon?"

"It was interesting. I've told you my family is more than comfortable financially because of my father's good head for business. He inherited his own father's small shoe company and has expanded it a hundredfold. But he also treats his employees well. He doesn't overwork them. They have fresh air and good illumination indoors. And he gives them ample time off to spend with their families."

"He's not likely to experience a strike, then."

"No, I doubt it. Now he wants to provide them with health services. He already purchases accident insurance from Travelers Insurance Company. But there is a new movement out west to establish a medical clinic for employees where they can be treated for common illnesses."

"Excellent idea. Even those earning the lowest wages would have access to a doctor."

"Exactly. He spoke with a senior physician at the hospital about it and wanted me along to listen and add my opinion."

His left hand lay on the seat between us. I covered it with my own. "Even though thee did not follow him into the shoe industry, thee can now take part in it. He must be happy and proud to be able to consult with his son." I'd met Herbert Dodge for the first time in April and had fallen for his warmth and twinkling eyes immediately. He'd clearly liked me, too. David's mother, on the other hand, didn't approve of me in the least as the object of David's affections.

"And I feel much the same toward the situation," David said. "Proud he is a decent caring businessman, and happy I can work with him at last."

"Thee could suggest to Herbert a midwife should be on staff at the clinic, too. I'd love to see all pregnant women have good antenatal care. Many choose not to because of the cost."

"Good idea. I'll tell him. His factory does employ quite a number of married ladies who do the stitching."

"Does thee think this new idea of providing medical services to workers will catch on across the country?"

"If it becomes widespread here in Massachusetts, and since it already is in the northwest, there might be a chance of it reaching inland from both coasts."

"Like when they drove the Last Spike in 1869, which connected the rail lines from the east and west."

"At Promontory Summit. You know your history well, Rosie."

I gazed at the wide river now next to us. "Doesn't every school child learn these things?"

"I suppose. Not all remember them, though." He pointed to the water. "Would you look at that moon?"

The full moon splashed a silver path from the distant bank across to ours. We rode along in silence for several minutes, comfortable simply being in each other's presence. We passed a boat yard and the Merrimac Hat Factory and continued on to the west. David whistled a tune I couldn't quite place.

"What's that thee is singing?"

"'Where did you get that hat?'" he sang out. "'Where did you get that tile? Isn't it a nobby one, and just the proper style?'" He stopped and grinned over at me.

"Is this a new ditty?" I smiled back.

"That it is. Joseph Sullivan composed and performed it last month in New York City. I took in the show at the Miner's Theater when I was in the city for that medical convention, remember?" He switched to whistling the tune and continued driving at a relaxed pace.

After some time he pulled to a halt near a square wooden platform built at the water's edge. A bench sat facing the river with a hitching post behind it. He jumped out and tied the horse to the post, then came around and helped me down.

"What is this delightful place?" I asked. I pushed my bonnet off my head, letting it hang down my back as I strolled to the edge of the large platform. An attached ramp perhaps half the width of the platform extended down to the water about twenty feet, with rope stretched on either side of the ramp at waist height to serve as a handhold. The ramp ended in a small dock, which bobbed up and down with the river's gentle movement. A metal cleat was inserted along the dock's edge.

"A friend of my parents built it as a place to tie up his boat when he sails inland and wants to stop for a picnic or to stretch his legs," he said. "Sometimes Mother and Father drive up here and wait for him so they can share a picnic by the side of the river."

"I love it." I took his hand. "Walk with me to the end." The two of us helped each other keep our balance as we made our way down the ramp, me clutching the rope on my right. I'd never been on a boat before despite living so near both the Powow and the Merrimack. I thought it might feel something like this with the water flowing under the dock and the faint rocking motion. A fish leapt out of the water and splashed back down, and an owl hooted in the trees. It looked like the moonlight on the water was a path leading straight to us. We stood in silence watching, our hands still clasped.

"Let's go up and sit on the bench for a spell." David drew me back up the ramp and to the bench.

I sat, but he remained standing. "Doesn't thee want to sit down?" I asked.

To my surprise he knelt on one knee, so my gaze went directly into his eyes. His hair was extra curly in the humidity and he was silent as he took my left hand with his right.

He took in a deep breath and let it out before speaking. "Miss Rose Margaret Carroll, I would be extremely happy if you would agree to take my hand in marriage. I love you and want to support you and be by your side always." Keeping hold of my hand, he drew a ring out of his left pocket and showed it to me on his open palm.

Marriage. Support. Always. My heart thrashed like a wild songbird in a net. My hand felt small and cold despite being held up by his warm, strong one. I stared at the slender golden band entwined in a love knot until I trusted myself to speak.

I met his gaze again. "My dearest David. Thee knows I love thee. This is the most special, the sweetest, the most memorable request anyone has ever made of me. In all my life." I squeezed his hand. "But ..." I couldn't continue.

His expression changed from hopeful to stricken. "But what? You'll say yes, won't you? Don't you want to be my wife?" He peered into my face as if understanding could be found there.

"Of course I do, with all my heart." It was my turn to take in a deep breath and then let it out. "But I have a confession to make,

155

and a fear to express." I tried to keep my voice from wobbling. He would have every right to retract his invitation to marriage after he heard what I was going to say, and I needed to accept that. I'd expected this proposal would come at some point, but didn't think it would be now. That we would be having this discussion tonight. That I would finally be telling him about my sordid past.

TWENTY

"A CONFESSION? YOU CAN never have done something I wouldn't embrace or forgive. Ever." His face now pale, he stared at the ring in his palm. "Let me put this on your finger so you'll believe me."

I shook my head. "Not yet. Come and sit next to me." After he closed his fist around the ring and slid it back into his pocket, I pulled him up and waited until he sat. I twisted to face him, remembering what Orpha had said to me recently. *You cannot let a painful experience in your distant past govern your future, you know. That would be giving it more power than it deserves.* It was time to take the power back. "Something horrid happened to me."

"I hate to hear that. Was it today?" He slid his arm along the back of the bench and touched my shoulder.

"No, when I was in my teenage years. I became enamored of a boy a bit older than I."

"In Lawrence?"

"Yes."

"All young people fall foolishly in love. This is nothing you need to confess, Rose."

I waited a moment before continuing. "Please hear me out. He wasn't a Quaker, but my wild cousin Sephronia introduced us. The boy was a bit wild, too, and I found him alluring. He was fun, and he made me feel attractive. My father did not approve, I can assure you, but I found ways of meeting the boy." I gazed at the river. A breeze carried the coolness of the water and I shivered. I looked back at David, lifting my chin. "Then one hot summer night he forced himself on me. It was awful, David. I tried to get away, but I couldn't." My heart began to race as if it were happening all over again. My hands grew clammy, and I had trouble swallowing.

"My Rosie. And you were only a girl." He edged closer and stroked my shoulder.

I was determined to finish my tale. "I was seventeen. Faith's age now. Hannah's age. I realized soon enough he'd impregnated me."

David's eyes went wide. "You poor dear. Did you ..." His voice trailed off as if he could well picture the choices I would have faced.

I held up a hand. "I miscarried, and early on. I never needed to tell my mother about either the deed or the pregnancy, and I thanked God for not making me bear the baby of that brute. I stayed well clear of him after that and moved to Amesbury after Betsy's birth to begin my apprenticeship with Orpha. She is the only person I have told, besides my sister. Until now."

David took my face in both hands. "You were young, and you were not to blame. It wasn't your fault that you trusted that scoundrel." He fixed his gaze directly on my eyes. "You know I don't care about what happened in the past. You know that."

My throat thickened. "I do. I'm touched thee says that."

"We Dodges mean what we say. Now will you accept?" He dropped his hands to take both of mine and squeezed them firmly, gently. He rubbed his thumb along the back of my hand.

"Not yet. I must discuss another matter." Despite his look of confusion, I went on. "Thee said thee wants to support me." I spoke slowly, as if that would give him time to absorb my words. "I do good work as a midwife, important work. My mothers need me, and I need them. I have given this much thought in recent months as we have grown closer. I do not wish to leave my profession."

He nodded, as slowly as I had spoken. "What I meant was to support you in your life, my dear, in whatever you choose to do. Should you need my support in the monetary sense, well, what is mine will of course be yours. And you might want to take some time away from work when our own little ones come along. But I wouldn't dream of asking you to give up your vocation."

I stared at him through wet eyes, my heart calming again. I wouldn't have to make the terrible choice between marriage and my calling, because I wouldn't be obliged to stop working after we were wed. How did I become so lucky to have this generous, caring man love me? "Thee is a strange and wonderful creature, and unique among thy sex. Thee is more sure about the rightness of equality than I, even. Is thee sure thee wasn't raised a Quaker?"

He laughed out loud. "I'm quite sure I was raised strictly in the high Episcopalian tradition at St. Paul's. But I grew tired of its elaborate trappings as an adult, and I rarely attend services these days. My father, however, attends the Unitarian church on Pleasant Street and is friends with the new pastor. I sometimes go along to their much more liberal services of a Sunday morning. Which irks Mother no end, as so much does."

I frowned. "Thy mother will be even more irked when you go to tell her of your proposal."

"My mother," he said. "My mother will simply have to adjust her expectations."

"It won't be easy, David. We are of different social classes. I barely made it through that dinner dance thee took me to in the spring, and Clarinda will expect me to participate in other like events as part of the family." This was a looming worry for me.

"Oh, hang social class. If I don't care and you don't care, and we have each other, how hard can it be?"

I doubted things would be that simple. But he was right. If we were united in love and purpose, we would manage.

"I know my father will be delighted at our union." David frowned. "But what about your father? When I drive to Lawrence to ask for your hand, will he refuse me because I'm not a member of the Religious Society of Friends?"

"I think our fathers are quite similar. Allan Burroughs Carroll will not object, as long as he knows I'm happy and will be entering into an equal partnership with thee. On the contrary I'm certain he'll be as delighted as Herbert. So will my mother. Both my parents are quite liberal in their thinking. I think thee will like both of them, and I know they'll like thee." I screwed up my nose. "My Meeting, on the other hand, will likely read me out."

"What does that mean?"

"It means being expelled for doing something unacceptable."

"And you don't care?" He tilted his head and studied my face.

"I do care, and after several months I can write a letter making amends. I believe they'll accept my request to be reinstated. Things are not as rigid as they once were, when marrying out was an act to be severely condemned."

"Marrying out. Meaning marrying a non-Quaker, I'd guess."

"Yes. I don't know why they were so strict about that in times past. It seems strange, because otherwise Friends are so strong for equality and acceptance. But truly times are changing, even for Quakers. I already know I have John Whittier's support, and I might not be read out at all." I fondled David's finger. "Thee might want to accompany me to Meeting for Worship before we wed. It is a highly peaceful and spiritual time."

"I might do that." He drew out the ring again. "Now, Rose Carroll, will you accept this token of my love, and say you'll be my bride?" The color was back in his face and the sparkle had returned to his eyes.

"I will, David Chase Dodge. Happily so."

He slid the ring gently onto my left hand, then lifted it and pressed his lips against the ring. "For now and for always," he murmured.

"For now and for always."

TWENTY-ONE

WE SAT A WHILE longer in the moonlight, talking about our future together.

"I want a passel of children," David said. "What do you think about that?"

"I agree. At least four?"

"Yes. And if they're all girls, I won't complain. I always wanted a sister, and somehow ended up with only the one brother."

I blinked at him. "I didn't know thee had any siblings at all. What's his name?"

David frowned at the river. "Wesley. But I don't want to spoil this lovely evening by talking about him." He cleared his throat and summoned a smile. "Tell me what a Quaker marriage ceremony is like."

"It's almost the same as any Meeting for Worship, except the marrying couple sits together on the facing bench. After some time of silence, they rise and say their vows to each other. Then they sign the wedding certificate."

"What's that?"

"It's a big piece of paper, like parchment, with a declaration of the marriage and the wedding vows written in ink. Sometimes the edges are decorated with drawings. After the couple signs, if anyone wishes to share a message about the bride or groom, they stand and say it. Sometimes this goes on for quite a while."

"Can non-Quakers attend?" A little smile played around the edges of his mouth.

"Most definitively." I smiled back. "After the Meeting is concluded, everyone present at the wedding also signs the certificate in witness to the union. The couple usually puts it in a frame and hangs it on the wall of their parlor for all to see. It's quite lovely, really." I turned my new ring on my finger and relished the moment. I decided not to dwell on the image of Clarinda's face when she heard of our plans.

"I like the sound of that, everyone witnessing the union," David said. "But if you are read out, how can we have a Quaker wedding?"

"What might happen is that they will read me out for becoming betrothed with thee. It's the Women's Business Meeting that decides these things, and several of our older female members are quite old-fashioned about marriage. But when I appeal, I can bring letters from other members, such as John. I do believe I would be reinstated, and then we can have a Friends ceremony."

"That's fine, then."

"When will thee go to Lawrence?" I drew my legs up and wrapped my arms around my knees. I'd never felt so comfortable around a man other than my father.

"Do you want to write to your parents first?"

"I shall, first thing tomorrow," I said. "I can just picture Daddy reading the letter. He'll wear a big grin and his spectacles will fog up with emotion." My father wore a full white beard and had a short, stocky build no taller than me. Both Harriet and I had inherited our height from Mother's side.

"Then I'll go mid-week." He stretched his legs out in front of him, crossing them at the ankle.

"The children will be happy to see thee there."

"That's right, I'd forgotten that was their destination."

"But let us not tell anyone until Daddy and Mother have agreed. Is that acceptable with thee?" I knew it would be hard not to bubble up with the news to Faith, but I also wanted things to proceed in the traditional order. There was enough of the untraditional about David and me, we could at least honor certain processes.

"Whatever you want, my Rose." He gazed at me. "Now I know something more of your past, I see this killing of a young pregnant girl must be extra painful for you."

"It is. That's one reason I want to get to the bottom of it, even though that is Kevin's job, not mine. To see Akwasi mistreated is also so hurtful. I'm completely sure he did not kill Hannah." I set my feet on the ground again.

"I do hope you won't take any risks looking into these things." He stroked my forearm, then wrapped his strong slender hand around mine, heating the ring with the warmth of his skin. "If anything happened to you, I'm not sure what I would do."

"I have a long life ahead of me, and I look forward to sharing it with thee." I laid my other hand on the side of his cheek. "I'll strive to be careful and circumspect."

"Speaking of circumspect, I'd better get you home before the hour grows indecently late." He checked his pocket watch. "Which it almost is, being well past nine."

Twenty minutes later we were about to drive past the police station when a police wagon pulled to a halt in front of us. Guy Gilbert went around to the back and opened the doors. He escorted a handcuffed Akwasi out and up the stairs. Akwasi's head hung and he dragged his feet.

David pulled his horse to a stop. He and I stared at each other.

"This is terrible," I said. "Something has happened. I have to go ask why they have taken him in again."

"And if Akwasi is handcuffed, it must be a real arrest, which means they must have found some kind of evidence. I agree. You should go in."

I jumped down, not waiting for his assistance, and hurried toward the stairs while David stayed with Daisy. Kevin descended from the cab of the wagon at the same time.

"Oh, no you don't," he said to me. "You're not getting him out this time."

"Why did thee arrest the poor man, Kevin?" I asked.

"Evidence has emerged, and it led us directly to Mr. Ayensu." He clasped his hands behind his back and rocked on his heels.

"What kind of evidence?" David asked.

"The gun. The very weapon he used to murder that girl."

"Where did thee find it?" I asked.

Kevin stared at me. "We found it hidden behind his workshop."

"But thee doesn't know he fired it, does thee?"

"Why else would it be there?"

I thought for a moment, narrowing my eyes. "Because the real killer planted it there, that's why. In fact, I saw someone rush around the corner of his shop when I went there earlier today."

Kevin smiled without including his eyes. "You go on and enjoy those fantasies of yours, Miss Rose."

"Now, see here, Detective." David stood tall and glared at Kevin. "Don't you dare speak with disrespect to my fiancée."

Kevin's eyes popped wide. "So that's the way it is, eh? Frankly, I don't care if she's your fiancée or Queen Victoria. We have us a suspect who was present at the scene and a murder weapon found in his possession, or very nearly so." He turned to go.

"But thee still has no motive," I protested. "Akwasi hadn't a reason in the world to kill Hannah."

"We'll find one. Never you fear."

———

We pulled up in front of my house. The lamps were lit within and the door stood open to the night air. I turned to David.

"Thy fiancée, am I?" I softened the question with a smile. "I thought we'd agreed to keep our engagement secret until we have the blessings of our parents."

"I apologize. I know you didn't want to let the news out." He pulled his mouth to the side.

"I confess I liked the sound of it."

"It's just that I won't stand for anyone being rude to you."

"Don't worry about it. And I don't think Kevin will be spreading the news of our betrothal around." My smile faded. "I hope instead he'll realize Akwasi had no motive, let him go, and work on finding the real killer. Or accept that Hannah's death was just a terrible accident."

"Those are my hopes, as well. Now get yourself indoors before the neighbors start to talk." He climbed out and hurried around to hand me down.

"As if I care what they say." I blew him a kiss as I headed for the house. I didn't care about the local gossips, although I probably should. I walked up the steps to the back door and paused on the landing. I held out my hand in the moonlight. The gold knot shone as if reflecting the warmth in my heart. I truly did feel that David and I together could surmount any obstacles.

"Rose, is that thee?" Faith called from within.

"It is I." I pulled open the screened door, an innovation that had done much to help cool the indoors while keeping the mosquitoes of summer out. Faith and Annie sat at the table, Annie glancing up from a book, Faith in front of a folio covered in penciled writing from her neat hand. A decimated bowl of popped corn occupied the middle of the table, with two peach pits sitting on a plate next to it.

"Annie is going to spend the night," Faith said. "She can have Betsy's bed."

"Good idea," I said. "It looks like school in here."

"It is, in a way," Annie said. "I'm working on my reading, and Faith is writing her article."

"What is thee reading, Annie?" The Bailey family, Faith in particular, had gladly taken on the task earlier in the year of teaching seventeen-year-old Annie to read. She'd been taken out of school by her French-Canadian family before she'd learned to read in that language and had been working in Amesbury ever since, so she'd never attended school in English, either.

She held up an open copy of *Little Women* with a shy smile. Her curly red hair was held back with a bright blue ribbon tonight, a color matching her eyes.

"Already? That's excellent," I exclaimed. "It was when, in April, when thee started off with Betsy's *First Reader*?"

Annie nodded. "I like seeing stories come to life. It's a bit hard for me yet, but Faith helps me when I stumble." She peered at the book. "Like this word, *tree-ah-soors*. What's that mean?" She pointed to a word on the page, still near the beginning of the tale.

Faith craned her neck. "That's a funny one. It's the word *treasures*. But the spelling doesn't look like the pronunciation."

Annie wrinkled her nose. "If you say so." She continued to read, moving her finger along under the line as she went.

I moved to stand next to Faith. "And thee is writing thy article already?" I pointed to the paper.

"Yes, I thought I could begin with a description of what it's like to work on the mill..." Faith peered at my hand, then turned her upper body to look up at me. "What's that ring?" Her eyes gleamed and she caught her lower lip in her teeth as she grinned.

Oh. So much for not letting the cat out of the bag. I gazed at the ring and then at the girls. "I think I should sit down."

Annie pushed out the chair across from her with her foot.

I sank into it. "I'm to be married." I held out my left hand and watched it shake at the momentous announcement. This would be the first time I would say those words, but certainly not the last.

Faith squealed and leapt out of her chair. "How splendid, Rose." She threw her arms around me and squeezed.

"To Mr. Dodge, I assume?" Annie asked, also beaming.

"Yes. Faith, I can't breathe," I said with a laugh. "But you two mustn't tell anyone until it's all right and proper. I'll write to Daddy and Mother tomorrow, and David will pay them a visit in a few days."

Faith stood back, clapped her hands, and sat. "This is such sweet news. I knew it would happen, I just knew it. Didn't I, Annie?"

Annie grinned. "We would have wagered on when he was going to spring the question, except you Quakers don't wager."

"I'm glad you girls were the first to know." Their faces were aglow. What young girl didn't dream of being in love and happy with her prince? My path to the castle had been slow, painful, and circuitous, and I hadn't cleared the moat yet. I sobered. "Actually, David let slip the words *my fiancée* to Kevin Donovan on our way home."

"Thee spoke with the police after thy romantic outing?" Faith narrowed her eyes.

"We were driving by the station when we saw Akwasi hauled out of the police wagon wearing handcuffs. Kevin said he has been arrested for Hannah's murder."

Annie frowned as she crossed herself and Faith's smile also slipped away. "Does thee think he was the killer?" Faith asked.

"No, of course not. Kevin said they found the gun behind Akwasi's shop, though."

"But how do they know that was the weapon that killed Hannah?" Annie asked.

"I don't believe they do. The coroner will perform an autopsy on Hannah tomorrow, and perhaps he will retrieve the fatal bullet from within her."

At these words Annie flinched. A devout Catholic girl, she hurriedly crossed herself again.

"I'm sorry, my dears," I said. "It's a fact of life that the soul's shell must be investigated if the death was not a peaceful one. But, of course, Hannah's spirit has been released to God. She no longer inhabits the earthly husk."

Faith straightened her back and patted Annie's hand. "And if the type of bullet matches the type of gun, it still doesn't prove Akwasi fired it, correct?"

"That's exactly right. Now, let's not talk further of these dark subjects. Tell me of thy article, Faith."

"I wanted to start it so I can have something to show to Lucy Larcom tomorrow. I'll want the readers to have a feel for the noise and vibration of the mill before I begin to lay out the facts—of which I have precious few as yet."

"I think that's a good idea. Both describing the atmosphere, and bringing a piece to show her that thee is serious about becoming a journalist. When does thee meet her?"

"John said to accompany him back to his home after Meeting for Worship tomorrow, that Lucy will be staying with him. Does thee think she'll take me seriously, Rose?"

I gazed at my dark-eyed niece, who could be lighthearted and young one moment and mature beyond her years the next. "Yes, I think she will."

Pops and cracks split the night air. The three of us hurried outside to see more colored displays decorate the sky. They came from high on Powow Hill, likely a late Independence Day celebration. I closed my eyes and prayed that never again would fireworks disguise a gunshot that took a person's life.

TWENTY-TWO

FAITH AND ANNIE SET out the next morning, Annie to her church and Faith to breakfast with Zeb and his family before Meeting. I ate my porridge, still savoring the feeling of being David's betrothed. It was curious about his brother, though. He'd never mentioned a word of this Wesley, and he'd seemed somehow troubled in thinking of him. I had faith he'd tell me when the time was right, and assumed the entire family would gather to celebrate our marriage, so I would meet the brother at that time.

I sat down with pen and paper to convey my happy news to Daddy and Mother. I thought for a moment, and first penned salutations and greetings to the children, saying I trusted everyone arrived safely and were happily enjoying farm life. I held out my left hand, admiring the ring, then wrote,

> *I am delighted to convey a joyful invitation I received last night. My dear friend David Dodge of Newburyport, of whom I have previously written, will be traveling to visit you in two days' time to ask for my hand in marriage. Please know that*

I have already accepted his proposal with a clear mind and a happy heart. We both know it is more conventional to do things in reverse—for him to ask thee first, Daddy, and then propose to me. But times are changing, and I welcomed his proposal.

He expressed no obstacle to my continuing to work in my called profession of midwife, and we enjoy an equal status in our respect and love for each other. While he is not a Friend, I foresee that he might come to appreciate the benefits of attending Meeting for Worship by and by, although of course I'll not pressure him to do so. I realize that I might be written out of Amesbury Meeting for becoming betrothed to a man who is not of our faith. I am ready, and will apply to make amends as soon as is appropriate.

David and I anticipate a small degree of resistance to the engagement from his mother, Clarinda Dodge. She had hoped David would wed his cousin. But we expect that hurdle shall be overcome with the help and support of his father, Herbert. We have not yet decided upon a date for the Meeting for Marriage. We'll pay you a visit in several weeks to discuss a felicitous date for the wedding to be set after the appropriate applications are made to both his church and to Amesbury Meeting.

Please welcome my dear David when he arrives. Daddy, I hope way will open for thee to give him thy heartiest blessing.

I ended with news of Faith looking forward to her meeting with Lucy Larcom today and signed the letter as the clock chimed nine-thirty. I blotted it, addressed an envelope, affixed a stamp, and slid in my message of joy. I donned my bonnet and glimpsed my gloves on the shelf but decided to forgo them because of the continuing warm weather. I'd be among Friends, and we were already unconventional enough. I wouldn't be judged for bare hands. I grabbed my birthing satchel and hurried out of the house. I planned to visit Georgia after Meeting to check on her well-being and that of the newborn. I doubted Georgia would care if I wore gloves, either.

I slipped the letter into a postbox I passed, imagining my mother's reaction when she opened it. I could almost hear her whoop of gladness, and could picture my father's broad smile. I thought the children would be delighted, too, since they all loved David.

As I walked up Friend Street toward the Meetinghouse, I spied Tobias approaching on Summer Street, his gaze on his feet. When I hailed him, he looked up.

"Off to worship, Rose?" he called.

"I am. Shall we walk together?" I paused until he joined me.

"I'm heavy of heart this morning," he said in a voice that sounded just as heavy. Under a tweed cap, dark patches beneath his eyes were signs of missing sleep and he looked far older than his twenty years.

"Missing Hannah?" I asked in a soft voice.

"Ever so much. And to be under suspicion of killing her is a pain almost too much to bear. I wanted her to marry me. Instead, first she rejected me, and then someone caused her to leave this earth forever. My heart will never recover."

"May God heal thee." We walked in silence for a moment.

"Rose, did thee perhaps hear from Faith about why Hannah had turned away from me? We hadn't argued or even had the smallest disagreement, and we'd been stepping out for several months. I'm at a loss to understand it."

"No, I don't believe Faith had any knowledge of it. I might not have told thee Hannah spoke with me that last morning." I quickly weighed whether I should tell him of her pregnancy and just as quickly again decided not to. It could ease his mind to know there was a reason for his rejection, but it might also make him feel much, much worse to know she'd had relations with another man.

"Independence Day."

"Yes. She seemed quite dejected about her life. I urged her to go off and have fun with her friends. Did thee see her at the fireworks?"

"No, more's the pity. Maybe I could have protected her. I went with some fellows with whom I work, but I never saw Hannah."

"About thy being under suspicion, Tobias."

"Yes?"

"According to Kevin Donovan, the police now think Friend Akwasi Ayensu murdered Hannah."

Tobias stopped short. "That gentle man? This can't be true."

"I'm afraid this is what the police are saying. Come along now, we don't want to arrive late." I switched my birthing satchel to my other hand and told him what Kevin had said about the weapon turning up behind the shop. "I agree, the arrest has to be a mistake."

He started walking again. "I moved to Amesbury for work, but also because it had a reputation for being a safe, just town where everyone was agreeable to each other. John Whittier had said as much to my father when he visited Milton once." He shook his head. "But now? Murder? Wrong accusations? Suspicion? It makes me want to flee back north."

"Thee knows Nora Walsh, is that right?"

"The girl who roomed with Hannah, yes." He curled his lip. "She's another one. All sweet and flirting one moment and dreadfully mean to Hannah the next."

"Nora told me you are sweet on her."

His mouth gaped. "Then she's dreaming. I never gave her the slightest cause to think that." He picked up his step and clenched his fists. "For her to claim so is a dishonor to Hannah. I'd dearly like to give Nora a piece of my mind."

I reached for his elbow. "Thee might be well advised to turn the other cheek, Tobias. She's young, far from home, and likely unhappy."

"I suppose. With any luck I'll never see her again. I've no cause to enter the Perkell boardinghouse now, nor to haunt the exit of the Hamilton Mill waiting for my girl." His voice broke at the end as we crossed Whitehall Road and then crossed Friend to enter the gate surrounding the Meetinghouse yard.

"Come and visit Faith and me at the Bailey home instead, will thee?"

He nodded without speaking and ran up the granite steps of the building. I paused, gazing at its simple white facade and dark green shutters. John Whittier had been on the building committee when Amesbury Monthly Meeting had resolved they needed newer, larger quarters than the former meetinghouse. The old location had been nearly across the street from John's home, but this spot on a low rise provided a better setting, with more light and air. I'd heard John had been adamant that the lines of the building, the tall windows, and the interior should be kept simple. Some other meetinghouses used the resources of their wealthier members to add fine paneling and other touches, but not this one. I preferred it that way.

I joined other Friends moving into one of the two worship rooms separated today by only a waist-high wall. Most First Days it was thus, but when we held our monthly business meetings, several men would ascend into the attic and use the giant pulley system to lower the dividing wall until it met the bottom section. The women held a business meeting separately from the men, which let us of the female persuasion control our own matters without the interference of males. I'd always found it odd that our belief in equality should lead to this separation, but it did result in giving women the confidence to speak up and come to a Divinely led sense of the meeting that spilled over into their daily lives.

John Whittier and several other elders of the Meeting, both male and female, already sat with closed eyes on the facing bench. I spied Faith sitting with Zeb, and slid into a pew next to them. I closed my eyes, shutting out the world. It was true what John had written in his poem, "The Meeting."

> *And from the silence multiplied*
> *By these still forms on either side,*
> *The world that time and sense have known*
> *Falls off and leaves us God alone.*

The Meeting had been silent for some time. I loved sensing the gradual quieting of the congregation. Once everyone had arrived, the rustling of clothing and creaking of benches began to still. So, too, did attenders' thoughts grow calm—or so I assumed. I felt the shared quiet deepen as we waited upon the Light together. I'd been taught if I discerned I'd received a message from God, I needed to hold that message and further determine if it should be shared, and then decide whether it should be shared silently or out loud. This process of discernment could go on so long sometimes silence reigned for the entire worship period. On other First Days, a dozen messages might be shared, the kind of service my irreverent mother had labeled a "popcorn" meeting. In Amesbury, one older lady often droned on for far too long, in my opinion, but who was I to judge?

This morning my own thoughts were not becoming quiet in the least. Images kept rolling through my brain. The moment Hannah died. The sight of Akwasi in handcuffs. The pained, grieving eyes of Edward Breed. Marie Colby's wasted body. But also the warmth and excitement at being David's fiancée. The beautiful newborn gaze of little Rosie and the joy on Patrick Hoyle's face at becoming a father. Even Annie's wonderment at finally being able to read. And then my thoughts slid back to the negative, worrying about Clarinda's reaction to our news, and wondering if she would express her disapproval in some unpleasant way. I kept shifting in the pew, adjusting my back, rubbing a small itch here, smoothing a wrinkle in my skirt there. I was not able to be still physically, either.

I finally opened my eyes and surveyed the large room. The light from the tall south-facing windows danced on the floor, light that was dappled from the trees in full leaf and wavy from the glass. Esther sat in a back pew with bowed head. Edward Breed had also slipped in and occupied a seat near the door. As I watched, Tobias stood and cleared his throat but kept his eyes closed. It was unusual for a young person to offer a message, and particularly one not raised up among Amesbury Friends.

"Jesus taught us to love our enemies," he began in a clear, strong voice. "And to turn the other cheek."

So he had been listening as we walked together. Someone murmured a low "Amen."

"Jesus also spoke truth to power. This morning I learned a great injustice has been done. May God guide those in power to free our dear Friend, Akwasi. May way open for them to find the troubled soul who took Hannah Breed from us." His voice cracked but he kept on. "May we love our enemies instead of killing them." The bench thumped as Tobias sat.

I shut my eyes again, hearing a sob from the direction of where Esther sat. What a fine young man Tobias was. What a terrible pity he had not been able to come to peace with Hannah before she was killed and that he'd lost his chance to share his life with her. And what a minister he was. Friends who worshiped in unprogrammed Meetings, as we did, have no priest. We employed no minister standing on a dais lecturing the congregation about what to do, how to act, who to believe. There were Quaker churches with programmed meetings and a pastor, but in our type of Meeting we believed we all ministered to each other. Still, some might evidence the gift of vocal ministry more than others, and I was glad to see this side of Tobias.

But how indeed would God guide Kevin to find Hannah's killer and thereby free Akwasi? And had her death been, in fact, a case of murder? I determined to quiet my thoughts and open myself to the Light that resides in all of us. The ending words to John's poem about Josiah Bartlett came to mind, the words Akwasi had spoken to me.

Whenever Freedom needs a voice, These sculptured lips shall not be dumb!

Freedom surely needed a voice at this time. Perhaps way would open for me to help ensure justice was served.

TWENTY-THREE

Faith, John Whittier, and I strolled slowly down Friend Street from the Meetinghouse toward his home. He'd insisted I come along to meet Lucy Larcom despite my saying it was Faith who was excited about being introduced to the famous writer. And excited she was.

"John, I have brought a bit of my own scribbling to show her," Faith said, fairly bouncing on her toes. "Does thee think that would be appropriate? Will she be displeased?"

"Why, I imagine she'll be highly pleased. She has always encouraged writers younger than herself." The tall poet swung his silver-tipped cane as he walked.

"Oh, good." She clasped the slim leather case she carried to her chest and quickened her step.

I reached for her elbow to slow her down. Elder John was frail. While he still went out, I knew his health had not been robust for some time. He was around eighty years of age, after all.

"What are thy scribblings about, Faith?" John asked.

"I aim to investigate some shady dealings at the mill and expose them in an article for the newspaper."

"This could be a risky business," he said.

"But aren't we taught to speak truth to power?" She tilted her head at him.

He picked his way with care along the brick sidewalk. "We are, and we should."

"Thee has much experience with that in the past, working bravely for an end to slavery," she said in an admiring tone. "Thee was almost burned in Philadelphia."

"Indeed. Garrison and I were working on our abolitionist newsletter and the supporters of slavery tried to burn down the newly built Pennsylvania Hall while we were within. We barely escaped."

"If there is a wrong here in our town, I want to help bring it to an end." Faith lifted her chin.

"That is a fine attitude for a young person," John said. "I only caution thee to proceed with care."

"I will, I will."

"I'll keep an eye out for her." I slid a glance at John. "Lucy isn't a Friend, is she?"

"No, but she conducts her life as if she were." He smiled into the distance, his dark eyes crinkling above a snowy white chinstrap beard. Then his expression sobered. "We do not have good news this morning about our Friend Akwasi, though."

"Indeed we do not," I said. "I continue to think the so-called evidence was planted behind his shop, and that the so-called witness is lying."

We arrived at the Whittier home and entered by the front door. John ushered us into the parlor on the right, where an older woman sat reading. Lucy Larcom wore a matronly black silk dress in an older fashion, with small covered buttons all the way down the front. Her slate gray hair was parted in the middle and pulled back in a sensible, almost severe style. She looked up and smiled, transforming a rather plain face with a prominent chin into a bright and welcoming visage.

"So, is this our budding journalist?" Lucy asked.

"That it is," John said. He made the introductions all the way around and bade us sit. "And Faith has brought some of her writing to show thee, Lucy."

"Splendid. Sit beside me here, Faith." Lucy patted the seat next to her on the settee.

Faith sat with a straight back, smoothing her case on her lap as if also smoothing her nerves. John lowered himself into his special chair with the writing tray that swung over the lap.

Lucy gazed at me. "And you're the midwife detective, I hear." Smile lines surrounded her intelligent eyes.

I sat across from them. "John, what has thee been telling her?" I smiled back at Lucy. "I did attempt to assist the police in the matter of two murders earlier in the year, Lucy. But I'm no detective. I help mothers bring their babies into the world. That's enough work for one woman."

Mrs. Cate appeared in the doorway with a tray holding glasses of lemonade and a plate of cookies. She set them down on a round table and bobbed her head without speaking when John thanked her.

"Please, refresh yourselves." John gestured at the table.

Faith selected a cookie, but instead of eating she pointed to a biscuit-sized hole at eye level in the door leading to the hall. "John, what is that hole for?"

He laughed. "That was so Charlie could come and go at will."

"Who is Charlie?" Faith asked.

"He was an African gray parrot I was given as a gift. I was fond of him but he was a rascally type. He'd fly up to the rooftop and cry out 'Whoa' to the passing carriages and horses. It caused all kinds of confusions."

"Does he still live?" I sipped my lemonade, which was indeed refreshing, cool and tangy. How funny that John's parrot was named the same as a new baby in town.

"No, I'm afraid not. He fell into the chimney one summer, and by the time we found him he was sufficiently weakened that his spirit was released to God several weeks later." He smiled, shaking his head.

"I remember Charlie," Lucy said. "Now Miss Bailey, why don't you show me what you've brought."

"I'll take my leave." I rose and extended my hand to Lucy. "It was an honor to meet thee, Lucy."

She took my hand and held it for a moment, gazing at my face as if she was peering into me. "Be well, Miss Carroll. Keep up the good work, both with your babies and with the detecting. I think you have a gift for it."

"I have told her she has the gift of seeing," John said, raising his eyebrows. "With a gift comes the responsibility to use it well."

———

After leaving John's house, I headed toward the Clarke home to visit Georgia. What an odd thing for Lucy Larcom to say after meeting me for only ten minutes, that she thought I possessed a gift for detecting. Orpha had told me the same in the spring, although she'd phrased it as a gift for seeing, as had John. At my own birth, which Orpha had attended as midwife, I'd been born in the caul, in an intact sac, an occurrence which many held great superstition about. I didn't believe in superstition as such, but as I'd mused when Orpha first told me, perhaps an infant whose first view of the world is through a translucent silvery membrane tries harder throughout life to see things clearly.

I tried to throw off the thought of having a gift and the attendant responsibility. I did my work as well as I was able, and I was grateful to be of assistance during the miraculous event that is childbirth. I did think the gift helped me understand the emotional ups and downs of my mothers, and it had certainly prodded me to do some detecting regarding the murders in the spring. I was curious and persistent, and always had been.

As I walked, I savored the feel of David's ring on my finger, smiling to myself as I rubbed it with my thumb. I didn't think anyone at Meeting had noticed. If they had, they'd kept silent about it.

Five minutes later the maid showed me into Georgia's room. A wicker cradle on rockers now sat next to her bed, and a breakfast tray rested on the bedside table. Georgia sat up in bed with plentiful pillows behind her. Her face and lips were pale but her hair was neatly pulled back and her nightgown and linens looked fresh. She smiled when she saw me.

"Come in, Rose, please." She waved me over.

"How fares thee, Georgia?" I moved to her side. The baby slept in the cradle, so I attended to her mother first.

"I feel a bit weak."

"It's from the blood loss. Does the bleeding continue?" I asked, touching her forehead with the back of my hand. I was relieved to find it of a normal temperature.

"A little. Like a monthly."

"That is normal. Let me feel the womb to be sure it is returning to size."

"All right." She folded back the coverlet.

She grimaced as I palpated her belly, pressing in to ascertain where the fundus was.

"I'm sorry for the pain," I said as I straightened. "But the top of the womb is in an appropriate place for a day after birth, and it all feels nice and firm."

Virginia bustled into the room carrying a pitcher. "I heard you were here, Rose. How goes the battle?"

"No battles, thank goodness, but I am well."

"Good. And has the new mother passed her test?"

I laughed. "She has indeed. But I want to stress what I said yesterday. Georgia, thee will need plenty of meat and milk to rebuild thy blood. When I see thee in two weeks I want some color back in thy cheeks."

"I will. I'm surely hungry enough. Little Rosie there seems to want to suckle all the time."

At that, the baby stirred and let out a good cry.

"Let me change her, sister, and I'll bring her to you." Virginia scooped up the baby and carried her to a dresser top laid out with a towel and a stack of diapers.

I accompanied her. "I'll take this chance to check the baby while she is unclothed."

Virginia deftly removed the squirming baby's wet wrappings and shirt, dropping them in a pail on the floor. Rosie had good color and reflexes. She wasn't the biggest baby I'd seen by a long shot, but she was of a healthy weight. And her eyes were clear.

There was definitely no gonorrhea here. Seeing this infant reminded me to keep alert about both Baby Charlie's eyesight and his mother's and grandmother's health. I'd go over to visit them all tomorrow if I could.

Being next to Virginia also reminded me of Nora. "Nora Walsh doesn't own a gun, does she?" I asked in a low voice.

Virginia kept her hand on the baby as she glanced sharply at me. "I certainly don't think so. What would a young girl be doing with a gun?"

"She told me she was accustomed to going hunting with her father, so she knows how to use one."

"So do I. I own a gun, but then I'm a mature woman with a business. Nora's a mill girl." She returned to putting a diaper on the baby, then wrapped the diaper in a wool covering.

I cocked my head. "Does thee keep thy weapon securely locked away?"

"Now what are you asking that for?" She quickly slid a clean shirt over the baby's head and maneuvered her little wriggling arms into the sleeves. After she picked up Rosie and tugged the shirt down to cover even her tiny feet, Virginia handed her to me. "If you're meaning did Nora steal my gun to shoot Hannah with, I won't hear another word about it. That's a ridiculous idea, Rose Carroll, and I'm surprised a nice Quaker like you would even consider it." She picked up the pail and huffed out of the room.

Of course she hadn't said whether she kept the gun locked up or not. I gazed at the baby, who gazed right back at me with deep, dark eyes. How did people traverse their lives from a state of pure innocence, like what I held in my arms, to feeling so harmed by spite, resentment, or fear they would commit an act as evil as murder?

———

I walked down the intricately designed brick front walk of the Clarke house, examining how the bricks formed a zig-zagging pattern. As I did, a large Rockaway carriage pulled past and turned into the drive, stopping under the house's *porte-cochère*. A liveried driver hurried around to help a lady out from the compartment. I swallowed when I saw who it was. This wasn't just any lady, but Clarinda Dodge, David's mother. I hoped to slip away down the street without being seen, but I was out of luck.

"Oh, Miss Carroll," she called.

I'd not yet convinced her to call me Rose. I smiled and gave a little wave.

She stood with hands clasped, clearly expecting me to come to her. So I did. I made my way around the side of the house, clutching my satchel. Feeling the ring burn into my finger. Ruing my decision not to wear gloves this morning.

"Clarinda, what brings thee here?" I gazed at her barely lined skin under a broad white summer hat, at her perfectly tailored pale-green dress, her dainty white shoes peeking out from the skirt.

"Why, Mrs. Clarke is an old friend of my younger sister's. Since my sister is abroad at present, I came to call and express my congratulations on the birth of the daughter." Her gaze fell to my satchel and the hand holding it. "Were you attending Mrs. Clarke?" she asked, her attention coming back to my face.

"I was. She is well, as is the baby." I cleared my throat. "Well, I'll let thee get on with thy visit, then."

"Rose Carroll, what a lovely ring you are wearing." She looked at me with a faint smile and blinked several times. "Might I ask its significance?"

She might as well have asked point-blank if her son had put it on my left hand. It had not been anywhere in our plans to have her learn of the engagement in this way. I opened my mouth and then closed it again. I thought as fast as I could. I could try to evade her inquiry, but she'd find out soon enough. And integrity was one of the Friends' values I cherished the most.

"Miss Carroll? I asked you a question."

"Thy son has proposed that he and I join in joyful matrimony." I shifted my bag to my right hand and extended my left, palm down. The golden knot on my ring winked in a ray of sun. "When I gladly accepted, he gave me this ring as a token of his love."

She stared at me for a moment. "Is that so?" She clipped her words as if her jaw was clenched even while speaking.

"It is very much so."

"He made this invitation without consulting me, you must be aware."

"I know David planned to inform thee and Herbert after he journeys to Lawrence to formally ask my father for my hand. I'm sorry thee had to learn of our plans in such an unconventional way."

"Your father is a farmer, I understand. And your mother some kind of wild radical who demands ladies be allowed to vote." She lifted her chin and looked like she'd bit into a sour lemon. "I've never heard of any match more ridiculous, more impossible."

I would not have my family maligned. "My father is indeed a farmer, and a hardworking, honest one, too. He is an esteemed propagator of new apple varieties. My mother also works hard, in her case to achieve women's universal suffrage." I grasped my satchel with both hands and stood my ground. "I ask for thy blessing on my union with thy son."

"We'll see about that." Her voice was low and cold. She turned toward the house and took a couple of steps. Halting, she faced me again. "If you want to rob my son of his rightful inheritance, that's your choice. But I doubt he'll go through with this so-called joyful matrimony when he learns he'll have to live on a physician's salary alone. Love is not the only determining factor that goes into a decision about a union. In fact, sometimes it isn't involved at all."

TWENTY-FOUR

I WALKED SLOWLY AWAY from the Clarke house, nearly stumbling down Powow Street, shaken by Clarinda's hostility. Was my life journey with David as secure as I'd let myself dream? Clarinda's rejection would cause David great pain and distress. I prayed he and his father would be able to smooth matters over with her. I could write a note forewarning him, but thought he'd hear it directly from Clarinda herself as soon as they next met. And surely he hadn't ever imagined his mother would cut him out of his inheritance if he married me. Or if he had, he hadn't mentioned it to me. I didn't care for riches, but he might have been counting on the money to help provide for our family to be.

At the moment I was also insecure as to my path for the rest of this day. I wanted to visit Akwasi in jail, but I wasn't sure if Kevin would even allow it. No stroke of insight about the killing had come to me in Meeting for Worship that morning, although I'd been able to calm my mind enough to feel somewhat restored by the time we had all risen from our seats, led by the elders.

My throat thickened with emotion and my whole body felt quavery from the confrontation with Clarinda. I thought I would head for home instead of the police station. I would have time to read, write a letter or two, and simply do nothing. There was no harm in taking a day of rest and ... The clatter of hooves behind me interrupted my thoughts.

"Whoa, Grover," Bertie said, pulling up next to me at the intersection with High Street. "Where does this Quaker walk to on a fine summer's day?" she asked, gazing down at me with her usual wicked smile.

"Bertie." I shielded my eyes from the overhead sun with my hand. "I am undecided, but I think I am heading home to do nothing. Where does thee ride to?"

"I was looking for you. What do you say we go to the beach?" She slid off Grover, wearing a fresh-looking dress in an aqua-and-white striped fabric. Her boater sported an elaborately tied aqua ribbon, and her bloomers were of a solid aqua.

"The beach? Does thee mean Salisbury?"

"Sure. Or Plum Island. You know, catch some ocean breezes, wiggle our toes in the sand, take in the salt air. It'll be good for you."

"I don't own a bathing costume, I'm afraid." And was I even in the mood for a light outing? Or maybe that was exactly what I needed.

"We don't have to bathe. I just want to get out of town for the afternoon." Bertie's eyes were bright.

The police station sat down the street at the end of the block. Maybe I had the strength to go if Bertie came with me. And two would be more effective than one. "I'd thought to visit the jail." I told her about Akwasi's arrest last night. "I'm not sure Kevin Donovan will let me see him, though."

"That detective?" She tossed her head. "He won't refuse the two of us. But if I accompany you, will you let me take you to the shore afterwards?"

"I will. I have some difficult news about which I'd like to consult with you, too."

"More difficult than solving a murder?" she asked.

"Difficult in its own way." I heard Clarinda's threat in my mind as clearly as if she still stood in front of me. I almost looked around to be sure she didn't.

Bertie murmured something to Grover and we set off toward the station, the horse clopping along behind. I filled Bertie in on the ostensible evidence against Akwasi as we walked.

She shook her head. "I've met Ayensu, and I agree he is an unlikely killer with, as you say, absolutely no motive. Doesn't Donovan see that the real murderer could have planted the gun on the African's property?"

"I think Kevin might be under some pressure to close this case, and Akwasi is a convenient culprit." After Bertie tied Grover to the hitching post in front of the station, I pushed open the door to find Guy seated at the reception desk.

"Don't tell me. You ladies want to visit Mr. Ayensu." He pulled a wry face.

"That's right, Officer Gilbert," Bertie said with a confident air.

He had to know he was no match for the combination of Bertie and me. "Let me find out if that can be allowed. Please take a seat." He gestured to the waiting bench and disappeared through the door to the back.

We sat and I inhaled the station's usual air—a mix of seasoned wood, stale smoke, and the metallic scent of gun oil.

"Hear that clock ticking?" Bertie pointed to the big clock on the wall. "Those are minutes we're not out enjoying the fresh air." She elbowed me.

"Thee didn't have to come in here." I elbowed her back and she snickered.

"I'm glad you know I was kidding."

"Maybe Kevin is at home with his family," I said. "I'm sure we can convince Guy to let us in."

Guy popped his head into the office. "Ladies, if you'll come with me?" He beckoned.

Bertie and I glanced at each other. "Well, that was easy," she whispered as we followed Guy into the back.

But he didn't lead us to the jail cell area, instead ushering us into Kevin's office, where he sat leaning back in his chair, hands behind his head, feet on his desk.

"Ah, ladies, come right in."

"Or not so easy," I muttered to Bertie.

"What can I help you with this fine summer morning?" He slapped his feet onto the floor and jumped up.

"We'd like to visit with Akwasi, Kevin."

He made a tsking sound. "Terribly sorry, can't let you do that. Ayensu's been arrested, like I told you last night, Miss Rose. Only his lawyer gets in." He almost had the word *satisfaction* chiseled into his forehead, he looked that pleased.

"Has thee arrived at a motivation for Akwasi to have shot Hannah to death?" I asked. I was sure my face did not look a bit pleased and I made no attempt to lighten my expression.

"As a matter of fact, I have." His voice gentled. "I'm sorry you were wrong about your Quaker friend, Miss Rose."

"Well, out with it, man," Bertie demanded.

He frowned at her and cleared his throat. "We have an eyewitness who says Ayensu was aiming at him and missed, shooting Hannah instead. So he's now charged with attempted murder as well as manslaughter."

I stared at him. "Who is this person?" I still didn't believe Akwasi capable of such a thing.

"He's a respectable and respected citizen in our town. I don't need to be telling you his identity. It'll come out in the fullness of time. We have the killer securely locked up and that's all you need to be knowing."

"Did anyone else see this reputed act?" Bertie asked.

"Not at liberty to say. Now, if there isn't anything else, I have other investigations to pursue."

He hadn't looked busy when we walked in. I thought of Hannah's father, waiting to take her body home. "Has the autopsy been completed?" When I saw him about to object, I held up my hand. "I ask because Edward Breed, as thee knows, awaits his daughter's body to transport her back to their island home. He was at our Friends Meeting this morning and I know where he is staying."

Kevin reached for a piece of paper on his desk and waved it at me, then laid it down. "Yes, it was complete, and he is free to take the body. He has already been here and I duly informed him of the same."

"Did the coroner find the bullet that killed Hannah?" I tried without success to read the script upside down. "Did it appear to match the gun?"

"Yes and yes. So you can get on with whatever other plans you have for the day. Case closed, Miss Rose, Miss Winslow."

Bertie folded her arms. "Not quite yet, Detective. Have you forgotten about the right to a trial by a jury of one's peers?"

Bertie and I stood on the sidewalk next to Grover in front of the station. "Who do you think this mysterious respectable citizen could have been?" she asked.

"I don't know for sure. But I wonder if it was Lester Colby. He pointed the finger at Akwasi that night. I thought it was because he doesn't like colored people, but later Akwasi told me Lester cheated him out of some money." I remembered our picnic by the side of the lake on Independence Day. "Last week thee said Lester was no good. Why?" I stroked Grover's smooth, warm neck.

"Hmph. I know some things about him. Like—"

Bertie halted when Benjamin Lehigh and Esther pulled up in a newer model trap. Benjamin jumped down and hurried around to help Esther descend. When he saw us he paused, gazing at the station door and then back at us.

"Good day, Rose," he said.

I introduced him and Esther to Bertie, and vice versa, and waited until they'd all completed the niceties. "Kevin told us of the new charge."

Benjamin looked grim. "Attempted murder. One more effort to frame our friend."

Esther pressed her lips together so hard they whitened.

"He wouldn't let us see Akwasi," I said. "He told us only you would be allowed in, Benjamin."

"I was afraid of that," he said. "Esther, will thee wait with these ladies until I ascertain if thee can accompany me?"

"All right." She lifted her chin and clasped her hands in front of her.

"Benjamin, see if thee can learn from Kevin who the accuser was," I said.

"I will." He hurried up the steps.

"I'm sorry thee had to hear Akwasi was arrested, Esther." I gazed at her.

"Not as sorry as I. We both thought living in the North would be safe and free. How can a place like Massachusetts harbor citizens with such a hatred for our kind?"

"There are wrong-minded people everywhere in the world," Bertie said kindly. "We have to keep seeking out the good ones, like Rose here, and her Quakers."

"You are both so kind, as has been the Society of Friends." Esther twisted a handkerchief in her hands. "And I suppose we're better off here than in many places. But still ..." Her voice trailed off. She stared at the ground.

The door to the station flew open and Benjamin ran easily down the stairs. "Thee can come in, Esther. We'll only have five minutes with Akwasi, though." He took Esther's elbow and they started for the building, Esther's hand held to her mouth.

"Did Kevin tell thee who the accuser was?" I called after him.

He turned back. "A Lester Colby."

TWENTY-FIVE

As one, Bertie and I turned to face each other.

"We've got to talk with him," I said.

"The beach is going to have to wait," she agreed. "Want to ride behind me?"

"I'm not wearing my bloomers. Can we walk instead? We should figure out how to approach him."

"We can do that. Come on, Grover." She untied him as he blew out a noisy breath, and we set out.

"We could frame it as a social call," I said.

"Except it isn't, and neither of us would be making such a call, anyway." Bertie waggled her eyebrows at me. "Do you engage in proper social calls?"

"Of course not. I could say I wanted to check on the newborn, except I already did that. And today is First Day, when all my clients know I don't work except to attend a birth or carry out the second-day visit. Does thee have any connection with Marie Colby or her daughter's mother-in-law, Catherine Toomey?"

"Mrs. Toomey from the Mercantile?"

"The same." We turned onto Powow Street and headed up the hill.

"I only know her to buy things from. But Marie Colby. Hmm. Was her maiden name Rousseau?" Bertie asked.

"French-Canadian? I don't know. Why?"

"I had a friend, Lisette Rousseau, whose big sister was Marie. I seem to remember her marrying a Colby, now you mention it."

Bertie was in her thirties. Marie could be as young as forty, even though the ravages of cancer made her appear older. It made sense that Bertie's friend's older sister might have been Marie Colby.

"Marie is quite ill, I'm afraid," I said. "It appears to be advanced cancer."

"I'm sorry to hear that. I haven't seen Lisette in ages. She must be sad. She always adored Marie and looked up to her."

As we passed Georgia's house, I checked for the Dodge carriage but it wasn't in evidence. Good.

"I attended a birth here at the Clarke home yesterday morning," I said. "And then a couple of hours ago when I was leaving after making my follow-up visit, I had quite the run-in with ..." I brought my left hand to my mouth. If I told Bertie about Clarinda, I'd have to tell her about my engagement. I felt the ring press against my lips and narrowed my eyes at Bertie.

She laughed. "Wondered when you were going to tell me about that ring."

"I can't keep a secret, can I?" My cheeks warmed.

"Not exactly. If you wanted to keep something secret, like, say, an engagement, Rosetta, you probably ought not wear that pretty ring out in public."

Bertie was the only person to call me by that nickname. "It's true. David Dodge proposed marriage to me last night. And I accepted." I rubbed the ring with my thumb.

"So you're to be Mrs. Dodge, the younger, now, eh? How does Mrs. Dodge, the elder, feel about this arrangement?"

"That was the run-in. Clarinda arrived to pay her respects to Georgia Clarke as I was leaving. She saw the ring, too, and surmised the same as thee. She wasn't a bit happy about it."

"I should say not. A society lady's son marrying an unconventional Quaker, and a midwife at that?"

"I confess I've been worrying about her reaction." I wrinkled my nose. "And now I've seen it. She threatened to cut off David's inheritance if he goes through with our marriage."

"Does he know that?"

"I don't think so." I blew out a breath. "But he might by now. She seems to have left." I pointed back to the empty *porte-cochère.*

"Listen. All will be well. I believe it. I'm not the religious sort, but I do believe things happen as they should. And I'm pretty sure you should marry that doctor of yours."

"Clarinda is a rather powerful force," I said as we turned right onto Lake Street.

"And he has a powerful love for you, Rose. I've seen it."

"I hope so." I did hope so. "But do I want to enter into a union with a mother-in-law who not only dislikes me but also disapproves of me?"

"You're marrying him, Rose. Not her. Don't worry so. It'll work out, I promise."

"I'm going to hold thee to that promise." I switched my satchel to the other hand. "Here we are." I pointed to the house.

Bertie whistled. "Quite a spread."

"Except we didn't come up with a plan."

"We've come to visit Marie. And then we can ask to have a word with Lester. I'll figure out some reason." She tied Grover to a fence post and followed me up the steps.

————

"Mrs. Colby isn't well," a white-capped young maid said after we'd rung the bell. "I'm not sure she's receiving visitors today."

"Will thee tell her it's Rose Carroll the midwife, and a special friend?"

"You're the one what helped our Baby Charlie into the world?" A smile split her broad face. "Do come in, then. He's a cute one, he is." She stepped back and motioned us in.

"He and his mother are faring well?" I asked.

"Oh, yes. Do you ladies want to see them, instead?"

"I won't disturb them. I did my post-birth check two days ago. But my friend Bertie Winslow here is an old friend of Marie's sister, and I promised her I'd introduce them."

"That's fine, then. I'll run up and let Mrs. Colby know." The maid turned and clattered up the stairs.

Bertie looked around and whistled. "Nice place they got here." She stroked the wood on the banister and peered at one of the framed portraits on the wall.

"It is." I glanced around. "Catherine must have gone home again. I didn't see a maid when I was here earlier."

The maid appeared on the landing above and motioned for us to go up. "She'll see you, certainly."

We followed her into Marie's room, where Marie sat in a chair near the window with a book on her lap. I introduced her to Bertie even as I noticed the smell of sickness in the air. It was nothing specific, only a hint of sourness, of decay.

"Of course I remember," Marie said. "You're Lisette's friend. Come and sit near me, Miss Winslow. Or is that Mrs. Winslow?"

Bertie snorted as she took a seat. "Still unmarried and happily so. Although I'm a little long in the tooth to be called Miss. Just call me Bertie. Rose here does."

Marie smiled and gave a hint of a shrug, as if arguing over social niceties took far too much energy from her sapped body.

"How is Lisette faring?" Bertie asked. "Last I heard she'd birthed a pack of babies and lived in Newburyport on the Chase farm."

"That is indeed her situation, and she's as rosy and red cheeked as the apples she raises. So are the children. Six at last count."

"Good for her. I'll have to ride over for a visit one day," Bertie said.

I remained standing, leaning against the window frame, patting my neck with my handkerchief. A hint of a breeze floated in, but it was a warm one, and Bertie and I had exerted ourselves walking up the hill. "How is thee feeling today, Marie?" I asked.

"About the same, although I sense my strength waning with each passing sunset."

"I should offer my congratulations on the birth of your new grandbaby," Bertie said.

"He's a sweet boy, and a good baby. Doesn't cry much, as long as he's fed and changed. My husband is quite taken with him."

"Is Lester at home today?" I exchanged a quick look with Bertie.

Marie frowned. "I think he might be out again, even though it's the Sabbath."

200

That was a disappointment, but there was nothing to be done about it.

"He's gotten himself all tangled up in this dreadful murder in town," Marie went on.

"Tangled up?" Bertie folded her hands in her lap, gazing at Marie.

"Oh, he's gone and accused some poor African of killing that mill girl. I don't have the slightest idea why he even wants to be involved. He should let the police do their job and come home to dote on Baby Charlie. Shouldn't he?"

"Of course." Bertie said. "Does Mr. Colby think he has facts about the case the police wouldn't be able to uncover?"

"I don't know. He wouldn't share that kind of thing with me, anyway. Says it will upset my well-being." She straightened in her chair. "What worsens my condition is him being gone during a happy family time. And only our blessed Lord knows how many more happy days I have left on this green earth."

———

I slid down off Star as the sun was beginning to lower behind the Bailey house. Bertie's boater hung from its strings down her back and we were both flushed and pink of cheek from our hour-and-a-half ride returning from the beach.

"That was great fun," I said. "We should go again next weekend." Grains of sand scratched between my toes inside my stockings but I didn't care. We'd stopped in at home after we left the Colby house for me to don my bloomers, leave my satchel, and fetch Star. Then we'd ridden side by side the ten miles straight east to Salisbury Beach. The shore had been full of folks seeking an ocean breeze and the fresh salt air. Men and children frolicked in the waves, while Bertie and I discarded our footwear and went for a long walk, lifting our skirts and laughing when the water lapped at our ankles.

"Good to get away from talk of murder, wasn't it?" Bertie reached down to stroke Grover's damp neck.

"This friend speaks my mind." I smiled up at her. "I thank thee for inviting me." Star nickered and tossed his black mane. "Star thanks, thee, too. He needed to stretch out his legs on a long ride."

"Let me know if you need my help." Bertie stopped smiling. "With anything."

"I will." I raised my hand in a wave and led Star around the back of the house. I took the time to wipe down his smooth gray coat and make sure he had fresh water and hay before heading into the house. The air wafting out as I pulled open the door smelled delectably of fish and herbs. I was famished from my afternoon of exercise and sea breezes. "What is thee ..." I began.

"Rose, look!" Faith sat cross-legged on the floor near the stove. A furry yellow bundle wriggled in her lap, and a saucer bearing traces of milk sat on the floor near her. "We have a cat. A kitchen cat." She held the little creature up to me.

I took it in my arms and petted its soft head. "This is a kitten, more like. Where did thee find him?" Purring like a tiny mill wheel, it twisted up to gaze at me with golden eyes.

"He's a she, and is from Zeb's mama cat. When I told him about the mouse we'd seen, he offered me one of the kittens. Isn't she sweet?"

"She is, indeed. Is her mama a good mouser?"

"Zeb said she is. We can keep her, can't we?"

"I don't see why not, as long as thee takes responsibility for making sure she is fed and has fresh water." I frowned at the door. "She'll need to be trained to do her business outside, I expect."

"Or we can put a box of sand down cellar. At least for the winter months. That's what the Weed family does."

"Good idea. Has thee named her?"

Faith pushed up to standing and took the kitty back. "She's Christabel, from the Coleridge poem. I love those verses, doesn't thee? They're so mysterious." She ran her finger under the kitten's chin along a pure white neck. " 'So halfway from her bed she rose, And on her elbow did recline, to look at the Lady Geraldine.' "

"Little Christabel, I hope thee is up to the task of scaring away all those mysterious mice, then." I moved to the sink and pumped water to wash my face and hands. The Christabel of the poem was, like Faith, the daughter of a deceased mother who was taking care of her father. I was sure that was in the back of Faith's mind despite her not mentioning it. When I turned back, wiping my hands on a linen towel, Faith was sitting with pencil in hand at the table in front of a piece of paper already full of writing. "Is thee making a fish soup for supper?" I asked.

She stroked the kitten's head in her lap. "Yes, but it's nothing heavy. Zeb's uncle caught a great deal of sea bass and was busy giving it away, so I gladly accepted one. I added various herbs from the garden and the juice of a lemon leftover from the lemonade. I'll put diced potatoes in by and by."

"I can help with the potatoes," I said. "The soup smells delicious. I commend thee."

She looked pleased. "And I had a couple of scraps of fish for Christy, here, too."

"How went the visit with Lucy?"

"Quite excellent." Faith was now all business. "She encouraged me in my writing. And she liked my idea of presenting the mill's history and what a girl's daily work is like as a backdrop to the results of my investigation. She's had the most interesting life, Rose."

I drew a cup of water and sat across from her. "Tell me."

"She was a mill girl herself, and her mama ran a boardinghouse for mill girls in Lowell."

"Like Virginia Perkell's."

Faith nodded. "Lucy began writing then, and published both prose and poetry in the mill girls' magazine, the *Lowell Offering*. Then she moved to Illinois to become a teacher. She came back to Massachusetts and taught at Wheaton Seminary, and she's an editor of children's magazines, too."

"That's quite a life."

"I know." Faith's eyes sparkled. "After her poem 'Hannah Binding Shoes' became famous, she left teaching to become an independent writer. She and John have written several books together."

"It was quite felicitous he invited thee to meet her. And how goes the second part of thy article?" I asked.

"I talked to a few other girls this afternoon. One thinks she also saw an exchange of money, but she refuses to be quoted for my article." She tapped the pencil on the table. "I wish our own Hannah were still here. She'd mentioned seeing something peculiar going on, but she never said who was involved."

"Her death is a pity for so many reasons." I shook my head. "I hope her father was successful in transporting her body back to Nantucket today. We know when the spirit is released to God, the body becomes only an earthly shell, but it still gives families great comfort to know their loved one's remains are buried nearby."

Faith gazed across the table at me. "I haven't been to visit Mother's grave in a while. I think I'll go soon. I want to tell her all about my article." She held up a hand. "I know she isn't there, don't worry. But it helps me to get my thoughts straight if I say them out loud. And I like to think she's listening from heaven."

TWENTY-SIX

FAITH AND I SAT outside on the steps reading in the last light of the day. A hearty breeze helped to cool the air. I'd leaned back against her knees and closed my eyes, tired after the fullness of the day, when I heard a clatter in front of the house. I opened my eyes to see Patrick jumping down from his gig.

As he ran toward the front of the house, I called out to him. He halted, glancing over, and rushed toward us. He nearly tripped over a stone but caught himself just in time.

"Miss Carroll, something's terribly wrong with Charlie. Can you come, please?" He rubbed his hands as if washing them, over and over.

My heart sank. "Is it his eyes?" I stood.

"How did you know? Yes, it is. They're all puffy, like, and exuding an awful substance."

"Let me get my bag. I'll be right with thee. I'll come out the front door." I glanced at Faith, who gave me a sympathetic look. I hurried into the house, washed my hands, and grabbed my bonnet and satchel.

Five minutes later I knelt next to Pearl's bed as she held the baby. Marie sat in a chair across the room, and Lester hovered on the other side of the bed. The windows were once again shut tight—what did this family have against fresh air?—and the air smelled sour.

I fixed my gaze on Patrick. "Please open the windows and curtains, Patrick. For good health, the air should circulate, especially on a fresh evening like this one." A few mosquitoes might enter, but that was a minor inconvenience compared to the unsavory stew of body odor, infection, and who knew what else.

"My grandmother never let anyone open windows," Lester said. "And she lived to be ninety-three."

"It's true that in years past, people believed it was healthier not to let in the air from outdoors. But that's been shown to be false, Lester," I said.

Patrick obeyed my request, bringing the instant relief of a clean night breeze. I picked up Charlie and carried him to the lamp on the dresser to examine him. His eyelids were now puffy and pink and lined with a conjunctival exudate. On his left eye, the lids were nearly sealed shut with the unpleasant-smelling yellow pus. At least the jaundice seemed to have passed. I looked around. I couldn't ask Marie to fetch anything and doubted if Lester was useful in the kitchen.

"Patrick, I'll need a basin of warm water, as soon as thee can."

"I'll get it." He strode out. Pearl watched him go. She turned her head with a furrowed brow to look at me.

"What's wrong with my baby?" she asked. "What's he got in his eyes?"

"Yes, what's my grandson got? Some kind of disease?" Lester asked. His nostrils flared and he stayed where he was, as if afraid of catching the illness. He'd removed his collar and his top shirt button was undone, but he still wore a linen coat, as if he'd come in recently from the outside.

Marie fingered rosary beads, her lips moving in silence, as she watched me, waiting. Tonight she wore a long flowered wrapper like she'd already been preparing for bed.

I gazed down at Charlie and then back at Pearl. "How has he been acting of late?" I shifted him to the crook of my left arm and felt his forehead with the back of my hand. I didn't detect the heat of fever, one small blessing. "I know he's only five days old, but has his behavior changed from the first few days?"

She frowned. "He's been more unsettled today, like he can't get comfortable. Even after I suckle him he's not happy."

Patrick returned with a bowl of water, slopping it over the side in his hurry. He stood, as if at a loss, until I pointed to the dresser.

I laid Charlie next to the water and took a cloth from the stack of clean linens that still remained from the birth. I wet the cloth and cleaned his eyes as well as I could, wiping from the inner corner to the outer as Orpha had taught me.

"Miss Carroll, please tell us what's wrong," Patrick pleaded, moving to Pearl's side and taking her hand.

"Some babies get a mild form of conjunctivitis and it clears up," I said. "This looks more serious, though. I'm sorry to say I believe he has the gonorrheal infection in his eyes." I laid a hand on Charlie's belly to make sure he didn't wriggle off the dresser, even though he seemed too listless to try. He wasn't unsettled at all right now. I turned to survey the room. Lester and Marie exchanged a quick look. Patrick's eyes grew wide.

Pearl's eyes went wide. "My little baby got the clap in his eyes?"

I wet a clean cloth, folded it, and laid it across Charlie's eyes. This was a sick baby; he didn't even protest. I brought him back to Pearl. She cuddled him, smoothing back his wisps of linen-colored hair. Returning to the basin, I washed my hands and dried them before facing this family with their portion of bad news.

Folding my hands in front of me, I said, "Charlie acquired gonorrhea from thee, Pearl, in the process of being born."

"But we've been taking that medicine you brought. It makes my stomach real upset, but both Paddy and me have been taking those capsules just like you said, three times a day."

Patrick nodded but said nothing. He smoothed Pearl's hair in the same way she was smoothing the baby's.

"Now see here, Miss Carroll." Lester took a step toward me, but Marie extended her pale, thin hand and stopped him. "What's this about the clap? I won't have you accusing my daughter of wayward behavior."

"I have not done so. As you all are aware, I'd not seen Pearl for prenatal care before the day of the birth. At my first examination, I…" I fixed my gaze on Patrick's intelligent, pained face. "Should I be explicit about the details?"

"No, please don't," Patrick said. "Simply tell him, I don't know, in a general way, if you can."

"All right. Pearl's birth passage was infected with gonorrhea. It still is. I told her and Patrick already."

Pearl turned her head to look out the window without speaking. Patrick gazed at the floor. Lester glared at Patrick.

"I knew the infection could be passed into the baby's eyes, but it was too late by then," I went on. "Catherine saw my reaction to the, uh, symptoms, and asked directly, so I told her. But I decided to wait and see how Charlie did before frightening you all with what I knew."

"But he'll be all right, won't he, Rose?" Pearl gazed down at the baby, then brought him up to her shoulder and stroked his back. "It's like what you told me about that infant *john-deese*."

"Jaundice, Pearl," Patrick said in a gentle tone. "It's called jaundice."

"Your ma said you had that and you got over it. And Charlie doesn't look as yellow any more. So our baby will get better from this sickness, too." She smiled up at Patrick. "Won't he?"

Patrick shifted his gaze to me and waited.

"He might not." I kept my voice as kind as I could even though I would not hide the likely prognosis from them. "His health might survive, but his corneas may be damaged." I focused on Pearl. "The corneas are part of the eyes."

"He'll be blind," Marie whispered. Her face grew even paler.

Lester laid his hand on Marie's shoulder. His own face grew red. He clamped his lips together and glared at me. Patrick bowed his head over Pearl and the baby.

"Yes," I said. "He could end up blind."

TWENTY-SEVEN

I GAZED AT PATRICK. "I know nothing to do for him except to use warm cloths to keep the eyes clean. If the condition worsens, I urge thee to take him to the hospital in Newburyport. Perhaps the doctors there know of some new remedy that can help." I wasn't hopeful about this, but I would ask David what he knew next time I saw him. "I'll take my leave now."

Pearl stayed with her head bent over the baby.

Patrick peered up. "Thank you for being honest with us, Miss Carroll. Shall I drive you home?" His light brown eyes held a sadness that pained me greatly.

"Thank thee, no. It's not far. I'll walk."

"I'll see her out." Lester hurried to the door and extended his arm, his face still red.

I followed him, watching as he trotted down holding his elbows out and breathing noisily with the exertion. He closed the outer door behind us with a thud and faced me.

"This is all your fault," Lester said in terse spurts. "You should have been able to do something at the birth." He leaned in toward me with a hot glare and breath reeking of tobacco and onions. "If we'd had a proper doctor to care for my girl instead of some midwife, the baby wouldn't be going blind." An owl hooted from across the road as a conveyance clattered up Prospect Street around the corner.

"Now see here, Lester." I backed up into the railing, holding my satchel in front of me for protection. "I was called to attend Pearl's birth by thy son-in-law. He could easily have summoned—"

"Don't you be calling me by my Christian name," he interrupted with a snarl. "You Quakers are some kind of witches. I knew it. First you insult my daughter's integrity and then you cause my little grandbaby to go blind."

I breathed in and out, taking an instant to hold this furious man in the Light. And myself, as well. I opened my mouth to reply and then shut it. There wasn't any point in arguing with him.

"Good night, then." I walked down the front steps half sideways, not wanting to turn my back on him in case he came after me. When he didn't, I paused on the walkway. "I'll pray for thy grandson's health."

"Your prayers aren't worth the paper they're written on. And listen to me. You'd better stay out of *all* my business, not only my family's. You and that niece of yours. I know you've been snooping around about the African's arrest. The police know he killed that girl and he's going to hang for it." He pointed his finger at me. "You might have to pray for your own damned health if you're not careful." He spat down the steps in my direction, then stormed into the house and slammed the door behind him.

I stared at the house for a moment before hurrying away home. Kevin might have told Lester about my questions. But what did he mean about praying for my own health? It sounded a lot like a threat. I'd have to be careful, but he certainly wasn't going to stop me from seeking justice. If Quaker martyr Mary Dyer wasn't silenced by the threat of hanging in Boston two hundred years ago, I wasn't about to keep quiet about murder, either. And I knew Akwasi's arrest did not represent truth.

———

The morning post arrived with a sizzling crack of lightning followed shortly after by a rumble of thunder. I watched the postman hunch into his slicker as he strode away. It had already begun raining when Faith had hurried down the path toward the mill a couple of hours earlier, but the skies now dumped sheets of water on the postman's head and everywhere else, splashing up from puddles in the path. I'd kept the windows open an inch at the bottom so the air indoors wouldn't become too close, and I could smell the sweet zing of the storm mixing with the scent of wet soil and soggy vegetation.

I'd spent the early hours cleaning and going over my accounts. I had a series of pregnant women coming for visits beginning in a little while, although I still reeled from Lester's threat of the night before. But what could he do, in truth? I couldn't control his daughter's ill health. Would that I could, would that there were some kind of medicine to cure the clap. But nothing could; there were only the capsules I'd given them to lesson the symptoms. And even if some treatment could banish the illness, Pearl had not sought care before the birth, so she couldn't have been treated, anyway.

I fetched the several envelopes from inside the front door where the postman had slid them through the slot. My gaze first lit on a postal card with a picture of the new Duck Bridge in Lawrence spanning the Merrimack River on the front, the bridge's sturdy trusses painted green. I turned it over to read a note penned by the children. Luke wrote that they'd arrived safely and he'd gotten to ride Father's young stallion. Matthew said he'd tasted goat's milk for the first time and was in charge of tending the flock, and Mark wrote that he'd helped Mother print one of her suffrage leaflets. Betsy's careful beginning handwriting said she missed Faith and me, and that Grandma had sewed matching dresses for her doll and her. I smiled and reread it. I'd had a happy childhood on the farm in Lawrence and was pleased my nephews and niece could enjoy the same.

The next letter got my heart beating somewhat faster and my cheeks aflush, as it was addressed in David's hand. I hurried to my desk for the opener and carefully slit open the envelope. I brought it to my face and sniffed, smiling as I caught a trace of the woody lavender scent David wore. Drawing out a folded sheet, I sank into a chair to read it.

> *Dear Rose,*
> *It is with great sadness that I write to you.*

What? What had happened? I raced on in my reading.

> *Mother said she spoke with you yesterday and that you have reconsidered my proposal. She said the pressure from your faith makes it impossible for you to join with me in tender matrimony. I cannot express the devastation in my heart that arose when I heard these words. I had thought we were united in our love and joy, and that we would face any obstacle together for the rest of our lives. I had hopes of raising a family with you, and growing old together.*

I stared at the letter. That lying woman! That monster. How could Clarinda tell such untruths to him? How could she dare to willfully, deliberately invent such a terrible story? Of course my hopes for the future were exactly the same as David's. How could he think they were not? I read on.

I beg of you to reconsider. But of course I will accept your refusal if I must. You should know I will never love another as I do you.

The poor man. His heart was broken. My poor dear, sweet David, to have to endure the thought that I would even consider for a moment withdrawing from our pact. Surely he would know if I were truly ending our betrothal I would have returned the ring. I wished I'd made a copy of my letter to my parents so he could see all Clarinda's words were falsehoods. Every single one of them.

Please write to me to say you have reverted back to our joyful agreement. But if by some means you cannot, I still need to read in your own words the confirmation of this dreadful news.
I remain ever your loving and adoring servant,
David

My eyes filled. I wouldn't write. I must get to him in person and tell him the truth. I wasn't going to the Dodge home, that was certain. If I met up with Clarinda, I was sure not to have a single decent word to say and might even be tempted toward some very unFriendly violence. That woman deserved a slap, or worse. I couldn't believe this thought even entered my brain, but it had.

Anyway, David would surely be at the hospital today. But how could I get there in this downpour? From the look of the dark sky, it might be raining heavily all day. Newburyport was a long ride on

215

my bicycle even in good weather. I'd have to take Star out again, but I'd get drenched. Even my wool cloak wasn't as waterproof as I would like, and it would be unbearably hot in this steamy weather. Perhaps Frederick had left some kind of oiled overcoat behind.

Thoughts racing, I paced in my room. I'd have to summon a conveyance, but even then I'd need to get down to High Street or even Market Square. The path in front of this house wasn't yet a street. Because they kept building new homes on it, though, I expected it would become a named road of the town soon enough. For now the narrow way definitely didn't carry conveyances roaming in search of paying fares.

I clenched my fists at Clarinda's audacity. Who did she think she was? She must be so accustomed to getting her own way in all matters domestic and social she thought she could run David's life as if it were a soiree of her rich, spoiled peers. I forced myself to sit. I closed my eyes and attempted to hold the situation in the Light. If I waited and listened prayerfully, surely I would discern the path I must take. But my thoughts refused to become still. My anger at Clarinda was mounting at the same time as my heart was rent over David's pain. And my own anguish.

The clock struck ten at the same time as the doorbell rang. Who…? I smacked my forehead. I had a client coming for prenatal care this morning. The last thing I wanted to do was muster my calm and professionalism to conduct a pregnancy examination.

I heard Orpha's voice in my head: "Your mothers need you to create an atmosphere of confidence and good health. If you make them feel safe during the months of pregnancy, their bodies will be able to stay calm and do the task of birthing when their time comes. But if you are anxious, tense, or worried, they'll mirror that. And a tense, fearful body retains the baby inside instead of letting the womb do its natural work of expelling the infant into the world."

Oh, Orpha. So much wisdom. I will see this client. But how will thee direct me in the natural work of love?

I took a deep breath and stowed the letter and postcard in my desk drawer. Today, this hour, right now, I needed to do my good work and make the woman standing on my doorstep feel safe and relaxed. Love would follow if it was meant to.

TWENTY-EIGHT

My morning stream of scheduled clients didn't abate until one o'clock. I had in fact managed to bury my raging emotions deeply enough to smile at the mothers. I managed to talk calmly and seriously with them about how their baby was growing and what they could expect during the birth, and to counsel them about eating well and drinking clean water.

By the time the last lady left, my insides growled for food and the sun fought to burst forth from the last of the clouds. I'd been wrong about the storm keeping up all day. The powerful winds had blown it out to sea, as often happened here. Our weather frequently came from the west, and Amesbury sat only one town inland from the Atlantic seaboard to our east. I went about opening windows in the house to let the breeze sweep through.

I sat in the kitchen with bread and cheese. Little Christabel lay asleep in a corner, her tiny furry body curled into a circle. As soon as I began to chew the first bite of my lunch, though, I set it down again. The dueling feelings of anger and despair reared up, roiling my stomach. My outrage at Clarinda's bald-faced lies. My worry for David's heart. I wasn't sure I could even manage traveling into Newburyport to find him and set him straight. Maybe I should write him a letter, after all. Then new uncertainties crept into my thoughts. Perhaps he secretly wanted to end our engagement so he wouldn't have to constantly battle his mother. Or it could be he was more fond of that cousin of his, Violet, than he'd let on, the one his mother wanted him to marry. But wouldn't I have sensed that in him? It was possible I wasn't as good as reading actions and unspoken motivations as I'd thought.

My doubts threatened to overwhelm me. I was paralyzed, glued to my chair. It had taken me so long to get over the hurt and shame of being abused as a young woman. I'd opened my heart and shown my most delicate and hidden thoughts to David because I trusted him. If that trust was now violated, I didn't think I could ever do it again. I would be content to remain a competent, trusted spinster midwife and devoted aunt. That should be enough for a woman. Shouldn't it?

Christabel reared her head and yawned wide, then began to lick her paw and rub it over her head. Had her mother taught her to wash, or was it instinctive? Was her mother missing her? I blew out a breath. I knew I didn't want to be a childless spinster. The thought of raising little Daveys and Rosies had filled me with warmth, and the prospect of sharing that undertaking with David had brought me great joy.

I decided against writing. With all these thoughts, I needed to see David and talk with him in person. When I saw him, way would open. I must have faith that it would. I swallowed hard and headed into my room to don bloomers and a bonnet. Star and I were going for another ride.

———

The Essex-Merrimack drawbridge across the Merrimack River to Deer Island was filled with vehicles traveling in both directions, so I pulled Star to a walk half an hour later. We followed a fanciful open surrey with both front and back benches and colored fringe dancing from its flat roof. A family in their summer finery rode within, the children occupying the back seat. They were pointing to the river and giggling about something. The boy, wearing a little white boater, turned his head to gaze out the back and widened his eyes. He nudged his sister, pointed at me, and called out, "Look, a lady riding like a man."

Indeed, I'd followed Bertie's example and taken to riding Star astride instead of sidesaddle, despite the stares and occasional expressions of disapproval. It was so much easier and allowed both more control of the horse and less discomfort of my top leg crooking over the top of the saddle.

The little girl widened her eyes at me and covered her mouth. Their mother twisted back from the front seat and appeared to admonish them to face front again, but not before she shot me a set of raised eyebrows. I followed them onto Deer Island, where, to my relief, they turned into the drive of one of the homes there. I continued onto the Chain Bridge, with its wrought-iron suspension chains supporting the passage over the river. The trolley from Newburyport clattered toward me, so I pulled Star to the right to give the trolley plenty of room.

I kept the horse at a walk once we left the bridge. My heart was beating too fast in anticipation of having the discussion with David. I wanted to turn Star around and gallop all the way home.

But instead I kept going, angling left up the tree-lined Mosley Avenue hill toward High Street, on which the Anna Jaques Hospital was located. It had been built only eight years earlier and David was always touting its modern facilities, from the chemist's laboratory to the indoor water closets to the telephone system. I hoped he'd be working quietly in his office and that I wouldn't have to track him down in one of the wards. It was two o'clock by now and he would have finished his usual rounds before noon. If he was seeing patients in his examination room, I should be able to catch him between appointments. It wasn't the best time or place to have a potentially life-changing conversation, but I felt an urgency to see him, to talk and resolve this business.

A black phaeton rode toward me down the hill with a beautiful roan in the traces. I pulled Star to a halt at the side of the road as I pushed my spectacles up my nose and squinted at the approaching conveyance. A jay squawked from the nearest elm and then fell silent. My stomach turned to ice. My hands numbed on the reins.

That combination of graceful Bailey buggy and roan mare belonged to only one man. David drove the phaeton but I did not lift my hand to hail him, for in the passenger seat rode a young woman in a sprigged lawn dress. A hat decorated with a white feather and purple ribbons sat jauntily on her head. His companion was none other than his cousin, Violet Currier, whom I'd met at Clarinda's *soireé* in the spring. The girl who was Clarinda's choice for David's bride.

Way had opened to a resolution of my doubts with nary a word of discussion. I wished I were anywhere but here. I wanted to slide off Star and disappear into the woods to my right. I yearned for a magic cloak of invisibility, a screen of smoke—anything to avoid

David seeing me. I averted my gaze, staring into the dark under-brush. When the clopping had passed and I thought it would be safe to continue, I glanced back at the road. Instead of having driven past without seeing me, as I'd hoped, David had pulled up directly across from me.

No. This can't be happening. I shut my eyes for a moment, but when I opened them he was still there, and now he was climbing down from the driver's seat.

"Rose," he said, hurrying over to me. "Were you coming to see me?" His eyes held both pain and hope. He reached up his left hand and covered mine where it lay on the saddle's pommel.

I took in a deep breath. I held myself in a moment of Light, discerning almost immediately I needed to tell the truth rather than making up a story or avoiding the subject. I exhaled. "Yes, I was. I was going to let thee know thy mother has been telling lies about me. But it appears thee is otherwise occupied. Please don't let me interrupt this pleasant outing with thy young lady there."

"But I'm not ... Miss Currier isn't ..." He looked at the buggy with despair, then back at me. "Rose, I love you. I want you to be my wife, no matter the obstacles. I'd prayed Mother's words weren't true but she insisted they were. I don't know why she was lying."

"No? Thee is aware she has never liked nor approved of me." I lifted my chin.

"I don't care about that. Please dismount and let me explain."

"And do you think I am the kind of person who would end our engagement through a third party?"

"Of course not!"

"I'm sorry, David. I must go." I didn't trust myself to say one more word without either bursting into tears or kicking him. Or both.

"But Rosie!" He squeezed my hand.

"Mr. Dodge," Violet called. "We shall be late."

I shook off his hand and clucked to Star until he broke into a trot. A trot to where, I knew not. Anywhere but here.

TWENTY-NINE

I took a long, slow ride home, traversing with my broken heart along Water Street and then back over the two bridges to Amesbury. Star and I plodded along the banks of the Merrimack west through Salisbury Point. I felt the ring through my glove. I should have thought to return it to David. How could he have changed so quickly, so thoroughly? Despite his protestations of love, there he'd been in his own buggy with the young lady of his mother's choosing. He had not been hard at work at doctoring, as I'd expected, but out for a summer's drive. And apparently on their way to some appointment or afternoon tea, since Violet had said they were to be late. I shook my head. Spinsterhood would be my fate, after all.

Star and I passed Lowell's Boat Shop, which only made me think of Patrick and poor Baby Charlie. I barely saw where I steered Star until he stopped, whuffing and stomping his front feet. I raised my head to see Orpha's front door. But of course. Where else should I go except to seek comfort from my teacher, my elder, my friend?

"Good boy, Star." I slid down and stroked his neck, then tied him to a tree, letting him stand in the shade.

When I knocked, though, no one answered. I didn't hear Orpha's great-granddaughters running about within, and her granddaughter Alma Latting didn't come to open the door. My heart sank. Perhaps the entire family had retired to the mountains or the countryside for the month and taken Orpha with them, although I wouldn't have thought she was quite strong enough for such an arduous journey. I rapped again and then tried the knob. When it turned, I opened the door.

"Orpha, is thee there?" I called. The hallway was dark and cool. "Alma?" I cupped my ear when I thought I detected a faint voice. "Hello?" I heard a sound like a chair toppling. Orpha's voice cried out, but it was still faint.

I shut the outer door and hurried down the hall into the parlor, then stopped short and gasped. Orpha sprawled on the floor on her front, her face turned to the side. A wooden chair lay half on top of her. Lace curtains filtered the daylight from outside but I could see her cheek was pink.

I hurried to kneel at her side. "Orpha, I'm here. It's Rose." I felt her brow, which was hot and damp.

She opened her eyes and gave me a wan smile. "Rose. Good of you to call."

I pushed the chair off her, not caring when it fell in the other direction. "Let's turn thee over, now." I helped her to turn onto her back. Her dress lay open all the way down the bodice and her hair was mussed and sweaty. Her thin stocking-clad legs stuck out from where her dress was hiked up to her knees. When she smiled again, it was lopsided, with one corner of her mouth drooping even as the other lifted. I grabbed a pillow from the settee behind me and gently lifted her head to lay on top of it. "How did thee fall?"

"I don't recall," she said. "But Esther wouldn't help me. She's gone to Bethlehem."

Esther? Bethlehem? Orpha had always been clear of mind. She'd stopped practicing midwifery because of her physical frailty, not out of any confusion or senility. That she suddenly wasn't making sense must have to do with her falling. Perhaps she'd hit her head. Or . . . a terrible thought passed through me. What if Esther had hurt Orpha? What if, as I had wondered a few days ago, Akwasi was Hannah's baby's father, and Esther had killed Hannah out of jealousy? I hated the idea, because I had liked Esther so much. The autopsy wouldn't have indicated if Akwasi was the father, because a fetus at that stage of development didn't yet have pigment in its skin.

I put the thought to the side. I had to focus on Orpha.

"Where is Alma?" I asked. I picked up her wrist and felt her pulse. It was racing.

"At the seaside." She slurred her words.

I thought hard. I remembered the grandmother of one of my clients who'd spoken in a similar manner, and also exhibited one side of her face drooping. A visiting physician had said it was the result of an apoplexy. I now feared Orpha had suffered the same, and that she'd fallen because of the brain attack. I fought back an emotional swelling in my throat. Here I'd come to seek solace from Orpha when she needed my help far more than I needed hers. My life wasn't about to end from grief. I prayed hers would continue despite this episode.

"I kept asking Esther to get me a cup of water from the bucket there in the corner, but she wouldn't."

There was no bucket of water here in the parlor. Orpha must be having some kind of vision or illusion, a hallucination.

"Is thee thirsty?"

"Oh, yes, dear."

"I'll fetch water. I'll be right back." I believed hallucinations and racing pulse could also be caused from the body not having sufficient fluids. Maybe getting some water into her would help.

I hurried into the kitchen and brought back a tin cup of water. "Let's get thee sitting up now, all right?" I put my arms under hers and hoisted her to sit against the back of the settee. Holding the cup to her lips, I watched as she drank deeply, a bit of the water dribbling out of the lax side of her mouth.

"I'm tired, Rose. So tired."

This was also unlike Orpha, who rarely complained about anything. I looked around the room. The settee wasn't wide enough to serve as a bed. While Orpha's legs were thin, she wasn't a slender woman. She carried the midsection heft of most mature women, with hers increased by her love for all things sweet. I wasn't sure I could maneuver her upstairs and into a bedroom alone. It'd be cooler down here, anyway.

"I'm going to make thee a nice bed on the floor here." I left her sitting, hoping she wouldn't keel over, and ran upstairs, bringing an armful of quilts back down. I laid out a thick pallet and helped her lower herself down. "How is that?"

"Like heaven, Rose, like I've crossed the dark river and gone up to heaven."

"Thee can be in heaven right here in thy parlor without having to cross the dark river." I smiled at her and smoothed her brow.

She gave me her lopsided smile and closed her eyes. "Esther did some writing, you know." She turned onto her side with a sigh, settling into sleep.

I sat back on my heels and frowned, narrowing my eyes. Writing. Did this hallucination contain a kernel of truth? I stood and looked around the room. After I put the chair back where it belonged, I lifted an empty tea cup and saucer from the small table next to Orpha's usual seat, a large upholstered chair. Under the saucer was tucked a folded piece of paper. I took it and the dishes to the kitchen, where sunshine streamed in. I opened the paper and read the penciled words.

You have been most helpful to Akwasi and me, Sister Orpha. But now we have fallen into an abyss of despair. With Akwasi's arrest, I no longer feel safe in Amesbury and am fleeing north to New Hampshire, where my sister lives with her husband and children in Bethlehem. I hate to desert my betrothed, but I will be no assistance to him if I am also accosted and falsely accused, which I fully expect if I stay here. I will endeavor to help from afar, as my sister's husband has some experience in the field of law.

You fell asleep in your chair as we were talking, so I did not wake you and I leave you only this note. Please thank Rose for us for all her help. Alas, it was to no avail.

I remain ever your humble servant,
Esther MacDonald

She'd added her sister's address at the bottom of the page. So Orpha wasn't making up Esther nor Bethlehem. Had she already experienced the apoplexy when Esther came to call or was it after that? But that was neither here nor there. Esther had left. My suspicion about Esther sprang up again. She could be lying in the note. But why?

Regardless, Alma was gone. I was going to need to care for Orpha. I smoothed the note on the table. My world as I knew it had crashed down around me. I hadn't lost my business, true, although how could I attend births if I was looking after an elderly friend? My efforts to find Hannah's killer would no longer be possible. Akwasi would either languish in jail or be tried and executed if found guilty. David—well, he appeared to have veered in a different direction. I felt I should have more faith in him, but look where that had landed me.

I'd have to get word to Faith somehow about my situation, but I didn't want to leave Orpha alone. I sank into a chair at the table and lowered my head onto my arms. Despite the now sunny day, darkness seemed to settle into every corner of my brain, nay, of my whole being.

THIRTY

I picked my head up off my arms. What was that sound? I swiped a drop of drool from the corner of my mouth, realizing I must have fallen asleep in Alma's kitchen. A clock in the house chimed four times as a scratching noise yielded to the back door opening. Genevieve LaChance, one of my former birthing clients, pushed the door open and then looked as surprised to find me there as I was to see her. She carried a basket covered with a white cloth and looked as healthy and sturdy as she always did. Almost like an angel, but one in a worn brown calico dress and oft-laundered apron.

"Genevieve," I began.

"Rose, it is nice to see you again," she said at the same time, and then laughed. "Are you conducting midwifery business with Mrs. Perkins?" Her French-Canadian lilt hadn't lessened since I'd helped her with the birth of her fourth child and first daughter last April.

"No. I'm not. And I'm happy to see thee, too." I cocked my head. "But what is thee doing here?" I sniffed at a delectable smell coming from the basket.

"My friend Alma, she asked me to look in on Mrs. Perkins while she and her family take a little vacation at the shore. I bring by meals twice a day and do for her grandmother. Today is the *potage* of chicken and fresh bread."

"That's awfully kind of thee. How is thy baby girl?"

"She's quite well, thank you. A bouncing thing, hearty and with more vigor than any of her older brothers. Still suckling like a champion, too, and she has her daddy wrapped around her little finger. I left her with her granny today."

"I'm exceedingly happy to hear of her good health."

She frowned. "But why do you sit at this table alone?"

I stood. "I came to call on Orpha. I didn't know Alma was gone. I'm afraid Orpha has had a crisis of health." I beckoned her closer and lowered my voice. "I found her on the floor perhaps an hour ago, incoherent and feverish."

"Oh, the poor dear. Has she the influenza?"

"I think it might be a case of apoplexy."

She peered at me. "*Apoplexie?* The hurt in the head?"

"Yes, but one that comes from within, as I understand it. It can cause death, but I think she might have experienced a mild attack. I pray she will recover."

Crossing herself, Genevieve said, "What can I do to help her?"

"Come with me. We'll see if she's still asleep." I pointed to the door to the parlor.

Orpha snored softly, still on her side on the makeshift bed on the floor. "I set up that bedding for her because I didn't think I could get her upstairs by myself."

Genevieve squatted and touched Orpha's forehead. "She's not having fever now." She sniffed. "But I think she wet herself."

I also detected the smell of passed water. "Can thee help me take her to the second floor into a proper bed and clean her?"

"Surely." She peered up at me. "But her room is down here, you know, off the kitchen. That'll make it much easier."

I shook my head. "I didn't know." Indeed, I'd only ever visited Orpha in her parlor. What a sensible arrangement to give the old woman a room where she wasn't forced to ascend or descend stairs several times a day. I followed Genevieve into a small but tidy bedroom. Windows on two sides allowed the air to move and the bed was neatly made. "This is perfect."

Thirty minutes later Orpha rested in her own bed in a clean shift. She'd awoken when we hoisted her up, but had not complained of our ministrations. After drinking another cup of water, she gave us her faint smile again. "You are both angels." She narrowed her eyes at me. "You'll help Esther, won't you? There's something about the Holy Land, but I can't quite recall. And her man, ah, ah . . ." She trailed off, looking confused.

"Akwasi. Yes, I'll help them both as much as I'm able." I squeezed her hand. "Now rest, dear Orpha." I laid my hand on her forehead, indeed now much cooler. "Rest now."

We went back into the kitchen. "Genevieve, thank thee ever so much. I'm sure she'll be able to eat again by and by."

"Who is this Esther, and why did Mrs. Perkins talk about the Holy Land? Is that part of the hurt to her brain?"

"Esther is the betrothed of a wonderful man, a Quaker, who has been wrongly arrested for murder." I hoped it was wrongly. And I hoped Esther wasn't the killer, either. Maybe I was blinded by my affection for Akwasi, and by John's. The incident with David and Violet flooded back into my thoughts. Apparently I'd been wrong about him, too. I wasn't sure I'd ever trust my own judgment again.

"The killing of that poor mill girl?" Genevieve asked.

"Yes, Hannah Breed. And now Esther has left town even as her man is in a jail cell because she said she didn't feel safe. They are both of African descent. She wrote in a note she was traveling to Bethlehem, a little town well north into New Hampshire. Named after the birthplace of Jesus, no doubt."

"That's a great pity. The poor woman, this Esther. I don't have the dark skin, but many in this town think I'm worth less than they are because my English is not good like theirs and my clothes are more Acadian than American." She tsked. "As if we all didn't come from some other country, whether in Europe or far Africa, except for the red-skinned ones."

"So true."

"Did you plan to stay and care for Mrs. Perkins?" she asked.

I gazed at the door and then back at her. "What else can I do? She's alone."

"Let me do it. My piecework business is quiet right now, and my mother has come down to live with us. She loves to spend time with the children."

"Oh, would thee, truly? I'm worried about being called to another birth and not being at home. And I still seek the truth about the murder."

"Of course I will. We have to care for our elders. It's the right way of it. But you must go and tell my family. I'll need the baby with me here, of course, so I can nurse her. Can you let them know?" She raised her eyebrows. "You know where I live, of course."

"I'll go there straight away. But what about notifying Alma? She'll want to know about this turn in events."

Genevieve opened a shallow drawer in the table and pulled out a card. "It's just here." She showed me the card, inscribed with the name of the Leavitt House hotel in Old Orchard Beach, Maine.

I committed the name to memory. "I'll send them a telegram." I handed her the card, which she laid on the table. "I thank thee greatly." I took her hand and squeezed it, but she dropped it and enveloped me in her arms, kissing me on both cheeks, then stood back. I felt my cheeks flush even as tears filled my eyes. I blinked them away, wiping one off my cheek.

"You and Orpha do much for others, Rose. I do this for you both."

———

I waited in a corner of the post office after first visiting Genevieve's home in the Flats and then sending the telegram to Alma in the telegraph office next door. I was grateful to have the use of Star today for all this travel here and there. I would be even more fatigued if I'd ridden my bicycle all over town.

Bertie would be closing the post office at five, which was in only a few minutes. I folded my arms and watched the last customers of the day hurry in to mail a package or pick up a letter before Bertie locked the doors. I covered a yawn even as my stomach let me know in no uncertain terms I hadn't eaten more than a bite of lunch, and that was hours ago. It had been a full and wrenching day, and it wasn't over yet.

Bertie followed the last gentleman in line to the door after she helped him, then locked it and drew the shade. She turned to me.

"You're looking a little peaked, there. What news, Rosetta?"

I shook my head. "I'm rather discouraged at the moment, Bertie."

"I can tell. What you need is a stiff drink." She laughed and rolled her eyes. "Yes, I know you don't imbibe, not even a drop, of that evil substance called alcohol. But why don't you come to my house and watch me have one. I've got some delicious new cheese and a basket of berries I picked yesterday. We'll have refreshments and you can tell me what's ailing you."

"I'd like that. But..."

"But what?"

"I'd hoped Kevin would let us in to see Akwasi today. The poor man. I've just learned Esther has fled to New Hampshire, saying she didn't feel safe here in Amesbury. I don't know if Akwasi even knows. I'm sure he's much disheartened."

"We'll never know if we don't try. Let us take ourselves yonder."

We left by the back door and slowly rode our steeds the few blocks to the station. Walking up the front steps was becoming a far too familiar activity in my life. Inside, Guy Gilbert sat at the desk again.

"Guy, we seek to visit Akwasi Ayensu." I kept my tone business-like and stood tall, with Bertie at my side.

He shook his head. "I'm sorry, Miss Rose, Miss Winslow. The detective said no visitors."

"Is Kevin here?" I asked.

"Gone out."

"Surely you can let us in for a few minutes, officer." Bertie set her hands on the desk and leaned in toward Guy. He scooted back in his chair and stood, now towering over my petite friend.

"Not possible. A rule is a rule." He glanced around and bent his head, facing us. "He's not doing too well, I can tell you that much," he said in a soft voice. "His woman hasn't been around, and his lawyer doesn't have any good news for him. The man only sits on his bed with his head in his hands. Not eating or nothing."

Who wouldn't be discouraged to be in such a situation? I thought for a moment. "Surely I can write a message to him."

"You can do that, yes." He proffered paper and pencil. "Here."

I knew Guy had a big heart and wished he could help us, and in a way I was glad he wasn't risking his job to do so. I took the paper and began to write, checking the slip of paper in my pocket halfway through. When I was done, I folded my note in half and wrote Akwasi's name on the outside, then slid it across the desk to Guy.

"I appreciate thy help, Guy." I said good-bye, as did Bertie, and we left the station.

"Too bad about the visit. Now for home?" she asked.

"Surely."

Ten minutes later, with Star and Grover drinking from two buckets Bertie had drawn, she and I settled into her leafy arbor in the back of the cottage she shared with Sophie. The garden was shady and welcoming, and smelled deliciously of the sweet peas clinging gracefully to strings trained up the wall of the house. She'd brought out cool lemonade for me and a glass for herself, into which I suspected she'd added alcohol of some kind. Cheese, rolls, and a bowl of blueberries sat on the small round table between us. I broke open a roll, spread a creamy cheese onto it, topped it with berries, and ate several bites before I spoke.

"That is perfect. I feel better already." I smiled at her. "I thank thee."

Bertie popped a few berries into her drink and sipped it. "What did you write to the prisoner?"

"I told him about Esther's trip north. I'd copied down her sister's address at Orpha's and I included that. So he knows she's safe and with family. I hope that sets his mind a little bit at ease."

"From the sound of it, he's got a case of melancholia, wouldn't you say?"

"Oh, yes. Wouldn't thee, arrested, in jail, persecuted for the color of thy skin?"

"Indeed." She regarded me. "You're getting to be quite the amateur detective. Who do you think killed Hannah?"

"It's such a confusion in my mind. I think Akwasi didn't. I think Tobias didn't. But either of them might have, I suppose. Last night Lester Colby threatened me, saying I'd been messing in his business. I don't know why he would have killed Hannah, but he could have. He was there directly afterwards. If he did, it could be because he's the father of her baby and she was threatening to tell."

"Lester Colby is a cheat and a liar. He has tried to put a few schemes past the United States Post Office. I didn't let him get away with it, of course. But I wouldn't be surprised that he continues his criminal ways."

"Or maybe Akwasi was the father, and his betrothed isn't the sweet woman she seems. Maybe she killed Hannah to get back at Akwasi."

"That's quite a muddle of ideas, Rose."

"I know. And there's another mill girl, Nora Walsh, who didn't like Hannah in the least and knows how to use a gun." I rubbed my forehead. "I don't know, Bertie. I seem to be doubting everything these days." I grabbed a quick look at Star. He was now contentedly munching on a portion of oats Bertie had also set out for the two horses. Why couldn't my life be as easy as theirs?

Bertie nudged my knee. "Something wrong with that handsome fellow of yours?"

I nodded slowly, meeting her gaze. "I think he lied to me. I think he's stepping out with his cousin, a pretty young thing named Violet." I twisted the ring and told her about Clarinda's lies and about encountering David on the road.

"And what about that?" She pointed at the ring. "I see you haven't take it off yet. He loves you, girl. He gave you a ring for a reason. Don't you think you might be mistaken about this cousin?"

I took in a deep, shaky breath and blinked away tears. "I don't know. Maybe it would be best for David if I gave up on him. Marrying a Quaker could present an impediment to his career."

"I think you need to give David a chance to explain himself before throwing this marriage proposal under the trolley." She bit into a bite of cheese and roll and swallowed before going on. "Now, tell me why Orpha had Esther's sister's address." She cocked her head.

"Poor Orpha. I found her today with an apparent attack of apoplexy. I think she'll be all right, but at first I thought she was rambling nonsensically, about Esther and a bucket of water and the Holy Land." I explained about Esther's note and the sister in Bethlehem.

Bertie snorted. "At least Orpha wasn't talking about drinking holy water."

I stared at her and then giggled. "Or Jesus coming to call." I covered my mouth with my hand but couldn't stop the laughter bubbling up.

"Or a dinner for twelve in Jerusalem, maybe?" Bertie laughed just as hard, and soon enough the two of us were bent over with tears streaming down our faces.

"Oh, my," I said, wiping my eyes. "We're terrible." More giggles came out.

"No." Bertie sniffed. "We aren't. We both love Orpha. But laughter is a good tonic, don't you think?"

"That it is, friend. That it is."

THIRTY-ONE

STAR TROTTED UP THE path to the Bailey house with a quickness to his step. I was also eager to arrive home. I planned to remove these layers of clothing, sponge off the heat and tensions of the day, and don a loose comfortable wrapper. I wanted to visit with Faith and go to bed early.

But from all appearances, Faith wasn't home. No lamp shone from within, and the solid door was shut fast, not swung open to let air in through the screen. I experienced a brief fear she might have come to some harm, after Lester's threatening farewell last night. But, no, Faith had likely dined with Zeb and his family, since neither she nor I had made plans for our own dinner. Zeb's family loved Faith as much as we loved Zeb. I was waiting for her to come home one day and report he'd asked her to join with him in marriage. With both of them Friends and both from families of modest means, the announcement would be joyously received by the families and the congregation. My earlier conflict with David, as well as our religious differences, flooded back into my brain, but

I shook my finger at myself. Laughing uncontrollably with Bertie had lightened my mood and I was determined not to sink back into the abyss. At least not tonight.

I slid off Star and led him into his stall. After I got him settled, and gave him fresh water and food, I headed into the house, removing my bonnet as I went. At the door I halted, spying an envelope sticking out from the gap between the door and the frame. I removed it and pressed my lips together when I saw my name in David's neat hand again. He must have come looking for me.

I stared at the envelope for a moment before I grabbed the house key out of my pocket, unlocked the door with a firm hand, and marched inside. I knew I needed to confront whatever was happening with David. I couldn't avoid it. I couldn't deny it. Bertie had helped me to regain more of the balance I was accustomed to feeling. Today was Second Day, and it'd been only two scant days earlier he'd proposed to me. Truly, how could all be lost so suddenly? Perhaps there was a perfectly logical reason for David to have quit work early and taken Violet for a buggy ride.

And then my anger rose up like the red flares of the fireworks. My hurt kept it company. I threw the letter on the table and unbuttoned the top few buttons of my dress. I paced the length of the kitchen and back over and over. Striding to the sink, I pumped cold water and doused my face and hands. I dried off and sank into a chair.

"Rose Carroll, thee is a Friend for a purpose," I told myself out loud. "Search for the answer. Listen for the small, still voice within. Wait upon the Light." So I closed my eyes and folded my hands in my lap. And waited.

I breathed in and out, listening to the sounds of the outer world: hooves, birds, voices in the distance. I felt the hard wooden chair beneath me. I caught a whiff of the rough kitchen soap we used for cleaning and the fruit sitting in a bowl on the counter. I saw nothing but the insides of my eyelids. I listened to my breath again and gradually felt myself quiet, the turmoil of life melting away.

Before my mind and heart had fully stilled, though, little Christabel wound her way through my ankles. She rubbed and mewed, and then jumped up on my lap. Once again laughter bubbled up in me as I opened my eyes and stroked her. Perhaps tonight's message was to accept life without judgment. I didn't need to condemn David before I'd heard his true heart, the key to which might be in this envelope before me. I would accept whatever the future held for Orpha, making sure I provided whatever assistance she might need. And in the matters of Akwasi, of Hannah's murderer, of Lester's anger, and of Nora's lies, I'd do my best to discern my best way forward and let the rest go.

But first this little animal needed some acceptance and, more importantly, dinner. I rose, sliced off a small hunk of whole-meal bread, and laid it in a bowl. I drew out the milk bottle from the icebox and soaked the bread. After I broke it up with a spoon, I set it on the floor for Christabel. She purred as she licked at it.

Now for the letter. I sat and opened it.

> *My dearest R,*
>
> *I came by to set things straight with you, but prepared this missive to leave in case you were out. I hate to see you angry with me for no reason and am determined to make it all right with you if you'll allow me. I have told my mother in no uncertain terms she is never to lie to me again. I have also let her know I will no longer provide transportation for that silly twit of a cousin of mine.*

I miss you. Please know my heart has never veered from you being its true north.

Your eternally loving husband-to-be,

D

THIRTY-TWO

I SAT WITH THE letter for some minutes as dusk began to fall around me. But this time it was the darkness of the sun setting, not of my mind. Smiling, I stroked the paper as if it were David's face. So his mother had tricked him into leaving his work and driving Violet somewhere, likely intending to foster their closeness. From David's words, it sounded like it had done exactly the opposite, leading him to assert his position with Clarinda. So I was not to remain a spinster, after all. I found it easy to accept his words, although a part of me wondered why I'd doubted him so quickly in the first place.

The evening having improved considerably, I lit a lamp in the kitchen and in my room and penned a letter back to him. I expressed my relief and apologized for my error and resulting anger. When I'd readied the missive for tomorrow's post, I strolled about the house feeling unsettled. It was curious Faith still hadn't returned. I picked up a book but laid it down again. I looked over at my client records but wasn't called to do work tonight. I dangled a piece of yarn for Christabel for a few minutes, watching her spring straight up off the ground to try to catch it, but she finally tired of the game and curled up to sleep.

I'd determined after my period of prayer to discern my best path forward in the matter of the murder. As I twisted the yarn back into a tiny ball, it occurred to me there was one avenue I could pursue this evening. Bonnet back on, I extinguished the lamps, grabbed my letter, and locked the door behind me. The moon hadn't yet risen, and I wasn't sure I should ride my cycle in the dark, so I set out on foot with a determined step, dropping the letter to David into the nearest postbox. It wouldn't go out until early morning, but this way I wouldn't forget to mail such an important message in case I was called out to a birth.

Virginia's boardinghouse wasn't far. Many disapproved of a single woman out walking at night alone, but it was early yet. And I'd traversed Amesbury's streets many times in the night going to and from births, although I always tried to hire a conveyance when the distance was far and the family did not provide a buggy and driver for me. I did have a moment of pause when I recalled Lester's threatening words, but I'd be out in public. What could he do? I wasn't about to stop going about my business because of him.

Fifteen minutes later I rang the bell and waited until Virginia pulled it open. She narrowed her eyes. "Rose Carroll. Did he get there so quickly?"

"Who does thee mean?"

She peered around me and then gazed at me with a wrinkled nose. "I just sent a boy to fetch you."

"Truly? I saw no boy, but I wanted to come and discuss a matter with thee."

Virginia let out a hearty laugh and stepped back. "Great minds think alike."

I followed her in. "Why did thee seek me?"

She beckoned me into the front parlor and closed the door after us. "Nora Walsh has gone out to see a friend," she whispered. "I want to search her room. I now suspect she was the thief and not Hannah. She protested far too often about Hannah. And since the poor girl's death, other small items about the house have gone missing, so Hannah certainly wasn't the one. Will you help me look for evidence?"

I stared at her. "This subterfuge makes me uneasy. Thee doesn't want to confront her directly?"

Virginia set her fists on her waist and shook her head. "I do not. It's my house and I mean to keep it a safe and honest one. But what did you come here to talk with me about?"

"I thought to inquire a bit more about Nora Walsh, actually, and her disagreements with Hannah. When I first met Nora, she expressed displeasure at having to room with Hannah. But why? She also told lies about Tobias being sweet on her. He denies it wholeheartedly. And then there were her accusations of Hannah stealing from her. I thought thee might have a better sense of her motivations."

"I might, and we might find it searching her room. Are you coming?" She opened the door and pointed to the stairs.

It seemed unethical to do so, but my urge to get to the truth was stronger at the moment. "Yes, I'll assist." I followed her up the narrow back staircase. "Virginia," I began in a soft voice, "Hannah's father mentioned she had been sending home a bit of extra money recently. Does thee know where she might have obtained it?"

She halted on the second-floor landing and twisted to face me. "She asked me if I had need for any help, that she wanted to assist her family beyond her pay from the mill. I discovered Hannah was a miracle with a needle, so I set her to doing some stitching for me in the evenings."

"I see." There was one of my questions answered.

"And by the way, I checked for my pistol yesterday after I arrived home. It was in the drawer next to my bed, right where I always keep it."

We made our way up to the third floor. The heat was far more oppressive than down below, where the larger windows and proximity to the ground let the air cool. Virginia opened a door at the end of the hall and lit a lamp. I stopped, astonished at the mess. Neither of the two beds were made. Clothes were strewn everywhere. And containers—there were wooden boxes, valises, cloth bags in every corner, all overflowing with objects.

Virginia pursed her lips. "This is entirely unacceptable."

"Thee doesn't clean the rooms?"

She shook her head. "No, the girls are to do that. It did not look like this when I let it to Nora at the beginning of May. I always check the room when a girl departs to make sure she's left it in good condition. The girl before Nora was neat as a pin, and so was Hannah." She shook her head and made a tsking sound. "In fact, it was reasonably tidy when I gathered up Hannah's things on Saturday."

"Where shall we start, and what do we seek?"

"Look for any silver spoons, salt cellars, that kind of thing. And see if you can find a collection of coins—the ones Nora claimed Hannah had taken from her."

"I'll start on this side."

"Good. That there was Hannah's bed." She pointed to a low narrow bed under the window. No bed linens or blankets covered the mattress's striped ticking. Instead I saw shifts, a coat, a pile of rags, and several dresses.

"Did Hannah's father take her belongings with him when he left here?" I shoved the clothing into a pile at the head of the bed and then selected one item at a time, smoothing it out and checking any pockets, then laying it neatly on the bed.

"That he did. She didn't have much. Two spare dresses, her winter coat, a warm hat, plus undergarments and stockings, that kind of thing. She owned a Bible, though, and a well-loved rag doll. He had quite the job of it not to weep when he saw those last two, I can tell you."

I kept working until I'd gone through all the clothing. "Nora has quite a lot of possessions for a poor Irish girl, doesn't she?"

"Far too many."

I started on a satchel that lay on its side on the floor, dumping the contents onto the bed with a clatter. I picked up a paper-wrapped parcel. It fell open to reveal a half-dozen leather-covered diaries. Fresh new ones, identical to the one Nora gave Faith as a gift. Had Nora stolen them?

Virginia straightened. "Would you look at this?" She held out a fancifully decorated hat with a green ribbon and a white feather. "My good Easter bonnet! She must have stowed it under the bed before I came up to gather Hannah's possessions for Mr. Breed."

"And take a look here," I said, pointing to the bed. A dozen spoons lay in a jumble, along with a small clock, a silver bracelet, and a porcelain salt cellar. A folded piece of paper was among the items, and I picked it out. "Are these the items thee has been missing from the house?"

Virginia folded her arms. "They are, indeed. That girl's a rotten thieving liar, and she'll not stay under my roof one more night."

A quick intake of breath came from the doorway. We both whirled to see Nora standing there with a hand gripping the door jamb, her eyes wide and terrified.

"Nora Walsh, you get in here and explain yourself," Virginia demanded.

Nora shook her head before she turned and ran down the stairs.

"Well, I'll be." Virginia stared after her.

A moment later a door slammed from below.

"Shall I go after her?" I asked, taking a step toward the door.

Virginia put her hand on my elbow. "Leave her. It's God's good riddance she's gone." Her nostrils flared. "And it'll be right and just punishment when she's hauled before the judge. She'll be on a boat back to Ireland before you can say Jack Robinson."

"Perhaps we should seek understanding before condemning Nora."

"Understanding, Rose? She's a common thief. That's as easy to understand as the First Primer."

"I have heard of an illness called kleptomania, in which people steal things they don't need. Nora hadn't sold your items. She seemed to want to keep things around her. Maybe growing up the eldest of ten children deprived her of any real possessions of her own. She might feel an uncontrollable urge to acquire worldly goods."

She stared at me, then threw back her head and laughed. "I think you're taking Christian forgiveness a step too far, there, Quaker Rose. I was also the eldest of many, on a farm in Maine, but I don't steal. I work hard and earn what I have. It's no illness, not some urge. It's a crime, plain and simple."

THIRTY-THREE

I WALKED HOME WITH a troubled mind. Why was Nora stealing, and where would she stay tonight? Virginia had left the house at the same time, bound for the police station to report the thieving. If Nora were found in town, she might well spend the night in a jail cell, which wasn't any kind of a place for a young woman to be. There didn't seem to be anything I could do, but I worried about her.

The waning moon, no longer full but still bright, made its appearance over Carriage Hill. I trudged along, turning onto High Street, where the overhanging elms and maples changed the moonlight to a distant glow. A wind picked up, rustling the branches like paper. Paper. I'd stuffed the folded piece of paper in Nora's room into my pocket, where it still sat. I'd have to return it if it was Nora's. If it was a letter of some kind, maybe it would provide an answer to why she felt compelled to steal other people's belongings.

The shadows were dark in this section of the road, with the few houses set far from each other and no streetlamps to guide my way. There was no sidewalk, either, and I was forced to travel along the side of the road. I tripped on an uneven section of the street and fell, reaching out my arms to stop my momentum. After I pushed myself back up, my hands stung with scrapes from the paving stones. I hurried on, coming to the intersection with Powow Street.

A horse approached, clopping down Powow Hill at great velocity, a carriage clattering behind it. The speed seemed reckless, as the carriage swayed to and fro. Was this an escaped animal, a horse that had not been properly tied up and had escaped without a driver? I tried to step back but a tall stone wall prevented me. The horse appeared aimed straight at me. I cried out and shrank as flat as I could against the wall. I heard a sharp quick sound like the crack of a whip, like a driver urging the steed to go even faster. What crazy person was this?

At the last minute, the horse veered back into the middle of the street. I briefly glimpsed the face of the driver under a black hat pulled low on his head. Still, they passed so close I could feel the heat off the animal and hear its heavy breathing. They careened left around the corner onto High, nearly toppling over in the turn, and headed toward Market Square.

I patted my heart, which was also galloping at high velocity, and blew out a breath. It had been such a close call. Who in the world would drive so recklessly? And was the driver actually aiming at me, or did he simply not see me there?

Now I really hurried home.

———

With the lamps lit and my hands washed, I commenced to pace anew. Where was Faith? I truly didn't want to venture out again, but it was past nine now. Even if she'd dined at Zeb's, they both needed to be up early in the morning for their jobs. I moved to the screen door and peered out, but didn't see her form coming up the walk. I grabbed the last meat pie and paced some more, then paused to help myself to a couple of cookies from the jar that I munched as I walked. My refreshments with Bertie had been hours ago, and not much, at that. I was going to have to do some cooking tomorrow if Faith and I didn't want to subsist on porridge and cheese.

Christabel ran up, so I lifted her into my arms and stroked her as I made my circuits. Her light yellow fur, almost a sandy color, brought me to mind of the reckless driver. I'd had only an instant to see his face, but it seemed to be clarifying in my memory now. And it included bushy sideburns the color of sand. Like Lester Colby's.

So it could have been malicious driving instead of careless. Lester had threatened me. What had he said? *You might have to pray for your own damned health if you're not careful.* How could he have known I was out walking at night, though?

He'd also threatened Faith indirectly. My heart turned to ice and I stopped still. Faith had gone to the mill this morning, and I hadn't even told her of Lester's warning. What if he'd accosted her after hours? What if she wasn't at Zeb's, after all? I brought my hand to cover my mouth.

The kitten twisted to look up at me and gave a little screech. I must have been squeezing her. She scrambled out of my arms up to my shoulder and jumped down from there.

Once again I felt paralyzed. How could I find Faith? I could go out on Star, but had no idea where to look. The mill? Lester's house? I could, of course, try Zeb's home first. But if Lester had a purpose to run me down, it wouldn't be safe to go out at all. I hurried over to the door to close and lock it. Maybe it wasn't even safe being home alone. If only the network of telephones were more widespread.

How I wished for David's strong arms and counsel at a time like this. How grateful I was for his refusing to allow me to back out of our commitment. But I didn't have any way of reaching him. I tried to take a deep breath and calm my mind, to return to that place of acceptance I'd found earlier. The problem was, I was accustomed to acting, not waiting. The patience required of Friends had long been a struggle for me.

The door rattled. I whirled. A scritch and a snick later, the door swung open to reveal a rosy-cheeked Faith. I rushed toward her and enveloped her in my arms.

"Rose!" She laughed and twisted away. "I'm glad to see thee, but this is quite the welcome." She leaned out the door and called, "Good night, my dear." She waved her arm, then turned back to me.

"I was so worried about thee." I smiled, but it felt a little shaky. "I can't tell thee how happy I am thee is home and safe." I took a closer look at her blushing face. "And happy, too, by the looks of it."

"I am happy. But why was thee so worried? I was only out strolling with Zeb."

"Sit down." I patted the table and took a seat.

She scooped up the kitten and stroked her as she sat. She rubbed foreheads with Christabel and giggled when the kitten licked her nose.

"I should have told thee this morning Lester Colby threatened me last night, and thee by association," I said.

Faith sat up straight. She stopped smiling. "Why?"

"He told me to stop snooping in his business is how he put it. But he mentioned thee, too. So when thee didn't come home, I feared he'd assaulted thee at work, or afterward."

253

"No, not at all. In fact, he wasn't even there today. Another manager stood in for him."

"Does he usually miss work?"

She shook her head. "Sometimes he takes his wife to a doctor, or is ill, himself. He doesn't tell me, of course, but word gets around."

"Of course." I rapped my fingers on the table. "I was nearly run down this evening as I walked home from Virginia Perkell's." I held up my hand. "Which is another story I'll get to. But a carriage came hurtling down Powow Street and aimed right at me. I'd have been maimed or even dead if it hadn't swerved ever so slightly before reaching me."

"Oh, Rose, that's dreadful. Some drunkard, no doubt."

"I'm not so sure." I told her about spying the sandy-colored sideburns.

Her eyes widened. "Like Lester's."

"Exactly."

THIRTY-FOUR

FAITH ROSE AND GRABBED a cookie of her own, then sat again. "Tell me about the visit to the boardinghouse. Why did thee go?"

"I sought clarity about why Nora didn't like Hannah, why she lied about Tobias's feelings. I thought Virginia might know more than I, since she is a stand-in mother to all her boarders. But when I got there, Virginia had already sent for me. She wanted me to help her search Nora's room while she was out."

"Oh? I spied Nora walking about town earlier with a couple of girls from the mill. They were heading toward the men's boardinghouse where Tobias stays. Did thee find anything?"

"Did we ever." I told her about the mess the room was in. "Virginia found her Easter bonnet and I uncovered silver and other items Nora had stolen from the house."

Her eyes widened and she whistled. "What an unscrupulous girl she is."

"Indeed. And I'm afraid I found other instances of the diary she gave you. I think she stole the lot of them."

Faith shook her head balefully. "She didn't need to do that." She stroked the kitten some more, who now slept purring in her lap. "Why Rose? Why would she steal and lie like that? Wouldn't her family have taught her to be honest?"

"Sometimes it's hard to know what causes people to act as they do, Faith. Hardship. Abuse. A feeling of not being wanted. A history of being deprived, whether of love or food or a clean quiet place to live."

"How will Virginia deal with Nora when she comes home?"

"I didn't finish my tale. Nora did come home, and found the two of us in her room talking about her thievery. She took one look and fled the house." The wind I'd felt while I was out picked up again and blew through the house, ruffling Faith's hair. I expected another storm was brewing.

"So Nora is out alone in the town? She must be terribly frightened."

I gazed at my niece with her kind heart, who thought not of Nora's crimes, but of a girl her own age stranded outdoors at night with nowhere to sleep. "She must be, indeed." I covered her hand with mine. As I shifted in my seat, I felt the paper in my pocket. I drew out the paper and unfolded it on the table.

"What's that?"

"I picked this up in Nora's room right before she returned and surprised us. I don't know which girl it belonged to. I stuck it in my pocket in the upset."

Faith leaned across the table, squinting as if trying to decipher the writing upside down. I peered at it through my glasses and read aloud what I saw.

Fourth Day, Seventh Month, 1888

"Hannah must have written this, since Nora wouldn't have used our terms for days and months. She wrote it the day she died," I said. "I suppose she never had a chance to post it." I read on.

Dearest Mother and Father,

I write to you today with difficult news. I know I have been remiss of late in my correspondence. Please know I think of you, as well as my brothers Asa and Jacob, every single day. I miss you all more than I can say. I have found myself in a situation impossible to resolve, one in which every turn seems wrong, at which I despair of finding a solution. The details are thus:

This spring I detected thievery and malfeasance being conducted by a manager in the Hamilton Mill where I am employed. This man is selling, to a private source, cloth we girls work long and hard to produce. He then keeps the money for himself. His name is Lester Colby.

At Faith's gasp, I peered up. "Thee was right about Lester."
She nodded. "As I suspected."
I continued reading aloud.

Because you, my dear and respected parents, have always taught me to honor our Quaker traditions and speak truth to power, I lingered one day after my shift and addressed him. I said what he was doing was wrong. He grew furious with me. He pushed me against a wall and

Here the writing was crossed out and smudged, as if Hannah had reconsidered what she wanted to say mid-sentence.

I am sorry to say he abused me terribly. And I now carry his child. I despair to discern the path I should take. I have deeply hurt the young man I have been stepping out with here, an honest hardworking Friend from New Hampshire, for whom I hold great affection. But I cannot tell him the shameful truth. How I wish I were back among you in my girlish state, helping thee in the kitchen, Mother, and walking with thee to Meeting for Worship, dear Father.

Please hold me in the Light of God and know I love you all with the fullness of my heart.

Ever your grateful and obedient daughter,
Hannah

I stopped, staring at the paper. Her signature was also smudged, perhaps by a tear. Now I fully understood poor Hannah's predicament. Her baby wasn't Tobias's or some other man's. It was Lester's, that apparently doting husband and grandfather. Had he also killed her?

Faith squeezed her eyes shut, her own tears leaking down her cheeks. She opened her eyes, now red-lined and despairing. "So not only did Hannah die, her baby was killed as well. And I have been working for this monster? Tell me, Rose, why didn't Hannah come to her friends? Or tell the police? Why?"

THIRTY-FIVE

THE MORNING SUN STREAMED in, accosting me. Faith and I had stayed up late talking and consoling each other. I blinked away what felt like sand in my eyes. I needed to rise and help Faith get ready for her work. Learning that her friend and fellow mill worker had been pregnant when she was killed had been a huge blow to my sensitive niece. I determined to ease this day for her as much as I was able.

I completed a simple toilet and headed into the kitchen to start the stove. We were going to have a proper breakfast of eggs, ham, bread, and fruit this day, with coffee to bolster us. I'd learned this from my mother. While she was an energetic fighter for women's rights, she also valued the home and hearth. Her solution for whatever plagued her family was a hot, filling breakfast. I didn't have time to bake a pie, as she might have, but I could pull together a good meal for Faith and myself. I was going to need the sustenance, too.

Faith wandered downstairs yawning, pinning up her hair as if still in slumber. She opened the door and stepped onto the landing, but quickly came back in. "It's blowing out there," she said, wrinkling her nose.

I turned my head from where I stood at the stove. "We're going to have a northeaster, I believe." We often experienced storms that blew from the northeast and twisted around, according to David, bringing downpours, heavy winds, and even tornadoes on occasion.

Faith came over to the stove and laid her head on my back, her arms around my waist. In a small voice she said, "I don't even want to go in today."

I flipped the ham in the skillet, and then twisted around. I put my hands on her shoulders and gazed into her eyes. "Thee is strong, and thee has the power of truth behind thee. I'll walk down to the mill with thee and then carry Hannah's letter to Kevin Donovan. Once inside the mill building, be sure thee stays in the company of other girls at all times. Do not let thyself be separated, or the others, either. If Lester calls one girl into his office for any reason, make sure she refuses and do the same thyself. Does thee understand?"

Faith's nostrils flared as she stared back at me. "I do." Her voice was strong now. "And I will. Thee is my pillar of iron, Aunt Rose."

"Not iron, surely. How heavy that would be to haul around." I laughed and turned back to the stove. "Now fetch the plates and let us break our fast."

Our moment of silent blessing before eating that morning lasted longer than usual. Soon enough, though, we had consumed the hearty breakfast and were out the door, which I locked carefully. We walked down the rainy hill in somber silence, Faith in her hooded cloak, me holding the largest umbrella we owned over both our heads. At the door to the mill, I held her hand and fixed my gaze on hers.

"Chin up," I said, delivering the stock phrase of my mother, her grandmother.

She nodded. "Chin up." She turned and joined the flood of women and men entering.

I bucked the tide and made my way back to the street, then put my head down against the wind and headed for the police station. It was only seven thirty, but if Kevin wasn't in, I'd leave the letter in the care of whoever was on duty. This news was too important to keep silent. Friends practiced silent worship, but when it came to injustice, we were far from quiet.

————

I was a block away from the station when a man's voice called to me. I glanced up to see Tobias hurrying in my direction.

"Good morning to thee, Tobias." I held up the umbrella so he could shelter under it, as well. "Is thee going to thy place of employment?"

He ducked under the umbrella and wiped the rain from his face. "No, I just came from Clarke's. I'm on the overnight shift."

I thought fast and made the decision to tell him what I'd discovered. "Let us stand there." I pointed to the storefront next door. Hargrove Milliners featured a green-and-white striped awning that provided cover from the windy downpour. Once under it, I put my umbrella to the side and took in a deep breath.

"I learned some disturbing news last night," I said.

He leaned toward me a bit, studying my face. "About my Hannah?"

"Yes. I found a letter at her boardinghouse that she'd written to her parents. It was dated the fourth of this month."

"The day she was killed," he whispered.

"Tobias, in the letter she said she'd confronted her manager at the mill, Lester Colby, about a crime she'd seen him commit. He took the opportunity to assault and abuse her."

His fists clenched and his jaw worked, but he waited in silence for me to go on.

"The reason she'd stopped seeing thee is that she was terribly distressed to discover she was with child. With Lester's child."

"No!" He shook his head, his face a mask of anguish. "What a monstrous thing to do to a girl, to one of his employees." He paced the length of the store and back. "If only she'd come to me. I would have married her. We could have raised the baby as our own. I'd have been proud..." His voice broke and he buried his face in his hands, his shoulders heaving.

It was my turn to wait in silence.

He raised his head and dropped his hands. "I'll kill him. I will find that man and kill him!" The despair in his face was replaced by a furious resolve.

I reached out and touched his arm. "Tobias, calm thyself. There is no need to resort to violence. I understand thy fury. But I'm on my way now to the police station with Hannah's letter. They'll investigate Lester's crimes, be sure of it."

"May I see the letter?"

"I'm afraid of damaging it with water. But do know she mentioned you. She told her parents she'd hurt thee and that she held great affection for thee. Keep that in thy heart."

He nodded slowly. "But why didn't she tell me?"

"When women are assaulted like that, even though they do nothing to invite it, it feels shameful to them." I knew this all too well. "Our society propagates that attitude, too."

"I wouldn't have blamed her for a moment." He swallowed hard. "Thee thinks the police will act on her accusation?"

"I'll see to it they do."

He gazed at me. "Thee seems troubled by other matters, too, Rose."

"It's true." He was an observant young man. I had no doubt my fatigue and concerns showed in my face. "I have had some personal troubles of late. One is that a dear old friend, the midwife who trained me, had an attack of apoplexy yesterday. After I go to the station I'm off to visit her."

"An old midwife. Is her name Orpha Perkins?"

"Why, yes, it is. Does thee know her?"

"No." Tobias shook his head. "But my grandmother does. They were great friends when they were young, she said. Granny told me to call on Orpha when I moved to Amesbury and I haven't made the time. But I shall."

"I know she'd love to see thee. Well, I'm off now. Be well, Tobias. And walk in peace." I watched him turn up his collar and trudge away in the rain.

————

For what seemed like the hundredth time this week, I ran up the steps to the police station. I had my hand on the door when Kevin hailed me from the street.

"You're here early, Midwife Rose. Come from a delivery, have you?" His tone was jolly, and when I turned to see him, his face was, too. His cheeks were full of color and his eyes sparkled, despite rain pouring down on his uniform coat and likely inside his collar.

263

"Not this time, Kevin." I opened the door and furled my umbrella. "What brings such joy to thy face?"

He waggled his eyebrows. "My little boy was telling jokes at breakfast. That lad can have us all in stitches, and he's not yet six. I'm a blessed man, Miss Rose, a blessed man."

I'd never seen him so jolly. "I'm happy for thee. And did thy wife like her bracelet?"

"She was well pleased with it." He narrowed his eyes at me. "You're not here with happy news, though, I dare say. Well, come in, come in, and tell me all about it."

A couple of minutes later we faced each other across his desk. He shoved some papers to the side and I laid the letter in front of him. I shook out the hem of my skirt, which was drenched.

"I found this letter last night in Hannah Breed's room at Virginia Perkell's boardinghouse."

"Mrs. Perkell delivered quite the accusation last night about young Nora Walsh. You were there, apparently."

"Yes. Did thee find Nora?" I realized the discovery of the letter's contents had put thoughts of Nora out of my mind.

"We did not. But all officers are on the alert for her." He picked up a pair of spectacles and hooked them around his ears.

"Thee wears glasses now?" I asked. I removed my own and wiped off the rain with my handkerchief.

"It's my aging eyes. I need these fool things to read with. Now, let's see what we have here." He bent over the letter.

I waited while he read. I hadn't thought he was so old as to need reading glasses, but maybe his ruddy cheeks and well-padded body made him look younger than he was.

He looked up, removing the spectacles. "This is interesting. And shocking."

"I'll add that my niece, Faith Bailey, also thought she saw a transaction going on between Lester and another man. She didn't confront Lester about it, but she said he saw her looking and seemed quite angry with her after that."

"Hmm."

"And on Sunday night I was at the Colby house." I told him about being summoned to check Charlie's eyes. "Lester saw me out and then threatened me, and Faith as well."

Kevin's eyes went wide. "You could have told me this yesterday."

"I thought it was more of an idle threat than a real one. Although last night a wild horse and carriage nearly ran me down. They were descending Powow Hill at far too great a speed and appeared to be aiming at me. I caught only a glimpse of the driver, but he resembled Lester Colby."

"You were alone?"

"I was walking home from Virginia's."

"Unwise under any circumstance to be out at night alone, Miss Rose." Kevin rapped on the table.

"Kevin, I did not come here to be scolded about my personal conduct. What is thee going to do about Hannah's allegations against Lester?" I stared at him. "The man impregnated her!"

"Calm yourself. I'm going to send a man over to the factory right now to fetch Colby in for questioning. That good enough for you?"

"That would be excellent. I trust thee will keep this letter safe? It'll be evidence in the case against him."

Kevin smiled. "You're sounding like my boss, now."

"Faith did say Lester wasn't at work at the mill yesterday. His home is up on Lake Street, if thy officer needs to search him out."

"Good to know. I thank you for coming in." He stood.

"May I visit with Akwasi for a moment?" I stood, too. "Since I have been so helpful to the local authorities?" I raised my eyebrows.

"You could if he was here. We transferred him to the Newburyport courthouse holding cells yesterday, since his trial is to begin tomorrow."

My chest tightened. We were no closer to freeing Akwasi than before. Unless...

"Kevin, perhaps Lester killed Hannah. Maybe he was afraid she'd tell others what he'd done, and why."

He pulled his mouth to the side and narrowed his eyes, then shook his head. "Maybe. I'll consider that as we question him. But it seems unlikely. He's in a good position. Mill manager, nice house on the hill."

"He's a new grandfather, too. But I have heard from his son-in-law that Lester's finances are not in a good position, in fact. And thee above all others should know that even people in so-called good positions can commit crimes. Please investigate him."

"All right. Is there anything else?" he asked.

I thought for a moment. "Did I ever tell thee I glimpsed someone near Akwasi's work shop? Maybe it was the person who planted the gun there, so Akwasi would be falsely accused."

"Maybe. Yes, you had mentioned it earlier. I hate to say it, but you've got a keen eye for this type of work."

"I simply hate to see crime go unpunished." I made my farewell and walked down the hall. I gazed at the door to the jail cells. Akwasi was now elsewhere, alone and awaiting trial on charges of murder, and I was helpless to change that. At least I believed Kevin took the accusations against Lester seriously. It was in his hands. And God's, of course.

THIRTY-SIX

THE RAIN HAD LESSENED to a drizzle by the time I reached Orpha's in the neighborhood of modest homes on Orchard Street. Genevieve opened the door to my knock, her infant daughter on her hip.

"Rose, here again so soon?" She stepped back so I could enter.

"I wanted to see how Orpha is doing, and to give thee a reprieve if thee would like it. How's our Elsie?" I chucked the baby under the chin and gave a little squeeze to her belly.

She giggled, then hid her head in her mother's shoulder before peeking out at me again. She had a healthy weight and color and sparkling dark eyes like her mother's.

"My girl is well and happy, thanks be to God. Here." Genevieve handed me the sturdy baby, who immediately reached for my spectacles.

I laughed and removed her hand. "And how is our Orpha?"

"She slept well. She's drinking water and ate a soft-boiled egg for breakfast. Come in and see for yourself."

"Elsie, let's go visit Nana Orpha." I squeezed her soft little belly again and was rewarded by the delight of another baby giggle.

"You go on back," Genevieve said. "I'll take this chance to clean up in the kitchen."

The baby, who didn't seem a bit worried to leave her mama, and I made our way to the back of the house and into Orpha's room. She lay with her eyes closed in bed, but her head and back were propped up with pillows. She wore a fresh blue shift and her hair was neatly brushed back. When Elsie made a peep, Orpha opened her eyes.

"Rose." She patted the bed next to her, so I sat, positioning Elsie on my lap, wrapping my arm around her. "No births this morning?"

"Not a one. How is thee?" I stroked Orpha's hand on the coverlet, her skin a soft parchment with dark raised veins winding through it.

"I'm still tired. Ginny said I had app … app …" Her speech was still a bit slurred, but better than the day before, although the droop to her mouth had not changed. She must have settled on calling Genevieve Ginny because it was easier to say. She smiled at the baby and extended a gnarled shaky finger for her to hang onto.

"Apoplexy," I said. "Yes, I believe thee did. But thy mind seems more clear now. Does it seem that way to thee?"

"A bit fuzzy yet. I suppose I'm grateful the good Lord did not take me into his arms. It wasn't yet my time, it appears."

"I'm also grateful." More than I could say. "Thy speech is better than yesterday, too. I think thee will continue to improve." I hoped so, anyway. "Can I fetch thee any sustenance? A sip of water?" A water glass sat on the table next to the bed.

"I'm not hungry, but water would be perfect." Her hand wobbled as she reached for the glass.

I steadied it and helped her take a sip, then returned it to the table. "We'll let thee rest again. I'm going to spell Genevieve, so if thee needs anything, call out for me."

"I shall. Thank you, Rose, dear." She closed her eyes.

"Come on, Elsie," I whispered.

Elsie still clung to Orpha's finger, so I detached her and headed for the kitchen. A small blanket lay on the floor.

"You can put her down there, Rose. You don't have to hold her all the time. Lord knows I don't." Genevieve laughed where she stood at the kitchen doing the washing up.

I laid the baby on the blanket, where she cooed and grabbed for her toes. I sat at the table. "Orpha does seem a bit better today."

"Yes. But she's a ways from taking care of herself."

"Indeed. Listen, I have no clients this morning. If thee wants to go out or take a break, I'll stay. I can watch Elsie, too, if that helps thee."

Genevieve turned and shot me a grateful smile. "That is a kind offer, and one which I'll gladly take. When you have children, you'll know how rare it is to be able to go out alone. I'll fetch some foodstuffs from Market Square and return in an hour or so." She dried her hands and removed her apron.

"No hurry."

"There's porridge on the back of the stove, although the fire has mostly gone out. You'll have to stoke it if you want anything warm to eat."

"I thank thee. I ate a hearty breakfast, so I'm fine. Does the baby need anything?"

"She just ate. She'll be fine for several hours." She showed me a stack of diapers in the next room, and a dresser drawer she'd lined with blankets as a makeshift bed the baby couldn't roll out of. "In fact, she'll have her morning nap soon. Lay her down in her drawer and stroke the bridge of her nose. She's an easy girl. She'll go right off. Or you can leave her right where she is if she falls asleep there. Her quilty is on the chair."

Genevieve donned a cloak and took the loan of my umbrella. I locked the door behind her and returned to the kitchen. Elsie had curled up on her side with her thumb in her mouth. I knelt and stroked from her forehead down onto her nose, and sure enough, her eyes drifted shut. This was the same technique I'd seen Catherine doing to little Charlie. I'd have to remember it for my own babies. When I stopped the movement, her eyes slid open again, so I kept it up until she was sound asleep. I laid the patchwork baby quilt over her, since the air was cooler on this rainy day than it had been.

I sat there watching her, this simple uncomplicated being. Soon enough she'd be having tempers and demands like any normal human. But for now, all she needed to be happy was her mother's breast, clean diapers, and plentiful love. How long before I would give birth to my own tiny creature? It seemed David and I were now back on the path to matrimony. I'd have to think hard if I was ready to take a break from my cherished profession a year after a wedding. Orpha had taught me the use of several herbs which seemed to have the effect of preventing pregnancy. But would I want to? I would need to discuss this with David.

My musings were interrupted by a pounding on the front door. I peeked in at Orpha but she also slept peacefully. Perhaps this was Alma already back from her vacation. But no, surely she'd have her own key to the house. Although the door had glass inserts on the top, the panes were clouded and etched with designs so all I could see was a figure outside.

I pulled open the door to see a wet and bedraggled Nora standing there. "Nora! Do come in. I was worried about thee." I stood back. "Did thee find a place to spend the night?"

She stepped in and waited until I closed the door before speaking. "You weren't so worried as to not snoop in my things." Her tone came out as harsh as a metal rasp. Her hatless hair was barely pinned in place, and her dress was dirty and wet. Of course she'd run out last night with nothing but the clothes she was wearing.

I looked more closely. A wild look filled her eyes. "Virginia had asked for my help," I said. "Now, can I fix thee a hot drink? Perhaps some breakfast?"

At that her face softened, but only for a moment before the hardness returned. "I'll get that later."

"How did thee know I was here? Or is thee here to visit Orpha?"

"I don't know any orphan. I followed yeh here. I was after watchin' the police, make sure they didn't nab me."

"What can I help thee with?"

Her eyes flashed. "You can help me get out of here, that's what." She pulled a gun out from the folds of her dress. And pointed it at my heart.

THIRTY-SEVEN

"NORA, PUT THAT THING down." I fought to keep my voice level. "Thee can't be having a gun in here." The baby in the kitchen. Why had I ever mentioned food? And Orpha in her room right beyond. Both sleeping with the peace of innocence.

"And why not? It's a pretty useful way to get what yeh want."

"If thee wants to leave, thee is welcome to. There's the door right behind thee."

She snorted. "Yeah, and walk into the arms of the police? I need money. I need transport to the rail station. I'm going out west."

"But surely stealing a few items won't merit a severe punishment."

"Yeh don't know anything. I done a lot worse than that."

Worse than stealing? *Oh, no. She didn't. Did she?*

"And there's nothing for me back home, especially when they find out I—" Nora cut herself off, shaking her head.

"That you what?" Had she killed Hannah? My thoughts came fast and furious. But no, they'd found the murder weapon behind Akwasi's shop. Or was it simply one of the same model?

She didn't answer me, but narrowed her eyes and stared.

"Where did you get that gun, Nora?"

"It's that old hag's pistol. She doesn't even know I took it, she's that dim." Even Nora's laugh was harsh.

"Virginia's?" Virginia, who had kept the weapon in an unlocked drawer.

She nodded with a satisfied look, but the aim of the weapon never wavered from my chest.

I needed to get her out of here. I had two cherished creatures to protect. "I'm happy to give thee all the money I have, but I didn't bring any with me today, I'm afraid to say." I tried to lighten my tone. "Shall we go together to my house and fetch some?"

"Ye're not gettin' my message. I can't go out. They were after lookin' for me all night. I hid behind some bushes for a long time. Now when it's daylight? I don't have a chance."

"How can you get to the train station, then, even if you had money?"

The wild look was back. "I'll think of something." She glanced around the hallway, dim except for the illumination from the door glass. A coat tree stood nearby. "Clothes. I need a hat, a cloak to hide in. A dry dress. And money. Is there any around here? Whose house is this, anyway?"

"Rose, are you there?" Orpha's plaintive voice called out. "Who's there?"

My heart sank further. If I endangered Orpha's and Elsie's lives, I would never be able to live with myself. If I even survived this morning.

Nora shoved the gun into my chest. "Who's that callin' out?" she demanded in a low voice.

"It's Orpha. She's an old, sick woman. I have to go to her. If thee will stay here, I'll bring thee money, a dress, a hat. I promise. It's all in the house."

"If you don't, I'll kill you, too." Her nostrils flared.

There it was. Lester wasn't the murderer. Nora was. "Did you kill Hannah?" I asked. I shivered from the chill of discovering what she'd done. Maybe I shouldn't have asked. Maybe she'd kill me, too, after I helped her.

"I did, at that. She found me astealin' and was going to turn me in. I couldn't have that, see? I can't help myself from takin' things." For a moment Nora's eyes took on a bewildered look. She shook it off. "But now I'm headin' westward. Gonna make up a new name for myself. Get out of this place."

"Rose?" Orpha called again.

"I'll be right back." I took a step back from the pistol.

"No, I'm going with yeh. Don't trust yeh an inch. Say, there's not one of those new telephone machines here, is there?"

Oh, only if there were. "No, of course not." Or was there? I realized I didn't know Alma's husband's occupation, or whether they were well off or struggling to get by. The house was modest in structure, true, but nicely furnished and well kept-up. Alma was a dressmaker by trade, but that wouldn't bring in enough money to afford a telephone.

"Then let's go. I want to be makin' my move." She took my shoulder and turned me around. "Listen to me," she whispered in my ear. "I'm after puttin' the gun in my pocket. But I can get it out right quick, like, and I'll shoot yeh dead if yeh try to trick me. Understand?"

"Yes." I swallowed and headed for the kitchen.

"Whoa up, here." Nora said, reaching for my shoulder and halting me. "Who's the wee babe?" Her voice softened.

"Her name's Elsie. Her mother will be back any minute. Let's get moving." I did not want this crazed young woman going near the baby.

"Rose, who's there?" Orpha's voice was insistent. "I need the bedpan, quickly."

"Yeh go on and see your crone there. I'll watch over the tiny one." She squatted next to Elsie. "But leave the door open." She kept her eyes on the sleeping baby.

"Try not to wake her, please." What could I do? There was no gun pointed at me, but I couldn't attack Nora for fear the gun in her pocket would fire. And she did have a fondness for babies. She'd gotten a wistful dreamy look in her eyes when she'd talked about her younger siblings. I'd have to trust she wouldn't hurt Elsie.

I hurried into Orpha's room, grabbed the pan, and slid it under her hips. A look of relief came over her face. When she was done I removed it and set it in the corner. I sat close to her on her bed.

"*Orpha, nous avons une visiteur qui veut faire mal.*" We have a visitor who wants to do bad. I knew my grammar wasn't perfect, but I also knew Orpha would understand.

Her eyes flew wide open. "*Mais, c'est qui?*" Who is it?

"*C'est la jeune femme qui a tué l'autre jeune femme.*" It's the young woman who killed the other young woman. I couldn't use names in case Nora was listening.

"*Qu'est ce qu'elle veut de nous?*" What does she want from us?

"*Elle dit qu'elle va partir au ouest, mais elle a besoin d'argent, d'une chapeau, et d'un, uh, un cloak.*" She said she's going to go west, but she needs money, a hat, and a cloak. I had no idea what the French word for *cloak* was, so I whispered it in English.

"*Il faut faire attention,* Rose." You need to be careful. Orpha had stopped slurring altogether.

"*Oui. Il y a de l'argent ici?*" Is there money here?

She pointed to the top drawer of the bureau across the room. I hurried over and drew out a small embroidered bag. "*Ici?*" When she nodded, I fished out a few greenbacks. I stared when I saw they were hundred-dollar bills. This must be Orpha's life savings. I kept one and stuffed the rest back into the sack, then buried it deep under the clothing in the drawer. I'd just shut the drawer when I heard a wail from the doorway. Nora stood there with Elsie in her arms. The baby was screwing up her face to cry.

"What are yeh doing there?" she snarled.

I held out the bill. "Money for thee."

She reached out and snatched it. "Hat, cloak, dress?"

"Let me ask Orpha. First, though, give me Elsie." I held out my arms. "She isn't acquainted with thee."

Elsie let out an unhappy cry and kept it up. Nora hugged her to her chest. "No. I know babies. And she's comin' with me."

I drew in a sharp breath. Behind Nora, I saw Orpha shake her head, fast.

"Oh, that would be a bad idea, Nora," I said. "Think of how difficult it will be to travel with an infant."

"I'll make my own decisions, thank yeh very much." She tapped her foot at the same time as she switched Elsie to her shoulder and patted her back. Elsie emitted a loud belch and then fell silent. "See? Now, get me the dress."

I looked at Orpha. "*Qu'est ce que je dois faire? Elle ne peut pas amener la petite.*" What should I do? She can't take the little one.

"*Avant tout, donne elle une robe d'Alma. N'importe quelle.*" First, give her one of Alma's dresses. It doesn't matter which one.

276

"*D'accord.*"

A frowning Nora had been looking back and forth between us. "The crone doesn't speak English?"

"No, more's the pity. She never learned," I lied. "But my mother taught me French. So Orpha was still able to tutor me in midwifery. I'll run upstairs and get thee a dress, shall I?"

"Go, and hurry. I'm after catchin' the noon train." Nora jiggled Elsie to keep her quiet.

"*Rose, il y a une machine à parler la bas en haute.*" There is a speaking machine upstairs there. Orpha's gaze burned into my eyes.

I waved my acknowledgment, trying not to react visibly, and rushed up the stairs. A speaking machine? Did she mean a telephone? I entered the first room, but it was obviously the little girls' bedroom, with dolls, toy wagons, and children's books strewn about. The next room held a marital bed and a wardrobe. I tore through the tall cabinet until I found a serviceable dress. It would be long on Nora. With any luck she'd trip and fall wearing it. My breath came short and fast.

I called down the stairs. "Still looking for a dress." I raced into the last room, which blessedly appeared to be an office of some kind. And there on the wall hung a wooden telephone box. I closed the door behind me, taking care not to make a sound. Thanking God I'd learned to use a telephone a few months ago, I removed the listening piece and clicked the lever on the side until the operator spoke.

"Rose Carroll at the Latting home. Seventeen Orchard Street," I whispered into the trumpet-shaped device on the front of the box. "Send the police quickly. A murderer is here. With a gun."

THIRTY-EIGHT

FOOTSTEPS SOUNDED ON THE stairs. I slid the piece back onto its hook and slid myself out of the room, closing the door quietly before hurrying toward the landing. Nora ascended toward me, still holding the baby.

"Were yeh talkin' to someone?" Her nostrils flared. "If yeh were, I'm tossin' this wee one down those stairs right now."

"Only to myself. There's no one here." I smiled, praying I didn't look nervous. "I kept saying to myself, *where are the dresses? Where are the dresses?* Alma is a dressmaker, so there's an entire room of cut-apart gowns but not a single one finished." I displayed the dress in my arms. "But here's a perfect traveling frock, doesn't thee agree?" I babbled on. "Let's go down and thee can change out of that wet one. It must be so uncomfortable." I tried to widen my presence in the passageway so she wouldn't think to come up and change her clothes in one of the second-floor rooms. If she found the telephone, we were all dead. I breathed out my relief when she turned and made her way down. I followed, smiling at Elsie's face over Nora's shoulder. We weren't out of this yet, and that sweet baby had to stay safe. She had to.

"Thee can change in the sitting room there." I pointed to the next room. "I'll just take Elsie."

"No. She's staying with me." Nora grabbed the dress and pointed to Orpha's room. "Yeh go in there with Frenchy or the baby dies." She pushed me in that direction and stayed on my heels until I was in. "Sit yerself down."

I perched on the bed next to Orpha and took her hand. Once Nora was gone, I whispered, "The machine worked."

Orpha blew out a breath, her shoulders relaxing, then put her finger to her lips.

Nora was so unstable, it was impossible to predict what she would do. One minute she was like an adoring big sister, the next a ruthless killer. I held her in the Light to be lenient with us, and most especially with Elsie.

In only minutes Nora was back, now in Alma's blue sprigged gown. She'd tidied her hair and wiped her face clean. She carried Elsie in one arm and the gun in the other hand.

"Hat." Her voice shook, almost as if the enormity of what she was about to do, and had done, had finally sunk in. She was only seventeen, after all. Her cheeks were devoid of the color they usually carried as she waved the gun in the air.

I sniffed. "Elsie needs a change."

As if on cue, Elsie began to whimper. Nora sniffed her, too, and frowned, but didn't lower the gun or make a move toward changing Elsie.

"Nora, that isn't safe, having a weapon so near a baby." I stood. "Won't thee reconsider taking her? I know how much thee cares for the wee ones. And thee will be far more free to make thy escape if thee leaves her here with us."

"*Oui*," Orpha said, looking sage despite her drooping mouth.

Nora jerked the gun toward Orpha. "So she understands English, after all."

Heaven help us. "Thee won't be able to move fast, and thee will have to find a bottle and canned baby milk to feed her on the journey. She's only ever been fed at the breast. We haven't even any clothing for her here." I stretched out my arms. "There's a hat and cloak on the coat tree in the hall. Take them and go. But leave Elsie."

At a rattle at the back door, Nora snapped her head about her like a fox in a trap. She shoved Elsie into my arms and fled into the hallway. In turn, I handed Orpha the baby and tiptoed after Nora. I heard the coat tree crash to the floor and felt a rush of cooler air from the open door. I dashed to it and stood outside on the landing, my breath coming as fast and furious as my thoughts had earlier.

Nora ran down toward High Street, clasping the hood of the cloak on her head. It was purely for disguise, because the rain had stopped. A horse and trap clopped by in the opposite direction, the driver glancing back at Nora. He shook his head and kept going. Two women on the sidewalk stopped and stared.

"Rose, what's happening?" a man called out.

I whipped my head in the opposite direction, where the voice had come from. Tobias hurried toward the house. "That's Hannah's killer," I cried, pointing toward her.

As he raced after Nora, I shouted, "Be careful. She has a gun!"

THIRTY-NINE

I WATCHED TOBIAS SPRINT down the road, fleet of foot. Nora was not only hampered by keeping the cloak secured to her head with one hand, but by having to lift her skirts with the other. She stumbled but didn't fall. She shot a look over her shoulder, then ran faster.

The clang of the police bell approached from behind me, growing ever louder. I kept my gaze on Nora. Would Tobias catch her? She'd killed once. I doubted she'd hesitate to shoot again. The buildings clustered close together here, family homes mixing in with small factories. People and animals were everywhere. I rested a hand on my chest, my heart thudding beneath it.

Tobias grew closer, finally nearly reaching her. He leapt and tackled her around the waist. Nora cried out. As they went down, the sharp report of gunfire resounded. I glanced quickly into the house. Orpha would be fine with the baby for a few minutes. I hurried down the front steps.

The police wagon roared up to the house, the horses noisily blowing through their flared nostrils. I pointed to the two figures wrestling on the ground about twenty yards distant and the wagon headed in their direction. The two women on the sidewalk clutched each other and shrank back against a low fence behind them.

The gun went off again. Tobias fell away from Nora and lay still. I ran toward him as Nora began to flee. Kevin and Guy jumped out of the wagon.

Guy pulled out his weapon, aiming it at Nora. "Police! Stop where you are or I'll shoot."

Kevin stared at me with alarm on his face and motioned for me to stop short. He also pulled out his weapon and pointed it at Nora, holding it with both hands, even as another police wagon approached from the opposite direction, three officers spilling out after it screeched to a stop. A horse whinnied. Nora whirled toward the new wagon, her gun pointed, then faced Guy and Kevin again.

"Drop the weapon and raise your hands above your head," Guy called out.

Would she? Or would she try to shoot? If she did, she'd surely be killed.

"It wasn't my fault," she cried. "I didn't mean to kill her." The hood of the cloak had fallen back, and her dark hair flew unpinned and wild about her face.

"Drop the gun, miss," Kevin said sternly.

I watched as Nora let the gun fall to the ground. She crumpled to sitting, her face in her hands. The officers rushed toward her. I glanced at Kevin, and he motioned me ahead, so I raced to Tobias. He lay on his side, his thigh bleeding heavily. His eyes were closed and his face ashen. Was there another wound? The gun had fired twice.

"Tobias, talk to me." I knelt and pressed on the wound with both hands.

Tobias opened his eyes. "I couldn't get the gun away from her, Rose. I'm sorry."

What a blessing he was alive. "Don't worry. The police have her." And they did. I looked over to see Guy haul Nora up and click handcuffs around first one wrist then the other, securing them behind her back.

"Good." He closed his eyes again.

"I need thee to stay awake, Tobias," I urged. "Does thee hurt anywhere else besides the leg?"

"No," he said in a voice I could barely hear, but he didn't open his eyes again.

"Kevin? Somebody? This man needs medical help!" The blood seeped out between my fingers. I doubled the hem of my dress and pressed that onto the wound. It wasn't clean, but would have to do. This dear courageous man must live. He must.

An officer I didn't know hurried up. He carried a black kit with crossed red bars on it.

"I'll take over, miss." He drew out a thick dressing.

On his signal, I scooted away and he placed the dressing on the wound and applied similar pressure. I wiped my hands on my dress and knelt again, at Tobias' head this time. I stroked it. "Thee was so brave, Tobias. Thee will survive. Thee will be fine."

FORTY

An ambulance had whisked Tobias to the hospital. I'd asked the driver to please bring Tobias's case to the attention of one Dr. David Dodge there.

The paddy wagon had taken a handcuffed Nora to the jail. She'd kept up her protests even as they latched the door of the back compartment. I didn't believe for a minute she hadn't meant to kill Hannah, but the court of law would decide that.

I trudged with heavy steps back to Orpha's house. My mood should have been more carefree. A murderer was behind bars. Tobias had not been killed. Akwasi would be freed. But I felt I'd imperiled Orpha and Baby Elsie. And there was still Lester's involvement in Hannah's assault and in the corruption at the mill. Life did not feel at all free of cares.

"Miss Rose," Kevin called out.

I turned and waited as he hurried toward me.

"I have to thank you," he said. "You bravely made that call. I'd like to know how you managed that under the eyes of a killer with a gun."

I smiled a little. "It involved a fake old French lady, some nerves, and a lot of lies."

He looked suitably confused.

"Come and meet the real brave one." I beckoned him to follow me. At Orpha's door, a wide-eyed Genevieve stood with Elsie in her arms. I introduced her to Kevin. "I want him to meet Orpha. Has she told thee what happened while thee was out?"

"No. I only came home to find her holding Elsie and the front door wide open." She looked from me to Kevin and back. "And then shots and police alarms out here."

"She and I can tell you both, then." I led the way into the house. A minute later Kevin sat in a chair in Orpha's room. I perched on the edge of her bed while Genevieve stood, doing the constant-movement dance of every parent to keep a baby quiet. I introduced Orpha and Kevin to each other.

"So what was this about a fake French lady?" he asked.

Orpha laughed, although it was still a shadow of her formerly robust guffaw. "Rose and I studied French together over the last few years, so we could better talk with our French-Canadian mothers."

"*Comme moi,*" Genevieve said with a smile.

"Exactly like thee," I said. "So Orpha and I used it as a secret language when Nora was here threatening us. Orpha told me there was a telephone upstairs."

"And you dared to use it with a gun-toting murderer in the house?" Kevin looked astonished.

"What else could I do? Nora asked for a dry dress, since she'd been out all night in the rain. I pretended I couldn't find it. I didn't stay on the line long."

"Long enough for the operator to get us an urgent message. But how did Mr. Cartland get involved?" he asked.

"I'd talked with Tobias earlier in the morning and somehow mentioned Orpha. His grandmother and thee are friends, he said."

"Cartland?" Orpha asked. "Why, yes, that would be my childhood friend Urania. Another Quaker, if memory serves."

"Tobias approached the house right as Nora fled," I went on. "He must have been coming to call on Orpha."

"He's another brave one," Kevin said. "If he survives his wound, I'll be sure he's publicly commended."

If. Tears came to my eyes and I covered my mouth.

"Oh, I'm sorry, Miss Rose." Kevin leaned over and patted my knee. "I'm sure he'll be fine. He's young and strong. Don't you worry, now."

"I apologize," I said. "It's been a wearing few days."

Genevieve frowned. "Where was Elsie during all this, when this killer girl was in the house?"

I glanced at Orpha, then back at Genevieve. I swallowed. "Nora said she was going to take Elsie with her. It was a frightening few minutes."

"Rose quite firmly and quite rightly convinced Nora it would be an extremely bad idea to take an infant on a long train journey," Orpha said.

When Kevin raised his eyebrows, I said, "She said she was going to go west, change her name, start a new life. The poor girl—"

"The poor girl? The one who was going to kidnap my little daughter?" Genevieve nearly screeched in outrage. "Who killed another young woman?"

"I only meant she'd experienced a hard life in Ireland," I said. "Of course that doesn't excuse her crimes, Genevieve. Please forgive me."

She nodded but clutched Elsie to her chest and didn't smile. I hoped she'd truly forgive me by and by.

"Did Nora tell you she'd killed Hannah?" Kevin asked, peering at me.

"She did. She said she'd stolen the gun from Virginia Perkell, and that Hannah was going to turn Nora in for stealing plenty of other things, too. As Virginia told thee, Kevin."

He nodded and stood. "It's been a pleasure meeting you ladies. I'm afraid I have a few things to attend to down at the station, so I'll take my leave."

Orpha extended a spotted, wobbly hand. "Thank you, Detective, for helping keep our town safe."

He squeezed it gently. "Be well, Mrs. Perkins. I thank you for assisting Miss Carroll."

Her eyes faded shut. She'd risen to the occasion, but she was still weak. I hated she'd had to go through the events of this morning.

"I'll go, too." I went to Genevieve and the baby and embraced them both. I pulled back and said, "I'm so, so sorry Elsie was in danger." I took a deep breath to try to master the tears springing up again, and swallowed down my suddenly thick throat. "I'm just so sorry."

"Don't fret, Rose. What's that English saying? All's good that ends good?"

"Close enough." Next I planted a kiss on Orpha's head. She smiled without opening her eyes.

———

Kevin and I walked side by side in silence toward the station. A gust of wind blew an opening in the clouds, showing a high, brilliant blue like a glimpse of a sparkling sea.

"What happened with Lester this morning?" I finally asked, pushing my spectacles back up my nose.

"We apprehended him on his way out of town. The mill had fired him yesterday morning."

"So that's why he wasn't on the job yesterday."

"Right. They apparently already suspected he'd been selling on the side. They were going to do their own investigation before they called us in. I spoke with Cyrus Hamilton, himself." He shook his head. "When I told him Colby had impregnated one of his girls, though, Mr. Hamilton was rightly incensed. Hard to bring decent Christian girls to work in your mill if that kind of shenanigan goes on."

"Kevin Donovan!" I stopped walking. "Assaulting and forcing any woman, no matter their age, to a man's sexual will is not a shenanigan. It's a travesty and a crime." I folded my arms.

"All right, all right." He waved his hand in the air. "Yes, I agree. Now can we get going again?"

I resumed walking. A buggy raced through a rain-filled puddle and sent up a spray of water that barely missed us. "So Lester was on his way out of town?"

"He certainly was."

"Was his wife with him?" I asked.

Kevin turned to look at me. "Why would she be?"

"Marie Colby is ill with advanced cancer. He kept saying he was going to take her to New York for treatment."

"She certainly wasn't with him. One keen-eyed officer had spied Colby heading for the station, and we found him trying to hide in a corner of one of the Boston and Maine cars before the train left.

He'd tried to disguise himself by rubbing coal dust into his sideburns. Oldest trick in the book, and not one we readily fall for."

Poor Marie. I hoped Patrick and Catherine Toomey would take care of her in her remaining days. We arrived at the station and stood out front.

"Will thee be releasing Akwasi soon?" I gazed at Kevin. The small exertion of walking several blocks had reddened his face and caused droplets of sweat to dot his cheeks.

"Already so ordered. He'll be delivered home within the hour. I'll pay him a call and apologize for the false arrest."

I frowned. "What about the gun that was found behind his house?"

"Colby confessed to planting it there. He told us right before your call he saw Miss Walsh shoot Miss Breed. It's a complicated tale, but the gist is that Colby threatened to reveal Miss Walsh's crime if she didn't allow him to have his way with her. However, she'd also seen his misdeeds at the mill and threatened him in return with making his thieving public."

My mouth fell open. "Truly? They each knew of the other's crimes?"

"Indeed they did."

"He tried to run me down in the road one evening."

"He must have been worried you'd figured out their little scheme, or that Nora would tell you and frame him for the killing. I'll add that to the list of crimes he's committed."

I nodded. "Good."

"Under Nora's pressure, he did say he had agreed to take the pressure off our lady killer by accusing the African. Colby owned a weapon of a similar model."

"I thought thee told me there was proof the bullet which killed Hannah came from that very gun found near Akwasi's shop." I pressed my lips together.

"We knew it was the right kind of bullet for that gun. But no, we have no way of verifying it came from exactly that weapon, although I've heard talk of them figuring out how to do that over in Europe. Would that we could do it here."

"That seems to be flimsy evidence for arresting a man on murder charges."

Kevin groaned. "Eyewitness, now proved unreliable. Bullet matched to wrong gun. Motive lacking. Yes, Miss Rose, this isn't my proudest moment."

"You'll be lucky if Akwasi's lawyer doesn't try to bring charges of false arrest."

"True. I was acting in good faith, but that's not always successful." Kevin removed his hat and rubbed his forehead. "I thank you again for bringing Miss Walsh to justice. I must get back to my desk now before the Chief finds something else to fault me for." He extended his hand.

I shook it. "Be well, then. I hope we don't have occasion to work on a case again for a long, long time. Perhaps never."

He laughed. "Whatever you say, Miss Rose." He turned and trotted up the steps. He paused at the top to face me. "Will I be receiving an invitation to your wedding?"

"That's entirely possible, Kevin." I turned, too, but headed for home. With all this commotion, I'd not even thought about my clients. If I'd been called to a birth, they were going to have to wait. I trudged along, replaying the scenes from the last few days in my head. I saw shadows on the walk, so the clouds must have finally blown through. My mood was anything but sunny, though. Death.

Betrayal. Sickness. Thievery. Rape. How had life in our safe, industrious town become so sordid?

I stopped and reversed direction. I knew what could lift my spirits.

FORTY-ONE

Twenty minutes later, Akwasi pulled open the door of his small house to greet me. His wide smile, which I hadn't seen in almost a week, lit up the day along with my spirits. The abrasion on his cheek was healing and he wore a fresh shirt that dazzled white against his dark skin.

"Rose." He extended both hands.

I held his hands in mine, feeling the calluses and strength of a man who did an honest day's work. "Did thee just arrive home?"

He nodded slowly. "But the officer who brought me did not know the particulars of why I was released."

"Hannah's killer turned out to be a disturbed mill girl. But she has been apprehended and arrested." I saw in my mind Nora holding both the baby and the gun, a gun also endangering Orpha, and a shudder rippled through me.

Akwasi peered at me. "Why do I sense thee was involved in this apprehension, Rose?"

"Because I was. It was a tense morning, and our friend Orpha was in danger."

"Orpha? That's terrible. She wasn't hurt, was she?"

"No, I assure thee she was not harmed. All's well that ends well, and Orpha is fine. In fact, she helped me find the way to let the police know of the girl's guilt and location." I briefly described the encounter with Nora, then squeezed his hands and released them. "I am sorry thee was wrongly accused and treated so badly."

"It is the fate of my people." For a moment his nostrils flared and he clenched his hands into fists. He let them go again almost as quickly, as if remembering Friends', our shared faith's, belief in nonviolence. "Perhaps things will change in the future. Perhaps they won't." He lifted a shoulder and dropped it. "For now I just want to return to my work, to my business, and also to my Esther's side."

I loosened my bonnet strings and pushed it back off my face as I nodded.

He smiled. "She will be so happy to know I am free. I shall journey to New Hampshire tomorrow."

"Good. Esther was very worried about thee, and became afraid for her own safety. That's why she left."

He nodded slowly. "A wise choice. I'll send her a telegram and let her know I am on my way to bring her home. I'll tell Friend John about my release, too."

"Excellent. I look forward to seeing Esther again, myself. For now, I think I'd better get home." The wind blowing the rain clouds away caught my bonnet and was about to fly off with it. I laughed and grabbed it in time.

"I thank thee for this visit, Rose. Thee is a good friend to call on me at this time. And thee spoke truth: all's well that ends well. Justice was finally served, even if it was forced to take the wrong path for some days."

My mood having lifted and my news delivered, I was walking along Patten's Pond when a buggy slowed next to me.

"May I offer this lovely and accomplished midwife a ride home?" David leaned out, smiling gently.

"I've rarely been offered a more welcome transport." I hurried around and climbed in.

I could tell he was about to bestow a kiss on my cheek when a bell and a shout rose up behind us. "Get the move on, there!" a driver shouted. David laughed and clucked to Daisy.

"Where was thee off to?" I asked, turning in my seat.

"I'm on my way to ask the second most important question of my life." His eyes sparkled.

"And what might that be?"

"To ask a Mr. Allan Burroughs Carroll if I might marry his daughter."

My throat swelled up with emotion once again as he pulled to a stop in front of my house. I sidled across the seat and let him put both arms around me, leaning my head on his shoulder. "David, I'm so sorry I doubted thee."

He hugged me tight. I brought my hands up to feel his strong arms.

"I wasn't going to let you go, you know," he said into my hair. "And I'm never going to, not for all eternity." He finally loosened his embrace and I sat back, his arm along the back of my shoulders. "And where were you coming from? Helping another lucky baby into the world so his first sight is your beautiful face?"

I reached up and tousled his dark curls, but I stopped smiling. "No, in fact I was out helping bring both a murderer and a rapist to justice."

The smile slid off his face, too. "Not again?"

"Again. As one of my clients said earlier, though, all's good that ends good. Both behind bars."

"Were you in danger, Rosie?"

"A bit. I was at Orpha's with an infant, a killer, and a gun. And Orpha, too."

He shook his head and squeezed my shoulder. "And you obviously triumphed. I hate it when you get in these situations."

I opened my mouth to object.

"No, let me finish. But I know it'll keep happening, and I'll simply trust you'll come out of it alive. I've never met a more competent woman in all respects, my dear. I'll not stand in your way."

"It'll have to be thus. And I thank thee for thy trust." I gazed into his deep blue eyes. "I shall try to earn it. But speaking of competence, did thee treat a young man who was shot in the leg not long ago? I asked the ambulance driver to request thy services."

"I didn't treat him personally, but when I left he was in the good hands of our best surgeon."

"What a blessing. Young Tobias Cartland was very brave this morning. He tackled that girl like he was catching a stray calf or something. He took her down, but was shot for his troubles."

"Do you mean to say the murderer is a girl?"

"She is, and a thief, too. Nora Walsh, one of Faith's fellow workers." I let out a long breath.

"Well, the young hero is going to recover nicely, I'm sure of it."

"All right, now, off with thee," I said. "I'm going in to take a good nap and not think about a single crime."

"May I kiss my fiancée?" He winked at me.

A man and a woman chose that moment to pass the buggy. The man grinned, but the woman tugged on his arm with scolding eyes staring back at us.

The kiss David bestowed on my lips lasted a good long time, and was the one thing that could lift my mood further. I stood in the hot July sunshine and watched him drive off, my hand raised in farewell. Before he turned the corner, he lifted his in return.

Our country was a week older. I felt a year older as I turned for the house. I'd only taken three steps when a fine carriage clattered to a stop. A man in livery stood up from the driver's perch.

"Miss Rose Carroll?"

"Yes."

"My mistress has need of your services in the matter of her confinement." He told me the name of one of my more financially comfortable clients, the wife of a mill owner. "She said to tell you that the appearance of her child appears to be imminent." His face showed no emotion.

"I'll be right with thee. Let me fetch my satchel." I could rest later. Another baby was making its way out of its mother and into our world. I smiled to myself. This was the work I was called to do. And the newborn's realm of home, hearth, and love would be a safe one. At least for a while.

ACKNOWLEDGMENTS

Thanks once again to editor Amy Glaser and the entire Midnight Ink crew for publishing this series. I'm so pleased to have Greg Newbold creating the art for the gorgeous covers. I'm grateful to author Tiger Wiseman for opening her Vermont home for a writer's retreat in the summer of 2015. During that week I wrote 17,000 new words and finished the first draft of this book. I also wrote furiously for a few days in my friend Patience Wales's home when she was away. I mentioned Chuck Fager, Alison Russell, Allan Hutchison-Maxwell, KB Inglee, and Sam Sherman in the Author's Note, but I want to thank them again for their historical expertise.

My older son, Allan Hutchison-Maxwell, read the entire manuscript and caught not only anachronisms but French misspellings, plot gaps, and more. Thanks, sweetie. Allan's grandfather—my father, Allan Burroughs Maxwell Jr.—is the model for Rose's father in this series. I know Daddy, a man who regularly wrote twelve-page single-spaced typed letters to me, would have been so pleased with my becoming an author had he lived this long.

As always, I want to thank the Wicked Cozy Authors for having my back: Jessie Crockett/Jessica Estevao, Julie Hennrikus/Julianne Holmes, Sherry Harris, Liz Mugavero/Cate Conte, and Barbara Ross. Independent editor Ramona DeFelice Long gave the book a close edit, and it's a much better book for her insightful comments and questions. Midwife and mystery fan extraordinaire Risa Rispoli vetted some of the birthing details in the book.

The character Catherine Toomey is the real life Cathy Toomey, a local real estate agent and a big fan and supporter of our town of Amesbury. She was the high bidder on my donation to the Pettengill

House charity for the right to name a character. Hope you like your 1888 self, Cathy!

My Quaker family, my Sisters in Crime family, my good friends, my family by blood, my partner Hugh—I love you all and thank you, always, for your support.

© Meg Manion

ABOUT THE AUTHOR

Edith Maxwell (Amesbury, MA) is the president of Sisters in Crime New England, a member of Mystery Writers of America, and a longtime member of the Society of Friends. She is also the author of the Local Foods Mysteries, the Country Store Mysteries, and the Cozy Capers Book Group Mysteries (the last two written as Maddie Day). You can find her at edithmaxwell.com, and blogging at wickedcozyauthors.com, killercharacters.com, and midnight writersblogspot.com.

Charles J. Schwahn and William G. Spady

Applying the Best
Future-Focused
Change Strategies
to Education

American Association of School Administrators
1801 N. Moore St.
Arlington, VA 22209
(703) 875-0748
http://www.aasa.org

Executive Director, Paul D. Houston
Deputy Executive Director, E. Joseph Schneider
Acquisitions Editor, Ginger R. O'Neil, GRO Communications
Editor, Barbara Hunter, Hunter Communications
Designer, Jim McGinnis, Mac Designs

Printed in the United States of America.

AASA Stock Number: 234-001
ISBN: 0-87652-233-9
Library of Congress Card Catalog Number: 97-78242

To order additional copies, call AASA's Order Fulfillment Department at
1-888-782-2272 (PUB-AASA) or, in Maryland, call 1-301-617-7802.

TOTAL LEADERS

Applying the Best Future-Focused Change Strategies to Education

Chuck Schwahn

I openly admit to being a learning addict. During my 8 years as superintendent of the Eagle County School District in Eagle and Vail, Colo., I read three to four leadership/change/futurist books per year. The rest of the time, I was busy attempting to apply what I had read. After leaving my "real job," I had more time to read and learn from the experts and found myself reading 20-30 books per year.

But in 1994, after reading and reflecting upon what I thought were two very good leadership/management books, I concluded that they had not added to my body of knowledge or understanding. All of the theorists and authors I consider to be my heroes and heroines seemed to have established a body of knowledge about the nature and critical roles of leadership and were only reinforcing each other. Apparently, *I had read it all* — for the time being anyway.

This new insight changed my work focus significantly. While continuing to read, listen, and learn about leadership, I — with the aid of my friend and colleague Bill Spady — began to think about how I could put all of my learning together in a way that would help the education and business leaders with whom I was consulting. My vision was to synthesize all of this literature into one comprehensive and useable leadership/change model. *Total Leaders* is the result of that vision.

Nothing made these pages without passing three tests. Test 1: Did my hero/heroine leadership experts agree that the information was right, important, even critical? Test 2: Did it work for me and my colleagues as we went about creating a dynamic and successful school system in Eagle County? Test 3: Did it seem to be working for the hundreds of leaders who have allowed me to be part of their own learning and development processes?

My life has been one of excitement and great fortune. I have been blessed with great learning experiences and great teachers. My desire to play college basketball took me to a small teachers college and, four years later, I found myself graduating and entering this most meaningful profession almost by chance. What a break! Although my consulting now involves working with business and industry as well as schools, my heart and mission is with education. I feel fortunate to have spent the majority of my career working in what I sincerely believe is the world's most important profession.

And I have been blessed with many GREAT teachers. Madeline Hunter taught me about students and learning, teachers and teaching, and about school structures that made teaching and learning effective. Dr. Hunter was one of the classiest people I have known.

Dwight Allen, while dean of the School of Education at the University of Massachusetts, taught me about innovations, risk taking, and change. Dwight had no fear and taught me to consistently view learning from the learner's point of view.

Ken Blanchard, my doctoral chair, taught me about leadership and change even before he became *The One Minute Manager*. Ken also taught me about core values, caring, and healthy relationships. His modeling is even more full of impact than his writings.

Bill Spady taught me about paradigm shifts and is the source of my vision of the ideal school and system. That part of my learning journey began more than 20 years ago when I heard Bill say that "our schools are operated in a way that makes *time* the constant and *student learning* the variable." So simple. So profound. So difficult for people caught in the old way of thinking. My work from that time on has been to make student learning the constant.

I sincerely believe that everything included here is right, important, even critical, and more significantly, I believe it is all doable. I trust that you will find our work of value to you as you lead your system into the Information Age and the new millennium.

Chuck Schwahn
January 1998

Bill Spady

As the development of this book unfolded, I realized that the original impetus for my writing a book on leadership surfaced nearly 30 years ago. It was in 1968 when I was teaching a graduate course in research methods to a cohort of sociology of education students at Harvard University.

The late sixties was an era of great unrest on university campuses across the country, and Harvard was no exception. Students were vigorously challenging the purpose and structure of American higher education, as well as the philosophy, roles, and competence of their professors. In responding to this challenge, our dean of education, Theodore Sizer, asserted that Harvard's Graduate School of Education played a unique role among education departments across the country. Its unique purpose was developing educational leaders.

Now there, I thought, was a proposition worth testing. So did my research students, many of whom were embroiled in the controversies of the time. We decided to turn the dean's declaration into a research project on Harvard's education graduates that would enable everyone to dig in and learn the realities of conducting research first hand.

Our first and biggest challenge was to define leadership. What did education leaders do that was different from what other educators did? What did teacher leaders, counselor leaders, curriculum leaders, and administrative leaders have in common? What distinguished them from other people in their states, organizations, and departments? To answer these questions, we absorbed ourselves in the day's major leadership literature.

In the end, we designed our study around two factors, which we saw as leadership essentials:

1. Leaders initiate improvements in their milieu or organization.

2. Leaders get results. By enlisting the support of others and sticking to their goal, they make something better and different happen.

All the rest, we asserted, was "details."

Nearly 30 years later, I'm prepared to say that Chuck Schwahn and I have filled in the wealth of details missing from that initial study. *Total Leaders* describes what the world's greatest experts say about leading successful change — the critical things leaders do between the time of "initiating" a change effort and seeing their intended "result" come to fruition. And it presents those details in a tight and compelling framework that shows that no one guru or school of thought addresses the total leadership and change picture.

The Total Leadership puzzle consists of five key pieces, each requiring a unique set of leadership skills, change conditions, and change processes. Deciphering the patterns in that puzzle from the countless details in more than 100 major books represented the key intellectual challenge of putting our framework together.

But working with Chuck, who is equally and passionately committed to this substance and enthusiastic about its potential impact on education, turned the challenge into fun. The more we discovered, the more things made sense and became exciting. And the more excited we got, the deeper our commitment to producing this book became.

This contagion of discovery, insight, and excitement fuels the commitment that drives us both. Chuck and I are unwaveringly committed to helping American educators develop the insights and take the steps that lead to new paradigm thinking and future-focused change. Our young people want it, our education colleagues deserve it, and our schools desperately need it.

It is in that spirit that we invite you to read and apply to your leadership work the wisdom of 100+ top thinkers found in this book. Our reward will be the realization of Total Leaders everywhere!

Bill Spady
January 1998

CHAPTER 1

Leading from the Future

■

Today's leaders are operating their organizations at the speed of change.

Daryl Conner

■

The Industrial Age officially ended in 1983 when Tom Peters and Bob Waterman's (1982) runaway bestseller, *In Search of Excellence*, was touted and quoted as the new paradigm of organizational leadership and effectiveness in major corporate boardrooms throughout the Western World. That is when the leaders of these organizations recognized that the old rules of organizational management, structuring, and functioning no longer applied.

Peters and Waterman's message was bolstered by William Ouchi's (1981) *Theory Z* explanation of Japanese business practices, Richard Pascale and Anthony Athos' (1981) treatment of the same subject, Philip Crosby's (1979) pioneering work on quality, and Alvin Toffler's (1981) second blockbuster, *The Third Wave*.

At the same time, huge, seemingly invincible steel mills and assembly plants had permanently closed. More people were driving fuel-efficient cars and watching color televisions made outside the United States. Reverence for the standardized, assembly-line model, "Made in America" way of doing things suddenly had eroded.

The paradigm had shifted, and, as Joel Barker (1988) would say a few years later, "everything went back to zero," or at least our allegiance to the past did. What once worked superbly by the standards of the day had almost overnight become the source of the problem, often because new technologies were driving a pace of change that no one had encountered before. To compete and stay in business, organizations had to become future focused, constantly monitor emerging trends, and operate on a set of principles no one had yet defined.

Education, on the other hand, responded quite differently to these same pressures for major change. Its response to the flood of reports issued in 1983 was almost exclusively "educentric" (Spady 1998). Encouraged by the overwhelmingly old paradigm perspectives of the *A Nation At Risk* report (1983), educators opted for trying harder with what they already had rather than working smarter with a new paradigm approach to schooling.

But elsewhere, the future was no longer an easily accepted extension of the past. It seemed alien and scary because two things had already become clear, spurred significantly by another blockbuster in its day, Alvin Toffler's *Future Shock* (1971). First, change was the new constant and the new definition of reality. Second, successful leaders were those who could get their organizations to the future first and keep them there.

Thirty years ago, before *Future Shock's* publication, people viewed change much more conservatively. In 1968, people saw change as an event that was predictable and dangerous. Today, that view has flipped 180 degrees as people view change as a continuous journey that is required to survive.

The Changing View of Change

Change in 1968	Change in 1998
A Destination	A Journey
An Event	A Process
Episodic	Continuous
Quite Predictable	Near Chaotic
Dangerous to Risk	Required to Survive

As everyone realized that change had become the constant and could not be avoided, leaders had no option. If they were going to lead, they had to take the helm of changing organizations. Those who did, and on whom the model in this book is based, had the awareness and motivation to recognize and adapt to this new context in innovative ways. Today, this new breed of leaders leads people in organizations where the meaning, function, and utility of the most accepted and revered structures and practices are subject to challenge.

We need to view, understand, and strengthen leadership in relation to these shifting and challenging conditions. Clearly, leaders exist to help their organizations succeed, but they must operate within the realities of the organization and its surrounding environment. Understanding those realities is the first essential step in understanding and applying what it means to be a "Total Leader."

The Realities Facing Total Leaders: A Synthesis of Futurist Literature

Fifteen years ago, we independently began to compile some key observations about shifts and changing trends. Because it was clear, even at the time, that the prevailing Industrial Age model of schooling was going to come under enormous pressure over the next decade, the trends we initially tracked had direct implications for schools and their students. When we formally joined forces and began to consult together, we quickly shared ideas and information and developed a working paper for school districts called "Future Trends" (Spady 1987).

Since then, the major futurist literature has mushroomed, portraying an evermore complex picture of the forces that shape every aspect of our world, careers, and personal lives. We have read hundreds of books and articles that have given us significant insights into the world that organizations face and the conditions for which students need to be prepared. The major works that influenced our thinking are listed in the bibliography.

Two years ago, we synthesized the major findings from more than 30 of these and other futurist books into a document called *The Shifts, Trends, and Future Conditions Redefining Organizations and Careers in the '90s* (Schwahn and Spady 1996), which portrays the challenging world in which Total Leaders lead. The following are some of its major themes. To those of you who keep abreast of headlines about corporate downsizing, expanding and contracting overseas markets, new labor-replacing technologies, and shrinking family incomes, many of these shifts and trends may sound like old news. This is no surprise because, as Alvin Toffler thoroughly documents in his 1990 bestseller *PowerShift*, the Information Age has arrived.

The High-Quality, Global Marketplace

A most fundamental feature of the Information Age is the high-quality, global marketplace that has influenced almost all businesses, no matter how small or local their focus. Without question, organizational leaders today are being strongly influenced by the following shifts and trends.

Quality as an entrance requirement. Quality products and services, once a distinct market advantage, are taken for granted today. Quality is literally the ticket to the game, as well as the key to playing it successfully. For organizations and their employees, quality must become a way of being.

Customers demanding value. If you expect to sell it, it needs to have value for the customer. That means both quality and a competitive price. Even the rich expect to get a good deal.

Transitory quality and success. Because of the constant pace of innovation and new developments, today's state-of-the-art can quickly become next month's also-ran. As paradoxical and challenging as it may seem, smart companies innovate while on top rather than trying to ride the crest of the wave of their success too long. The same applies to employees who are constantly learning, upgrading, and preparing for the future.

The seamless world economy. With the growth of advanced communications and technologies, national economic borders are disappearing. The world is increasingly one large marketplace where ownership, resources, production, marketing, and sales can be dispersed throughout the globe. Even the smallest, most locally focused businesses are a part of this global web.

New players entering the marketplace. As markets and production become more global, the concentration of economic power is shifting dramatically. Formerly underdeveloped countries in Asia and Latin America are emerging as major world production centers and markets, while traditional economic giants struggle with widespread downsizing and unemployment.

"Glocalism." While living in a world economy, we must still communicate and sell to customers who are members of local communities and cultures. Hence, markets must simultaneously satisfy both global and local values and tastes.

Being "green." Social awareness about the fragility of the environment has become a norm. Consumers demand that companies act responsibly toward the environment and reward those companies by patronizing them.

Doing well by doing good. Being socially conscious and showing concern is not only the right thing to do, it results in customer support and financial profitability. Companies that invest in enhancing and supporting the common good appeal to the deeper sense of right and morality in their potential customers, thereby generating highly beneficial goodwill.

English as the common language. From travel to business to sports to science, English is becoming the common global language.

The Adept, Empowered Employee in the Nimble Organization

Enormous pressures exist on individuals and organizations to be future focused, capable of change, and light on their feet. Individuals who achieve these strengths become invaluable assets to their organizations and may represent the difference between the organization's thriving and going out of business.

As a result, businesses must learn to use and capitalize on the unique strengths of their employees, just as employees must continually reassess their capabilities, talents, and potential contributions to their organizations. The dynamic that will result is dramatically different from the fixed skills/fixed career employment and organizational patterns of the now-departed Industrial Age. No book makes this theme of continuous learning, adaptation, and improvement clearer than Peter Senge's (1990) *The Fifth Discipline*. Significant trends related to nimble organizations are:

Change: The only constant. For organizations and their employees, change is inevitable, improvement imperative, and survival optional. Survival results from the ability to adapt in constructive ways and be more productive. Individuals and organizations that want to be successful face the challenge of continuously learning, improving, and changing.

Mass customization. The market presses for products and services that meet highly specific needs. Nimble organizations must find ways of meeting those individual needs quickly on a mass scale. Advanced technologies in the hands of adept employees can achieve the mass customization necessary for capturing and sustaining viable markets for the organization's products or services.

Small is powerful. Smaller organizations consistently beat larger organizations to the future in almost every way. Smallness encourages clearer focus, better communication, less bureaucracy, and more rapid decision making and response to changing conditions and opportunities.

Competence as capital, knowledge as power. The knowledge and technology explosions have shifted the nature of work and the determiners of organizational success. In the 1990s, an organization's greatest asset is its people's expertise and commitment. Recruiting, developing, and using competent, growth-oriented staff has replaced the accumulation of capital as an organization's best assurance of staying competitive.

Empowered people produce. Empowering qualified people to have more control over their work is morally right and profitable. Empowerment honors the intrinsic motivation of people to use their expertise to best advantage and gives them a direct stake in achieving personal and organizational success. Empowerment works best when employees deeply identify with organizational purpose, have a clear vision of where the organization wants to go, have a strong commitment to getting there, and receive the necessary organizational supports.

The precarious intermediary. Whether in sales, management, or clerical work, a combination of automation and advanced communications technologies allows both producers and consumers to get things done either directly or on-line, thereby rendering the middle person an increasingly endangered species. As a result, self-motivated, continuously improving individuals are becoming consultants (to their former employers) or small business entrepreneurs. To survive, they make every day count and embody quality and professionalism at their best.

From competition to cooperation. Organizational success requires competing successfully in the marketplace through focused, cooperative endeavors among staff. The win-lose psychology of the Industrial Age has given way to the new win-win empowerment strategies. Success depends on finding ways of channeling individual contributions into a total team effort, rather than having individuals and divisions compete against each other.

Unit-based management. Large organizations are decentralizing into smaller units capable of focusing and applying their expertise to specific market opportunities. Hierarchical direction and oversight are being replaced by vision-driven teams of empowered, expert employees that enjoy greater autonomy and increased responsibility for the results they achieve.

The 24-hour economy. As the marketplace and telecommunications become more global and sophisticated, traditional work schedules are disappearing. Business can be transacted at any time from anywhere, giving organizations and employees greater flexibility over work roles and schedules — the greater the technological expertise of an employee, the wider the range of work role and scheduling options.

The feminine factor. A large proportion of new businesses are owned and operated by women. These businesses not only serve as a source of employment, they represent a new, congenial, relationship-oriented approach to management that balances the traditional command/control approach so widely accepted in male-dominated organizations.

Value-added decision making. Organizational success is ultimately linked to defining a mission consistent with one of three distinctively different market positions. Organizations must either add value for the customer by providing low-cost, hassle-free service; produce the leading product in the field; or provide a unique solution to the customer's problem. Organizations that clearly make decisions consistent with one of these three missions are destined to be more successful than those that try to pursue mixed missions.

Transformational Technology

Today, individuals and organizations have powerful and efficient tools that were almost unimaginable a decade ago, yet are vulnerable to imminent obsolescence. Clearly these constantly advancing technologies have already begun to transform the very meaning, structures, and processes of work and recreation. And the potential for further transformation seems to be exponentially related to the pace of advances in the current state of the art. Two books that capture the profound implications and complexities of this major trend particularly well are Nicholas Negroponte's (1995) *Being Digital* and Michael Dertouzos' (1997) *What Will Be*. They and others note several important developments:

The Internet. The Internet and other closely related electronic communications systems give tens of millions of people access to vast arrays of immediate and inexpensive information, which reduces the need for hard copy media and stimulates the market for related hardware, software, and operator expertise. In addition, the Internet dramatically facilitates the emergence and growth of information-based cottage industries across the country.

Interactive machines and tools. Interactive machines (and the computer processors and software that drive them) are getting continually smarter and more versatile, enabling users to communicate with and more directly control the machine's processes, functions, and output. With "smart" machines and "smart" operators to get the most from them, output and productivity soar.

Digital information. As digitized, binary electronic impulses become the common form of transmitted information, and as the electronic processors of that information become more sophisticated, the distinctions begin to blur among telephones, televisions, faxes, home entertainment systems, printing presses, and computers. Consumers benefit from the marked increase in speed, versatility, and quality of digital processors. Congressional passage of the Telecommunications Act of 1996 officially endorsed the potential inherent in becoming digital.

On-demand interactive communication. As communication technologies become smarter and more versatile, control and power shift to the smart user, who can control not only what transmissions to access, store, and use, but when and where to do so.

Fixed schedules for broadcasting and observing programs or any other information source are giving way to user-flexible and user-influenced communications, creating a major quandary for those who depend on selling advertising time.

Meaningless miles. With the rapid expansion of on-line and satellite technologies, increasing numbers of face-to-face interactions are no longer necessary. "Friction-free" transactions enable work, business, purchases, sales, conferences, education, training seminars, research, publishing, and a host of other common activities to be handled from remote locations. Outsourcing work to New Delhi is as fast as outsourcing to a provider two miles away.

High-level thinking. As machines are built to do more sophisticated things faster, non-thinking, repetitive jobs continue to be eliminated. The economy of the Information Age requires highly skilled, self-directed learners and thinkers who can't be replaced by a more sophisticated robot, suggesting that the right kind of education can forge a tight link with a high-paying career.

The paperless environment. With increasing sophistication in technologies, digital media, and software comes the disappearance of now familiar tangibles and the needs to store and safeguard them. Paperless offices, paperless wallets and address books, and just-in-time delivery head the list of innovations that use electronic memory to supplant paper records and reduce costly inventories.

Virtual reality. Virtual reality simulations enable consumers to experience almost anything in detail from their own homes, including the tangible features of products, which they can examine and order at their own convenience.

Technology saturation point. A two-sided coin, technology offers astonishing benefits at the cost of redefining human existence. Those who stay on the cutting edge of technological advances and their applications can devote so much time to the endeavor that they surrender control over their lives and forfeit the quality of interpersonal relationships, conventional forms of interpersonal communication, cultural and personal development, and balanced, healthy lifestyles.

The Virtual Workplace

When you pull together the trends and implications described so far, the transformation of the workplace comes as no surprise. Increasingly sophisticated technology makes work and productivity less dependent on fixed physical locations, face-to-face interactions, and schedules, enabling small-scale, highly niche-oriented business to emerge everywhere and highly innovative leaders to succeed.

Among the many books that address this phenomenon well is John Naisbitt's (1994) *Global Paradox*. He and others offer four keen insights.

First, through the power of communication technologies, more people are already working outside of the conventional 40-hour-per-week job schedule and structure. Flexible schedules, job-sharing and teaming arrangements, and off-site locations place a premium on worker autonomy, responsibility, and the ability to get the job done well with minimum structure and supervision. These conditions enable capable and adaptable contractors or consultants to deliver goods on terms that work best for them.

Second, those with the necessary education, technological tools, expertise, and motivation are choosing to isolate themselves from the intensity, frustrations, and dangers of urban life by moving to and conducting their work from more congenial, remote, idyllic rural settings. This is a key feature of a more general "cashing out" process that has people opting for early retirement over greater income but continued career pressures.

Third, sophisticated networking and outsourcing strategies can launch temporary organizations capable of accomplishing just about anything without making major investments in employees, equipment, materials, or facilities.

Fourth, alliances, networking, and contracting for services enable organizations to grow, build capacity, and stay flexible and market responsive. But these strategies give others access to proprietary information and unique skills that they can later exploit to their own advantage. Hence, "owning" and safeguarding ideas and expertise are becoming increasingly problematic.

The Changing Milieu of Public Education

While the aforementioned themes and trends clearly represent major forces shaping organizations and careers in the 1990s, they are by no means a complete picture. Along with these themes and trends, a special set of challenges faces public education.

The maldistribution of wealth. Rich countries, including the United States, and their better educated citizenry are getting richer while the poor continue to bear children in disproportionate numbers, thereby lessening their per capita incomes even further. Wide economic disparities across a country's social and ethnic groups is the leading predictor of political unrest and revolution and will continue to shape internal as well as international politics and policies beyond the 1990s.

The persistent inequalities of education and training. The demands for high levels of education and technological literacy are increasing at the same time that indicators of educational achievement for young people from low socioeconomic backgrounds are falling or barely holding steady. This will continue to widen the gap between those qualified for entry into the high-tech workforce and those lacking the skills to do so and to further exacerbate the inequalities of wealth.

The move toward individual responsibility. Social programs are under attack for lack of effectiveness, governments are operating in the red, tolerance for those needing governmental assistance has waned, and admonitions for citizens to take responsibility for their lives are heard across the political spectrum. The implementation of mandatory "workfare" programs in some states reflects this new paradigm of "caring": that it's necessary for individuals to first pull their own weight rather than depend on society to care for them.

The graying of America. The over-70 segment of the population will continue to increase for the foreseeable future, resulting in a continued shift of products, services, political influence, and demands for public resources toward the elderly, which will continue to imperil the funding levels of public education

The diversification of America. If current trends persist over the next decade, the population balance in the United States will shift to a non-Anglo majority during the first half of the 21st century. Paralleling this trend is a political reaction against the public funding of social and educational programs targeted to those population groups. As a result, schools must find and implement new ways to effectively teach an increasingly diverse and under-served population.

The transparency of organizations. Society's demand for greater organizational openness and accountability is reinforcing a major theme in effective organizational change and adaptability: namely, honest, open communication is a key to effective leadership per-formance, organizational credibility, employee trust and motiva-tion, and organizational innovation and productivity. Schools must strengthen their communications resources to inform and effectively involve the larger community in order to gain needed support for public education.

Paradigm paralysis in education. The technologically, economical-ly, and culturally driven forces for fundamental societal and institu-tional change have unleashed a powerful, ideologically grounded political backlash against change that is felt most strongly in the education arena. Despite the shifts and trends noted here, local and state policies are pressuring educators to stick with traditional methods and processes and to disavow anything that might carry the label new or progressive.

Enter the Total Leader

All of these trends demand a lot of people in leadership positions. The essence of a Total Leader is openness, flexibility, empowerment, and a capacity to manage increasingly complex and dynamic changes. Total Leaders share similar characteristics, which will be explored in this book:

They are purpose-, value-, and vision-driven. Strategic, Information Age Total Leaders focus organizations on their funda-mental purpose for existing, their core values, and the vision of what they ideally want to become. These, in turn, become the key motivators of highly competent, empowered employees. By contrast, Industrial Age managers lead through hierarchical con-trol and focus organizations on past practices, precedents, and formal policies and procedures.

They are visionaries. Visionary leadership, a key component of Total Leadership, is about working with organizational members and constituents to create and communicate a concrete picture of an organization operating at its ideal best in a world of complex, dynamic change and to identify and define the processes and strategies needed for translating that picture into concrete action.

They rely on future forecasting. In an era of rapid and constant change, organizations must keep a steady eye on the future and chart their course on a clear picture of the conditions that will most likely affect their clients, markets, and processes. Staying in business is often a matter of continually engaging in competent and insightful trend tracking and aligning the organization with the results of those analyses.

They are lifelong learners. With knowledge doubling every two years and new technologies emerging monthly, Information Age leaders and employees are never finished learning. The key for Total Leaders is to provide useful learning experiences for themselves and their staffs and to establish clear and compelling ways for the organization to benefit from what everyone learns. Developing strategies for decision making based on new learning and developments is key to personal and organizational health and success.

Total Leaders in Education

Education leaders find themselves in an enormous quandary. As we have seen, they and their constituents live in a high-quality, global marketplace that:

- Is extraordinarily dynamic and driven by transformational technologies that are almost obsolete the moment they are installed;
- Demands organizations be client centered and nimble or face extinction;
- Offers employment conditions with limitless challenge, flexibility, and opportunity for the able, adept, and highly motivated but with increasingly limited opportunities for others;
- Contains an exploding knowledge base with limitless access;
- Functions within a society becoming more diverse and unequal every day and more divided about what to do about those differences and inequalities;

- Holds powerful political and cultural pressures for everyone to pull his or her own weight or reap the consequences; and
- Changes constantly.

It is in this milieu that school leaders are being asked to lead and for this milieu that their schools are presumably attempting to prepare young people. But education leaders must lead amidst the enormous inertia surrounding the basic structures, processes, roles, practices, and institutional forms that constitute public education — an inertia that Spady (1998) describes in *Paradigm Lost: Reclaiming America's Educational Future*. That inertia, described by Spady as "educentrism," is embedded in the laws and regulations that define education; institutionalized in the structures, cultures, and practices of public education; and ingrained in the minds of all who have spent their youth (and adulthood) in schools. When addressing educational change, we automatically start with what exists and try to improve it. We are stuck in an educentric paradigm. We simply know what schools are, what they do, how they're to be structured, and how they operate because that's how they were when we and our parents went there.

In the face of change, many Americans believe that at least schools should remain familiar and predictable. This acceptance and advocacy of the prevailing paradigm of education reflects thinking that is neither critical in an analytic sense nor systemic in an organizational sense. This helps explain why so much failed educational change is superficial, piecemeal, episodic, situational, and/or cosmetic.

Despite this paradigm inertia, we believe that the change forces surrounding education are compelling its local and state leaders to examine and alter the most basic features and assumptions of the existing system. To facilitate that process, we encourage leaders to look at their schools as a "systemic educational iceberg" as shown here. Their challenge as future-focused Total Leaders is to melt the iceberg.

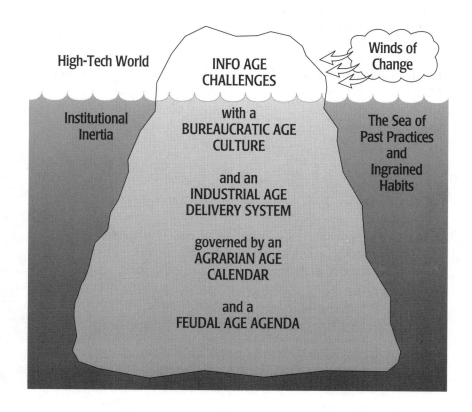

High-Tech World

INFO AGE
CHALLENGES

Winds of
Change

Institutional
Inertia

with a
BUREAUCRATIC AGE
CULTURE

The Sea of
Past Practices
and
Ingrained
Habits

and an
INDUSTRIAL AGE
DELIVERY SYSTEM

governed by an
AGRARIAN AGE
CALENDAR

and a
FEUDAL AGE AGENDA

Understanding the Educational Iceberg

To understand the educational iceberg, start by recognizing the numerous Information Age challenges you and your students now face. Heed Toffler's reminder that the Information Age isn't in some theoretical future; it is here embodied in the shifts and trends described earlier. But the systemic iceberg is influenced little by the winds of change blowing in the real world as long as it drifts in the sea of past practices and ingrained habits.

What resists the force of the wind are layers of established practice that reflect major eras of the past:

- A Bureaucratic Age culture that thinks and acts in terms of time, programs, procedures, means, teaching, and resources rather than standards, achievement, purposes, ends, learning, and results.

- An Industrial Age delivery system that operates like an assembly line with students and teachers moving from segment to segment through the curriculum at a uniform rate for the prescribed amount of time.
- An Agrarian Age calendar running from September until June around which everything is defined, including opportunity, access to instruction, curriculum, grade levels, reporting systems, credit, teaching assignments, and contracts.
- A Feudal Age agenda of sorting and selecting the faster from the slower, the academic from the practical, and the motivated from the uninspired, all under the assumption that only some children can learn the hard stuff.

Are there alternatives to this archaic collection of self-limiting, counter-productive features? Absolutely! Many of them are spelled out in Spady's book and resonate with the essence of Lewis Perelman's (1992) book *School's Out*, namely, that with today's technologies and information systems anyone can learn anything at anytime from anywhere.

What does it take to design and implement such an Information Age learning system? We'll discover the answer as we explore Total Leadership, the focus of the chapters that follow.

CHAPTER 2

The Essence of Total Leaders

---

*Total Leaders are individuals who embody all
of the performance abilities and attributes
needed to erect the pillars of productive
change and carry out the essential processes
that make successful systemic change happen.*

A long with futurist literature, we've been studying major books on
leadership and organizational change. Most of them focus on the
business world rather than education because, until recently, the
challenging realities business faced attracted most of the world's best
organizational researchers, consultants, and writers. Business encountered a simple reality: Maintaining the status quo was not an option; it
was the kiss of death.

Now it's education's turn.

The 100 or so books we have synthesized and applied in our work
focus on leaders who have decisively moved their organizations off
dead center and out of their comfort and danger zones in the face of
challenging realities. We're not talking about technical tinkering or seg-
mental change (see Spady 1996c and 1998); we're talking about productive change that is comprehensive, systemic, and paradigm breaking. Productive change is defined by five explicit criteria:

It takes. Things that matter actually change.

Results improve. It leads to consistently improved outcomes.

Functions improve. It involves more effective ways of operating.

It enhances. It motivates and benefits all those involved.

It lasts. The improvements keep on improving.

Our experience suggests that only when all five criteria are met do organizations experience and sustain productive change.

Not all leaders highlighted in the literature operated in the same ways to achieve productive change, and not all of the experts and gurus who describe their efforts emphasize the same things. For example, there are significant differences between the works of Warren Bennis and W. Edwards Deming, between Kenneth Blanchard and Michael Hammer, or Stephen Covey and Peter Senge, or Peter Drucker and Tom Peters. But our continuing analysis of all their work and our ongoing commitment to integrate and apply the best of it to education began to reveal patterns, complementarities, and similarities that intrigued us. It seemed to us that they all had something important to contribute to the total picture of leadership and change, but no single person was describing the picture in its entirety. When we finally found enough consistency and replication across these many studies and books, we formed our own synthesis picture of the Total Leader.

The Grounding of Total Leaders

Today's leaders aren't what they used to be. We've found that they're more, and they're less, than they were in previous years. While this is an especially challenging era for education as well as business leaders, it is not an impossible one in which to lead adaptable, productive organizations. As Daryl Conner (1992) notes, today's leaders are operating their organizations "at the speed of change" and being driven by the major shifts and trends described in chapter 1. Moreover, today's leaders are expected to involve and empower their people, to be visible to their employees and constituents, to act with integrity, and to be accountable for their organization's performance and results.

This leadership pendulum is making a big swing from an older, entrenched authoritarian style in which decisions were viewed as black and white, to one in which decisions are seen as situational, paradoxical, and even non-rational and shaped by a democratic or participative style (Wheatley 1992). Today's leaders must be more like Jesus than John Wayne, more Ghandi than Vince Lombardi, and more Mother Theresa than Machiavelli. Total Leaders are capable of striking the beneficial balance. They strive to be decisive and build consensus, embrace core values and be tolerant, exercise productive power and empower others, evaluate and coach, be firm and care about others, and remain concerned about the bottom line while supporting creativity.

The Key Paradigm of Total Leaders

The common theme running throughout futurist and leadership literature that has most influenced our work is the inevitability of change. It's everywhere. You can't deny or hide from change. It's constant, accelerating, and here to stay. In this new era of rapid rather than gradual change, organisms and organizations face a certain reality—either adapt, change, and survive, or die. Considering the alternative, change doesn't look that bad, particularly to Total Leaders.

Openness to change creates and sustains personal and organizational health and security. It is through this paradigm that Total Leaders perceive their world and act on it. The statement's essence is the phrase, "openness to change." One can begin the statement with this phrase, pick and combine either verb in the statement with either adjective and either noun, and come up with a series of smaller statements that are all true for Total Leaders. For example, openness to change creates organizational health. Or, openness to change sustains personal security. And so forth.

In a world of constant change, Total Leaders view stability as the source of the problem, not the solution. In heart, mind, and action, they are change agents. Total Leaders pull into the parking lot on Friday mornings wondering what they can still do this week to create significant change. Others pull in wondering how to keep the lid on until next week, at least.

The Key Purposes of Total Leaders

Total Leaders are purposeful visionaries; they look outside of "the box" for possibilities and solutions, take initiative, are persuasive, and get results. They also balance overt attention to customer and client needs with a concern for the internal quality and effectiveness of their organizations.

This simultaneous external and internal focus is reflected in Total Leaders' two fundamental reasons for being.

Their externally focused purpose is *to create quality products and services that meet or exceed the present, emerging, and future needs of customers.* Fulfilling this purpose is key to ensuring their organization's reputation, competitiveness, and future security.

Their internally focused purpose is *to empower and motivate employees to give their best to accomplish their organization's mission and vision.* Fulfilling this purpose is key to ensuring their organization's vitality, health, and effectiveness.

These two purposes serve as a Total Leader's overriding priorities and decision screen. Total Leaders use this screen before setting priorities and agendas, and when assessing their organization's productivity and health. Despite daily distractions, they consciously use these purposes to set their calendars and focus their time and attention. This way they can readily assess which of their meetings, activities, and travels have been worthwhile and which were a waste of time. Of course, these two purposes also serve as Total Leaders' major criteria in evaluating their own job performance and effectiveness.

The Key Premises of Total Leaders

Premises are the fundamental assumptions and beliefs on which people ground their behavior and work. These beliefs serve as filters for perceiving and interpreting what exists and what choices are available, and as important shapers of behavior. For example, supervisors who believe that most people are naturally lazy and irresponsible will usually end up treating their employees accordingly and using tight direction, close supervision, and extrinsic rewards as motivators. On the other hand, those who, like Peters and Waterman (1982), believe that most people are conscientious and want to do a good job, behave consistently with that belief.

Total Leaders take the time to deeply reflect on and identify what their key operating premises are, and come down strongly on the side of employee empowerment. They believe that:

- All members of the organization have the right to find meaning in their work;
- Employees want to contribute, be responsible, and achieve at high levels, and will if given the opportunity; and
- Leaders have the power and responsibility to create and maintain a culture of innovation, cooperation, success, and sustained organizational health.

Total Leaders see the personnel glass as half full rather than half empty. With these three premises, they are psychologically positioned to tap and use the inherent talent, motivation, and pride in their employees, and to lead rather than coerce. Without premises like those of Total Leaders, effective leadership over the long haul is impossible.

The Key Principles of Total Leaders

While premises may operate at an unconscious level most of the time, guiding principles are different. They are the fundamental, self-imposed rules of behavior that form our internal compass and decision screen. We are aware of them whenever we face a difficult problem or have to make a tough decision. Not only can Total Leaders proudly describe and explain the key principles that guide their behavior, they also define their personal integrity around these key principles. Total Leaders know when they are being true to those principles, and they feel pain and guilt when they are not. Because so many people depend on knowing what the leader's operating principles are, these principles must be made public. How else can leaders or their subordinates be empowered or held accountable for their decisions and actions?

Our reading of the literature indicates that Total Leaders consciously and consistently act on four key leadership principles:

- Honest communication, which keeps all organizational members informed, focused, and motivated. Total Leaders are honest without being brutal.
- Win-win relationships, which foster the dignity and contribution of each individual. Total Leaders believe that success is not a "zero-sum" game.
- Acknowledged power, which results in empowered and committed personnel. Total Leaders don't believe they actually make people powerful or actively empower them. Instead, they believe that a tremendous amount of power lies within each person and that their role is to create work environments that let that power and capability emerge.
- Shared rewards, which match group and organizational accomplishments. Total Leaders distribute the organization's tangible and intangible rewards proportionately to those who make the contributions and generate the success. Shared rewards is a direct response to the disproportionate salaries and benefits that some

executives receive compared to their main line employees, and an acknowledgment of the contribution rank and file employees make — 50 times greater — to the organization's successes.

The Five Pillars of Productive Change

Long before our analysis and synthesis of this massive literature began in earnest, we focused on defining and implementing what we now call the pillars or essential conditions of productive change. These are the make-it or break-it factors that have to be in place in order for significant change to take hold in an organization. We thought there were four of them—vision, ownership, capacity, and support—and we knew that all four had to be strong and in place or change efforts would falter.

Our more recent analysis and synthesis efforts, however, indicate that we were on the right track but one pillar short. Purpose, which we initially perceived to be a part of vision, is not only a distinct pillar of productive change, it is the *key* to lasting change and the glue that holds change efforts together.

The ultimate goal for Total Leaders then is to establish and sustain the five pillars of change throughout their organizations. These pillars are:

Purpose — "It has meaning for me." Purpose is the deep reason the organization exists, which employees must share in order to find value and meaning in their work and constituents must endorse in order to identify with organizational aims.

Purpose lies at the very heart of both organizational change and organizational success. Establishing purpose is a Total Leader's most basic and important task. When purpose is clear, heartfelt, and personally fulfilling, it is the driving force of successful change. With it, employees and constituents can easily recognize, identify with, and embrace what the organization is there to accomplish.

Vision —"It's clear and exciting." Vision is the Total Leader's blueprint and road map for change. A clear and compelling vision statement brings the purpose to life, provides a concrete description of what the organization will be like when operating at its ideal best, and gives everyone in the district and community a clear direction to pursue and standard against which to measure their performance and results.

Ownership — "I want to be part of it." Ownership is the strong identification with, investment in, and commitment to the organization's purpose and vision statement.

The motivational fuel of successful change, ownership is the result of employee and constituent investment in and commitment to what their organization is doing. This heavy involvement of employees and constituents in both designing and carrying out an organization's purpose and vision makes the organization theirs, not just the leader's.

Capacity — "I can do it." Capacity is the knowledge, skills, resources, and tools needed to successfully make the changes implied in the organization's stated purpose and vision statement.

Capacity is the "know how" and "how to" pillar. It embodies the entire array of knowledge, information, understanding, skills, processes, technologies, and resources that enables employees to carry out the desired change competently. Purpose, vision, and ownership primarily affect employee motivation to engage in productive change; capacity is about the ability to do so.

Support — "Our leader is helping us do it." Support comprises the policies, decisions, attention, resources, and procedures that enable employees and constituents to make and sustain the changes implied in the purpose and vision.

What Might Happen Without the Five Pillars of Productive Change?

The five pillars of productive change are the key elements that make up the chemistry needed for successful change to occur. Leave one element out and the balance is destroyed. For example,

- Without purpose, the organization lacks the reason to change.
- Without vision, the organization lacks a clear road map for change.
- Without ownership, the organization lacks the commitment needed for change to succeed.
- Without capacity, the organization lacks the ability to succeed.
- Without support, the organization lacks the opportunity to succeed.

Total Leaders constantly work to keep this chemistry balanced in their organizations.

Support is the organization's "proof of the pudding" — its willingness and ability to put itself and its resources squarely behind its declared purpose and vision and the people it's counting on to make them happen. Support reflects Total Leaders' commitment to and involvement in the change process.

The Five Performance Domains of Total Leaders

Ultimately, Total Leaders are defined by what they do to activate and apply the paradigm, purposes, premises, and principles described earlier in establishing these five pillars of productive change. All the ideas from the major studies, books, gurus, and training programs about leadership and change today fit into five broad clusters that we call *domains of leadership performance.*

After establishing the nature of each leadership domain, we described them as authentic, visionary, cultural, quality, and service. Each domain has its own set of proponents, experts, and practitioners, and each embodies a distinctive set of leadership performance roles and skills.

The Authentic Leadership Domain

The authentic leadership domain is about establishing and embodying purpose, values, and meaning throughout the organization. Authentic leaders engage employees and other constituents in reflecting deeply on and clarifying their organization's fundamental purpose and mission, the core organizational values and professional principles that embrace that purpose, and how their work as individuals can fully embody and support that purpose.

Authentic leadership establishes the moral and philosophical bedrock on which the organization operates and defines the absolute core of why the organization exists. Authentic leaders carry out three interrelated performance roles:

- Creating and sustaining a compelling personal and organizational purpose;
- Being the lead learner; and
- Modeling the core organizational values and principles of professionalism.

Each of these performance roles of the authentic leaders is described in Chapter 3.

Among the experts whose work emphasizes the authentic leadership domain are Kenneth Blanchard and Norman Vincent Peale (1988); William Bridges (1980); Tom Chapell (1993); Robert Cooper and Ayman Sawaf (1996); Stephen Covey (1989 and 1991); Covey, Roger Merrill, and Rebecca Merrill (1994); Victor Frankl (1984); Howard Gardner (1995); William Glasser (1994); Daniel Goleman (1995); John Kotter (1996); James Kouzes and Barry Poser (1993); Peter Senge (1990); Margaret Wheatley (1992); and David Whyte (1994).

The Visionary Leadership Domain

The visionary leadership domain is about creating innovative possibilities that shape organizational direction and performance. Visionary leaders involve employees and other constituents in a thorough investigation of the challenges and opportunities facing their organization's future and the potential courses of action.

Visionary leaders look far beyond the tried and true, develop the future-focused and creative orientation on which their organizations depend in a world of constant change, and establish the concrete, innovative road map of where their organizations must go and how they must operate to meet the changing and escalating needs and expectations of their customers.

They do so through three interrelated performance roles, which are described in Chapter 4:

• Defining and pursuing a preferred organizational future;
• Consistently employing a client focus; and
• Expanding organizational perspectives and options.

Among the experts whose work emphasizes the visionary leadership domain are Warren Bennis and Burt Nanus (1985); Gerald Celente (1990); Peter Drucker (1992); Andrew Grove (1996); Gary Hamel and C. K. Prahalad (1994); James Liebig (1994); Dudley Lynch and Paul Kordis (1988); Gareth Morgan (1993); Burt Nanus (1992); Morris Schechtman (1994); Michael Tracey and Fred Wiersema (1995); and Fred Wiersema (1996).

The Cultural Leadership Domain

The cultural leadership domain is about developing meaning and ownership for innovation and quality throughout the organization. Cultural leaders reach out to and actively engage all employees and constituents in ongoing activities that highlight the integrity and importance of the organization's declared purpose and vision, foster healthy and positive values and relationships among employees and constituents, and directly encourage employee and constituent ownership in charting and implementing the organization's course toward productive change.

Cultural leadership is people-oriented and creates an optimistic, inclusive, participatory, and healthy organizational climate. Cultural leaders carry out three interrelated performance roles, which are described in Chapter 5:

- Involving everyone in productive change;
- Developing a change-friendly culture of innovation, healthy relationships, quality, and success; and
- Creating meaning for everyone.

Among the experts whose work emphasizes the cultural leadership domain are Stephen Carter (1996); Stephen Covey (1989); Thomas Crum (1987); Terrence Deal and Alan Kennedy (1982); Robert Heller (1995); Eric Hoffer (1963); Ralph Kilmann and colleagues (1985); Ed Oakley and Doug Krug (1991); Thomas Sergiovanni (1990); and James O'Toole (1995).

The Quality Leadership Domain

The quality leadership domain is about building continuous improvement capacities and strategies throughout the organization. Quality leaders build the personal and organizational capacity to achieve and sustain continuous improvement and productive change. They must also initiate and actively participate in ongoing activities that continuously expand the pertinent knowledge and skills of employees, set high standards for quality results throughout the organization, and use timely and accurate information to continuously improve the organization's capacity to operate effectively.

Quality leadership is focused on improving personal and organizational productivity and excellence, and on stimulating employees to grow and develop as people. It does so through the actions that quality leaders carry out through the three interrelated performance roles described in Chapter 6:

- Developing and empowering everyone,
- Improving the organization's performance standards and results, and
- Creating and using feedback loops to improve performance.

Among the experts whose work emphasizes the quality leadership domain are Kenneth Blanchard and colleagues (1985); Peter Block (1987); James Collins and Jerry Porras (1994); Philip Crosby (1979 and 1989); W. Edwards Deming (1986); Max DePree (1989); Lloyd Dobyns and Clare Crawford-Mason (1991); Robert Kaplan and David Norton (1996); William Ouchi (1982); Richard Pascale and Anthony Athos (1981); Tom Peters (1992); Peters and Robert Waterman (1982); and Mary Walton (1986).

The Service Leadership Domain

The service leadership domain is about supporting empowered workers to accomplish the organization's purpose and vision. Service leaders make the tough decisions and create enlightened policies, expanded opportunities, necessary resources, and flexible procedures that maximize employees' talents and teamwork, consistently support their best efforts, and accomplish the organization's purpose and vision.

Service leadership focuses on ensuring that organizational structures and procedures clearly help productive things happen. It does so through the actions that service leaders carry out through the three interrelated performance roles discussed in Chapter 7:

- Supporting and managing the organization's purpose and vision,
- Restructuring to achieve intended results, and
- Rewarding positive contributions to productive change.

Among the experts whose work emphasizes the service leadership domain are James Autry (1991); Warren Bennis and Patricia Biederman (1997); William Bridges (1991); Peter Drucker (1995); Robert Greenleaf (1991); Michael Hammer and James Champy (1993); Paul Hersey (1984); Hersey and Kenneth Blanchard (1972); George Labovitz and Victor Rosansky (1997); and Douglas Smith (1996).

How the Domains and Pillars of Change Connect

Unique things emerged from our study of the five domains and their performance roles. We realized that each domain was explicitly connected to one of the five essential pillars of change. In fact, a specific pillar of change was each domain's key reason for being. And it became clear that Total Leaders must operate in all five domains.

In other words, each domain of leadership performance has an explicit purpose, and that purpose is to establish one of the essential pillars of change. Until all five pillars are established, one cannot be a Total Leader or successfully achieve and sustain productive change. Something critical would be missing! These five sets of critical connections are outlined in Figure 2.1 and detailed in the rest of this book.

As our work progressed in building a comprehensive synthesis of the literature, we made three further discoveries.

FIGURE 2.1 The Performance Domains and Purposes of Total Leaders

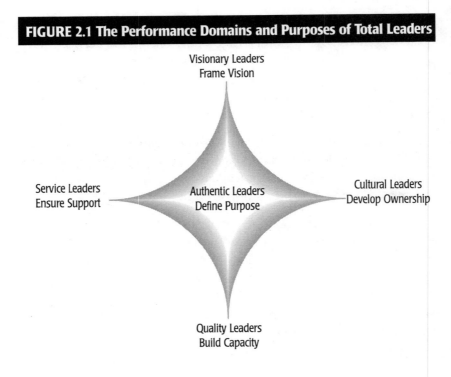

Visionary Leaders
Frame Vision

Service Leaders
Ensure Support

Authentic Leaders
Define Purpose

Cultural Leaders
Develop Ownership

Quality Leaders
Build Capacity

First, in exercising these performance domains, Total Leaders consistently advocate and operate according to a definable set of values and principles.

Second, there are two kinds of leadership described in the literature. One is about helping organizations operate more effectively at what they have been doing. The other, Total Leadership, is about helping organizations undertake and achieve future-focused, continuous, productive change. This second kind of leadership dominates most of the literature we have reviewed, is inseparable from the change process itself, and represents the essence of this book.

Third, there is a definable set of actions carried out within each performance domain that enables leaders to achieve a key pillar of change.

These five purposeful, simultaneous sets of actions are what we call the processes of change. As portrayed in figure 2.2, there is a distinctive process connected to each domain that allows the organization to establish a particular pillar of change.

These five processes — consideration, exploration, enrollment, development, and orchestration — are essential for Total Leaders to implement. Without them, achieving productive change is next to impossible.

Each of these processes is defined and described more fully in the following chapters.

FIGURE 2.2 The Total Leadership Change Process Connection

Performance Domain	(uses)	Change Process	(to achieve)	Pillar of Change
Authentic Leadership		Consideration		Purpose
Visionary Leadership		Exploration		Vision
Cultural Leadership		Enrollment		Ownership
Quality Leadership		Development		Capacity
Service Leadership		Orchestration		Support

The Moral Foundation of Total Leaders

In *Principle-Centered Leadership*, Stephen Covey (1990) teaches us that a clear set of positive values, when consistently acted upon, are at the heart of living a happy and successful life, and that core organizational values and leadership principles are at the heart of effective leadership. For Covey, it all begins from that values base; without that base, we lack a true north on our personal or organizational compasses.

Total Leaders intentionally create that values base. They involve the total organization in inquiring about, reflecting upon, and defining core organizational values, and they make those values part of the dialogue when considering important decisions. Because of their moral foundation, they are able to lead moral and ethical organizations.

In addition, Tom Chapell (1993) shows us in *The Soul of a Business* how we can "do well by doing good." Chapell clearly demonstrates that leaders can act on a strong moral foundation and still have a very attractive bottom line, even over the long haul. In today's society, when businesses are beginning to be rewarded by customers for modeling morality, we may even be at a point where the bottom line is enhanced by a strong moral foundation.

Our experiences clearly indicate that, by contrast, those individuals and organizations that have not taken the time to be explicit about their values are just not value-driven decision makers and tend to lose the trust of their employees and customers in the process.

Total Leaders have the advantage of standing on and working from a moral foundation made up of three elements:

Personal values. Personal values are compelling standards related to what individuals believe to be right, fair, honorable, important, and worthy of consistent attention and action. For example, if you value the inherent worth of people, you will find a way to treat everyone with whom you come into contact with dignity, even when a person has harmed you or your organization. Personal values are the first step in forming the moral pillar of authentic leaders described in Chapter 3.

Core organizational values. These are values that are widely under-stood, publicly endorsed, and consistently acted upon by the organization and each of its members. For example, if your organization values openness, you will have no qualms about making all the clauses of your contract public, even when you know that you may be perceived as greedy by some constituencies.

Principles of professionalism. These principles are ethical rules or decisions and performances that transcend personal considera-tions and circumstantial pressures and that promote the higher good of the organization and its clients. For example, if you value the professional principle of alignment, you will select the person whose competences, background, and personality best fit the job, even when a personal friend has seniority and expects the posi-tion to be his or hers.

The major difference between personal values and core values is that the latter are embraced by everyone in the organization and not just isolated individuals. Our analysis indicates that Total Leaders go well beyond simply using their personal values, the organization's core values, and the principles of professionalism as their personal deci-sion screen. They also:

- Model the core values and the professional principles for others and are aware that they are modeling with a purpose;
- Formalize and communicate their core organizational values so that everyone knows what's important, what's expected, and how peo-ple will be held accountable for upholding the values;
- Use their core values as a screen for all important decisions to ensure that they will always be, and be seen, acting on them; and
- Make value-based decision making the norm throughout the orga-nization so that their moral foundation will have a life of its own.

Our synthesis of the leadership and organizational change literature shows a strong consensus regarding these core values and principles of professionalism, which are consistently associated with effective leadership and with effective organizations that are built to last and provide a great deal of meaning and satisfaction for their employees.

Ten Core Organizational Values of Total Leaders

The 10 powerful core organizational values consistently embraced and modeled by Total Leaders are:

- Reflection
- Honesty
- Openness
- Courage
- Integrity
- Commitment
- Excellence
- Productivity
- Risk Taking
- Teamwork

Some of these core values may not appear to be values, but rather psychological traits and orientations. What elevates them to the values status is that Total Leaders, through modeling and influence, make them an organizational norm. For example, when Total Leaders behave openly toward new ideas, it could be argued that they just happen to have that psychological disposition. But when they make openness to new ideas a visible everyday practice and an organizational norm, we believe that openness becomes a value.

Ten Principles of Professionalism

The principles of professionalism are a bit different from personal or core organizational values. They are about how leaders think, decide, and behave as ethical professionals. While closely associated with, complementary to, and supportive of core values, the principles of professionalism of Total Leaders provide the moral and procedural rules by which organizational members are expected to behave.

Productive change efforts strengthen as well as benefit from the consistent application of principles of professionalism. Our reading of the literature indicates that they can serve as both the criteria for defining and judging professionalism in today's complex world, and as the operating ethos of genuine learning organizations. Because these principles are particularly powerful when translated into formal agreements or covenants about how people in organizations will make decisions and act, Total Leaders may establish them as the organization's expectations for behavior and/or even establish them as the organization's moral contract with itself.

The 10 powerful principles of professionalism are:

- Inquiry
- Connection
- Future-focusing
- Clarity
- Inclusiveness
- Win-win
- Accountability
- Improvement
- Alignment
- Contribution

Throughout the next five chapters, each of these principles and core values will be defined and explained in relation to the particular leadership domain and change process with which it has the strongest connection.

Profile of Authentic Leaders

The guru   Stephen Covey

An exemplar   Mahatma Gandhi

An antithesis   Richard Nixon (enjoyed temporary suc-
                       cesses until his core values were
                       exposed)

Mind set   It is only when one has become an
                       authentic, value-driven person that he or
                       she is able to morally and effectively
                       lead others.

Purpose   To establish a deep and compelling
                       organizational purpose.

Focus   Personal values and life mission
                       Core organizational values
                       Doing well while doing good

Change belief   Change happens when there is a com-
                       pelling reason to change.

Performance roles   Creating a compelling purpose
                       Being the lead learner
                       Modeling core values and declared
                       principles

Key sources   *Credibility* (Kouzes and Posner 1993)
                       Executive EQ (Cooper and Sawaf 1996)
                       Principle-Centered Leadership (Covey
                           1991)
                       The Soul of a Business (Chapell 1993)
                       *The Seven Habits of Highly Effective
                           People* (Covey 1989)
                       The Fifth Discipline (Senge 1990)
                       Leading Change (Kotter 1996)

CHAPTER 3

The Authentic Leadership Domain: Total Leaders Defining Purpose

---

Total Leadership starts with and revolves around authentic leadership. Its moral and psychological character and influence pervade everything an organization does.

T om Chappel calls it *The Soul of a Business*. Ken Blanchard and Norman Vincent Peale see it as *The Power of Ethical Management*. To Stephen Covey, it's *Principle–Centered Leadership;* to Daniel Goleman, it's *Emotional Intelligence;* and to James Kotter, it's the essence of *Leading Change*. For Robert Cooper and Ayman Sawaf, it all adds up to *Executive EQ*, and for James Kouzes and Barry Posner, it comes down to a single word, *Credibility*. We call it:

Authentic leadership, the true heart, soul, and purposeful central domain of Total Leadership.

Total Leadership starts with and revolves around authentic leadership. Its moral and psychological character and influence pervade everything an organization does. The purposeful way in which all five Total Leadership domains are carried out depends on the character and actions of leaders who are authentic in every sense of the word.

The Essence of Authentic Leaders

Authentic leaders are masters of personal meaning and purpose. There is nothing pretentious or artificial about them. Their essence is value based and personally grounded.

The Logic Behind the Authentic leader

The logic of the essence of the authentic leader can be described by the following.

- You have to be a person to be a leader.
- Who you are as a person will ultimately be reflected in your leadership.
- If you don't have your personal act together, don't expect to have your leadership act together.
- Developing yourself as a leader begins with personal reflection, personal assessment, and personal growth.
- Organizational change will reflect the personal change and character you model in both your personal and leadership life.

The categories we used in the first half of Chapter 2 to define the grounding of Total Leaders equally apply to all of us as persons. Although we might not have framed and articulated these categories so precisely, we all operate from a fundamental paradigm perspective about life, have deeply grounded purposes for our lives, operate from premises and assumptions, and act and make decisions consistent with certain key principles.

A difference between us and authentic leaders may be that they have consciously and deeply reflected on these matters, achieved the blend of personal and leadership orientations shown in the sidebar below, and developed their inner being around that blend. For others, these remain the profound first steps in becoming the leader they want to be.

The Blend and Consistent Alignment of Personal and Leadership Grounding

How closely do your personal and leadership orientations lie? Here's one way to compare them.

You as a Person	You as a Leader
Personal Values	Moral Compass
Personal Ethics	Leadership Principles
Life Purpose	Organizational Purpose
Personal Vision	Ideal Organization
Personal Integrity	Organizational Culture
Personal Reputation	Organizational Reputation

The specific nature of the personal characteristics that define the authentic leader are beautifully described in Cooper and Sawaf's (1996) book, *Executive EQ*. At their core, authentic leaders manifest high levels of:

- Self-awareness of their feelings and actions.
- Self-control of their feelings and gratification needs.
- Sensitivity and empathy toward others.
- Trustworthiness toward and in relationships.
- Openness to new ideas and experiences.
- Integrity to walk their talk and talk their walk.
- Intuition that puts them in touch with their subconscious "flow."
- Resilience and adaptability in the face of disappointments.
- Renewal and optimism when faced with the challenge of change.
- Laughter and fun, especially when the going gets tough.

In short, authentic leaders are those who many seek out to be their best friend. They have their inner and interpersonal acts together as reflective, open, and honest human beings. But authentic leaders are more than morally and psychologically healthy people. They lead by example and by establishing the most important thing in an organizational change process: its purpose.

The Purpose of Authentic Leaders

As we explained in the latter half of Chapter 2, the fundamental purpose of authentic leaders in a productive change process is to orchestrate and shape their organization's purpose defining process. Quite simply, people and organizations do not change if they perceive everything to be going well today, with similarly bright days waiting ahead.

Change is much more attractive when people feel threatened or when they sense an opportunity. Purpose defines and reflects those reasons to change. In today's world, the threat is always there, even when one is on top. The case that Andrew Grove (1996), Intel's CEO, makes about this in his book is simple, *Only the Paranoid Survive.*

Purpose is the absolute bedrock of everything related to organizational effectiveness and productivity. As Total Leaders view and use it, purpose:

- Is the declared reason the organization exists;
- Defines what the organization is there to accomplish;
- Focuses all organizational decisions and actions;
- Inspires and embodies core values and principles of professionalism;
- Gives meaning to the work of organizational members;
- Provides the rationale for the organization's vision, expectations; intended outcomes, and priorities;
- Conveys to customers and constituents what the organization stands for;
- Builds employee and client trust, identification, and motivation; and
- Lies at the heart of organizational change and success.

In its broadest sense, purpose comprises three key elements that are explained later in this chapter: beliefs and values, mission, and organizational (i.e., student) outcomes. Without these, employees go through the motions or do their own thing, constituents wonder about the course of the organization, and change efforts falter due to apathy and distrust. Defining a compelling purpose is the authentic leader's most basic and important task, and they do it through the major change process we call *consideration.*

Opening Our Eyes to What Exists

Of the five change processes — consideration, exploration, enrollment, development, and orchestration — consideration is the most central and fundamental.

Consideration is the introspective, honest, and empathetic search for, dialogue about, and acknowledgment of two things:
- Changes, new conditions, and new realities facing an organization and its employees, students, and constituents; and
- Truths, meaning, values, and purpose on which an organization's effectiveness and success ultimately rests.

When led by capable authentic leaders and shaped by core values of reflection and honesty, the consideration process engages organizational members and constituents in a truthful, ongoing search for the deeper essence, meaning, and values that define and embody their organization's ultimate reason for existing, that is, its purpose and mission.

For many people, this process of serious, collective introspection, self-examination, and revelation represents an exciting time of major focusing and growth. For others, however, the consideration process brings risk, vulnerability, and uncertainty. This combination of potential opportunity and threat occurs because consideration involves raising and dealing with issues such as:

- Discovering what needs to be accomplished,
- Waking up to reality,
- Looking beneath the surface of issues and problems,
- Acknowledging the unacknowledged,
- Shedding light on things long kept in the dark,
- Searching deeply for underlying causes, meaning, or explanations, and
- Becoming sensitive to painful organizational issues and experiences.

Some organizational members and constituents openly welcome this kind of dialogue and revelation; others fear it. Consequently, wise authentic leaders establish an organizational safety zone. This zone is a location, process for, and set of formally acknowledged and endorsed ground rules that directly encourage, honor, and protect each individual's right to discuss sensitive issues and feelings openly and honestly without fear of criticism, censure, or recrimination.

Otherwise, serious introspection and the open expression of ideas, values, and feelings that consideration requires can be too easily pooh-poohed or negatively exploited by those less sensitive to their essential role in fostering productive change.

With such a zone in place, which Spady (1996c and 1998) calls the learning circle, the consideration process allows the members of an organization to perceive, acknowledge, and eventually move beyond what many may have experienced as a familiar, comfortable, but stagnant personal and organizational dead center.

This dead center keeps people and organizations stuck in one place, inhibits their effectiveness, and diminishes their integrity and well-being. By breaking the psychological and behavioral inertia that pervades so many organizations, the consideration process ultimately allows organizational members and constituents to overtly acknowledge that "something different and better is needed here, and we'd better start searching for what it is."

This collective recognition that has worked in the past is no longer working well and will not work in the future requires lots of courage and character, and is usually mixed with both anxiety and enormous relief. Fortunately, it encourages everyone to take a hard look at what's true about their strengths and limitations as individuals, and what they can willingly and successfully contribute to defining and achieving the organization's ultimate purpose. When handled well, this hard and deep look allows people to see familiar things in new ways and to use those new perspectives to develop ideas, consider possibilities, acquire different thinking, and discover the deeper purpose of making major change.

Consideration is an ongoing component of a productive change process, not a discrete stage or event in that process. It continues as long as the overall change effort lasts and directly supports the functioning and success of the other four change processes: exploration, enrollment, development, and orchestration.

The Moral Foundation of Authentic Leaders

As they carry out the performance roles to orchestrate the consideration process, authentic leaders rely on a moral foundation for their success. Besides specifically employing the core organizational values of reflection and honesty, they also place special emphasis on the inquiry and connection principles of professionalism.

Authentic leaders use ...
- *Core values of reflection and honesty*
- *Principles of inquiry and connection*

Reflection is the process of using a values decision screen to review, assess, and judge the decisions you and your organization have made or will make, and the actions you and your organization have taken or will take. When this process is encouraged, honored, and endorsed by the organization, reflection becomes a core value. Reflection is essential to both Total Leadership and productive change because it fosters as well as reflects a thoughtful, sensitive, logical, and empathetic orientation to people, issues, and situations. Reflection encourages a deep internal and external probing of past actions, possibilities, and solutions, and discourages impulsive, arbitrary, and simplistic decision making and behavior. Simply put, Total Leaders are reflective people.

Honesty is being truthful while being sensitive to the thoughts, needs, and feelings of others. The absence of manipulation and deceit, honesty is embodied in communication that is open, frank, and sincere. Honesty is the bedrock of trust, consistency, loyalty, and trustworthiness without which healthy relationships and productive organizational action are difficult to generate and impossible to sustain. Total Leaders are honest even when it causes them to risk themselves, because their organizations' welfare depends on it and because their integrity demands it.

Inquiry represents the honest search for personal and organizational purpose, rich and broad perspectives on complex issues, and a deep understanding of ideas and possibilities. It means being open to all that is out there. It involves a deep personal reflection about, and a rigorous analysis of, purpose and meaning, information, theory and research, ideas, beliefs, and values.

Total Leaders think of inquiry as both a state of mind and a way of operating. Inquiry prevents organizational members from making snap decisions, from getting boxed in by outdated traditions and practices, and from missing out on newly discovered processes or technologies. Inquiry has to do with studying and learning, with testing theories, with knowing and applying the research regarding leadership and your profession, and with listening to the recognized experts in your field. Inquiry allows Total Leaders to become aware of others' options before making important decisions, and to identify insightful and creative opportunities for productive change.

Connection represents one's deep and genuine relationship with, and appreciation of, the value, intellectual, and feeling dimensions in oneself and others. Connection is about your "EQ," the emotional equivalent of your IQ (see the Cooper and Sawaf elements on page 77). Connection is the awareness of the many dimensions of human talent, respect for the exploration and development of these dimensions in self and others, and sensitivity to both the similarities and differences among people along these three dimensions. Most of all, it involves responding in words and deeds, positively and empathetically, to the expression of these dimensions in oneself and in others.

Connection compels people to pay attention to and acknowledge what is going on with themselves — thoughts, feelings, experiences, actions, results — among their work mates, and within their organization as a whole. Total Leaders are aware of the power of emotional intelligence, have a "high EQ," and realize that people can increase their EQs with study, work, and connection.

Together, these four moral foundation elements strongly bolster the orientations and activities that consideration demands of organizational members.

Here are the kinds of situations in which you might be challenged to apply these four Moral Foundation elements:

Reflection: You become aware of new research about how children learn and you realize that your schools and teachers are out of synch with these findings.

Honesty: You are evaluating a teacher who has become a rather close friend and you do not believe he is meeting your high standards.

Inquiry: Your system does not have a clearly articulated set of beliefs regarding children and learning or teachers and teaching. You want to create a consensus about what the members of the organization believe about these two key issues.

Connection: You are meeting with angry parents from a different culture than yours, and you do not understand why they are making such a big issue now over something you think has happened regularly without incident in the past.

Critical Performance Roles of Authentic Leaders

To implement the consideration process as effectively as possible, authentic leaders implement three major sets of responsibilities, which we call performance roles. These broad arenas of action enable authentic leaders to make the decisions and carry out the plans that constitute the consideration process and achieve the pillar of change to which it is linked, organizational purpose. The three critical performance roles of the authentic leader are:

- Creating and sustaining a compelling personal and organizational purpose.
- Being the lead learner.
- Modeling core organizational values and the principles of professionalism.

The 15 Performance Roles of a Total Leader

- Creating and sustaining a compelling personal and organizational purpose.
- Being the lead learner.
- Modeling core organizational values and personal principles.
- Defining and pursuing a preferred organizational future.
- Consistently employing a client focus.
- Expanding organizational perspectives and options.
- Involving everyone in productive change.
- Developing a change-friendly culture of innovation, healthy relationships, quality, and success.
- Creating meaning for everyone.
- Developing and empowering everyone.
- Improving the organization's performance standards and results.
- Creating and using feedback loops to improve performance.
- Supporting and managing the organization's purpose and vision.
- Restructuring to achieve intended results.
- Rewarding positive contributions to productive change.

As in the other four leadership domains described in the following chapters, the first of the three performance roles listed is most central to carrying out its domain's particular change process and for achieving its essential pillar of change. The other two performance roles directly support and complement the first. However, we'll give specific attention to all three roles in each domain because they constitute the heart of Total Leadership in action.

Performance Role 1: Creating a Compelling Purpose

All 15 performance roles of the Total Leader are important, but creating a compelling purpose is the top priority. Not only is this performance role the most closely associated with the purest definition of leadership, it is also a prerequisite for the other 14 performance roles since an organization's compelling purpose virtually drives everything else it does.

When Total Leaders create a compelling purpose in a manner that builds commitment, the other 14 performance roles can easily flow from it. But if an organization lacks a compelling purpose, the other 14 are very difficult or impossible to implement successfully. This will become evident as we identify and describe each role in the chapters that follow.

Our analysis of the leadership and change literature indicates that Total Leaders lead effective, dynamic, and enduring organizations that:

- Have a clear and compelling purpose, which they involve all stakeholders in creating and maintaining;
- Embody the values of the staff in that purpose; and
- Align all the organization's functions and decisions with the purpose.

When an organization has a compelling purpose, everyone knows the direction in which the organization and its people are headed. The purpose will help everyone determine what they should be doing, and equally important, inform them of what they can stop doing.

When the organization is a school or a school district, that compelling purpose is contained in three distinct and complementary components: values and beliefs, the mission statement, and student outcomes. These elements are not just catchy phrases that look good on your district stationery or on bumper stickers. They form an important decision screen that helps everyone in the district discriminate between what is right and wrong, and what is honored and what is not accepted. If any one of these three elements does not discriminate, it isn't doing the important job that was intended. For instance, if the mission is ". . . to enable all students to . . . ," then schools should not continue to grade students on the bell curve.

The leadership gurus cited in earlier chapters suggest that one can begin to create a compelling purpose by identifying values and beliefs, that is, those things we honor and believe and, therefore, how we do things. Those values and beliefs consist of:

- Premises (or assumptions) about the beliefs surrounding students and learning, teachers and teaching, and effective schools and organizations.
- Core organizational values that guide the thinking and actions of organizational members.
- Principles of professionalism that set standards for decision making, actions, and accomplishments.

An example of a key premise advocated by many school systems with which we have worked is, "All students can learn and succeed, but not on the same day in the same way."

The Case for a Compelling Purpose

In the absence of organizational purpose, leadership does not exist. And if the purpose is not compelling, why would anyone want to follow?

The second component of a compelling purpose is a clear, concise, easy-to-remember mission statement that answers the questions of why the organization exists and its fundamental business. When school communities take the time to study future conditions like those outlined in Chapter 1 before creating their mission, they frequently develop one such as, "Equipping all students to succeed in a rapidly changing world."

To be effective, mission statements must be brief, discriminating, challenging, and exciting. If the mission statement isn't driving all decision making throughout the district, it simply isn't having the impact that it should. One true test of a mission statement's influence is to realize that if organizational members can't easily state the mission, then the organization doesn't have one.

When a district has identified its beliefs, values, and mission, it's ready to derive a set of student outcomes, or what graduates should know, be able to do, and be like when they leave a school system.

Most systems with whom we have worked identify outcomes that have to do with their graduates being what Spady (1994, 1996a, and 1998) calls role performers in life, such as lifelong learners, involved citizens, quality producers, community contributors, and the like. These broad outcome labels are, of course, further developed to clearly specify what a lifelong learner must know, be able to do, and be like. Student outcomes are much more compelling and significant to constituents and students when written about life roles and role performance abilities than when developed around course or program content.

Performance Role 2: Being the Lead Learner

Authentic leaders lead the quest for continuous personal and organizational learning. For them, learning and being a lifelong learner are as natural as breathing. Even if they didn't have an organization to lead, they would be reading a book, listening to someone, trying new things in an attempt to find better ways to do things, or simply observing some phenomenon to see what they could learn from the experience.

But lead learners *do* lead organizations and they realize that in a rapidly changing world, continuous learning is required, not just of the authentic leader, but of the total organization. Effective organizations, especially those effective over time, are learning organizations (Senge 1990).

The learning of the authentic leader has impact. More than simply adding knowledge, impactful learning:
- Clarifies or challenges one's values,
- Changes one's world view,
- Changes one's expectations,
- Changes one's vision, and
- Changes one's behavior.

Authentic leaders are totally open to new learning, even learning that can be quite painful given that it's not always easy to have one's values challenged or to admit to an inaccurate world view.

Lead learners are intentional about creating learning organizations. They don't leave anything of this importance to chance. They model lifelong, self-directed learning. And because they know they are models who want to make continuous learning an organizational norm, they use what they learn and let others know they are doing so. They can be seen carrying around good books, talking about what they have most recently learned or heard, and encouraging others to attend seminars they have enjoyed or to check out tapes they have found interesting.

Lead learners encourage and support the learning of others. In doing so, they provide resources and rewards for learning. For them, not being a self-directed, continuous learner is not an option.

In addition, lead learners create a culture of learning and innovation. They make learning and talking about learning a norm. They want everyone to be learning, even when no one is watching. They create this culture of learning and innovation by being collegial, by encouraging the creation of collegial groups, and by encouraging teams and teamwork. They know that people grow faster, feel more professional, feel more job satisfaction, and are more productive when they are members of collegial teams.

Lead learners are future focused because they realize that they are competing for the future. For them, studying the future and deriving future conditions for leadership and for their industry or profession is not only rewarding but also exciting and fun. That's why they encourage and expect everyone in the organization to be tracking trends, why they share their "future conditions" information with their colleagues, and why they will create and pursue new visions based upon their study of the future.

Both lead learners and learning organizations are data driven. They gather, study, analyze, and learn from data about their organization including its processes, products, production, and quality. And they gather, study, and analyze data from outside their organization including theories and new research on improvement, expert opinions, and the thinking of gurus and trend setters.

The world is exciting for lead learners. They know that they are competing for a share of their industry's foresight (Hamel and Prahalad 1994), they know that new learning is not a zero-sum game, and they want to be leading an organization that is *Built to Last* (Collins and Porras 1994).

Performance Role 3: Modeling Core Values and Principles

If creating a compelling purpose is the most important thing authentic leaders do to generate productive change, then modeling the core organizational values and principles of professionalism is the second most important. Why? Because, as we said at the beginning of this chapter, authentic leadership, the central domain of Total Leadership, comes down to credibility.

With credibility, as Peters and Waterman aptly demonstrated in 1982, leaders can mobilize and channel enormous reservoirs of hands-on/value-driven good will and loyalty, which is the motivational engine that drives personal and organizational success. Without it, it's doubtful that they can get much off the ground, let alone claim the title of leader.

It is no accident, therefore, that we chose the term *authentic* to describe this domain of Total Leadership. Authentic means genuine, real, heartfelt, honest, open, unadulterated, and trustworthy, and this is the performance role that most embodies those qualities and gives Total Leaders their moral foundation and moral compass.

Authentic leaders model core values and principles in a number of ways. They:

- Walk their talk,
- Get going when the going gets tough,
- Arrive first and leave last,
- Put up and pull through when challenged,
- Honor their commitments and their colleagues' trust,
- Give 110 percent all the time,
- Bear the responsibility and give others the credit,
- Do unto others far better than is often done unto them,
- Stand by their word,
- Root for the underdog,
- Always come through, all things being equal,
- Ask of others only what they unfailingly demonstrate,
- Go the extra mile, and
- Are honest.

As stated in Chapter 2, authentic leadership and its three performance roles lie in the center of the productive change process. What happens in each of the other four domains is directly influenced by and aligned with this value-based operational core. The core values and the operating principles of professionalism that reside within the authentic leader are carried into the exploration process of visionary leaders, the enrollment process of cultural leaders, the development process of quality leaders, and the orchestration process of service leaders through the universal presence and influence of this single performance role.

Who the Total Leader is defines what the Total Leader can and will ultimately do, which makes modeling core values and principles the centerpiece of any leader's profile of effectiveness.

Profile of Visionary Leaders

The guru	Warren Bennis
An exemplar	Walt Disney
An antithesis	George Bush (had solid values, but never got the "vision thing")
Mind set	Vision and leadership are synonymous. If you're not a visionary, at best, you're a manager.
Purpose	To create an inspirational and concrete picture of the organization's preferred future.
Focus	Shifts, trends, and future conditions Emerging and future needs of clients Creating scenarios of alternative futures
Change belief	Change happens when people are able to see a concrete picture of the future.
Performance roles	Defining a preferred organizational future Consistently employing a client focus Expanding organizational options
Key sources	*Leaders: Strategies for Taking Charge* (Bennis and Nanus 1985) *Competing for the Future* (Hamel and Prahalad 1994) *The Discipline of Market Leaders* (Treacy and Wiersema 1995) *Customer Intimacy* (Wiersema 1996) *Visionary Leadership* (Nanus 1992) *Built to Last* (Collins and Porras 1994) *Trend Tracking* (Celente 1990)

CHAPTER 4

The Visionary Leadership Domain: Total Leaders Framing Vision

---

■

---

*If your vision sounds like motherhood and
apple pie and is somewhat embarrassing, you
are on the right track.*

Peter Block

■

Gerald Celente calls it *Trend Tracking.* Peter Drucker sees it as
Managing for the Future. To Gary Hamel and C.K. Prahalad, it's
Competing for the Future; to James Liebig, it's about *Merchants of
Vision;* and to Dudley Lynch and Paul Kordis, it requires the *Strategy of
the Dolphin.* For Gareth Morgan, it requires *Imaginization.* And for
Joel Barker it comes down to *Discovering the Future: The Business of
Paradigms.*

But Burt Nanus most accurately describes it. *Visionary leadership is the
future focused, creative, imaginative domain of Total Leadership.*

The meaning of and innovative way in which all five Total Leadership
Domains are carried out depend on the character and actions of visionary leaders. Their creative influence is everywhere.

The Essence of Visionary Leaders

The essence of visionary leaders is paradigm-breaking imagination and
innovation. They excel at creating novel possibilities that others don't
see; chart new directions and destinations for their organizations; and
thrive on translating shifts and trends into productive options for organizational transformation. They turn issues and problems inside out
and upside down before declaring a preferred course of action, and
they never mindlessly opt for the way they've always done things
before.

Visionary leaders create organizational direction and a clear picture of the preferred future. We learned in the last chapter that people and organizations don't change unless there is a compelling reason to change. But even if they perceive a reason to change, they cannot and will not change unless they can see and feel a picture of a preferred future.

Organizational vision is the concrete picture and a manifestation of the organization's compelling purpose. It is what the organization will look like when it consistently and creatively acts on its core values and principles of professionalism, and meets its compelling purpose. It's vision that brings excitement to the productive change process.

It takes a shared vision for an organization to embrace change. Note that the word used here is embrace, not tolerate or go along with. Warren Bennis (1985), who may be the leading authority on organizational vision, states that, "Vision is the single most empowering and motivating factor in human organizations. It can bond diverse people together."

Visionary leaders are not unrealistic romantics. By imaginatively using the kind of information presented in the first chapter of this book and focusing on the conditions their organizations will inevitably be facing in the future, visionary leaders:

- Are more realistic than those leaders focused on past accomplishments.
- Care enough about the people in their organizations to give them a proven recipe for survival and security, namely, personal and organizational change.
- Have more than an equal stake in their organization's success and for getting it to the future first.

Moreover, their innovative nature is balanced by a self-interested pragmatism: Visionary leaders want to see their ideas work! They know that that means setting directions and goals that are within the reach of their colleagues and constituents, even though they may not fall within their current capabilities. Because of their ability to look far beyond the givens in typical situations, visionary leaders are invaluable to organizations facing the challenge of continuous change.

The Purpose of Visionary Leaders

The fundamental purpose of visionary leaders in a total change process is to orchestrate and lead their organization's vision framing process. They use their skills to:

- Involve their employees and other constituents in a thorough investigation of the challenges and opportunities facing their organization's future;
- Develop potential courses of action open; and
- Translate those options into a clear and compelling vision of what their organization can and should become when addressing these future realities and functioning at its ideal best.

This concrete, detailed, compelling document is their organizational vision. It is a highly motivating statement of what they want their organization to look like and be doing when accomplishing its purpose as well as operating at its highest performance. This vision statement demonstrates the quality and depth of the ideals that the change effort will embody when fully in place. With it, their ideal future comes to life in the present. Without it, the specifics of their declared purpose and intended change remain obscure, people hesitate to try anything new, and no one is ever quite sure where they stand as things unfold or unravel.

Expanding a Vision of the Possible

Of the five change processes, exploration is the most paradigm breaking and innovative.

> Exploration is the open, thorough, and stimulating search for, dialogue about, concrete formulation of preferred pictures of the possible for the total organization and its employees and constituents functioning at their best to achieve the declared purpose.

When led by capable visionary leaders, the exploration process expands people's perspectives of the operational options and possibilities open to their organization and what is possible and desirable to include in their organizational and personal vision statements. Such a process encourages people to examine cutting-edge ideas and developments in a whole range of arenas related to their organization's purpose and to openly discuss how they might lead to new ways of designing and conducting their work.

Without a serious and thorough exploration effort, an organization's vision will be limited primarily to images of the known and familiar, the very things it is intended to transcend. This effort must stimulate and encourage staff and constituents to search out new possibilities that lie beyond their current patterns of thinking and action because, to be transforming, a vision must be ahead of its organization's present capacity to operate.

Exploration Implications for School Districts

Our extensive experience with the strategic design process in which exploration is embedded suggests that school districts should invest the time in having employees and constituents ask:

- How are the realities our students will face after they leave school different from our prevailing educational expectations, programs, and patterns of action?
- What are the assumptions in this new work about students, parents, staff, and other constituents, and how are they different from what we have believed and acted upon to date?
- What kind of information do we need to gather that is consistent with our district's purpose and operating essentials?
- What's in the professional literature that could guide us?
- What models and strategies of more effective practice exist and seem applicable to our situation?
- How are we, our students, and community members unique?
- What would we look like if we were implementing everything we know about students and learning?

The more intense and extensive a district's exploration effort, the more likely it is that staff and stakeholders will become exposed to a wealth of new information and possibilities that is exciting and overwhelming in content and quality. Early on, the district should begin developing a comprehensive and sound framework of key ideas or themes around which to organize its new information and develop a plan for acting on them. The frameworks in Spady's work (1996b, 1996c, and 1998) can be useful in this regard.

The Moral Foundation of Visionary Leaders

Like all effective leaders, visionary leaders operate from a clear moral foundation. In this case, their foundation comprises the core values of openness and courage and the principles of professionalism we call future focusing and clarity. All four of these elements clearly strengthen Total Leaders' capacity to effectively carry out an insightful, paradigm-breaking exploration process.

> *Visionary leaders use ...*
> * *Core values of openness and courage*
> * *Principles of future focusing and clarity*

Openness is grounded in a sense of psychological security. It reflects a willingness and desire to receive, consider, and act ethically on information, possibilities, and perspectives of all kinds. Openness pertains both to individuals and to the organizations in which they engage. By being open-minded, open in their communications, and open in their willingness and desire to have their ideas and actions challenged and judged, Total Leaders elevate openness to the status of a value and make it an expected norm in day-to-day interactions. In so doing, they make it both permissible and desirable for divergent and unconventional viewpoints to be offered and considered.

Courage is the willingness of individuals and organizations to risk themselves despite the likelihood of negative consequences or fear of the unknown. Courage allows individuals to express viewpoints, make decisions, and take actions that, while supported by sound information and logic, either have never been tried or run contrary to widespread opinion, customary practice, or the viewpoints of those with greater organizational power and influence. Total Leaders are not afraid of making mistakes or failing. They demonstrate the courage to act on their convictions and to make tough choices that have the potential for productive change. Total Leaders also have the courage to admit when they are or have been wrong.

Future focusing involves conducting a thorough and consistent study of the shifts, trends, and future conditions that redefine a profession, industry, and/or organization, and taking a visionary and far-reaching view of emerging possibilities, potential innovations, and promising strategies. At its inherently creative, imaginative, and adventurous core, future focusing is about thinking and acting "outside the box" of conventional experience and ways of operating. It stresses the creation, discovery, and exploration of new paradigms, frameworks, models, and options. Total Leaders realize that future focusing is the critical first step in effective vision building and they ask, encourage, and maybe even insist that everyone in the organization be a trend-tracker, futurist, and lifelong learner.

Clarity is embodied in the open, honest, and comprehensible communication of one's direction and priorities, the information needed for making sound decisions and taking positive action, and the expectations that surround work and personal relationships. Clarity is about making important information and viewpoints known and accessible to those who depend on them to accomplish their goals.

Here are the kinds of situations that challenge you to apply these four Moral Foundation elements.

Openness: In the past you have taken a hard stand against the charter school movement. You now begin to hear reports of a number of very successful charter schools in your state. A group of parents who wish to start a charter school in your district have been meeting.

Courage: You are being pressured to pull books from the library that are unacceptable to a strong political group in the community.

Future focusing: You are beginning a strategic planning process for your system and need to identify outcomes for your graduates.

Clarity: Your mission statement is about a half-page long, and few people can remember it. You sense that it is not influencing the important decisions being made in your district.

Clarity is rooted in a strong desire to be honest and is the antithesis of manipulation and deceit. Clarity requires that everything in your leadership and change effort be written and communicated in crystal clear language, be agreed upon by everyone with a stake in its success, and be communicated and shared proactively with all employees and constituents. Total Leaders continually work to improve their communication skills. They learn to write and speak with clarity, but that's not to say that their communication is formal and humorless. Since nearly everyone likes to find a bit of levity sprinkled into even the clearest of communication, clarity doesn't always require formality.

Critical Performance Roles of Visionary Leaders

To carry out the exploration process effectively, visionary leaders undertake three major performance roles. These broad arenas of responsibility and action enable visionary leaders to make the decisions and carry out the actions that constitute the exploration process and achieve the pillar of change to which it is linked, organizational vision. The three critical performance roles of the visionary leader are:

- Defining and pursuing a preferred organizational future.
- Consistently employing a client focus.
- Expanding organizational perspectives and options.

Performance Role 4: Defining and Pursuing a Preferred Future

Although the leadership and change literature is inconsistent with its definition of mission and vision, we believe that mission is a statement of purpose, and vision is an idea, picture, or image of the future — a sense of what could be.

Simply stated, vision is the mental picture of a preferred future of a department, an organization, or a world. It's the mental "tape" that Jack Nicklaus plays before beginning his backswing, that Michael Jordan plays when he goes up for his fade-away jump shot, and that Gail Deevers plays when she kneels in the blocks waiting for the gun to sound for the 100-meter hurdles.

The 15 Performance Roles of a Total Leader

- Creating and sustaining a compelling personal and organizational purpose.
- Being the lead learner.
- Modeling core organizational values and personal principles.
- Defining and pursuing a preferred organizational future.
- Consistently employing a client focus.
- Expanding organizational perspectives and options.
- Involving everyone in productive change.
- Developing a change-friendly culture of innovation, healthy relationships, quality, and success.
- Creating meaning for everyone.
- Developing and empowering everyone.
- Improving the organization's performance standards and results.
- Creating and using feedback loops to improve performance.
- Supporting and managing the organization's purpose and vision.
- Restructuring to achieve intended results.
- Rewarding positive contributions to productive change.

The tape that school leaders play in their minds could include the ideal student learning experience, the ideal school, the ideal school district, or the ideal leader.

Personal values and the organization's core values and mission help leaders, their employees, and their organizations focus. While values and missions (although powerful for creating a moral foundation) are abstract, vision is concrete. Former Apple CEO John Scully believes that leaders "have to be able to make the abstract recognizable, because only then can people accept or reject it." If vision creates focus, then concrete vision creates clarity of focus. It focuses energy, motivation, actions, learning, and investment (Peters 1994).

When does one know that he or she has a good vision, one that will pull people and make them want to be part of the action? For starters, valid and viable visions are based on an insightful analysis of world and industry shifts, trends, and future conditions like those presented in Chapter 1. Future conditions regarding values, lifestyles, technology, demographics, and politics and power combine to make up a comprehensive analysis (Hamel and Prahalad 1994). If a vision is to be futuristic, then its grounding must be based on the best approximation of the future.

Visionary leaders make no small plans. If a vision can be achieved at the time a leader creates it, then it's probably not a vision. Powerful visions present significant challenges and run well ahead of the organization's capacity to achieve it. For example, NASA estimated that they knew about 15 percent of what they needed to know in order to get to the moon and back safely when President Kennedy communicated that bold vision for the U.S. space program.

Peter Block (1987) believes that "If your vision sounds like motherhood and apple pie and is somewhat embarrassing, you are on the right track." Visionary leaders are then, he suggests, "ready to bet the farm."

For a vision to be powerful, it has to be useful. Useful and powerful visions are:

- Describable in that they are clear, concrete, and easily communicated,
- Desirable, representing a preferred future that excites and enthuses,
- Doable but not without risking and heroic efforts, and
- Directing for the individual and organization.

Visionary leadership experts suggest that visions be stated in the present rather than the future tense as if an organization is already accomplishing them. For example, a classroom teacher's vision might be as follows:

"My classroom is an adventureland of learning. The students eagerly participate in our wide array of projects proving repeatedly that they all can learn and successfully demonstrate things of significance to a high level, even though they differ a lot in the time needed and approach that works best for them. I continue to remind them of the major competence outcomes toward which we are all working so that they know what's important to demonstrate at the end and know what they need to do to learn it. We consistently apply each lesson, activity, and larger project directly to one or more of these real-life performance abilities. And they remind and demonstrate to each other in focused work groups what it means to do well on those outcomes and ways they can improve on what they're doing or have just done.

"I consistently find ways to provide extra help, suggestions, and exercises to the few students who don't get things the first time, including having other students show them some of their learning strategies. We all share in giving support to those who make visible improvements in their work, knowing that successful learning is the strongest promoter there is in more successful learning. Because they understand and continuously apply clear performance standards so well in their everyday work, they find it easy to provide progress reports on their work to their parents every few months."

A paradox, however, surrounds the framing of an organization's vision. As Bennis says, "Great paintings were not painted by a committee, and visions seldom come from the herd. They are usually the creation of one person. But successful visions require commitment, ownership, and a broad consensus."

What are visionary leaders to do in the face of this paradox? We suggest they:

- Show how the vision manifests employee values, core organizational values, and mission.
- Encourage everyone in their organization to enhance, extend, develop, and personalize the vision.
- Always say "we" and "our," not "I" or "my" when communicating about the vision.
- Give (and give away) credit to all contributors.

Total Leaders need to see themselves as seekers, consensus builders, communicators, clarifiers, modelers, and keepers of the vision.

Performance Role 5: Employing a Client Focus

When visionary leaders create a compelling purpose or a concrete picture of their organization's preferred future, they do it with their customers and clients in mind. Their practices, policies, procedures, decisions, and actions are *all* based on what's best for the customer.

When we ask, "Who is the *end user* of my work?" we can usually identify an external customer. But when we ask, "Who is the *user* of my work?" we frequently can identify an internal customer, someone in the organization who directly relies on our work in order to accomplish theirs.

For example, end user clients of second grade teachers are their students and parents; but these teachers' internal clients include all the rest of the teachers in the system who will eventually build on what those students learned in second grade. The same applies to visionary leaders. Their focus is on both their external and internal clients.

Visionary leaders ask their colleagues and themselves repeatedly if they meet or exceed their customers':

Present needs. Wal-Mart is an example of a company that meets the expressed needs of its customers. While not innovative or one-of-a-kind, Wal-Mart products are good name brands sold cheaper than the customer can get elsewhere. Likewise, school districts that have a sound curriculum meet the needs articulated by success-oriented parents, university admissions offices, and students who have college aspirations.

Emerging needs. This means surprising and pleasing customers and clients with new products and services even before they ask. Chrysler's minivans hit the market well before soccer moms asked for them because Lee Iacocca and other Chrysler leaders sensed an emerging need and designed a vehicle to fit that need. In fact, minivan sales are the main reason for Chrysler's successes during the past decade. Likewise, school districts that have created exciting and successful magnet school programs are meeting the needs of a set of students and parents who, until the magnet school option was presented, probably didn't even realize that their desires could be met within the structure of the public schools.

Future needs. Intel and Microsoft know about potential future needs, even before their customers do. Before one of their breakthrough products hits the market, they are well on their way with the development of even newer products/services that will make this "new" one obsolete (Grove 1996). Likewise, school districts that study the shifts, trends, and future conditions before identifying student outcomes consciously and systematically focus their internal and external adult clients on the future needs of their student clients.

Clearly, visionary leaders are listeners, trend trackers, and futurists. As Peters and Waterman (1982) pointed out, visionary leaders get "close to the customers" to hear what they say about their needs, desires, hopes, and dreams. They study what's happening in the profession or industry, their society, and other nations. And they draw conclusions about what the future holds for them. Specifically, visionary leaders:

- Have frequent face-to-face meetings with their customers, and make sure that everyone else in the organization does so too. In a school, for example, if a sizable percentage of the graduation classes are college bound, visionary school leaders make sure that their teachers have face-to-face dialogues with college teachers. If a sizable percentage will seek employment right out of high school, then they meet regularly with promising employers. And they devote 90 percent of their time to asking and listening.
- Systematically involve both their organization and customers in a study of their customers' future needs. For school districts, this can be done through the consideration process described in the previous chapter and the exploration process.
- Create long-term strategic alliances with their customers and suppliers. For educational leaders, this means treating students, parents, the community, colleges and universities, and employers as customers whose satisfaction depends on your success. Parents and the community also double as "suppliers," as they supply the students and most of the district's personnel.
- View disagreements with customers and clients as a stimulus for growth. They look for win-win solutions to problems and win-win rewards from opportunities.

In sum, these four strategies lie at the heart of an effective visioning process. They also reflect the sensitivity and empathy that visionary leaders bring to their relations with customers — an ability to discover and act on future possibilities through the eyes of their customers, even before they become aware that those possibilities exist.

Why is this performance role so critical to the success of Total Leaders? Because they know that customers and clients vote with their feet and that customer satisfaction is best measured by repeat business. Because customers, have so many options in today's world, they frequently don't give organizations a second chance. This is true for schools as well. Until the 1990s, employing a client focus looked like a minor issue to educational leaders. Schools had few, if any, competitors. Today, private schools, charter schools, vouchers, home schooling, and virtual schools on the Internet are a growth industry. Whether they turn out to be better remains to be seen, but more potential public school clients are voting with their feet and ballots. The demand for something different is here, and visionary leaders within the educational community will be the ones who find ways to meet that demand.

Performance Role 6: Expanding Organizational Perspectives

Defining and pursuing a preferred organizational future, the key performance role of visionary leaders, is impossible to carry out successfully without simultaneously implementing this performance role. Expanding organizational perspectives and options embodies the heart and soul of the exploration process. At its core, this process and this performance role are about what visionary leaders call breaking paradigm: Transcending and reconstructing the patterns of assumptions, beliefs, and interpretations that cause individuals to see and act on the world in particular (and limiting) ways.

Breaking constraining paradigms is the focus of Joel Barker's (1988) tremendously popular and impactful work. He coaches people to see and understand things in ways that they simply couldn't perceive before because of the blinders, preconceptions, mind sets, or limiting perspectives they had. Paradigm-breaking experiences, sometimes called revelations, great ah-ha's, hits, or mind blowers, result in thinking, "Wow! I see this thing in a whole new way now."

Visionary leaders are, at their core, paradigm breakers.

For example, John Carroll (1963) was a visionary leader who stood the prevailing paradigm of education on its head and provided the theoretical grounding that eventually led to the major reform efforts of mastery learning, effective schools, accelerated schools, and outcome-based education. (See Spady 1998 for an explanation of how this learning success paradigm evolved.)

Carroll based his analysis on a simple proposition: Aptitude is the rate at which people learn new things; some faster, some slower. Theoretically, all students can learn clearly defined things equally well, but the time they need to do it will vary because their aptitudes vary. This calls into question how schools are organized. They make time the constant and learning success the variable. To be effective, they need to reverse this relationship.

Today, that reversal would be a paradigm shift in a new way of viewing and doing teaching and learning.

Try Out a New Paradigm

All school leaders need are some simple tools and examples to easily open up a dramatically different set of possibilities and options for their internal and external clients to consider and eventually implement.

In this example, consider education being organized around a new set of expectations, instead of the current ones.

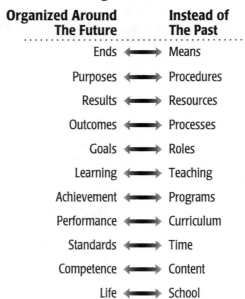

Imagine Education...

Organized Around The Future		Instead of The Past
Ends	⟷	Means
Purposes	⟷	Procedures
Results	⟷	Resources
Outcomes	⟷	Processes
Goals	⟷	Roles
Learning	⟷	Teaching
Achievement	⟷	Programs
Performance	⟷	Curriculum
Standards	⟷	Time
Competence	⟷	Content
Life	⟷	School

What you're likely to find in the examples in the left column is that (1) each operates around clearly defined expectations and performance criteria that determine what given levels of success mean rather than around ambiguous or comparative standards; (2) the time needed to reach a given level of performance and the methods used, is usually flexible and/or learner specific; and (3) all participants can reach the highest possible performance levels and are often given multiple opportunities for doing so.

These three features alone portray dramatic differences between current thinking and future possibilities that could be the focus of an option-expanding discussion in your schools. It is up to Total Leaders to begin such a discussion.

Profile of Cultural Leaders

The guru

Terry Deal

An exemplar

Red Auerbach and the Boston Celtics

An antithesis

Jerry Jones and the Dallas Cowboys

Mind set

Organizational culture is the critical variable in the long-term success of organizations.

Purpose

To establish, monitor, and model positive organizational norms, values, and principles.

Focus

Human relationships
Creating project teams
Visible symbols of organizational culture

Change belief

Change happens from the inside out when individuals are involved in, and thereby become committed to, the change.

Performance roles

Involving everyone in productive change
Developing a change-friendly culture
Creating meaning for everyone

Key sources

Corporate Cultures (Deal and Kennedy 1982)
Enlightened Leadership (Oakley and Krug 1991)
Integrity (Carter 1996)
Man's Search for Meaning (Frankl 1984)
The Heart Aroused (Whyte 1994)
The Balanced Scorecard (Kaplan and Norton 1996)
Leading Change (O'Toole 1995)

CHAPTER 5

The Cultural Leadership Domain: Total Leaders Developing Ownership

■

Whether or not leaders are perceptive enough to recognize it, organizations have cultures, which take root, grow, evolve, and silently control the attitudes and behaviors of organizational members even when, and perhaps especially when, no one pays them any special attention.

■

Stephen Carter calls its essence *Integrity.* Thomas Crum sees it embodied in *The Magic of Conflict.* To Terry Deal and Alan Kennedy, its focus is *Corporate Cultures;* for Robert Heller it involves *The Naked Manager for the Nineties;* who, as Roy Kilmann and his colleagues show, must be involved in *Gaining Control of the Corporate Culture.* To Victor Frankl, it's manifested in *Man's Search for Meaning;* and for Ed Oakley and Doug Krug, it's a matter of *Enlightened Leadership,* which Tom Sergiovanni calls *Value-Added Leadership.*

From our reading of these works, we have concluded that the essence of the issue is *cultural leadership, the participatory, interpersonally motivational domain of Total Leadership.*

Cultural leaders bring the value and purpose dimensions of authentic leadership to life in a direct, interpersonal way. The quality and consistency of cultural leaders' relations with others are key in determining how well the other four domains of Total Leadership are carried out and how strongly those domains motivate organizational members to involve and invest themselves in the organization's change efforts.

The Essence of Cultural Leaders

Cultural leaders shape the orientations, quality, cohesiveness, and energy of their organization's culture — those often unspoken values, beliefs, norms, symbols, actions, and pressures that exist beyond an organization's policies and rules and that powerfully influence how its members:

- Relate to each other,
- Do their business,
- Value and reward each other's productivity and contributions, and
- Participate in the organization's social, recreational, and work life.

The skills and qualities of cultural leadership are needed for carrying out the enrollment process that is necessary for developing ownership of organizational purpose and change. Cultural leaders are, therefore, highly perceptive and aware people. They easily place themselves in the shoes of their peers, constituents, and employees, and readily recognize that it's critical to have an organizational culture that strongly influences people's sense of esteem and belonging.

Whether or not leaders are perceptive enough to recognize it, organizations have cultures, which take root, grow, evolve, and often silently control the attitudes and behaviors of organizational members even when, and perhaps especially when, no one pays them any special attention. Just as high blood pressure is said to be the silent killer because many people do not recognize it, negative cultures can be the silent killer of organizations, draining energy and commitment without the leader's recognition.

People who work in an organization often find it difficult to describe precisely what their culture is because they live with it every day and grow accustomed to its presence, much like fish in water. Certainly this is the case for most educators who have lived in and with our current educational system since they were five years old.

Cultural leaders avoid this problem by intentionally influencing their organization through the power of their presence and example, messages they convey, input from external sources they solicit, decisions they make, people and efforts they recognize, and principles they advocate and consistently uphold. Peters and Waterman use the term hands on/value driven to capture this essence.

Because cultural leaders are extremely sensitive to the pulse and climate of their organizations, they can readily identify the major tangible forms that a culture takes. Thanks to the pioneering work of Deal and Kennedy (1982), we recognize these tangibles as:

Organizational heroes and heroines. These are people who are ultimately revered by other organizational members for what they have contributed to the organization's standing and reputation. A leader should know who they are, how closely they align with the organization's core values and compelling purpose, and whether they are positive and change-friendly or negative and cynical. Cultural leaders deliberately elevate those who exemplify the organization's core values and purpose to hero/heroine status.

Rituals and ceremonies. These are special events in which the organization's core values and compelling purpose are celebrated and reinforced. Leaders should be aware of these events, their frequency, and whether the established procedures and ceremonies are consistent with the core values, compelling purpose, and vision. Cultural leaders deliberately create and reinforce rituals and ceremonies that embody and reinforce their organization's core values and purpose.

Traditions. These are ways of thinking and doing that get handed down from year to year in the organization. It's helpful to know if traditions have been assessed and acted upon for their impact on an organization's core values and purpose. For example, does a school have a single valedictorian for the senior class or does it recognize a number of students for meeting very high standards? Cultural leaders deliberately act to reinforce contributions and actions worthy of becoming honored organizational traditions.

Symbols. Symbols are material objects that represent meaning, values, purpose, honor, and status within the organization. A leader should know what his or her organization's symbols communicate about beliefs, values, and purpose. For example, which symbols does one see entering a school, a district office, or the superintendent's office? Trophies and records demonstrating athletic power? Engraved listings of past National Honor Society members? The largest desk with the largest office and the best view? Cultural leaders establish symbols that directly embody the organization's highest values and contributions to its compelling purpose.

Stories. Stories are the recounting of significant events in the organization's history and the roles people played in shaping the outcomes of those events. Leaders should reflect on what stories are retold, the heroes and heroines of those stories, and their meaning. Are the people wearing the "white hats" the defenders of the core values and ultimate organizational purpose, or are they the people who resist change? Are there stories about the leader's integrity, risk-taking, and courage? Cultural leaders monitor stories and reinforce the ones that bolster the organization's values, purpose, and vision.

The organization's culture is embodied in the daily actions and decisions of its leaders and members. That's why cultural leaders are hands on/value driven and consistently:

- Involve organizational members and clients in identifying what they see as an ideal culture,
- Assess their present culture and the gaps between it and their ideal,
- Identify the beliefs, behaviors, and norms that need to change, and
- Monitor and shape their culture over time.

The Purpose of Cultural Leaders

The fundamental purpose of cultural leaders in a productive change process is to orchestrate and shape their organization's ownership developing process. Organizational change has little chance of succeeding unless those affected by the change, both internal members and external clients, feel invested in the proposed changes and are willing to give their best efforts to making them happen. Various aspects of that psychological investment are called ownership, buy-in, commitment, motivation, involvement, and engagement.

Regardless of the term, the essence of this critical pillar of change is the feeling within organizational members and clients that they can identify with and are a part of what is going on. This feeling of belonging, being connected, participating, and contributing is the motivational fuel of productive change. With it, organizations move mountains. Without it, they barely make it up a mole hill. True cultural leaders have the orientations and abilities to create a culture of genuine engagement in which people feel a part of the decisions and actions that most affect their jobs, performances, and results.

By openly and sincerely enlisting all organizational members and clients in defining the purpose and framing the vision, and by visibly using their input and insights in the change process, cultural leaders establish the psychological connection that makes ownership possible. This act of reaching out and bringing people into the organization's decision making process is called enrollment.

Enrollment builds identity, allegiance, motivation, commitment, and a stronger base of expertise, and it uses the invaluable perspectives and expertise of those outside as well as inside the organization to do it. If the organization's leaders don't engender these feelings in others, they face the grim prospect of carrying all its changes and challenges exclusively on their shoulders. They also leave untapped what several authors describe as the almost limitless reserve of employee goodwill that could exist.

Casting the Net Widely and Deeply

Of the five change processes, enrollment is the most personally motivating

> Enrollment is the open, continuous, and enthusiastic recruitment, inclusion, and involvement of all of the organization's employees and constituents in its productive change effort.

When led by capable cultural leaders and shaped by the core values of integrity and commitment, the enrollment process represents the open arms approach to welcoming and fully engaging both internal and external clients in an organization's productive change process.

For educators, that means including in the process teachers, staff, students, parents, board members, employers, and other community constituents. This inclusion process is the only way to ensure that they all understand, contribute to, and take ownership for the change effort, and enlist their support and involvement when the effort is challenged.

Enrollment is based on four fundamental assumptions that embody the professional principles of inclusiveness and win-win. These key assumptions are that:

• All constituents, both outside and inside the organization, have a major stake in what the organization does, and they all contribute to and benefit from its success.

- External clients and customers bring to the organization fresh, badly needed perspectives, resources, talents, and support that are vital to defining and carrying out the organization's mission.
- The we/they, insider/outsider, closed-system attitude that characterizes most organizational hierarchies must be broken down if the inherent power and benefit of this connection is to be realized. Organizational barriers only hinder organizational success.
- Leaders can only "win" if they reach out and involve every one of these constituencies in shaping the organization's direction and success. Sincere outreach efforts transform organizations into collaborative communities.

People-focused and people-intensive, the enrollment process generates many of the same kinds of issues, opportunities, tensions, risks, and emotions inherent in the consideration process. But the issues can be even more intense as they go beyond ideas, values, and information to highly sensitive matters of people, power, and professionalism. That's why leaders expect attitudes among all parties about developing strong working relationships with each other to range from mild uncertainty and apprehension to strong suspicion and mistrust. Therefore, at the outset of this process, cultural leaders need to help everyone understand that acknowledging these feelings of apprehension is the first step in creating the communication and empathy that are vital to getting past them. Successful enrollment requires that these assumptions and operating principles be openly acknowledged, discussed, and endorsed since they are keys to developing a genuine sense of community and cooperation within the organization.

School leaders, then, have to actively recruit parents and other constituents, as well as reluctant colleagues, in the productive change effort. Otherwise, leaders run the major risk of these key constituents:

- Not understanding or sharing the purpose or vision,
- Having no ownership in the purpose or vision,
- Lacking the capacity to help implement the purpose or vision, and
- Offering no support when tough questions and implementation challenges arise.

Clearly, without the skills and a deep commitment to implementing and sustaining an expansive enrollment process, leaders are unlikely to motivate their employees and constituents to undergo the challenges inherent in a long-term productive change effort.

The Moral Foundation of Cultural Leaders

Although organizational culture is awash in symbols and manifestations of core values, there are two particular core values that underlie the culture shaping efforts of cultural leaders: integrity and commitment. The two key principles that drive their ownership-developing decisions and actions are inclusiveness and win-win.

Cultural leaders use . . .

- *Core values of integrity and commitment*
- *Principles of inclusiveness and win-win*

Integrity is the long-term expression and embodiment of honesty, fairness, trustworthiness, honor, and consistent adherence to high-level moral principles, especially those core values and professional principles recognized and endorsed by the organization. Integrity emanates from a keen sense of right and wrong and a strong sensitivity to the likely consequences of one's decisions and actions on the interests and welfare of others. Some of its common opposites are selfishness, expedience, manipulation, and deceit. Total Leaders reflect deeply on their values and principles, are open to their organization and the public about them, and consistently model them.

Commitment is reflected in people's willingness to devote their full energies and talents to the successful completion of undertakings they have agreed to pursue, despite challenges and adverse conditions that may arise. Commitment often requires setting aside personal comfort, convenience, and, at times, welfare and self-interest, to fulfill agreements. Commitment is strongest and comes easiest when there is tight alignment between personal and organizational values. Therefore, Total Leaders insist that their organization's values and principles be extensions of their personal values, that they select and develop others with similar values, and that they help others find meaning in and become committed to their work.

Inclusiveness is embodied in consistent commitment to maximizing the range of opportunities for success available to organizational members, the number of people included in relevant and meaningful organizational decisions, and the level of member and stakeholder participation and input in decisions that affect their welfare.

At its core, inclusiveness is about outreach, communication, recruitment, acceptance, involvement, and the development of ownership among organizational members and stakeholders. Its participation dimension involves including organizational members and constituents in planning and decisions. Its substance side involves taking advantage of the broad range of ideas and possibilities that these individuals will suggest, and using their input in decision making, planning, and implementation. Total Leaders include people in the process to gain their commitment, to ensure follow-through, to help everyone find meaning in their work, to be politically correct, and so forth; but it all starts with the Total Leader's firm belief that people have something to offer that will enhance the outcome for everyone involved.

Here are the kinds of situations that might challenge you to apply these four Moral Foundation elements.

Integrity: As superintendent, you have frequently stated that you are concerned about curriculum and instruction. It's Friday, and you are developing your work schedule for the following week.

Commitment: You are scheduled to present at a national conference in an attractive city. The day before you are to leave, you become aware of a difficult personnel problem involving one of your principals.

Inclusiveness: You are beginning a strategic planning process for your system and need to assemble a team to identify learner outcomes for your graduates.

Win-Win: As a new superintendent, you are being given most of the credit for turning an underachieving school district around. A reporter asks you how *you* did it.

Win-win embodies a commitment to achieving and experiencing mutual benefit in the agreements people make, the relationships they establish, and the rewards they obtain from the contributions they make. Win-win is about enhancing one's status and well-being through sharing with others, publicly recognizing and honoring the value of others' efforts and contributions, and defining self-interest and success in terms of the common good. Win-win emanates from, and projects a view of, human nature as positive, cooperative, and deserving of dignity and recognition. Its antithesis is selfishness, insensitivity, exploitation, and win-lose, which usually degenerates into lose-lose.

Win-win leads to more win-wins. If people get a fair and profitable shake with you and your organization, they'll quite naturally want to come back for more of the same. Win-win is the heart and soul of healthy relationships and an organizational culture that evokes trust and makes people want to be involved and contribute.

The Critical Performance Roles of Cultural Leaders

To carry out the enrollment process and to achieve the pillar of change to which it's linked, constituent ownership, cultural leaders use three performance roles:

- Involving everyone in productive change.
- Developing a change-friendly culture of innovation, healthy relationships, quality, and success.
- Creating meaning for everyone.

Performance Role 7: Involving Everyone in Productive Change

Involving everyone in productive change is one of the most important things Total Leaders do to ensure that change gets started and achieved.

Strategically, involving everyone in productive change is the precondition to carrying out four of the six previously discussed performance roles (creating a compelling purpose, defining a preferred future, employing a client focus, and expanding organizational perspectives). Unless one attends to this first, it will be impossible to create and sustain a compelling organizational purpose or to define and pursue a preferred organizational future. Hence, three of the five essential pillars of change—purpose, vision, and ownership—will not materialize.

Not an event controlled by the leader, productive change is a process in which all organizational members and clients are directly involved. As noted in the previous section, without such involvement, input, and agreement, the most vital conditions for change simply collapse and organizations are left standing at the starting blocks.

Cultural leaders are able to avoid this pitfall because of their ability to see change from the perspective of the organizational members and clients who will be directly affected by whatever changes occur. Change is too frequently represented as "what we want those other people to do." In education, this is called "fixing the teachers" but leaving the rest of the system untouched.

The 15 Performance Roles of a Total Leader

- Creating and sustaining a compelling personal and organizational purpose.
- Being the lead learner.
- Modeling core organizational values and personal principles.
- Defining and pursuing a preferred organizational future.
- Consistently employing a client focus.
- Expanding organizational perspectives and options.
- Involving everyone in productive change.
- Developing a change-friendly culture of innovation, healthy relationships, quality, and success.
- Creating meaning for everyone.
- Developing and empowering everyone.
- Improving the organization's performance standards and results.
- Creating and using feedback loops to improve performance.
- Supporting and managing the organization's purpose and vision.
- Restructuring to achieve intended results.
- Rewarding positive contributions to productive change.

Cultural leaders know that real change happens from the inside out, with the paradigm perspectives, beliefs, values, and goals of the individual. Therefore, they take the point of view of those facing the change by using what Cooper and Sawaf (1996) call *Executive EQ,* their sensitivity and empathy toward the attitudes, hopes, fears, and needs of individuals, teams, and divisions within their organization. They know that when people begin to see things differently through new eyes and paradigms, they can open up emotionally as well as intellectually to the potential need for and benefits of change. Then, with a new perspective and a safe place to explore change, individuals can participate in a process with confidence that it will "work" for them.

Cultural leaders cultivate this safe place by helping others address and positively respond to questions about:

Their psychological readiness for change. How secure do I feel as a person and member of this organization? How does the change fit with my personal values? What's in it for me? What might I gain, and what do I stand to lose? Is the potential reward worth the obvious risk? Do I have the skills and knowledge to change?

The organization's culture. Are the heroes/heroines in this organization innovators and risk-takers? If not, what do they represent? What happens around here to people who try new things and fail? What happens around here to people who try new things and succeed? Do the things people admire and celebrate here support change? Are the leaders people we can trust?

The organization's structure. What happened to the last major change effort this organization tried? Is the organization structured to accomplish its declared purpose? Is it aligned with its declared vision? Have the leaders aligned the organization's resources and rewards with its declared vision?

With a safe psychological place established, cultural leaders can carry out the enrollment process: recruit, include, and involve all of the organization's members and clients in the consideration and exploration processes needed to launch productive change. In this way, they can define a purpose and frame a vision that will benefit from everyone's participation, input, understanding, and support.

Performance Role 8: Developing a Change-Friendly Culture

The literature strongly suggests that cultural leaders consistently work to develop a culture that has two highly visible, mutually reinforcing features. First, the culture is empowering and promotes personal initiative, improved performance, and organizational effectiveness. Second, the culture is change-friendly and openly encourages new ideas, dynamism, and lasting organizational health.

Empowering cultures—and the cultural leaders that shape them—espouse, embody, and reward four key things:

Innovation. Employees risk trying promising new ideas, keep what works, and discard what doesn't. When mistakes happen, they don't treat them as failure or blame people, but rather, do their best to learn from them.

Cooperation. Employees cooperate in the workplace so that they can compete successfully in the marketplace. Teaming and helping others look good are encouraged and rewarded in this culture.

Quality. Employees know that quality is no longer a market advantage but a ticket to the game. They carefully monitor products and processes to continuously improve them.

Success. Employees recognize that it's the norm to plan well, work hard, work smart, and win. When they don't win after doing their best, they study how to not make the same mistakes again.

These four attributes directly reinforce what appear to be five dominant norms that cultural leaders reinforce in change-friendly cultures:

- They strongly focus on customers and clients because the needs and priorities of their customers change with the times. They keep their fingers on their pulse or risk losing them.
- They enthusiastically study the future, partly because it's fascinating and informative, and partly because their careers depend on it. They openly discuss the latest research, trends, and theories and how they can be applied.
- They demand a flat, nimble organization by cutting down the decision-making layers in the organization and placing authority close to where the action is. That way, they can respond more rapidly and creatively to challenges.

- They value risk-taking and "good shot" failures. Because they focus so much on the best information around, they're willing to try things that show real promise. If those attempts don't work, they figure out why.
- They get creative people working together. They know that five smart people working together can tackle a problem better than one person. They feed off each other's insights and share the risks and rewards.

From our perspective, education leaders can benefit enormously from the emphasis cultural leaders place on these attributes and norms because the public schools are now finally facing the market forces that have compelled business and other public institutions to become empowering and change-friendly. If this seems like speculation, consider that the fastest growing segment of the K-12 education market is home schooling. This growing market is followed by private schools, charter schools, and virtual schools on the Internet — all alternatives to the unchallenged monopoly public schools once enjoyed.

School leaders can benefit from the lessons learned by another former public monopoly, the U.S. Postal Service. Twenty years ago, who would have believed that anyone could take on the postal service? It was the only game in town, a government monopoly that received large subsidies from the U.S. Treasury.

Then came along United Parcel Service, Federal Express, a host of smaller private carriers, computers, and fax machines, and suddenly, it was a whole new ball game. Literally overnight, "truly important" mail or packages arrived by private carrier, fax, or the Internet. The postal service, an inefficient bureaucracy, handled the junk mail, monthly bills, and Christmas cards.

The postal service realized they had to change to survive. They became change-friendly and began to offer the same services that their competitors had used to break their monopoly. Today, their services and prices are designed to win and retain customers. The U.S. Postal Service is now one of the world's best national delivery services.

Today's public schools find themselves in a similar situation. College-educated parents, home schooling, and charter schools represent the growth industries of the education world. No longer immune from the market forces that have finally caught up, schools, like the postal service and a number of other public institutions, have a choice: deny and belittle the competition, or change and become competitive.

If Smith and Clurman (1997) are right, our response to this challenge may be related to age. The older we are in outlook, the more inclined we are to see change as a threat to our sense of security. The younger we are in outlook, the more we, like Total Leaders, are likely to see it as an opportunity.

Total Leaders are eager to meet the challenge of competing and winning so that public schools can learn to do better for *all* of their students. It simply requires cultural leaders who recognize that change is here to stay and are eager to create empowering, change-friendly cultures in their schools.

Performance Role 9: Creating Meaning For Everyone

Because, by nature, cultural leaders are hands on/value driven, they are the key ambassadors of the organization's core values, principles of professionalism, and compelling purpose. All the core values and principles of professionalism shown at the end of Chapter 2 embody the essence of the organization's culture, which gives work so much of its meaning and intrinsic worth.

These 10 core values also serve as the bedrock of purpose. Together, these values and purpose give things meaning. And when things have meaning, they bolster personal identity, motivation, and empowerment. Once these conditions are met, cultural leaders know that quality and productivity are sure to follow because people are willing to thoroughly invest themselves in their work.

Cultural leaders are creators and promoters of meaning. And the cultural leader in education has a head start because of the profession's inherent meaning in educating children and young adults to be successful in life. Meaning is everywhere in education, and cultural leaders never let us lose sight of it. They understand and continuously communicate that meaning comes from:

A compelling purpose. People find meaning in doing work that is significant and makes a difference in the lives of others. Organizations that lack such a purpose will only be motivating for those who want to do their own thing. There's a difference between motivating a few high performers and focusing the energy and resources of everyone in the organization.

Seeing and being part of the big picture. People find meaning in doing work that is part of something lasting and bigger than themselves. This is illustrated in the story about the person who walked by a construction site and noticed three people at work, seemingly on the same task. The passerby greeted the first person and asked him what he was doing. "I'm a bricklayer," he replied tersely. "I'm laying bricks." He moved on until he met the second person to whom he asked the same question. "I'm a bricklayer," he replied, "and I'm building a very large wall." When he got to the third person and asked the question, he was told proudly with a sweeping gesture: "I'm a bricklayer, and I'm building a magnificent cathedral!"

Challenge and high expectations. Meaning comes from challenge and high expectations. If work is routine and something that anyone can do, what deeper meaning is there? And if high-quality products or services are not expected, who can take pride in what they're doing and put forth a best effort? For educators, this is a key issue: Challenge is everywhere, but public education doesn't consistently create, demand, and hold everyone accountable for meeting high expectations.

Being in control and responsible. Meaning is heightened when one knows he or she is in control, responsible, and will be held accountable. Good people and quality performers wouldn't have it any other way. Denver Broncos quarterback John Elway likes being in control and being held responsible when his team is down by four points at the two-minute warning. Teachers feel a strong sense of responsibility when they know they have the nation's future in their hands.

Being part of a team. For most people, winning at something as an individual is fun. But winning as a member of a team is multidimensional fun. For example, when a professional golfer wins a tournament, there's jubilation for a moment or so, but he or she quickly retreats back to previous reserve and composure. The winner checks and signs the score card and submits to the TV interview with little emotion. But watch the final results of the Ryder Cup and you'll see the winning team of golfers hugging, shouting, rolling in the grass, and throwing each other in a pond if there's one nearby. Being part of a recognizable team is emotionally enervating and meaningful, and cultural leaders deliberately work to create teams.

Feedback/keeping score. Ken Blanchard, author of the widely read *One Minute Manager* (1982), believes that "feedback is the breakfast of champions." Without some form of keeping score or track, how can anyone know how well they're doing? And without knowing how well they're doing, how can they work toward continuous improvement? Cultural leaders create communication/feedback loops that tell their people how well they are doing. They know that keeping score creates meaning, that meaning enhances productivity, and that being productive in an important endeavor creates meaning. It's a non-vicious, highly empowering cycle that is knowingly created by savvy cultural leaders who want to help everyone find meaning in their work.

Cultural leaders know that today is a great time to be leading. They recognize that helping people find meaning in their work is the moral thing to do and is productive for the organization as well. Education is full of opportunities for people to find meaning. Cultural leaders help make it happen.

Profile of Quality Leaders

The guru	W. Edwards Deming
An exemplar	U.S. Postmaster Marvin Runyon (who turned the post office around)
An antithesis	Montgomery Ward department store (an old standard not able to keep up)
Mind set	High-quality products and services are no longer a market advantage but an entrance requirement.
Purpose	To establish policies, procedures, and practices that guarantee the continuous improvement of products and services.
Focus	Client requirements Quality standards Statistical/objective measures
Change belief	Change happens when individuals and teams have the capacity to implement the vision.
Performance roles	Developing and empowering everyone Improving organizational performance Creating and using feedback loops
Key sources	*The Empowered Manager* (Block 1987) *The Circle of Innovation* (Peters 1997) *Quality or Else* (Dobyns and Crawford-Mason 1991) *Out of the Crisis* (Deming 1986) *The Deming Management Method* (Walton 1986) *Quality Is Free* (Crosby 1979) *Taking Charge of Change* (Smith 1996)

CHAPTER 6

The Quality Leadership Domain: Total Leaders Building Capacity

---

You can't manage quality — quality is an output.
You can only manage systems.

W. Edwards Deming

Peter Block calls it *The Empowered Manager.* James Collins and Jerry Porras see the issue as being *Built to Last,* and Philip Crosby calls it *The Art of Making Quality Certain.* But to W. Edwards Deming, the issue is about leading organizations *Out of the Crisis,* which to Lloyd Dobyns and Clare Crawford-Mason comes down to *Quality or Else.* Richard Pascale and Anthony Athos identify it as *The Art of Japanese Management;* while Tom Peters sees it as *Liberation Management.* And Mary Walton personalizes it as *The Deming Management Method.* All their work focuses on one thing: quality leadership, *the empowerment and continuous improvement domain of Total Leadership.*

Total Leadership is about creating and sustaining productive change. Change is productive when it involves more effective ways of operating and leads to consistently improved outcomes. The knowledge, skills, strategies, standards, and expectations that it takes to achieve these improvements is the domain of quality leaders. They focus on and achieve these improvements through a process called development to establish a key pillar of change: greater organizational capacity. Without improved capacity, organizations lack the ability to implement and sustain productive change.

The Essence of Quality Leaders

Quality leadership is about developing organizational and staff capacity to change and improve. We learned in the previous chapters that people and organizations do not change unless there is a compelling reason to change, unless they have a clear picture of that change, and unless they are committed to making the change. But even then, people and organizations cannot change unless they have the capacity to do so. Quality leaders must have the orientations and abilities to stimulate employees to grow and develop as people and to establish ever higher expectations and standards concerning product and service quality and their abilities.

W. Edwards Deming, the most noted of all quality gurus, believed strongly that the organization itself is the major part of any quality or production problem (Walton 1986). Deming believed and proved that workers could and would change if quality programs started at the top and leaders implemented the kinds of organizational processes that strengthened and supported the workers' abilities.

Deming believed that 85 percent or more of the problems in any organization are caused by the organization itself and 15 percent or fewer are caused by the workers. Later in his career, he changed those figures to 94 and 6 percent.

Quality leaders know and act on their role as the standard bearers of excellence in their organizations. Doing things fast is no substitute for doing things well — excellently the first time, and even better after that. Quality leaders are able to develop, empower, and build the capacity of individuals, teams, and the total organization to change, to implement a total quality management (TQM) approach, and to continuously improve. They know that people are an organization's greatest resource, that the real capital of their organization goes home every night, and that the drive for quality in a world of constant change can never stop.

Nowhere is the need for quality leaders more apparent than in schools and school districts. Educators are members of the world's most important profession and operate a people-intensive business. Student learning success certainly deserves at least as much quality emphasis as the Ford Taurus!

There are four basic aspects of any quality paradigm: understanding client needs, setting quality standards, measuring product quality, and modifying the processes to ensure improved results. Quality leaders do them all.

Understanding Client Needs

Quality leaders go directly to clients to inquire about their needs. In understanding client needs, educational leaders face a special problem because they have so many different clients. It isn't just the customers and the suppliers, as is the case with most businesses. Education's clients include students, parents, communities, employers, universities, and society as a whole (Bonstingl 1992).

For example, if a district has 70 percent of its students go to college, the district should recognize universities as one of its prime clients and conduct systematic research on (1) what it takes for students to be successful there, (2) how well the district's graduates are doing once they reach college, and (3) which factors seem to underlie success and failure. Quality leaders use such data to evaluate and improve their high school programs.

Setting Quality Standards

The ultimate concern of quality leaders is student performance on the district's declared outcomes and the ability of their schools to achieve them for all students. So quality leaders insist that quality standards be attached to each student outcome for each level of schooling. And they insist on establishing and implementing quality standards for teaching, school-level leadership, and the superintendency, all of which are tied to results.

Quality leaders would wholeheartedly agree with the frustrating insights of a teacher from New York State with whom we worked several years ago. At the end of a seminar on setting and achieving quality standards, she observed: "Bs, Cs, Ds, and Fs represent the degree to which students don't meet our high standards, but we think it's okay and give them anyway."

Measuring Product Quality

Feedback is the key to improvement. Without it, any attempt at continuous improvement will be haphazard at best. Careful measurement of product quality provides decision makers with the feedback information that supports continuous improvement. During the past several years, education has made great strides with authentic performance assessment and performance portfolios for students.

When clear quality standards are established, the foundation has been laid for a measurement system that directly reflects intended outcomes. Even more encouraging are the efforts of some school systems that apply performance assessment and portfolio processes to educators as well as to student outcomes. Quality leaders applaud this trend.

Modifying the Process

Feedback on performance allows for data-driven decision making and change. Leaders are aware of the power of intuition, insight, and gut feelings, but quality leaders know that concrete information about performance results makes for sound continuous improvement decisions. If they're not getting the expected results, quality leaders will insist that their organizations modify what they are doing and continue to study the results of these changes to determine what works best. While quality leaders allow workers to lay out their own work so that they can improve their processes (Deming 1986), they insist that those decisions be based on the best data possible.

The Purpose of Quality Leaders

As we explained in the latter half of Chapter 2, the fundamental purpose of quality leaders in a productive change process is to orchestrate and shape their organization's capacity building process. Quite simply, organizational change has little chance of succeeding unless those entrusted to implement the change have the tools, understanding, and technical abilities to execute the proposed changes. Developing and strengthening these abilities is what quality leaders do best. Their focus on capacity building requires that organizations improve:

- Technical knowledge,
- Employee skills,
- Tools and technologies,
- Timely information,
- Production processes,
- Decision making,
- Design frameworks,
- Performance standards,
- Training systems,

- Feedback loops,
- Implementation strategies,
- Improvement processes, and
- Communication networks.

These 13 factors define and embody the conditions that enable employees to implement the declared purpose and carry out desired changes competently. Remove an element or two from the list, and organizational effectiveness begins to wane.

Being sensitive to these issues, quality leaders know that purpose, vision, and ownership fuel the affective and motivational side of change, but without these critical technical elements, even the most noble and compelling change efforts will falter. When quality leaders focus on and strengthen these elements, organizations will have the ability to succeed. But without them, change becomes a nightmare of errors, frustrations, and disappointing results.

As decisive, results-oriented, and hard driving as they can be, quality leaders also know that they can't get quality on the cheap or in a hurry. Capacities of this scope and depth cannot be developed and refined overnight. They take time to build, especially when change efforts involve new paradigm thinking, new technologies, and fundamentally different ways of operating. That's why quality leaders are the champions of ongoing professional development. They fight for the budget dollars to conduct quality staff development and work extra hard to ensure that people's technical understanding and expertise don't lag behind their motivation to succeed. That's why quality leaders' continuous improvement agenda requires constant attention, limitless energy, and the resources to keep the organization's capacity growing.

Developing the Capacity for Success

Of all the five change processes, development is the most technically demanding.

> Development is the focused, deliberate, continuous unlocking, building, and improvement of individual's and teams' perspectives and talents needed to create, sustain, and renew personal and organizational success.

The purpose of development is to translate staff and constituent willingness and motivation into the concrete capacities — knowledge, ideas, skills, information, tools, and competences — that enable them to make productive contributions to the organization. The massive literature we've reviewed clearly shows that lasting improvement is impossible without building and strengthening personal and organizational capacity.

First and foremost, capacity development is about all participants becoming responsible for being:

• Continuous learners who are accountable for regularly improving their decision making, actions, performance, and contributions to the organization; and
• Quality performers who are committed to applying standards of excellence to all their productive endeavors and to achieving the organization's declared purpose.

This continuous learning/continuous improvement orientation is essential to establishing what Senge (1990) regards as genuine learning organizations.

There are four major aspects to the development process that reflect the critical pillars of change that underlie everything described in this book:

• All participants must be given an opportunity to acquire the knowledge and skills needed to shape and fully understand the organization's declared purpose and vision. Without a clear picture of what these critical purpose-defining and direction-setting components are and mean to the organization and how to develop them, participants can't see where they are headed, why it's important, and what they intend to accomplish by participating in the organization and its change efforts. And without both clear purpose and vision and the skills and knowledge to back them up, participation can be unfocused, scattered, and even counterproductive.
• By participating actively in shaping the purpose and vision from the ground up, participants know that the vision is their own. They understand and identify with the vision, and are committed to making it work. Even though they may borrow elements from other people's work to shape their purpose and vision, the decision to borrow and incorporate is theirs, not someone else's. This ownership-developing process is vital to having an organization pub-

licly acknowledge its values, assumptions, and priorities and to developing a culture that embodies them. It is also vital to being able to implement a vision.

- Development requires the capacity to execute the vision. Otherwise, it's an empty promise that offers opportunities and delegates responsibilities that participants lack the skills and tools to fulfill. Successful performance is an inseparable combination of commitment and ability. Neither is a substitute for the other. Hence, the single most important thing that can be done during this process is to strengthen the knowledge base and competences of the many people who will be involved in the larger change effort over the long haul. The second most important thing is to strengthen the tools and technologies the organization uses to pursue and achieve its purpose. In the beginning, that strengthening process must focus on what is needed to make the productive change effort successful. Then, it can focus on the tools and skills needed for successful program implementation.
- Development depends on organizational support, the determination by those in authority to make the decisions, create the opportunities, devote the time and resources, and coordinate participants' efforts as they build the purpose, vision, ownership, and capacity necessary for successful planning and implementation. Without this support, and the opportunities and encouragement it provides, the participation and contributions of employees will wane, especially among those who volunteer their time to go the extra mile. Total Leaders know that providing support is a matter of "putting up" or "shutting down," so they find ways to create opportunities for and reward those who make exceptional personal investments.

The Moral Foundation of Quality Leaders

Besides being the champions of the four arenas of the quality paradigm, quality leaders operate on a moral foundation that supports this paradigm. Our reading of the literature strongly suggests that quality leaders openly endorse, consistently model, and clearly exemplify the core values of excellence and productivity and the professional principles of accountability and improvement. Together, these four moral elements define and shape their commitment to continuous improvement — of themselves, their employees, and their organization's processes and products.

Excellence represents a desire for, and pursuit of, the highest quality in any undertaking, process, product, or result. It represents a dedication to monitoring and responding constructively to whatever is done or created to ensure that there is a way for it to eventually meet or exceed the highest attainable standard of performance and consistency. Excellence requires that you be acutely aware of the present and emerging needs of your customers — outside and inside the organization — and that you meet or exceed *their* expectations. Total Leaders are able to set quality standards for all significant processes and products, create feedback loops for themselves and others, and consistently improve the quality of their products and services.

Productivity is reflected in the optimum use of available time, resources, technologies, and talent to achieve desired results. In addition to the simple notions of hard work and improved technologies, productivity is about using the often untapped motivation, creativity, and abilities of people to generate more "smart work," "fun work," and commitment to quality results. When work is aligned with personal values and interests, it becomes meaningful. This condition sparks the internal motivators in people, which in turn increases both their productivity and work satisfaction. Total Leaders do not, however, achieve productivity on the backs of their people. They realize that the unhealthy stress that results from long hours with difficult tasks will eventually be counterproductive to long-term health and productivity.

Accountability is a matter of taking responsibility for the content and process of decisions made, actions taken, and the resulting outcomes. It is being cognizant from the beginning about the need to make agreements and engage in activities with the full expectation that they must be carried out in the most competent and conscientious manner possible. Accountability is also about making sure that those agreements are kept. At its essence, it is inseparable from the deepest meaning and implications of professionalism and the core value of integrity.

Accountability applies at a personal level, at a collective/team level, and at an organizational level, and it emanates far more from within the individual or group than from the outside. Hence, accountability should not be mistaken for compliance with external standards and demands. Total Leaders not only accept accountability, they seek and embrace it. Consequently, they believe that what they do and what they produce is so important that they want their employees, their customers, and the public to know of their standards, goals, and accomplishments.

Improvement represents a commitment to continuously enhancing the quality of personal and organizational performance, the processes used to generate results, and the results themselves. Embracing and applying this principle of professionalism implies that standards exist (or can be defined) toward which your organization and its members can direct their sights and efforts. Defining and communicating those standards is a key component of improvement.

Here are the kinds of situations that might challenge you to apply these four Moral Foundation elements:

Excellence: You realize that about one-third of your graduates who choose to attend colleges and or universities drop out before completing their second year.

Productivity: You are aware that one of your schools is getting significantly better student learning results than another with a very similar student body.

Accountability: You have agreed with your board of education that improving student achievement is the top priority and that it will be a significant part of you personal evaluation.

Improvement: You believe that the Total Quality Management concept should be applied to your school district, but you have no clear-cut quality standards for principals and teachers.

Underlying the improvement principle are: (1) a commitment to quality and the core value of excellence, (2) a belief that everything an organization does and produces can be done better or more effectively, and (3) a conviction that continuous improvement and achieving quality should be carefully designed and monitored processes that fuel an organization's ability to meet the constantly rising expectations and challenges from its constituents and external environment.

Total Leaders insist that quality standards be developed for all significant processes, products, and services; feedback loops be established that inform everyone of the degree to which quality standards are being met or exceeded; and that feedback be used to continuously improve the processes designed to create products and provide services.

The Critical Performance Roles of Quality Leaders

To carry out the development process effectively, quality leaders implement three critical performance roles. These broad arenas of responsibility and action directly enable them to make the decisions and carry out the actions that constitute the development process and achieve the pillar of change to which it is linked, organizational capacity. These three critical performance roles of the Total Leader are:

- Developing and empowering everyone.
- Improving the organization's performance standards and results.
- Creating and using feedback loops to improve performance.

Performance Role 10: Developing and Empowering Everyone

This is the most central performance role to the success of quality leaders, and it contains a unique challenge. If beauty is in the eyes of the beholder, then the psychological condition that is called "empowerment" is in the perceptions and feelings of the empowered. The very word empowerment implies that if the "empoweree" doesn't feel empowered, they are not — no matter what leaders may say or do. With that clarification, we define empowerment as being in control of the variables that one perceives to be important to one's success.

But this empowerment condition is not like blessing people and sending them forth to be forever empowered. Empowerment makes little sense if the empowered don't know what to do with their power.

The 15 Performance Roles of a Total Leader

- Creating and sustaining a compelling personal and organizational purpose.
- Being the lead learner.
- Modeling core organizational values and personal principles.
- Defining and pursuing a preferred organizational future.
- Consistently employing a client focus.
- Expanding organizational perspectives and options.
- Involving everyone in productive change.
- Developing a change-friendly culture of innovation, healthy relationships, quality, and success.
- Creating meaning for everyone.
- Developing and empowering everyone.
- Improving the organization's performance standards and results.
- Creating and using feedback loops to improve performance.
- Supporting and managing the organization's purpose and vision.
- Restructuring to achieve intended results.
- Rewarding positive contributions to productive change.

As noted in the previous section, it takes a compelling organizational purpose to set the direction that empowered people take. But before individuals can be effectively empowered, they must have a maturity level that reflects four key things that quality leaders strive to have in place:

- The ability to set high yet attainable goals so that purpose and high-quality standards can be met.
- The ability to take responsibility for achieving the purpose and the standards.
- The willingness to take responsibility so that they are motivationally focused on achieving the purpose and standards.
- A receptivity to coaching (Hersey and Blanchard 1972) so they can acquire the skills and understanding necessary for achieving the purpose and standards.

Because quality leaders are so concerned about personal and organizational effectiveness, they are intentional about empowering people. They do not wait for someone to come to them to ask to be empowered. They are proactive about it and take the initiative to carry out eight essential steps. They:

- Explain and define empowerment to everyone.
- Say they want it and make it an organizational value and norm.
- Set ambitious, vision-based goals.
- Determine the maturity level of the individual since not everyone is ready to meet the four criteria yet.
- Observe, monitor, and coach, but not before people are ready.
- Provide support for performance success including structure, training, and dollars.
- Reward and celebrate the successes of those who are empowered.
- Help the empowered create bold new visions of the possible.

This approach rests on the conviction that genuine empowerment exists when one:

- Has a compelling organizational purpose in place,
- Puts people in control of the variables that they perceive to be important to their success,
- Moves decisions to the point of implementation,
- Has individuals and teams lay out their own work, and
- Allows people to express themselves through their work.

When people require new knowledge and skills above and beyond the maturity qualities, quality leaders leap into action on another front: competence development. Quality leaders believe that professional competence and growth are the responsibilities of both the individual and the organization. Each has a big stake in the outcome. Organizations need the increased capacity of their employees, and employees need to remain marketable in a work world that no longer affords lifelong employment in a single organization.

Therefore, quality leaders work closely with their employees to develop and implement professional development programs that:

- Focus on building the capacity to implement the organization's purpose and vision.
- Align with the organization's reward system.
- Take into account the experience and characteristics of adult learners.

- Include a strong hands-on coaching component.
- Are facilitated by the organization's heroes and heroines.
- Keep all employees on the cutting edge of their performance capabilities and current in the job market.

Performance Role 11: Improving the Organization's Performance

If we asked a cross-section of leaders to pick the one performance role on which their career success ultimately depends, we'd guess that improving the organization's performance would be their choice. Everything else looks to be an enabling factor in getting this ultimate improvement to happen. This performance role is why one signs up to be a leader.

But what specifically do you need to change to get your organization's performance to improve? If the answer is unclear, consider the following.

In *Competing for the Future*, Hamel and Prahalad (1994) introduced the notion of core competencies: "A bundle of skills and technologies that enables a company to provide a particular benefit to customers." In our language, the particular benefit they refer to is the organization's mission, its unique market niche, and the reason the organization exists. Its core competencies, then, are the unique tools and techniques it uses to achieve that mission. For Sony, it's pocketability. For Federal Express, it's on-time delivery. For Motorola, it's mass customization, and for schools, we hope it's learning success.

With this important notion in mind, let's focus on schools. The premises, definitions, and logic of this book clearly indicate that improving educational performance — achieving productive change — comes down to improving learning results for all students. Without becoming mired in discussing which results are most important for students in the long run and whether or not schools do much to develop them, we'll simply start the improvement effort here.

From a school leader's perspective, improving organizational performance is about improving student learning.

School leaders can start with a key concept and concrete framework. The concept is called the conditions of success, comes from Spady's (1998) *Paradigm Lost,* and relates to factors that directly determine whether a successful learning result is likely to happen. For example, if students aren't given enough time to reach a given performance level on an outcome, it doesn't matter how good the curriculum is, how good the facilities are, how good the teacher is, or how well constructed the assessment is. The critical condition of success called time for learning was inadequate and caused lower than desired/deserved results.

Quality leaders in education are savvy about these conditions of success. The concept gives them a powerful rationale for deciding whether proposed improvements are likely to address direct causes or only indirect influences of student learning. The differences are quite clear from the four kinds of conditions of success that Spady identifies:

Beliefs and priorities, namely paradigm perspectives, assumptions, beliefs, philosophy, defining orientations, attitudes, and criteria for decision making held by those who work directly with students.

Operating principles and processes, which are the standards and criteria for action and decision making, and the techniques and strategies that instructional personnel use in planning, teaching, teaming, assessing, grading, and advancing students through the curriculum.

Organizational structures, or the patterns of organizing and allocating time, space, staff, students, curriculum, and learning resources that directly affect student opportunities to successfully learn what is essential.

Support conditions, which are the resources, processes, and strategies used to mobilize interest and participation in instructional effectiveness efforts.

If improving student learning is the goal, then school leaders should focus first on the likely direct causes. They are reflected in the operating principles and processes and organizational structures, so the initial focus should be on these. But beliefs and priorities and support conditions are important indirect influences since they bear on how the operating principles and processes and organizational structures are implemented.

Performance Role 12: Creating and Using Feedback Loops

When thinking of quality leaders, it's easy to conjure up pictures of people with green-billed caps pouring over statistics, as we can imagine W. Edwards Deming doing. Quality leaders know that there is another aspect of feedback that is more subjective, spontaneous, and "qualitative." Quality leaders communicate regularly with individuals and teams and informally let them know how important their role is, when and how they make contributions to the organization, how those contributions add value for the organization, and how their participation on teams creates synergy.

But quality leaders also know that occasional qualitative feedback is only part of the quality equation. Because they are thoroughly grounded in the power and crucial role of systematic objective feedback that includes performance targets, measures, data, and communication as the basis for continuous improvement, quality leaders make sure that individuals and teams create and use feedback loops on a regular basis. This information also informs them about the quality of their products and/or services, and about the effectiveness and efficiency of their processes.

Their rationale is simple. Quality leaders consider feedback a key personal motivator, especially for those who are already achievement oriented. They want to know how they're doing, where they stand, whether they're having a good week or year, and how to make it better. It's natural for such achievement-oriented people to want to better their previous best and compete favorably when compared to others.

As a part of this performance role, quality leaders also embrace accountability for the quality of products and services, for organizational processes, and for how people do things. But these processes, like the conditions of success, are only the "means" part of the equation. Being accountable for the means is meaningless unless you're also accountable for the ends. That's why, for example, it does little good to have teachers using Madeline Hunter's model perfectly if their students can't demonstrate the intended learning outcomes.

Creating a Feedback Loop

Creating a feedback loop is a rather logical but somewhat complex process. Whether building widgets or educating children, there are six steps to designing and implementing a sound feedback process. School districts that have defined their student outcomes and performance standards and built a system for authentically assessing them will have a head start in creating feedback loops that are objective, meaningful, and growth-producing. These steps involved are:

Clearly identify the product/service. While some educators might struggle to identify their product, the verdict is already in: it's *student learning*. When educators have clearly defined student outcomes, their product is students' demonstrations of those outcomes.

Set quality standards, with a heavy-duty focus on customers and clients. For educators, quality standards often come in the form of rubrics that help practitioners determine the degree to which student demonstrations of learning meet predetermined high-level performance criteria.

Identify the data needed to measure quality standards. For teachers, these data may be the number or percentage of students who are demonstrating particular outcomes at given levels of proficiency. Teachers will need to specify which students are able to do which things at which levels.

Determine how to collect, analyze, and communicate those data to all decision makers. This step requires decisions about (1) where and how students will be assessed, (2) how the performance data will be compiled, (3) what form will make it easiest to use for teachers, principals, and the district office, (4) who is to receive the data, (5) and when the data will be available for review.

Establish a process to ensure that the data are being used effectively. Just because people are receiving student performance data doesn't mean they are using it, or using it effectively. Quality leaders make sure that everyone in their charge uses this feedback to determine what to change that has the potential for improving quality and productivity. If the feedback received isn't used for making improvement decisions, then the previous steps have been a waste of time.

***Continuously improve the effectiveness of the feedback loop and the process of production*.** This step is why one does the previous five. After receiving objective feedback about the product (i.e., student outcome performance), school leaders are positioned to determine: (1) how well things are going, (2) what the probable causes are for the good and bad news, and (3) what part of the process of education needs to be changed to continuously improve your product. Even if the feedback is positive, quality leaders will push individuals and teams to set even higher productivity and quality standards. That's what continuous (quality) improvement is all about.

Quality leaders know that feedback loops are the backbone of continuous improvement. What Deming and his colleagues taught the Japanese about quality and feedback after World War II is even more necessary in schools today than it is at Ford, Sony, and Nordstrom.

Profile of Service Leaders

The guru	Robert Greenleaf
An exemplar	Mother Theresa
An antithesis	Karl Icahn (former chairman of Eastern Airlines)
Mind set	People are our most important resource, and they'll do the "right thing right" if they get support.
Purpose	To align the organization and its reward system to directly support its vision.
Focus	Organizational alignment and restructuring Worker and staff needs Leadership density
Change belief	Change happens, and is sustained, when people are supported in making the change.
Performance roles	Managing the organization's vision Restructuring to achieve intended results Rewarding positive contributions
Key sources	*Servant Leadership* (Greenleaf 1991) *The Power of Alignment* (Labovitz and Rosansky 1997) *Stewardship* (Block 1987) *Managing Transitions* (Bridges 1980) *Synchronicity* (Jaworski 1996) *Reengineering the Corporation* (Hammer and Champy 1993) *1001 Ways to Reward Employees* (Nelson 1994)

CHAPTER 7

The Service Leadership Domain: Total Leaders Ensuring Support

---

"The main thing, is to keep the main thing, the main thing!"

George Labovitz and Victor Rosansky

James Autry sees it as the balance between *Love and Profit.* Warren Bennis and Patricia Biederman see a key aspect of it as *Organizing Genius.* To William Bridges, it's a matter of *Managing Transitions,* while Peter Drucker calls it *Managing in a Time of Great Change.* Robert Greenleaf call it *Servant Leadership,* but Paul Hersey describes it from the perspective of *The Situational Leader.* George Labovitz and Victor Rosansky boldly declare its essence to be *The Power of Alignment,* while Douglas Smith says it's a matter of *Taking Charge of Change.*

They refer to what we call service leadership, *the strategic alignment and management domain of Total Leadership.*

Because Total Leadership is about creating and sustaining productive change, it can't succeed without service leadership. Using a powerful process we call orchestration, service leaders do everything possible to establish organizational support, the fifth and final pillar that underlies successful change efforts. They are committed to ensuring that their organizations are structured and aligned to achieve their declared purpose and vision. They make sure their organizations really do change.

The Essence of Service Leaders

Service leadership is about being "in service" to the organization's declared purpose and vision. Because they are change agents, service leaders create the conditions, procedures, incentives, and structures that enable genuine change to happen. The previous four chapters discuss how essential it is to have a reason to change, a clear picture of the change, commitment to change, and the ability to make the change. But those changes won't last until service leaders enter the picture and close the circle by establishing the direct organizational supports that make deep and lasting change possible.

While the term service sounds soft, the duty is hard. When service leaders recognize that aspects of their organization are diminishing or impeding the organization's success, they are the ones who insist that changes be made. This can be a thankless and unpopular task. But service leaders choose these tough assignments.

As the name implies, service leaders have hearts of gold, but they also have nerves of steel. When push comes to shove and the integrity of organizational purpose and success are at stake, they're the first to step up. They're not looking for a fight, but rather for successful change. Sometimes the two go hand-in-hand despite the best efforts of Total Leaders to get the roadblocks surrounding purpose, vision, ownership, and capacity out of the way.

If this sounds more tough-minded than kindhearted, service leaders will be the first to say that the compassionate thing to do is to deal with issues and get to the bottom of problems, not ignore them. To sidestep issues that impair the effectiveness of the organization and its members is no act of kindness. The organization suffers, its productive members suffer, and those contributing to the problem suffer because no action is taken to get them on a more productive and fulfilling track. Service leaders both tell it like it is, and deal with what they say. Hypocrisy isn't in their vocabulary or character.

So far, this book can be summarized into four simple propositions:

- Leadership involves the ability to create and gain consensus around a compelling vision.
- Management involves the ability to make that vision a reality.
- Both are essential to productive change.
- Service leaders are exemplary managers.

The Purpose of Service Leaders

The fundamental purpose of service leaders in a productive change process is to ensure that organizational support for change abounds. Quite simply, organizational change has little chance of succeeding unless those entrusted to implement the change have the opportunity to do so without encountering organizational obstacles including procedures, misallocated resources, poor communication and coordination, inadequate technologies, disorganization, rivalries, and a host of other liabilities.

Getting organizations aligned and structured to establish this support is what service leaders do best. Their focus on effective organizational functioning requires that they constantly address and align the policies, decisions, resources, and procedures that make it possible for employees and constituents to achieve and sustain the changes implied in their stated purpose and vision.

Support is demonstrated by the organization's willingness and ability to put itself and its resources squarely behind its declared purpose and vision and the people it counts on to make them happen. Support reflects Total Leaders' true commitment to and involvement in the change process, specifically their willingness to make decisions, commit people and resources, and operate in ways that align with organizational purpose and vision, and encourage and enable employees to carry out the changes everyone has committed to.

With adequate and consistent support, change will last. Without it, anxiety, cynicism, and a major retreat to the status quo will occur.

Consequently, service leaders must have the orientations and abilities (1) to ask organizational members what needs to be done to support their success, (2) to cultivate their desire to contribute their best, and (3) to remove organizational obstacles to their doing so. This is the heart of the change process we call orchestration.

Translating Vision into Concrete Form

The orchestration process is foremost about formally designing and executing what the organization's productive change effort exists to accomplish.

Orchestration involves the explicit, concrete, aligned design, implementation, and management of the structures and processes that directly support the organization's declared purpose and vision.

Orchestration also involves getting things to work effectively by establishing and managing the roles, mechanisms, structures, and programs that directly support the declared purpose. And it's about clearly defining and making concrete what it actually looks like to accomplish your purpose, implement your vision, have strong ownership, and possess strong capacities.

The most important asset in the orchestration process is consistently applying the professional principle of alignment to daily decision making. Alignment is the powerful standard and criterion for determining whether plans and actions match and directly support the declared purpose and vision. If what you're doing doesn't match, orchestration requires managing it and bringing it into alignment.

This is a tough duty because the organization's status quo is bound to be disrupted by the realignment and restructuring that will occur. In education, that is the operational equivalent to melting the iceberg described in Chapter 1. People's definitions of their work, careers, and status within the organization will inevitably be disrupted, which is why the other four pillars of change are so critical to the change effort.

In thinking about the orchestration process, keep in mind that it involves both designing and doing. It's a good idea to test the feasibility of the most important ideas on a trial basis before committing to them. After the ideas are tried out, they can be rigorously evaluated and openly discussed. If things don't turn out as anticipated, look for the reasons and revise things accordingly, using the feedback loop strategy described in Chapter 6.

Sending up these trial balloons early in the change effort is a smart idea, particularly if they meet three key criteria:

- They are grounded in the solid research and theory that surfaced in the consideration and exploration processes.
- They receive rigorous and informed scrutiny during the trial stage.
- They have their pros and cons shared openly with colleagues and stakeholders against some clearly defined expectations or criteria.

For example, educators frequently try out new concepts, such as new ways of grouping students, in an alternative school or a designated "experimental" program in order to test their effectiveness and suitability for wider use in the district. Often trial balloons of this kind are encouraged by awarding mini-grants to teachers or departments within a building. The purpose of the grant is to acknowledge the effort being made to innovate, to note that the district will be paying special attention to how things go, and to set expectations for the staff involved to share the results of their work with others. These same three criteria should be applied with even more intensity and care the longer a productive change effort continues. These criteria will ensure soundly grounded decisions and actions, an honest assessment of consequences, and a demonstrated desire to learn and improve from the results. That's a lot of benefit from three common sense criteria.

When applying these three criteria, school leaders need to take special note of the core values of risk taking and teamwork and the principles of alignment and contribution. Colleagues need to focus on this moral foundation since it's the strongest assurance of carrying out purposeful, ethical, informed, and responsible decision making and action during what could be a tense and challenging time for the organization.

Finally, to avoid the risk of being overwhelmed with data and detail, you must keep the big picture of the organizational purpose and vision as simple and focused as possible.

The Moral Foundation of Service Leaders

Service leaders operate from a moral foundation that places risk taking (to step up and take the road less traveled) and teamwork (everyone pulling together without special status or credit) at the pinnacle of their core values chart. These values are manifested in their commitment to two particular principles of professionalism: alignment (getting the whole herd headed in the right direction) and contribution (giving the very best). Consequently, they willingly and by nature choose to do the "heavy lifting" of Total Leadership, much like offensive linemen in football do the heavy lifting for the point makers — without the glory or headlines.

Risk taking is inseparable from change and improvement because both require extending beyond the tried, true, and familiar to do (different) things a different way, often without the assurance of success. Risk taking involves taking initiative, innovating, breaking the mold, speaking out, and a variety of things that foster and support the other core values, but may disrupt the status quo and invite criticism from those invested in present practices.

Total Leaders model risk taking and, most often, they make those risks public. Effective risk taking is not without planning. Total Leaders lower their and others' risk levels by insisting that good thinking precede risk taking. Mistakes and failing are accepted, and even valued, by Total Leaders, but only when the risk to innovate and change is thought through before making the jump. A bit of a paradox here, but Total Leaders are also not afraid to follow their intuition and their gut feeling about what is possible, even when there is not much evidence available to support them.

Teamwork is less about everyone doing everything as a coordinated team, and more about working collaboratively and cooperatively toward achieving a common recognized end, with individuals going out of their way to make the performance or results of others easier and better. Teamwork requires large doses of selflessness and the ability to anticipate and empathize with the needs and priorities of the total endeavor as well as those participating in it. Total Leaders openly acknowledge that "no one of us is as smart as all of us," and they know that the complex tasks of today's organizations usually require the efforts of an effective team. They also know how to create teams, how to facilitate and lead teams, and how to reward team efforts so that teamwork becomes an organizational norm.

Alignment represents the purposeful, direct matching of decisions, resources, and organizational structures and processes with the organization's declared purpose, vision, and core values. Alignment is about making something totally congruent or parallel with something else. It is also about using consistency, logic, and common sense in planning, decision making, and implementation. Clearly, alignment requires both personal conviction and the same kind of analytical orientation embodied in the inquiry principle.

Without alignment, change efforts are likely to be inconsistent, illogical, and haphazard. In fact, without alignment between your organization's vision and its processes, policies, and structures, you can't expect the desired change to stick. Total Leaders know that leadership is about vision building and that new visions nearly always require new structures, new processes, and sometimes even new organizations. They also know that managing change is fundamentally about alignment of the organization with its declared purpose and vision.

Contribution represents freely giving and completely investing one's attention, talent, and available resources to enhance the quality and success of meaningful endeavors. Contribution is about caring, selflessness, responsibility, and dedication. It is also about giving your best all of the time, with no anticipation of special rewards or recognition. Teachers who work day after day with little or no recognition are excellent examples of this definition of contribution.

Contribution is inseparable from what it means to be a true professional. It occurs most naturally when people simply pay close attention to what is happening around them and respond as competently and responsibly as possible when new opportunities arise or things go awry. When organizational crises arise, contribution, not simply employment or participation, spells the difference between failure and success. Without the extra investments of time and talent by employees in the face of such circumstances, few organizations would sustain themselves. Total Leaders create a professional culture that makes contribution an expectation and a norm, and rewards it as the highest level of Abraham Maslow's (1954) hierarchy of needs.

Here are the kinds of situations that might challenge you to apply these four Moral Foundation elements.

Risk taking: You have been asked to teach a course on leadership for your district's staff development program, and you know you will be expected to model effective staff development techniques.

Teamwork: You sense that two or three members of your administrative team have hidden agendas, and you believe that openness and trust have suffered as a result.

Alignment: You have created a dynamic new vision of teaching for your school system and you want to apply this vision to teacher selection, development, and out-counseling.

Contribution: A principal in your district has established an outstanding reputation, and her state association has asked her to be a presenter at a series of seminars for aspiring leaders. She comes to you to request professional leave.

The Critical Performance Roles of Service Leaders

To carry out the orchestration process effectively, service leaders implement three critical performance roles. These broad arenas of responsibility and action enable them to make the decisions and carry out the actions that constitute the orchestration process and achieve the pillar of change to which it is linked, organizational support. These three critical performance roles of the Total Leader are:

- Supporting and managing the organization's purpose and vision.
- Restructuring to achieve intended results.
- Rewarding positive contributions to productive change.

Service leaders recognize that the performance role of supporting and managing the organization's purpose and vision is key to establishing the support pillar of change, but they know restructuring and rewarding positive contributions also play a critical part.

- Creating and sustaining a compelling personal and organizational purpose.
- Being the lead learner.
- Modeling core organizational values and personal principles.
- Defining and pursuing a preferred organizational future.
- Consistently employing a client focus.
- Expanding organizational perspectives and options.
- Involving everyone in productive change.
- Developing a change-friendly culture of innovation, healthy relationships, quality, and success.
- Creating meaning for everyone.
- Developing and empowering everyone.
- Improving the organization's performance standards and results.
- Creating and using feedback loops to improve performance.
- Supporting and managing the organization's purpose and vision.
- Restructuring to achieve intended results.
- Rewarding positive contributions to productive change.

Performance Role 13: Supporting the Organization's Purpose and Vision

"The main thing, is to keep the main thing, the main thing!" say Labovitz and Rosansky (1997). Without immediate, enthusiastic, and visible support, a newly formed compelling purpose and vision will have the shelf life of a ripe banana. Why? Because after that stimulating meeting in which people created an exciting reason for being and picture of a perfect organizational future, they return to the same offices the next morning. The people they meet on their way into the office are the same people they left the day before; the people waiting outside their offices don't even know they have this new vision; the mail in their in-boxes was sent before the vision was drafted; and their desks and surroundings look just like they did when they left.

It's reality time. They either start putting off the old "urgent" stuff to do what they just learned is the "truly important" stuff right now (Covey, Merrill, and Merrill 1994), or they can kiss their new strategic design good-bye. Framing the vision is one thing; keeping and managing it is another. And that's what service leaders were born to do.

The service approach to management is all about alignment, the direct matching of one thing with another. What needs to get aligned with the new vision are four things: structures, policies, processes, and people (Schwahn 1993). Here's what each entails.

Structures. New visions invariably demand new ways of getting things done, which in turn, demand new organizational structures. For example, if a value/belief about student learning is that schools control the conditions of student success, and the new vision is about continuous progress and performance-based learning, then the practice of grading in ink on specific days and averaging those grades is out of alignment with the vision and must be changed. And similar changes in the traditional structure of the organization will probably need to occur if practice is to be wholly consistent with the vision. Making changes of this kind requires risk taking of the first order because such changes represent major departures from the familiar and tried and true.

Policies. New visions frequently require establishing new policies and priorities and abandoning some long-established ways of doing business. For example, if a vision is for everyone to be empowered and encouraged to improve, but the staff evaluation policy is a deficit model that punishes people for unsatisfactory performance, it has to go. Otherwise, leaders can't expect people to take the risks necessary for dynamic, paradigm-breaking empowerment.

Processes. The way a leader effectively operated in the past is probably aligned with the old vision but not a new, future-focused one. For example, a principal may have previously hired teachers simply because he thought that they would be good. But now, the principal has embraced the idea that all students can learn and that having students learn something well is more important than exactly when they learn it (Spady 1994). To bring his selection processes and practices in line with these new beliefs, the principal will have to establish a process that results in his hiring not just a good teacher, but a good teacher whose beliefs are consistent with those of the system.

People. Everyone in the organization needs to implement the new vision. If only those who find the new vision comfortable or exciting implement it, then creating and sustaining productive change will be impossible. That is why implementing the organization's vision must become the key role and goal of every supervisor in the system. Service leaders make supporting and monitoring the implementation of the vision the central part of the supervision process. When each supervision session begins with the question, "Tell me about the things you are doing that are helping us to put our vision into practice?" the service leader clearly signals that the organization's purpose is important and real. By using these sorts of questions, supervisors communicate their excitement to the supervisees, who also become excited. We strongly believe that dialogue-initiating questions such as these need to be asked at every level of the organization, starting with the school board's evaluation session of the superintendent.

Managing for alignment around these four areas of organizational functioning is where the heavy lifting takes place for Total Leaders, but leaders can lighten their load by employing the strategies that service leaders use to manage the vision. They include:

- Aligning the organization and its people (Labovitz and Rosansky 1997);
- Having a bias for action (Peters and Waterman 1982);
- Creating feedback loops;
- Encouraging risk taking for promising innovations;
- Rewarding positive contributions;
- Making strategic resource allocations;
- Encouraging, coaching, developing, empowering, and, sometimes, outcounseling employees.

Being keeper of the dream and keeper of the vision is at the core of service leadership. When all organizational stakeholders are meaningfully involved in creating a compelling purpose and a picture of their preferred future, service leaders can assume that this is what everyone wants — that the organization's stakeholders have formed a compact. At that point, service leadership is about supporting everyone to move in that new, exciting direction.

Performance Role 14: Restructuring To Achieve Intended Results

For the past decade, the term restructuring has become a buzzword in almost all fields of endeavor. But, like most terms that become indiscriminately used by people trying to prove that they are keeping up with the times, restructuring has come to mean almost anything that has to do with change of any kind, whether it is as trivial as technical tinkering or as profound as paradigm transformation. But not so for service leaders. They know that:

- A structure is a tangible, fundamental pattern of organizational action.
- Structures get created to accomplish specific organizational ends.
- Structures that make sense for accomplishing a given end may not work effectively if that end changes.
- Structures can take on a life of their own, known as institutional inertia, which makes achieving new ends very difficult.

Restructuring is a matter of repatterning the organization's major actions around its highest priority purposes and intended results; otherwise, those ends will not be realized. This is why service leaders were born to restructure to achieve intended results.

Because they inherently start with the end in mind, service leaders use purpose and vision as both their starting point and their bottom line. By aligning (i.e., designing) "back from where they want to end up" (see Spady 1994, 1998), they approach their work with a perspective that is revolutionary to those accustomed to starting with the present and planning forward.

But for service leaders, there's only one place to start: the organization's priority results. For educators, that means having all students demonstrate the district's exit outcomes successfully.

Service leaders design their way back, step by step, from their desired end to where they need to start their implementation, just like mountain climbers do when they plan a climb from the peak back. At this initial design stage, everything but the end result is off the table; otherwise, old baggage and structures may be imposed on a result that may require completely new paradigm perspectives and possibilities. This challenge and opportunity is especially clear in education. It's the difference between designing curriculum from future-grounded outcomes and developing outcomes for the existing curriculum.

Here's how a service leader might address this challenge with his or her colleagues and constituents.

"Our district has used a highly future-focused strategic design process to develop an organizational mission that declares that we exist to 'equip all our students to succeed in a changing world.' That got us thinking and planning around the conditions and challenges our students will face once they've graduated, rather than around the curriculum structures and programs that we have inherited from past generations and various kinds of regulations and 'mandates.'

"What we recognized once we started looking at the futures research and other educational reform literature is that our students will have to become competent at a whole range of complex performance abilities if they're going to be successful adults. That's why we developed a framework of learning outcomes that emphasizes these real-world performance abilities. And for us, that's definitely the good news.

"The bad news is that these intended performance outcomes are dramatically different from the way our curriculum is focused and organized, what we teach, how we teach, what we test, how we test, and how we group, promote, and accredit students. Right now we structure everything around fixed, predetermined blocks of content and time, even though we know that content and competence are different, that different approaches are needed for developing competence, and that student learning progresses at different rates and in different ways.

"Therefore, we've got to fundamentally redesign and restructure what we're doing around what we've already said are the highest priority results we want for our students. This means shifting our emphasis from content to competence, from time to standards, and from curriculum categories to authentic performance areas. And we're going to have to restructure how we organize and use time, when we make critical learning experiences available, how we use staff and other adults in the community to accomplish our outcomes, and how we're going to handle the assessment and reporting of things we say reflect 'the real world.' How are we going to do that if our students are spending all their time sitting at desks in classrooms?"

This scenario illustrates that service leaders develop, advocate, and unwaveringly employ the basic, common sense logic of alignment. They seek to organize themselves and their processes around the desired results. If service leaders say they want their students to be quality producers, then they define high levels of quality in everything students do, hold those levels out as performance expectations, and give students unlimited experiences in producing things of significance.

Performance Role 15: Rewarding Positive Contributions

People mostly do what they are rewarded for. And when the rewards are for doing things consistent with their personal values and mission as well as those of the organization, it's almost certain that people will make positive contributions. Rewards are especially meaningful if they are near or at the top of Abraham Maslow's (1954) needs hierarchy. People do what meets their psychological needs, what is consistent with their values, and the things for which they are rewarded.

Service leaders believe in shared rewards be they monetary, emotional, or psychological. Shared rewards are not only powerful staff motivators, they also clearly demonstrate authentic leadership. Sharing the rewards of success is simply the moral response to organizational accomplishment.

Because service leaders reward positive contributions for productive change, they must first be able to spot a positive contribution. Specifically, they look for contributions consistent with the organization's declared values, mission, and vision:

Hard work. Who's doing the heavy lifting? It's a bit old fashioned, but hard work is still hard work! And it's a contribution to an organization that is nearly always critical and deeply valued. Success usually *is* hard work that is made meaningful through the alignment of productivity, values, and rewards. Hard work, however, should not be confused with being overworked. Service leaders don't reward workaholics. They believe that their employees have responsibilities elsewhere in their lives that require commitment and time. Hence, they reward those who work both hard and smart more than those who work long and hard.

Risk taking and winning. Risk taking and winning happen when everything comes together. Risk taking and winning usually create a breakthrough that shows the way for future successes. It doesn't get any better than taking a creative, insightful, and challenging chance to produce a breakthrough product — especially when that product is a breakthrough learning system for children.

Risk taking, losing, and learning. If a school leader or school system has never failed, it's obvious that they haven't taken significant risks. At the same time, they probably haven't gotten a lot better at what they're doing. Anything more than tinkering or a technical change requires risk, and risk means making a few mistakes, even when you have a good batting average. Losing isn't so bad if one takes the time to learn from it, and that's what service leaders honor as long as a thoughtful effort was behind the loss. Although we don't agree with the adage that says we learn more from our failures than our successes, we do admire Thomas Edison for learning hundreds of ways not to make a light bulb before he discovered the one that worked.

Committing fully in team efforts. "The Lone Ranger" has been replaced by the staff of "ER," the popular drama about a hospital emergency room, as the fictional hero/heroine of our day. The Lone Ranger has also been replaced by teams in most effective and enduring organizations. Most significant work in today's world is done in creative teams because projects are too large and complex for one person to do well on his or her own.

Challenges to the status quo. It takes courage to take on city hall. Most of us choose to blend in with the norms of the group and organization we're in. But telling the leader that he "has no clothes on" is sometimes what is needed to keep the organization on track and meeting customer needs. Teachers and principals who point out the places where schools continue to do things that are inconsistent with what we know about students and learning have demonstrated courage, taken a risk, and changed the course of the most important business in the community — education.

Doing it on time, with quality and a smile. Most good organizations, including schools, are privileged to employ a number of people who continue to do what is expected with superior quality and, in the process, to make the organization a better place for everyone.

The natural. Some people just seem to win more often than others. They are naturals who just seem to have it. And they are naturals who sometimes work hard and *always* work smart. The service leader wants to keep the natural around, even to the point of providing a bonus for renewing his or her contract.

Clearly, service leaders are about rewarding positive contributions, so they have to know a good contribution when they see one. But they also have to know a reward as their employees see one, for rewards are in the eyes of the beholder. When service leaders are unsure of how people would like to be rewarded for their contributions, they ask them. Invariably, employees begin by talking about money as the ultimate reward. Service leaders know that everyone likes money, but they also know that money does not tend to be a long-term motivator, especially for anyone who is having his or her basic needs met. After an employee receives a raise, and it makes her feel good for a week or two, then it's back to business as usual. However, when her organization or boss gives her that raise, it's a symbol of the *value* of the contribution. Chances are that the value shown will influence an employee much longer than the dollars that were symbolically attached.

Service leaders are either very aware of the powerful motivators at the top of Maslow's hierarchy, or they are unconscious appliers of his theory of motivation. They somehow know that opportunities for recognition, esteem, and actualization are the most powerful motivators for people working at their productive and creative best. That's why they consistently reward both teams and individuals with the motivator and the message as shown on page 119.

Clearly, service leaders recognize that the most powerful motivators are free. They work to pay fair salaries and provide fair benefits. They lobby their organizations for the welfare of their people. But beyond that, they work through the motivators of opportunity, influence, freedom, responsibility, and recognition.

Rewarding with the Motivator and the Message

Do you recognize these powerful motivators and messages? Using these consistently can encourage people to work at their productive and creative best.

The Motivator	The Message
Recognition	We want others to know about your success.
Advancement	Let us help you with your career path.
Freedom	You set the agenda . . . we'll get the resources.
Responsibility	This is big . . . and we need you to do it.
Attagirls/Attaboys	I saw and appreciate what you did.
Influence	We want you to help us make our big, important decisions.
Dollars	This organization shares the rewards of its success.

CHAPTER 8

Applying Total Leadership to Your Schools

A fter reading all the information, insight, and knowledge in this book, it's now time to consider some commitments about becoming a Total Leader. So far, we know:

- What the leading futurists say about the future conditions that will define organizations and careers in the 21st century (Chapter 1),
- How the best leaders in the best organizations think (Chapter 2), and
- What the best leaders in the best organizations value and do (Chapters 3 through 7).

If you have not read much of the leadership, change, and futurist literature of the past decade, but only read this book, you are now caught up. If you have read most of these best-sellers, you now have a framework with this book on which to hang everything you have learned.

While the first two chapters presented the mind set of Total Leaders, the remainder of the book gave the knowledge, insights, and strategies required to make productive change happen, which is the goal of every successful leader today. We discussed that each of the five leadership domains contained:

- A pillar of change,
- A critical change process, and
- Three performance roles.

Total Leadership happens when the pillar of change, the change process, and the performance roles of each leadership domain are focused on a comprehensive strategic design. This concentrated leadership focus gives Total Leaders and their organizations their best shot at productive change. A tall order for any leader, but Total Leadership provides the best formula known for getting things done — in an ethical manner and in a way that makes the organization even stronger when meeting its next challenge (Collins and Porras 1994).

Where To Start With Strategic Design

Strategic design has two major components. First, a Total Leader and his or her organization must develop a strategic direction. Second, when that direction has been set and clarified, the Total Leader must create strategic alignment around that strategic direction.

In short, one is a systematic, future-focused plan; the other is its implementation. Strategic direction is identifying what you want to get, and strategic alignment is structuring to get what you want.

We've helped more than 50 school systems identify their strategic directions and learned some key lessons, many of which are summarized in the Figure 8.1.

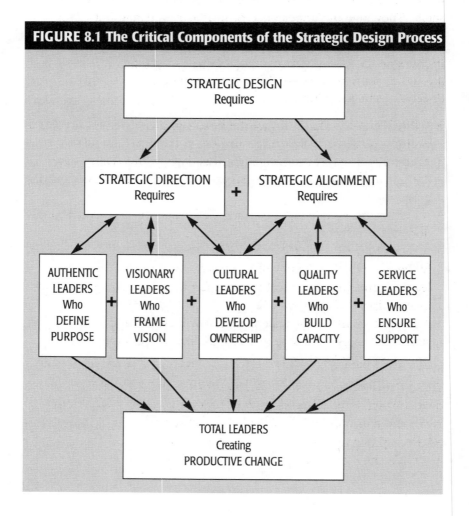

FIGURE 8.1 The Critical Components of the Strategic Design Process

The authentic, the visionary, and the cultural domains of Total Leaders are where strategic direction happens. Authentic leaders create compelling purposes, visionary leaders create inspirational visions, and cultural leaders create committed stakeholders. Systems without a strategic direction are managed but not led, and focused on means rather than ends, on policies rather than products, and on the familiar rather than the new and challenging.

Similarly, the cultural, the quality, and the service domains of Total Leaders make strategic alignment happen. Cultural leaders create employee ownership and commitment for the implementation, quality leaders build capacity for it, and service leaders ensure the support that makes it happen. Strategic directions without the necessary organizational alignment to make them happen end up as plans on a shelf. They give the appearance of productive change but never result in genuine implementation.

In our strategic design process, Total Leaders lead their systems through a planning process that results in the creation of five key direction-setting products:

- A brief but powerful listing of the beliefs and values that serve as a decision screen for all decision makers in the school system.
- A future-focused mission statement that briefly and clearly states the purpose of the school system and the reason the school district exists.
- A framework identifying the spheres of living and the future conditions that students will face once they leave school.
- A set of future-focused student performance outcomes that explicitly identify what students will be able to do with what they have learned, and what they will be like after they leave school and are living full and productive lives.
- A future-focused vision statement that will clearly and concretely state what the school system will look like in the future when operating at its ideal best.

These five products are the outcomes for the five key steps in the direction-setting component of the overall strategic design process. When the five steps are completed, the school system will have created a comprehensive decision screen that, when applied systematically, consistently, and creatively, ensures total system focus.

Most importantly, these five direction-setting documents serve as the basis for all decisions regarding curriculum and instruction, student assessment and credentialing, student placement and advancement, and the instructional delivery system. In short, they direct everything that affects student learning — the only reason the school system exists.

Using All 15 Performance Roles To Achieve Strategic Design

The Total Leader uses all 15 performance roles to create and implement a strategic plan — that is, to set a strategic direction and to create strategic alignment. Total Leadership is the surest way of transforming an organization to make it serve the critical emerging and future needs of students, parents, and society.

Our approach to strategic design has a strong bias toward participation and involving everyone in productive change. The most effective and efficient way to gain the commitment of the staff and stakeholders is to involve them in the design process. Our process is based upon the belief that:

- Groups have a collective wisdom,
- Involvement leads to commitment,
- Involvement is an effective means of communication, and
- Involvement is an effective means of educating the staff and the community.

We've found a strong correlation between the percentage of people involved in creating a compelling purpose and commitment and the follow through it generates. If a leader involves a dozen or so people, there will be a struggle to implement the plan. If a leader involves more than 1,000, there will be support and follow through.

In starting the strategic design process, it's effective to have groups respond to a set of basic, yet profound, strategic design questions that prompt deep thinking.

Each of the following questions is tied directly to one or more performance roles of the Total Leader, which are referenced in parentheses.

What are our strongest beliefs and values about learning and teaching?

Stephen Covey (1991) suggests, and we agree, that all good planning begins by identifying what we *believe* and *value*. Total Leaders begin the strategic direction-setting process by helping the group identify their strongest beliefs and values regarding students and learning, teachers and teaching, and effective schools and effective organizations. (Creating a compelling purpose, Creating meaning for everyone)

What is the fundamental reason our school system exists?

Logic dictates that once beliefs and values have been identified and clarified, the strategic design group is in a position to identify the mission of the school system — a clear and inspirational statement of why the system exists. But before this can be done with the necessary future focus, the strategic design group must do a thorough study of the shifts, trends, and future conditions that are redefining organizations and careers in the 21st century. (Being the lead learner, Modeling the principles of productive change, Employing a client focus)

Most of the systems with which we have worked created a future-focused mission that centers on equipping all students for the future. For example, the mission of the Evergreen School District in Vancouver, Wash., is "Equipping all students to succeed in a changing world."

In which spheres of living do you want your children/students to be successful after they finish school?

To serve the student, who is the primary client, we continue the process by asking participants to identify the spheres or arenas of life and living that are important to students' future life success once they leave the schools. (Employing a client focus, Expanding organizational options).

The identified spheres of living (e.g., work, relationships, family) determine the significant life roles of successful, fully functioning adults.

What are the key conditions and challenges students will face in these spheres that they will need to successfully meet?

Next, the planning group, with input from experts on each life role, identifies the conditions students are likely to face in each particular sphere after they leave school. This process, too, begins with a thorough study of shifts, trends, and future conditions. (Being the lead learner)

Identifying future conditions is a prerequisite to determining student learning needs. For example, math and science will be important in most workplaces, but what math will be required? How often do we use what we learn in algebra when we work in a high-tech organization like the 3M company? What type of math does the workplace require? Most people will be surprised by the response of someone who knows today's workplaces well. (Expanding organizational options)

What will graduates need to be able to know, do, and be like to successfully meet these conditions and challenges?

Discussing what graduates should be like when they live full and productive lives can be a sensitive issue in some communities. But the "be like" of students, based on the research presented by Goleman (1992) and Cooper and Sawaf (1996) is even more important than the "know" and "do" part of student outcomes. One's values, "be likes," and emotional quotient are too important to be ignored by schools. (Modeling the core values, Employing a client focus)

We have yet to find a school staff and community that have not been able to create a solid consensus around 10 universally endorsed values and their definitions: honesty, integrity, trustworthiness, loyalty, fairness, caring, respect, citizenship, pursuit of excellence, and accountability. While the value labels and definitions differ among communities, the essence of these 10 universal values seems to be the desire of parents no matter what their culture, religion, or socioeconomic status.

The next step in the strategic direction-setting process is to synthesize the future conditions, the universal values, and answers to the last question into student outcome statements. For example, some districts have chosen the student outcome label, "concerned citizens," which means that the system and the community want their graduates to live their lives as concerned citizens. The citizen part of this label comes from the life role of the same name, and the "concerned" part of the label comes from the universal values or the "be likes" that the school and community desire to foster.

Although the outcome label does set a general direction for student learning and performance, it's not specific enough to drive curriculum and instruction. For the outcome to be functional, the strategic direction-setting process must spell out what concerned citizens actually do. For example, here's how the South Washington County Schools in Cottage Grove, Minn., stated their student outcome for the civic sphere:

"Our graduates will be able to demonstrate that they are prepared to be informed, contributing citizens who:

- Promote an orderly society and use the democratic process for managing change,
- Participate in the political process by voting, volunteering, and providing input to leadership,
- Interpret the historical and theoretical foundations of the democratic political process, and
- Evaluate information to create and implement solutions concerning social, political, economic, and environmental issues."

South Washington County identified seven other similar student exit outcomes, each related to a significant life role. (Creating a compelling purpose, Employing a client focus, Creating meaning for everyone)

The beliefs and values, the mission, and the student exit outcomes constitute the compelling purpose of a school system. In effect, every activity to this point in the process could be attributed to the Total Leader's creating a compelling purpose.

What will our school system look like when we are operating at our ideal best?

The next stage, vision framing, is more the responsibility of the staff than the community. What the schools and classrooms will look like when everything is perfect, what the system will look like when everyone acts on everything the education profession knows about students and learning, teachers and teaching, and about effective schools, should be a professional decision. That's not to say that other stakeholders should not be involved in the vision framing process, but rather that their role should be more limited than when they were helping to create the system's compelling purpose. (Defining a preferred future)

While the organization has one set of beliefs and values, one mission, and one set of student exit outcomes, visions that are aligned with these elements need to be everywhere. Schools, departments, individual teachers — actually every program and person in the system— need to be pursuing their own creative and challenging vision. (Developing a culture of innovation) But it all begins with a *system* vision. People need to know the school district's vision so that they can create personal visions that will accomplish the larger system vision. (Creating meaning for everyone)

Total Leaders create their organization's future (Liebig 1994); they "act rather than being acted upon, and they begin with the end in mind" (Covey 1989). Total Leaders identify many alternative futures for their organization and then choose that which will best meet their clients' needs, namely, the future needs of students. (Defining a preferred future, Employing a client focus, Expanding organizational options) Educators can begin the vision building process by answering some key questions: How do you picture students demonstrating their learning — what are they actually doing? What are students doing when they are learning? Where is the learning taking place? How are students grouped? What are teachers doing?

Don't Forget Strategic Alignment

Often, the good intentions and excitement created by the strategic direction-setting process flounder or fail because leaders do not follow through with the alignment part of their responsibility. The quality and service domains of Total Leaders are where strategic alignment happens. Quality leaders develop powerful people, and service leaders support positive contributors.

Total Leaders are visionary leaders who create an organizational vision and then encourage, support, and, if need be, demand that there be compatible, compelling, and challenging visions throughout the organization. Visionary leaders insist that everyone in the organization be working toward attaining the preferred future. When individuals and teams are driven by a compelling purpose, they quite naturally find meaning in their work and are ready to be given the freedom to use their own motivation and power to pursue their vision.

Let's continue examining the relevant questions and the performance roles of Total Leaders within the strategic alignment process.

What attitudes and skills do we need to acquire to implement our challenging vision?

The quality leader knows that empowered people are a prerequisite to consistent quality and productivity (Glasser 1994). And because effective visions are those that run well ahead of the capacity to attain them, quality leaders make learning opportunities available to everyone. For example, if the inspirational vision of the system is that all students are able to demonstrate high-level outcomes, then principals and schools will have to create new instructional delivery systems and teachers will probably have to learn the skills required to individualize and personalize instruction. Building individual and organizational capacity is the essence of the quality leader (Developing and empowering everyone, Improving organizational performance)

How can we create an attitude for and a system of accountability?

A critical, but often forgotten, step in the strategic alignment process is to create a culture and system of accountability throughout the organization. Once an organization has identified what it wants to produce (i.e., students able to demonstrate challenging learning outcomes), the leaders have to track the progress of students and the organization. Students, parents, and taxpayers deserve accountable schools, and schools and teachers cannot consistently improve if they do not hold themselves accountable for what and how students learn. Student assessment and the creation of feedback loops are critical roles of Total Leaders who also create feedback loops for themselves and help everyone else to do the same. They then monitor and use the feedback to improve how they do things and they make sure that everyone else is receiving and using feedback too. (Creating feedback loops)

What can we do to ensure that everyone is on board and implementing our new vision?

Many educators seem to think that implementing the system's compelling purpose and vision are optional. Total Leaders aren't afraid to let those who haven't gotten on board know that they need to do so. They clearly state their message, which is that implementing the vision of quality learning for all students is the reason we all are allowed to work here. (Managing the vision.) They also use the supervision process to reward those who do the hard work required when challenging individual and organizational visions. (Rewarding positive contributions) Total Leaders probably spend about 95 percent of their time encouraging, supporting, and rewarding the great people who are part of the profession. But they also realize that they are not an employment agency focused on the employee. They are educators in the business of student learning, and those not contributing to that end will find themselves confronted by the Total Leader. (Modeling the core values)

How can we restructure to align our district's programs and support with our new vision?

Total Leaders know that they have the power to align the structure, the policies, and the procedures of their organization with its vision. They know that structure, policies, and procedures are not neutral forces — they will either support, or be inconsistent with, the system's compelling purpose and vision. They can help the organization or they can make it difficult for anyone to buck the tide. For example, if a vision has to do with creating feedback loops for continuous improvement, and the student evaluation policies aren't aligned with authentic or criterion-defined assessment practices, it will be impossible to provide principals and teachers with the data necessary to improve student performance. Or, if a belief is that student success breeds more student success, yet the organization still hires teachers who grade on the curve, then the leader can't expect that belief to become part of the organizational culture. (Restructuring to achieve productive change)

Total Leaders are authentic leaders and service leaders. They walk their talk and they align structures, policies, and procedures with the organizational vision, even when it will make them unpopular and open to personal risk. (Managing the vision, Restructuring to achieve productive change) They know that the main thing is to keep the main thing (student success) the main thing.

Final Thoughts

At this time, *Total Leaders* represents the best of what we know about leadership and about organizational change. Although most of the thinking on these topics today comes from business and industry, we've done our best to show that it can easily be applied to educational leaders. And it is a *must* that educators make those applications.

Total Leaders does not suggest anything that is not tightly aligned with the best of what our profession knows about students and learning, teachers and teaching, and effective schools. We are leading the world's most important profession, and in doing so, we must take advantage of the best we know about effective leadership and systemic change. It's our choice to learn and apply to schools what Motorola knows about mass customization, what 3M knows about innovation, and what Nordstrom knows about quality and service.

The mission of our profession couldn't be more important or meaningful. Our times and challenges demand that education and educators reinvent themselves by adopting new ways of thinking and acting that take advantage of the best we know about our profession and our professional role as educational leaders. It is our hope, therefore, that all educators will become Total Leaders.

Bibliography

Aburdene, P., and J. Naisbitt. (1992). *Megatrends for Women*. New York: Villard Books.

Autry, J. (1991). *Love and Profit*. New York: Avon Books.

Barker, J. (1992). *Future Edge: Discovering the New Paradigms of Success*. New York: William Morrow and Company.

Barker, J. (1988). *Discovering the Future: The Business of Paradigms*. St. Paul, Minn.: ILI Press.

Belasco, J.A., and R.C. Stayer. (1993).*Flight of the Buffalo*. New York: Warner Books.

Bennis, W., and P. Biederman. (1997). *Organizing Genius*. Reading, Mass.: Addison-Wesley.

Bennis, W., and B. Nanus. (1985). *Leaders: The Strategies for Taking Charge*. New York: Harper & Row.

Blanchard, K.H., and N.V., Peale. (1988). *The Power of Ethical Management*. New York: William Morrow and Co., Inc.

Blanchard, K., P. Zigarmi, and D. Zigarmi. (1985). *Leadership and the One Minute Manager*. New York: William Morrow and Co.

Block, P. (1987). *The Empowered Manager*. San Francisco: Jossey-Bass.

Bonstingl, J.J. (1992). *Schools of Quality: An Introduction to Total Quality Management in Education*. Alexandria, Va.: Association for Supervision and Curriculum Development

Boyett, J.H., and H.P. Conn. (1991). *Workplace 2000: The Revolution Reshaping American Business*. New York: Dutton Press.

Bridges, W. (1991). *Managing Transitions*. Reading, Mass.: Addison-Wesley.

Bridges, W. (1980). *Transitions: Making Sense of Life's Changes*. Reading, Mass.: Addison-Wesley.

Burton, T.T., and J.W. Moran. (1995). *The Future Focused Organization*. Englewood Cliffs, N.J.: Prentice-Hall, Inc.

Carter, S. (1996). *Integrity*. New York: Harper Collins.

Celente, G. (1990). *Trend Tracking*. New York: John Wiley & Sons.

Chappel, T. (1993). *The Soul of a Business*. New York: Bantam Books.

Collins, J.C., and J.I. Porras. (1994). *Built to Last: Successful Habits of Visionary Companies*. New York: Harper Collins Publishers.

Conner, D. R. (1992). *Managing at the Speed of Change*. New York: Villard Books.

Cooper, R., and A. Sawaf. (1996). *Executive EQ*. New York: Grosset/Putman.

Covey, S.R. (1991). *Principle Centered Leadership*. New York: Summit Books.

Covey, S. R. (1989). *The Seven Habits of Highly Effective People*. New York: Simon and Schuster.

Covey, S.R., A.R. Merrill, and R.R. Merrill. (1994). *First Things First*. New York: Simon & Schuster.

Crosby, P.B. (1989). *Let's Talk Quality*. New York: McGraw Hill.

Crosby, P.B. (1979). *Quality Is Free: The Art of Making Quality Certain*. New York: McGraw Hill.

Crum, T.F. (1987). *The Magic of Conflict*. New York: Simon and Schuster.

Davis, S.M. (1987). *Future Perfect*. Reading, Mass.: Addison-Wesley.

Deal, T., and A. Kennedy. (1982). *Corporate Cultures*. Reading, Mass.: Addison-Wesley

Deming, W.E. (1986). *Out of the Crisis*. Cambridge: Massachusetts Institute of Technology.

DePree, M. (1989). *Leadership Is An Art*. New York: Doubleday.

Dertouzos, M. (1997). *What Will Be*. New York: HarperCollins Publishers.

Dobyns, L., and C. Crawford-Mason. (1991). *Quality or Else: The Revolution in World Business*. Boston: Houghton Mifflin.

Drucker, P.F.. (1995). *Managing in a Time of Great Change*. New York: Truman Talley Books.

Drucker, P.F. (1992). *Managing for the Future*. New York: Truman Talley Books.

Feather, F. (1994). *The Future Consumer*. Los Angeles: Warwick Publishing Group.

Frankl, V.E. (1984). *Man's Search for Meaning*. New York: Simon & Schuster.

Gardner, H. (1995). *Leading Minds: Anatomy of Leadership*. New York: Basic Books.

Gates, B. (1995). *The Road Ahead*. New York: Viking Press.

Glasser, W. (1994). *The Control Theory Manager*. New York: HarperCollins.

Goleman, D. (1995). *Emotional Intelligence*. New York: Bantam Books.

Greenleaf, R. (1991). *Servant Leadership*. New York: Paulist Press.

Grove, A.S. (1996). *Only the Paranoid Survive*. New York: Doubleday.

Hamel, G., and C.K. Prahalad. (1994). *Competing for the Future*. Boston: Harvard Business School Press.

Hammer, M., and J. Champy. (1993). *Reengineering the Corporation*. New York: Harper Collins.

Heller, R. (1995). *The Naked Manager for the Nineties*. London: Little Brown and Company.

Hersey, P. (1984). *The Situational Leader*. New York: Warner Books.

Hersey, P., and K.H. Blanchard. (1972). *Management of Organizational Behavior*. Englewood Cliffs, N.J.: Prentice-Hall.

Hoffer, E. (1963). *The Ordeal of Change*. New York: Harper & Row.

Kaplan, R., and D. Norton. (1996). *The Balanced Scorecard*. Boston: Harvard Business School Press.

Kilmann, R.H., M.J. Saxton, and R. Serpa. (1985). *Gaining Control of the Corporate Culture.* San Francisco: Jossey-Bass.

Kotter. J.P. (1996). *Leading Change.* Boston: Harvard Business School Press.

Kotter, J.P. (1995). *The New Rules.* New York: The Free Press.

Kouzes, J.M., and B.Z. Posner. (1993). *Credibility.* San Francisco: Jossey-Bass.

Kuhn, T.S. (1970). *The Structure of Scientific Revolutions.* Chicago: University of Chicago Press.

Labovitz, G., and V. Rosansky. (1997). *The Power of Alignment.* New York: John Wiley & Sons.

Laszlo, E. (1994). *Vision 2020: Reordering Chaos for Global Survival.* Amsterdam: Gordon and Breach Science Publishers.

Liebig, J.E. (1994). *Merchants of Vision.* San Francisco: Berrett-Koehler.

Lynch, D., and P.L. Kordis. (1988). *Strategy of the Dolphin.* New York: Fawcett Columbine.

Maslow, A.H. (1954). *Motivation and Personality.* New York: Harper & Row.

Matejka, K., and R.J. Dunsing. (1995). *A Manager's Guide to the Millennium.* New York: American Management Association.

Morgan, G. (1993). *Imaginization: The Art of Creative Management.* Newbury Park, Calif.: Sage Publications, Inc.

Naisbitt, J. (1997). *Megatrends Asia.* New York: Touchstone Books.

Naisbitt, J. (1994). *Global Paradox.* New York: William Morrow and Company.

Naisbitt, J., and P. Aburdene. (1990). *Megatrends 2000.: Ten New Directions for the 1990's.* New York: William Morrow and Company.

Nanus, B. (1992). *Visionary Leadership.* San Francisco: Jossey-Bass.

National Commission on Excellence in Education. (1983). *A Nation at Risk.* Washington, D.C.: U.S. Department of Education.

Negroponte, N. (1995). *Being Digital.* New York: Alfred A. Knopf.

Oakley, E., and D. Krug. (1991). *Enlightened Leadership*. Denver: Stone Tree Publishing

O'Toole, J. (1995). *Leading Change: Overcoming the Ideology of Comfort and the Tyranny of Custom*. San Francisco: Jossey-Bass.

Ouchi, W.G. (1981). *Theory Z*. New York: Avon Books.

Pascale, R.T., and A.G. Athos. (1981). *The Art of Japanese Management*. New York: Warner Books.

Perelman, L.J. (1992). *School's Out*. New York: Avon Books.

Peters, T. (1994). *The Tom Peters Seminar*. New York: Vintage Books.

Peters, T. (1992). *Liberation Management*. New York: Alfred A. Knopf.

Peters, T., and R. Waterman. (1982). *In Search of Excellence*. New York: Harper & Row.

Petersen, J.L. (1994). *The Road to 2015*. Corte Madera, Cal.: Waite Group Press.

Peterson, P.G. (1996). *Will America Grow Up Before It Grows Old?* New York: Random House.

Schechtman, M. (1994). *Working Without a Net*. New York: Pocket Books.

Schwahn, C.J. (1993). *Making Change Happen: An Action Planning Handbook*. Dillon, Colorado: Breakthrough Learning Systems.

Schwahn, C.J., and W.G. Spady. (1996). *The Shifts, Trends, and Future Conditions that are Redefining Organizations and Careers in the '90s*. Dillon, Colorado: Breakthrough Learning Systems.

Senge, P. (1990). *The Fifth Discipline*. New York: Doubleday.

Sergiovanni, T.J. (1990). *Value-Added Leadership*. New York: Harcourt Brace Jovanovich.

Smith, D.K. (1996). *Taking Charge of Change*. Reading, Mass,: Addison-Wesley.

Smith, J.W., and A. Clurman. (1997). *Rocking The Ages*. New York: Harper Business.

Spady, W.G. (1998). *Paradigm Lost: Reclaiming America's Educational Future*. Arlington, Va.: American Association of School Administrators.

Spady, W.G. (1996a). *A Strategic Process for Developing Future-Focused Student Learning Outcomes*. Dillon, Colorado: Breakthrough Learning Systems.

Spady, W.G. (1996b). *Action Steps for Leading and Implementing Productive Change*. Dillon, Colorado: Breakthrough Learning Systems.

Spady, W.G. (1996c). *Guidelines for Leading and Implementing Productive Change*. Dillon, Colorado: Breakthrough Learning Systems.

Spady, W.G. (1994). *Outcome Based Education: Critical Issues and Answers*. Arlington, Va.: American Association of School Administrators.

Spady, W.G. (1987). *Future Trends*. Dillon, Colo.: Breakthrough Learning Systems.

Theobold, R. (1987). *The Rapids of Change*. Indianapolis: Knowledge Systems, Inc.

Toffler, A.. (1990). *PowerShift*. New York: Bantam Books.

Toffler, A. (1981). *The Third Wave*. New York: Bantam Books.

Toffler, A. (1971). *Future Shock*. New York: Bantam Books.

Toffler, A., and H. Toffler. (1995). *Creating a New Civilization*. Atlanta: Turner Publishing, Inc.

Treacy, M., and F. Wiersema. (1995). *The Discipline of Market Leaders*. Reading, Mass.: Addison-Wesley.

Walton, M. (1986). *The Deming Management Method*. New York: Perigree Books.

Wheatley, M.J. (1992). *Leadership and the New Science*. San Francisco: Berrett-Koehler Publishers.

Wiersema, F. (1996). *Customer Intimacy*. Santa Monica: Knowledge Exchange.

Whyte, D. (1994). *The Heart Aroused*. New York: Doubleday.

Wilson, W.J. (1996). *When Work Disappears: The World of the New Urban Poor*. New York: Alfred A. Knopf.

About the Authors

Chuck J. Schwahn

Charles (Chuck) Schwahn has made his professional life a study of leadership and effective organizations. For the past 20 years he has worked with businesses and schools throughout North America providing consultation and training on the topics of leadership, change, personnel practices, and future-focused strategic planning. His work with businesses and school systems is based upon his study of leadership and his successful 8-year experience as superintendent of the Eagle County School District, Eagle and Vail, Colo.

Chuck, who is the author of *Making Change Happen*, received his doctorate from the University of Massachusetts where Ken Blanchard of *The One Minute Manager* fame was his doctoral chair.

A South Dakotan for much of his life, Chuck is one of 10 children, born and raised on a Sioux Indian Reservation. He is enjoying a successful career that has placed him in nearly all of the critical roles in education. He has taught middle school and university students and has been a high school coach, an elementary and secondary school principal, an assistant superintendent for curriculum, instruction, and personnel, and the director of a state service center for organizational development.

Chuck has been married to his favorite teacher, Genny, for 37 years. They have one daughter, Lori, and one adorable grandchild, Spencer. Chuck's interests include reading the latest literature on leadership and the future, cutting and chopping firewood, skiing, golfing, and hiking.

Chuck can be reached at (605) 673-3723 May 1 through December 1 and (602) 977-7956 January 1 through April 31.

William G. Spady

William (Bill) Spady is internationally recognized as one of the major theorists, writers, developers, and leaders in future-focused outcome-based educational reform efforts worldwide. He is also a noted authority on strategic design and alignment strategies, systemic change, and leadership development.

Bill has authored two other books for AASA: *Paradigm Lost: Reclaiming America's Educational Future* (1998) and *Outcome-Based Education: Critical Issues and Answers* (1994). He is senior partner with Chuck Schwahn in ChangeLeaders, a consulting company dedicated to developing Total Leaders and fostering organizational transformation in education and business.

A native of Milwaukie, Ore., Bill holds three degrees from the University of Chicago — in humanities, education, and sociology. Between 1967 and 1973 he held academic appointments in the Sociology of Education at Harvard University and the Ontario Institute for Studies in Education. He served as a senior research sociologist at the National Institute of Education from 1973 until 1979 when he joined the staff of the American Association of School Administrators as an associate executive director. Bill left AASA in 1983 to become director of the Far West Laboratory for Educational Research and Development.

Bill has two adult daughters, Jill and Vanessa, and a host of highly involving hobbies and pursuits, including classical music, stereo systems, history and science documentaries, skiing, bicycling, golfing, windsurfing, and fond memories of 30 years as a classical trumpeter.

Bill can be reached at P.O. Box 4388, Dillon, CO 80435 or by phone at (970) 262-1935.

Acknowledgments

"To steal from one is plagiarism; to steal from everyone is research." We confess. We have done an enormous amount of research in putting *Total Leaders* together and, therefore, we owe our profoundest thanks to more than 100 authors for sharing their unique insights and rich experiences with us in their writings. Some of them we know personally; most we don't. But without their ideas, we could not have been so bold as to write this book, let alone call it *Total Leaders*.

Our genuine admiration and thanks go also to the many organizational leaders who have allowed us to help them chart their direction, development, and eventual success over the years. We have learned much from them — their beliefs, values, strategies, actions, and results all helped shape our understanding about Total Leadership.

We also know that *Total Leaders* would not have been possible without the commitment and support of three key people at the American Association of School Administrators. Gary Marx became interested in this work several years ago and encouraged us to develop it. Then in 1997, Paul Houston and Joe Schneider gave us the green light to develop our work into this book and a larger collaborative relationship with AASA. We thank each of them and are honored that AASA has chosen to make this book one of its member service publications.

Writing books is not easy. In this case, we had much needed encouragement and insight from several friends and colleagues from the start. Chief among them is Ron Brandt, retired executive editor for the Association for Supervision and Curriculum Development. Ron responded thoughtfully again and again to frameworks, outlines, and early chapters. We also received insights from Karen and Larry Gallio, from Kandace Laass of the U.S. Chamber of Commerce, from Bruce Wenger, and from Genny Schwahn, whose faith in us bolstered our spirits, and whose delicious food helped us keep our dueling computers running 14 hours a day.

While it is customary to thanks your editors, in this case, thanks is not enough. *Total Leaders* was produced in record time because of the tremendous energy, talent, and commitment of Ginger O'Neil and editor Barbara Hunter, who helped us find better words, organization, and formatting, and provided encouraging insights. We'd gladly do it all over again with them, but on that they get the last word.

Finally, we thank you, the reader, for taking the time to acknowledge our work. For us, *Total Leaders* is the result of a 30-year journey. We now look forward to hearing how you apply the wisdom of our 100+ gurus to improve the schools in your district. Know that we will be cheering for you along the way.

Chuck Schwahn

Bill Spady

January 1998